THE MAN FROM ROCK BOTTOM

BY STEPHEN ERIC JOHNSON

Book Cover Design Artwork & Interior Images: Pierre Joubert

Editors: Austin Hatch & Abigail Bunner

Additional Contributors: Tara Richter

Publisher: Richter Publishing LLC www.richterpublishing.com

ISBN-13: 978-1-954094-49-9 Paperback

DISCLAIMER

This book is a work of science fiction. This information is provided and sold with the knowledge that the publisher and author do not offer any legal or medical advice. In the case of a need for any such expertise, consult with the appropriate professional. This book does not contain all information available on the subject. This book has not been created to be specific to any individual's or organization's situation or needs. Every effort has been made to make this book as accurate as possible. However, there may be typographical and/ or content errors. Therefore, this book should serve only as a general guide and not as the ultimate source of subject information. This book contains information that might be dated and is intended only to educate and entertain. The author and publisher shall have no liability or responsibility to any person or entity regarding any loss or damage incurred, or alleged to have incurred, directly or indirectly, by the information contained in this book. You hereby agree to be bound by this disclaimer or you may return this book within the guarantee time period for a full refund. All characters appearing in this work are fictitious. Any resemblance to real persons, living or dead, is purely coincidental. The opinions and stories in this book are the views of the author and not that of the publisher.

DEDICATION

To my parents, my siblings, and my friends (if you don't know who you are, please ask): for enduring long.

TABLE OF CONTENTS

ACKNOWLEDGMENTS

With thanks to the hardworking folks at Richter Publishing.

CHAPTER 0: AS ABOVE, SO BELOW; AS BELOW SO ABOVE

Location: En Route to Earth; Pan-Galactic Republic Flagship *Questing*
Perspective: Garfi Lett, Master of the Ministry of Defense

With a scarred face nearly without the capacity for expression anymore, Garfi Lett shifted his gaze between the various screens of the ship's command center. Assorted crew went about their duties in a state of perpetually controlled chaos all around the central gradine on which he stood. On his immediate left was a view of what lay behind the ship, the freshly installed solar energy collector and microwave transmitter visibly humming as it sent streams of nigh-unlimited energy off toward the power-thirsty planets of this sparsely inhabited solar system. To his right, however, was the ship's destination: a small planet, dark and pulsing with unnatural life, save for a single shining point along its equator.

This shimmer was the last city on Earth. The city made for humanity because of the efforts of their would-be savior, the one Master of the Ministries, who dared to believe in them, who felt that they were worth saving. That Master, however, was not Garfi Lett.

"The essence of humanity is weakness," Garfi declared in his calm, deep, resonant voice. "If they are not afraid, they are angry. And still afraid. And if they are not angry, they are arrogant. And angry. And afraid."

Of course, as the Master of the Ministry of Defense, Garfi spoke with the voice of experience: ages past he'd been created by the gene-forgers of the tarig species, one of their many living constructs, creatures designed and fielded when that ancient, terrible race of conquerors couldn't be bothered to deal with situations themselves. He knew how to take the measure of an opponent at a heartbeat, and humanity had only been the latest of so many opponents now past.

The tarig and their all-encompassing empire were also past, of course, long ago destroyed through a combination of their own internal strife and the enthusiastic efforts of the freedom fighters and resistance forces that rose from their former subjects. Still, some of their creations lingered, Garfi among them, doing his best to serve the Pan-Galactic Republic that had sprung up from the unity and idealism of those formerly subject species. Doing his best to somehow achieve atonement for his many sins as a war-slave of the Tarig Empire. Bringing peace out of war whenever it was possible.

With the humans, though, Garfi didn't think peace was possible. Not after what they'd done. Best to leave them, either to find their own light, or to die, lost in the dark.

What little expression was left to the patchwork man's face showed his fear as he turned his head. Fear for the small, soft-furred, gracile biped standing next to him.

"Please don't go down there, Sin," Garfi begged, his old, old eyes showing all the horror of ten thousand years engaged in the cruel business of waging war. "They'll kill you," his eyes shifted past his friend, back to the benighted planet that was their destination. "And then they'll die, too."

At first Garfi thought his little friend hadn't heard, or simply wasn't going to answer. He knew the law of silence, however, and contented himself with it while their ship progressed ever nearer to the human home-world.

Finally, Scintillant Camor, Master of the Ministry of Life, spoke.

"One of the most long-running and successful governments of Earth's past made use of a philosophy called Legalism," began the purple-furred I'dray in a voice soft as down-fluff and sweet as new-picked wineberries. "Its tenets for managing a population can be summed up thusly: punishment produces force; force produces strength; strength produces awe; awe produces virtue; thus, virtue has its origin in punishment."

Scintillant shook his head, the quirk of his long, delicate muzzle and softly glowing eyes conveying ultimate pity, ultimate compassion. "Can you imagine growing up under generations of such a philosophy, Garfi?" His eyes flicked to the patchwork man's face, his expression turning wry. "No, you don't have to imagine, you were there, right at the beginning. Compared to you, I'm just an infant, and my sorrow almost as uninformed."

3

Despite his words, however, the delicate-seeming biped's jaw set, his eyes turning forward, peering toward the benighted little world that had been covered in so much light less than a human generation ago.

"Most of history is driven by the actions of a few individuals," he said at last. "Most people just want to *be*, while great powers clash above their heads. Humanity hasn't had a fair chance for their heroes to really shine; villains are far more reliable. Now they're going to get that chance: with the power station set up, Sunflower City is ready to bloom in earnest. I've got four of the finest peacekeeper veterans in the entire Pan-Galactic Republic, each dividing up the city into districts of command and gathering the best and most merciful that humanity has to offer for training in the fine art of keeping the Republic's peace. One of them is Sergeant Benjuro Clee," he added, casting a sidelong glance at his old friend, smirking a little at the subtle signs of shock-of-recognition and admiration on the other male's face. "There's Doctor Salvee for management and distribution of life-essentials, of course, Gret to cover auditing, and...the Professor has his classes on Republic Cultural Integration."

Garfi couldn't help but let the faintest smirk of his own touch his inflexible lips at the brief pause.

"You can't pronounce his name either, huh?" Then his expression hardened. "Earth has had a Link connection for almost a local year now, Sin, while you started gathering humans to live in that city of yours. That class teaches the bare minimum that anybody needs to know to join the Pan-Galactic Republic properly, and only one human has signed up so far. One."

"Up until now, Sunflower City's mostly just been populated by humanity's old leadership, along with their staff," Scintillant answered dismissively. "The ones who got them into their present mess. Gathering them up first was essential to getting any work done. They're contained now, set up in nice places to live and out of positions where they can do any more damage. And consider which human it was who signed up: the Man!"

Despite his skepticism, Garfi Lett gave the slightest grunt of acknowledgement, but not surprise, at this revelation: of course, if anybody signed up, it would be the Man.

"Right now, we've got the peacekeepers and your citizen-mercenaries working full time to bring in boatloads of refugees from the rest of the planet," Scintillant continued, "and Salvee and Gret are working overtime with the City Central Computer System and any native humans they can get on board to get them settled into proper housing with necessary resources: food and water, safety, education, and recreational facilities. We've got all the pieces in place now, Garfi, everyone all working together to help lead humanity into the light. Maybe for the first time ever. And we *have* to succeed here, Garfi." The look on the little I'dray's face as he said these words made the strings of Garfi's multiple hearts twinge. "If we can't save humanity, even if it's from themselves, what's the point of our entire way of life? What we're doing here is the whole purpose of the Pan-Galactic Republic being created in the first place, playing out in miniature."

"Maybe," said the patchwork man, shaking his head, obviously unconvinced. "Maybe not. Think about this, Sin: every sapient species, somewhere in their religions, has some mythology built up around a messiah, someone who'll save them from their sins. Out of all those tens of thousands of different cultures, each with their own ideal savior, humanity's the only one that killed theirs. Repeatedly." He sighed, his eyes turning down. "I'm serious, Sin, you fail here, and nobody will pick things up. This is the last chance this planet gets."

Squaring his shoulders as he drew himself up to his not-considerable full height, Scintillant Camor looked toward the shining city as it filled the screen.

"Then I guess we just won't fail."

Location: Earth; Sunflower City Main Aquatic
Loading Dock
Perspective: Barika Das

So close, packed in so tight...it was almost impossible to breathe.

With knuckles as drained of color as her cheeks, Barika Das gripped the rail of the flat-bottomed watercraft, praying to whatever gods might be listening to end this trial soon.

Behind her, she could hear the cacophony of humanity, a multilingual mélange of profanity, threats, curses, crying babies, wailing children, groans of the elderly, and there, behind it all, the sound of her own family, coarse and cruel.

The marriage had been arranged, of course, because her parents were poor, but had a good name and lineage. Her betrothed came from a family of the lowest orders but had more than enough money to buy their way up in the world. Now, though, none of that mattered, not after the End had taken away everything so many years ago.

Everything, that is, but her personal, private hell.

Fortunately, everyone was packed in too tight to do more than cast threats, most people too seasick even for that. Even more fortunately, most of the passengers of this little craft were children, which further lessened the overall hostility. Most fortunately of all, even as she cast her eyes up from where she'd just finished feeding the fish, Barika's view was filled with the brilliance of the great city, their salvation. Bright as a star fallen to Earth, as a jewel pulled up from the deepest depths and polished to perfection by a maker more than human. Glorious, and full of promise.

The promise of an end to the End.

CLUNK!

The impact shook them all, and then suddenly – blissfully! – the rocking of the waves came to a complete and utter stop as one of the loading mechanisms hoisted the too-small craft right up onto the dock. The great doors at the far end of the boat dropped with a reverberating *CLANG*, revealing the glorious entrance to the city across the docks.

Everyone surged forward, jostling and shoving and working their elbows to get to the front, to head straight toward the great glowing gates where it was said anybody could register as a citizen of the Pan-Galactic Republic, receive a place to stay and food to eat, all for free. Of course, after the horrors of the End, atrocities inflicted by humans on humans, nobody really believed that anything was free: there was always a catch. Compared, though, to what waited on the other side of the waters dividing the great shining city from the shadows of the endless night that had once been Earth...no, there was no comparison, and no price too high.

Even so, as everyone else disembarked, Barika hung back, waiting, watching. Perhaps it was because she was still recovering from seasickness. Perhaps she just didn't relish the thought of rejoining her family, her mother-in-law and husband and their hangers-on. Whatever the reason, she stayed where she was, letting the shadow of the boat's pilothouse cover her, hiding her from sight, from memory. Instead, she let her eyes follow the milling crowd of children walking uncertainly toward the entry gates to the city, feeling a softness inside of her that she'd forgotten for far too long. These children would never face the same horrors that she had endured. They would never...

Suddenly her breath caught, and Barika froze as two vast, dangerous-looking figures stepped from the pilothouse. Framed in the light of the City, Barika could make them out quite clearly: one was a small humanoid, gilled and finned, seated inside a giant plastic bubble, which itself was attached to immense robotic arms and legs; the other, meanwhile, was a creature as tall as the tallest humans, but with a body as broad in the shoulders as it was tall, with skin made of shale-like scales, and a face composed of transparent gel in which a sphere of electricity sparked and jolted.

"Human-made garbage," growled the second alien as it kicked the inner hull of the little landing craft, its words formed from the sound of lightning striking the inside of its gelatinous head-parts. "How do they survive such conditions?"

"But they *did* survive," came the reply of the being in the bubble-robot, its voice a sweet, high tenor, and as it spoke, Barika realized she could understand them; she'd heard of the translation filters that Republic personnel often implanted into their bodies or hid in their clothes where they couldn't be seen, and wondered if this was how this marvel was made possible. "We owe them that much respect."

"Yes, that much," the stone-scaled creature admitted with a soft grunt. "Pity we mercs won't be around for long: I don't think these humans are ready to accept peace just yet, not even after all they've endured. But Master Lett wants us out, to give the experts a chance to make this mess work. What can you do?"

"Nothing," admitted the one with the mellifluous voice. "Not without making things worse, anyway. We must simply trust that-"

The pair cut off their conversation sharply, both of them turning to look at the assembled humanity gathered below the lights of the city gates. Barika looked, too, and couldn't quite stifle the deep, despairing groan that what she saw coaxed from her innermost parts.

Striding into the middle of the crowd of the recently disembarked in the unloading area was a man, tall and thin, dressed in the robes of a priest, though it was hard at that distance to see what sect he represented. Nevertheless, Barika knew what was coming next, a scene she'd already endured far too many times among the communities of humanity: that was a Preacher Man, and soon he was going to start preaching, and then everything would go to Hell.

"My brothers, my sisters!" rose the Preacher Man's voice. "My brothers and sisters of humanity! Of the rich, pure soil of our dear Earth! How long are we to suffer these unholy and these impure elements? How long are we to prostitute ourselves to the alien and the invader?"

He strode to the fore of the line of citizen-aspirants, and everyone with sense quailed and fell back, not wanting to draw the ire of the Preacher Man and the mob that was even then starting to form in earnest all around. They'd all been raised on the words of the traveling Preacher Men, the lone sources of humanity's cultural unity during the End, and to listen to one too long was to feel your mind go fuzzy, your heart enflame, and soon the murmur of the crowd's discontent bound them from a mass of individuals into a single, outrage-roused whole.

Only Barika remained unmoved, her and the children. They, because they were too innocent for the complexities of the hate-filled gospel of a Preacher Man. She, because the scene was all too familiar.

"By the word of God Almighty, we will not be made slaves nor whores!" railed the Preacher Man, his arms raised high, the cries of the crowd around him rising higher still.

As the two Republic soldiers raced from the deck of the boat and other figures joined them from all sides, acting fast to quell the mob before it got out of hand, Barika's attention turned away from the Preacher Man's words. Instead, she looked toward the knot of children that had been making their way toward the gates. Now they were surrounded by shadow-shrouded humans clad in black, bearing guns. Cowering, fearful, they were being led away into the darkness of the bottommost level of the city, away from the gates, away from safety.

For them, salvation was lost.

Now that she was looking into the darkness, Barika could see other crafts: small transports like hers, fishing boats, even little rubber rafts. Some came to one of the legitimate docks, the well-lit places where those who wanted to join the Republic were meant to land. Others, though...others went into the darkness, the places where even the light of the city's heaven-thrust spires couldn't quite reach.

Darkness sank into Barika's heart as well as she stepped off the boat's gangplank, then turned away from the great glowing gates and began to walk along the shore. Made of shaped rock, she saw that the edges of the artificial island on which Sunflower City had been built looked almost natural. Perhaps in time and with the lashing of waves, they'd even become truly natural-looking beaches, as rock yielded to tide.

Trees rose up around her, and sweet, fragrant flowers, and before she knew it, Barika was walking in a fairy forest, a place that was so perfect, so wonderful, it couldn't possibly have been real. There were even the sounds of birdsong. Birds! She hadn't heard birds in years! And now she was hearing songbirds in the dark of night, on the island of a city built by aliens to house the remnants of humanity, plucked from the jaws of doom.

Unable to resist, Barika followed her ears, her eyes lifting, moonlight catching the flitting forms of little passerines. They were soon joined by corvids, raptors, avians of both the night and the day. The birds weren't alone, either: alongside them flew other shapes, leather-winged and sharp-voiced, the night fliers and the day fliers sharing the same space without conflict.

Then she stepped out into a clearing at the base of a moon-dappled, grassy knoll. Looking up, she saw what was drawing the birds and the bats. There, seated at the top of the hill was a funny little man, dressed in a full-body, baggy-looking suit, complete with a rounded helmet shaped something like a bucket. A strange patchwork quilt of a map was laid out before him.

Unable to help herself, Barika drew closer, and saw that the short, slightly pudgy man's garb looked like a very old, very faded hazmat suit, something like what had once been worn by world militaries when they'd had to operate in contaminated areas...before there was anything but contaminated areas, of course. Except this suit was ill-fitting, and the man himself cut an odd figure, making him look something like a clown, but without the greasepaint creepiness.

This little man was harmless. That was something Barika could feel deep inside herself.

However, his companions were anything but!

Just as she neared the top of the crest, Barika came up short with a soft, fearful *gasp*. From one side of the man came a vast shape, broad wings outstretched like thunderheads, a sharp, wicked *hiss* of fury filling the night. Moments later, a second of the darkling beasts stepped up from the other side, a low, crouching figure on all-fours, its muzzle sharp, its gleaming teeth sharper as it growled, low and menacing.

Just moments before the creatures leapt and Barika was doomed, the little man's head turned slightly, his hand lifted. That gesture was enough, and instantly the two creatures pulled back into the glow of the camp light by which he was making notes on his overly complicated map. Revealed by that light, Barika could see at once that what she'd thought were monsters were only a swan and a big, fluffy dog. The swan studiously ignored her as it waddled away. The dog, on the other hand, gave her a sheepish grin and wag of its tail.

"Hey-o," said the plump little man, rising slowly, gingerly to his feet as he turned to face Barika.

As he stood, the light of his lamp falling on him fully, Barika saw with a start why the animals around him had been so protective: there was a wide half-oval tinged in darkening crimson dotted across his body from hip to shoulder, front and back. Bite marks! The mystery of how he'd survived such a bite was at least partially revealed, however, by the strange armor plates visible through the holes in the hazmat suit. They pulsed like something alive, glistening wetly, and as she watched, extended tiny tendrils that were already hard at work sealing up the tears in the heavily faded beige-yellow of the man's suit.

"Black widow shark," he said by way of explanation, seeing her wide-eyed concern, then dismissing it as though such an encounter were...were *commonplace*. He'd faced one of the monsters of the wasted lands, and...

"You're still alive," she almost whispered.

"Yeah," he admitted with a shrug, his helmeted head turning away, bashfully avoiding her gaze even as he sank back down, worn out. "Not much choice."

Following the line of his softly glowing visor, Barika blinked: curled up right next to the camp light were two children, brother and sister judging from their family resemblance. An assortment of critters were cuddled up close beside them as though in a family-friendly animated feature.

The story of what had to have happened flooded into Barika's mind. Black widow sharks were one of the many monsters of the End, and like all monsters, they were creatures made to hunt, kill, and most of all, *terrorize* humanity, keeping the humans disorganized and easily dominated by those with power. The few survivors of their attacks described their tactics with shuddering horror: they would snatch people who wandered too close to the water, drag them down, and surround them in mucous-encased bubbles. Then the horrible, midnight-skinned monsters would circle their struggling, helpless, doomed captives, letting them panic, and in their panic, use up what little air they had just that much faster. Finally, just at the moment when the air was about to run out, just when fear had seasoned their meat to perfection, the creature, part shark, part crustacean, part freak of nightmares, would strike.

To have taken two children back from a black widow shark, this cute, short, plump, utterly unassuming little man in the silly, ill-fitting outfit had to have gone into the water, into the dark, right into the lair of the beast. And won.

"You can call me Aracuan," said the funny little man, who Barika was starting to realize wasn't nearly as funny – or harmless – as she'd initially thought.

"Barika Das," she answered, holding out her hand. Instead of taking it, he put a slender, bright orange hardcover book into her grip instead. A copy of "Old Possum's Book of Practical Cats," by T. S. Eliot. A real paper book!

"I read it to them until they fell asleep," he explained, and though the softly glowing visor hid his eyes from view, she somehow got the impression that he was smiling at her, gentle and shy. "Then I took away the bad dreams," he paused when he saw her confused expression. "It's something empaths can do," he explained, "to help people heal. Scintillant Camor, my mentor, taught me, but, well." She heard the sound of him clearing his throat, his voice growing slightly husky. "The nightmares have to go somewhere. It's okay, though: I've got plenty already. What's a few more, give or take? So," he cocked his head to one side, conveying so much in body language for someone without a visible face, "what brings you out here, Miss Barika Das? Shouldn't you be at the gates to Sunflower City, getting registered? Getting somewhere safe to sleep, with good food to eat and safe water to drink? Somewhere far away from Rock Bottom," he added, motioning toward the lowest level of the

14

city, where the light of its gleaming spires didn't quite reach. "You only go there if you don't have anywhere else."

"I," she began, her own voice almost as husky as his, thick with emotion, then started again, "I just couldn't."

Her eyes met the man's visor, which seemed to soften with compassion. Impossible, of course, since it was just metal and plastic. Still, the impression remained.

"People who hurt you are waiting back there," he said, a statement more than a question. She nodded. "You don't know how to leave them," he added. She nodded again. "Nowhere to go. No power. No choice. No safety. So, you left them, wandered out here, not caring where you went."

"And found you," she finished, her free hand resting on the head of the immense, fluffy dog, a smile coming to her face as it leaned into her touch, looking up at her with endearing amber eyes.

"Well," sighed the man, leaning back on his hands as he continued to sit on the soft green grass, "maybe you can do something for me. And in the process, you can do something for you as well." She didn't object, so he continued. "First, do you want to be a citizen of the Republic?"

"I suppose," Barika replied with a shrug of her own. "There aren't that many other good options for me right now."

"Is that good enough, Central?" Aracuan asked the empty air. A moment later, a glowing, friendly blue rectangle materialized between them.

"Good enough for government work, Igor," said the round-edged rectangle in a pleasantly neutral, slightly feminine-sounding voice. "Or is it Aracuan now?"

15

"Aracuan, if you please," replied the man, who then motioned between Barika and the hovering construct. "Miss Barika Das, meet the City Central Computer System, or just Central. She – sorry, I mean they – Central doesn't exactly have a gender – is the guiding intelligence behind all of Sunflower City's operations. They keep tabs on everyone and everything within their sensor range, all part of fulfilling their primary mission."

"Serving the people of this city," Central finished. "That is my one concern. My sole objective. My purpose. You do not need to fear me, Miss Das: I am not a person, and so I do not experience the frailties of people, or their corruption. I do not get bored. I do not require sleep. I am incapable of experiencing spite, or anger, or sorrow. I experience some very basic emotions, such as satisfaction in a job well done, but they are unable to interfere with my functions, nor can they bias me in serving the people under my protection. As a new citizen of the Pan-Galactic Republic, that now includes you."

"And also, these kids," added the man, slowly, painfully getting to his feet, picking up his tatterdemalion map as he rose and slowly, carefully folded it before packing it into a pouch above his thigh. "I had them swear in like you before they went down for their naps. They need to be taken somewhere safe, and the Education Center is as good a place as any. Central, can you take Miss Das there?"

"I can, and I will," replied the computer construct, as a glowing blue line appeared on the grass. "Just follow the guideline as soon as you are ready."

With that, the solid light construct burst into a shower of pixels. The blue line, however, remained.

"If you want to save yourself, Miss Barika Das," said the man, gently shaking first one and then the other child until they began to stir into wakefulness, while all around him the animals began to slip silently into the dark, "go into the Education Center, hand over the kids, and tell whoever's at the front desk that you want to work. They'll give you an initial aptitude test, then they'll send you to your new home with some materials to study. Read whatever they give you thoroughly, but don't worry too much about memorizing it: they just want to see how well you adapt to new ideas. Once you feel ready, go back, and take the follow-up test. You should get a call for an interview soon after. If it's for a really good job, you'll meet with Scintillant Camor himself: I hear he's arriving in Sunflower City tonight."

Before the two children had quite come fully awake, still on the edge of dreams, he snapped off the camp light and slipped it into another pouch, then began to limp his slow, careful way down the hill and into the deepening shade of the forest.

"You can keep the book, Miss Barika Das," he said over his shoulder before he vanished from sight. "Take care. Be safe."

Blinking like the children, and like them feeling as though she'd just come out of a dream, Barika reached down, taking a small hand in each of hers, letting the boy, the older of the two, take the book: they'd liked it, after all, so they might as well keep it.

"Well," she said with an air of determination, and took her first step along the guideline, which began to snake off toward the brightness of the city, "I suppose we'd better get going."

CHAPTER 1: TEN DAYS LATER

Location: Earth, Sunflower City, Central Spire
Perspective: Scintillant Camor

Right now, I'm looking out over the City through the clear, clear glass of this office's massive window. It's beautiful, beautiful enough that I just *have* to put that mental capitalization on it, on the City, to mark the place as important.

We built this city, *the* City, Sunflower City, for humanity. Its wide, open avenues for foot traffic, dotted with trees and shrubbery and tempting grassy swards abloom with ambrosial, kaleidoscopic blossoms. Its infinitely complex series of interconnected magnetocentric flight paths for gravitic aerocar travel. The clickways made of fitted, textured diamond of myriad colors that glow to guide travelers to their destinations. The spires above, shining with solar radiance as they collect and distribute the microwaves caught from the energy beamed directly from the sun. Its planarian engines ever shifting the City's many layers like a living thing (and it might as well be alive!), reacting to the needs of its inhabitants for rain or shine to enhance or quell their moods even while joining with the natural rhythms of their planet itself. Its ample places of cultural diversity, of libraries and museums, of forums and plazas, coliseums and auditoriums, dance halls and concert halls and theaters and *more*.

We, the builders of the Pan-Galactic Republic, *we* built this, for *them*. "Give me your tired, your poor" indeed!

(Ah, but apologies to Emma Lazarus: her poem is beautiful, and I appreciate its nuances ever more deeply as I learn more about Earth's languages and cultures and long, sad history.)

Did we do the right thing?

Now I'm looking at my violet eyes, their slightly luminous irises clearly visible in reflection in the glass before me. Then I focus my attention back a bit, taking in the whole picture.

Hmm...I look *good* in this suit. I'm going to have to introduce this fashion style to the rest of the Republic: humans know how to dress!

Behind me, also reflected in the glass, is an office. It's designed by humans, built for humans, something that human executives use to show off their wealth, power, and prestige, and to intimidate, browbeat, and bully their visitors. There's a massive desk so tall it comes up past my chest, carved out of carefully varnished, well-polished, and so, *so* dark hardwood. Behind it – and right behind me – is a chair so immense, I almost got trapped the last time I tried to sit in it. And it wasn't comfortable, either! Just sticky with its soft, black, dead animal skin covering, the stink of the dye that tinted it, and that of its previous owner, infused into its cushions. The stink of his cruelty, and his greed, and his love for the fear of his victims.

That stink has infused this room, permeated every fiber of the expensive carpet, every disposable tile of the cheap ceiling. I didn't choose this office, I certainly don't want to hold any interviews of potential employees in this office, and I will never, ever, *ever* allow my daughter in this office so long as I draw breath. But it was all that the humans had available, an import from one of their old cities, like far too many of the things to be found in the City, leftovers from a collective culture that nearly killed every last one of them.

Why oh why did we not start over from scratch when we were building this place!

The first candidate is coming! I can hear her soft foot tread in the outer office, where once there was a secretary and now there's just my dear, darling daughter, sitting behind a cute little desk in her perfect little office dress, modeled on human lines, to show her off as the perfect little businesswoman that I know she'll be one day (if she wants, of course; presently she does, but she has plenty of time ahead in which to change her mind). *That* desk I chose, and all the little furnishings. As for the disgusting shield-wall of a desk that had been there, intended to intimidate and demoralize anyone trying to get past the outer guard to this executive office, and every last little detail and decoration left behind by the humans who vacated the premises, I and my daughter and a few good friends spent a happy morning dumping it all in the bay, to be collected and ground up into teeny tiny pieces by the scavenger robots before being carried off to the great recycling facilities floating over what was once the Great Pacific Garbage Patch.

That was fun!

I only wish we'd had time to do the same to this stupid nasty desk...ah, and now she's approaching the inner office door, and I can tell from the sound that her shoes are worn through in two places on the left shoe, one on the right, and here I am in a tailored pinstriped business suit and an office that stinks of Evil.

This is absolutely unacceptable!

So, when the human woman who is to be my first interviewee for the day walks through the door to my office, I've improvised as best I could under the time constraints.

I understand that many humans think we l'dray are "cute," and that we look somewhat like Earth foxes, if those foxes were people, with proper hands and walking on plantigrade feet. Perhaps my iridescent purple fur and bright violet eyes throw off terrestrial expectations, but when the woman opens the door and walks in, I'm sitting in that big chair, which I've cranked right up to its greatest height, while hugging the white tip of my fluffy tail to my chest, hunched over just slightly to better round my shoulders, my bare feet dangling above the floor and kicking slightly, like a child sitting in his daddy's seat.

She takes one look, and I can tell I've achieved the right effect because she just stands there, her face immediately letting me know that she's now completely put off her guard at the contrast between the office and its inhabitant. Not a *perfect* effect, but needs must.

"Hello, Miss Barika Das," I say, hopping to my feet, ears erect, tail flicking behind me as I stride forward, extending my center-self toward her, sharing my joy at getting to meet her, even as I take her hesitantly extended hand in both of mine. "I'm so glad that you came to see me."

And I *am*! Of *course* I am! Miss Barika Das comes from a family of refugees, like most of humanity these days, the few who weren't from their political classes, or the ranks of their ultra-rich, or their criminals (all of those, of course, came through their recent trials quite well). She's one of the many who took the battery of aptitude and excellence exams that my colleagues in the Ministry of Understanding have been trying to administer to humanity, to find out who can fit into the present systems of the Republic without needing too much adjustment. It's only the first wave of testing, of course, and not precisely tailored to humans yet, but Miss Das was one of the highest scorers of the last batch, which means she went well out of her way to study and prepare: she *wants* to work.

And if she wants to work, I want to give her a job!

Now I'm close to her, and as I stop projecting my center-self quite so aggressively, I start sensing more about her. She's dressed neatly in a plain but well-kept business dress, her hair is trimmed short, her skin is a color not too dissimilar from rich, red clay, and she's wearing a careful application of the cosmetics that humans love so well, probably a little more than would be considered normal. I'm no perfect judge of human aesthetics, at least not yet, but I think she's reasonably attractive for her species: she's fairly symmetrical, and she's obviously in decent physical condition, albeit a bit underfed yet in spite of our efforts at providing sustenance to the newly arrived of the City; she must have been nearly *starved* when she first got here.

She'd be more attractive if she wasn't hiding so much hurt inside, the same way she's hiding the bruises of recent violence under her neat clothes and slightly too-heavy makeup.

So, I open my center-self to her. Just enough to touch her mind, to touch her center-self, just a little. Not enough to interfere with her feelings, but enough to sound the metaphoric waters of her psyche and see what sort of person lies beneath the outer façade.

Sometimes...

Oh!

Sometimes the ability to share the feelings of others is just too much.

"Please, have a seat," I invite her, drawing my center-self back in, stepping to one side and gesturing to the room at large, drawing her attention away from me for the time I need to conceal my reaction to sharing in her center-self. I haven't put any chairs near mine, mostly because I spent all my time for impromptu decorating to move the big ugly chair out from behind the desk and into the middle of the soft, plush carpet with its sunk-in stink of emotional ugliness. There are chairs around the room, though, smaller and less comfortable ones, obviously made to enhance the size and importance of whoever was sitting in the big ugly chair, driving home that man's power and the smallness and weakness of his visitors.

Miss Das stands there, bewildered. Instead of taking my open invitation, she keeps looking around the room, looking to the obvious chair in its center, and then looking back to me, the last a little embarrassing, since I had to lean most of my weight on the door handle just to keep from falling down flat after that emotional ordeal, sharing in her years of neglect, abuse, and suffering in a matter of seconds. Every time her lovely brown eyes pass over me, I can feel her wanting so badly to smile and then shift into the baby talk that most sapients like to lavish upon small, cute things, creatures that can't talk back, but must simply endure the silliness with as much dignity as they can manage under the circumstances.

Fortunately, I'm a l'dray, noble and proud: I take that sort of reaction as a compliment.

Finally, however, I can't hold back the grin, though I do try not to show as much of my rather sharp teeth as I might have with someone I know better.

"Would it help, Miss Das, if I let you pet my head?" I ask her. "I can tell you'd like to, and if it helps you to relax, I don't really mind."

"Oh!"

Ah, *that* got her attention. Now she's the one who looks adorable, flustered and off-kilter. I don't bother restraining my chuckle, and then reach out and pull over a pair of the smaller chairs, indicating one to her; they're not very heavy, so even I can manage them without too much difficulty. As I move them, I make sure to angle my chair slightly so that we're not facing each other directly, deflecting some of the heavier emotional energies that might pass between us. Hers is closer to the door, too, and the tilt of her chair ensures that I've given her a clear avenue of escape, something to relax the hindbrain instincts, telling her inner animal that even if things get to their worst, she can still make a break for it.

"I-I'm sorry, Mister Camor," she stammers, dropping into the proffered chair with a remarkable lack of grace. "I didn't mean to..."

I touch my finger to the lips of my slender muzzle, another human gesture I'd picked up from my subliminal training programs as well as from my numerous in-person experiences. She takes the hint promptly and hushes before she embarrasses herself further, clutching her hands together on her lap, her body tense, almost quivering in the anxiety of the moment.

"Everything is all right, Miss Das," I tell her, putting my chin on my fist as I lean on one of the arms of the uncomfortable little chair. "You're not in trouble, and I was quite serious when I offered to let you pet me: I often get that reaction from other species, sapient and non, and I'm used to it. I'm not offended, and I do like the physical contact: it allows my empathic abilities to work more smoothly."

There was the expected flickering on her face, showing off a complex and quite interesting array of emotions, each melding together until it took my centuries (Earth centuries, that is) of experience to start sifting through them.

"I should give you some explanations before we begin, Miss Das," I tell her. "Just so you know what I know already, and we don't waste your valuable time more than absolutely necessary. Various personnel from the Ministry of Understanding have been keeping tabs on you since you entered the testing center to try yourself against our battery of exams. They've given me all the information they could compile on such short notice, which ended up being a reasonably sized dossier, from which I've gotten an idea of your general background. Nothing especially invasive, just what could be found in the public archives about your present living situation, and what little could be recovered from Earth's records.

"You should also know that, because of my abilities as an experienced I'dray empath – specialists like me are called Gentle Ones, by the way – I can sense everything you feel, at least when I'm concentrating, and you'll probably find yourself being more," I pause, frowning a little in thought, "*open* with your emotions, with yourself as well as with me. This is normal when you're around l'dray in general, and so we're all used to it, and only a tiny number of malcontents among our population take any offense from it. But then," I give her a gentle smile, "I suppose there are people like that in every society, everywhere."

Saying that, I lean forward, steepling my fingers as I fix her brown eyes with my violet ones, feeling the slight flicker within her as she notices that my eyes are actually glowing softly (something that often surprises people on their first meeting with a l'dray in the flesh).

"Now that you know what I know, Miss Das," I begin as kindly as I can, "and how I know it, why don't you tell me your *real* reason for wanting to take a job with the Pan-Galactic Republic?"

"Mister Camor…"

I tap my forehead suddenly, cutting her off as I then held out my hand, palm extended.

"Please forgive me," I add. "I forgot to mention, you've already got the job, if you still want it at the end of this interview, and nothing you say here will change that…unless it's 'no.' If you weren't fully qualified, and I didn't think you'd be a good match, I would never have invited you here. I still feel that way, even after shaking your hand, and feeling your center-self."

I lower my hand and use it to rub my chin fuzz as I regard her, once more resting my elbow on my knee.

"But you *hurt*, Miss Das," I tell her, and as I say the words, I open my center-self in invitation, even knowing that it will hurt if she chooses to accept. "You hurt so deeply. You've *been* hurt so deeply. Recently, too, and for a very long time before. Physically, yes," and her hand goes unconsciously to the nearly concealed bruise on her face, "but in your

27

center-self as well, in places where the wounds don't fade easily, and the scars not at all. Your..." I hesitate as I grasp for the words in her language, "your atman; your psyche; your soul; your...*you*. The center-self is that place deep inside," I add in explanation, "the place where you draw all your inner reserves. It's the one place in the whole universe where you can be you, where nobody can touch you without your permission."

She tenses, and I feel a flicker of something almost like guilt. Poor, poor human, having to hide your center-self all the time, never allowed to be fully honest. To be caught being honest is a crime worse than murder!

Then I have her eyes with my own once more, drawing her in. Allowing her to feel that I am no threat, except to endanger her pain.

But that is certainly the worst of all threats, isn't it?

Will she allow herself to be healed?

"What you feel, Miss Das, I feel also," I say softly, sharing my own piece of truth with her; sharing my vile transgression of daring to show feeling; sharing all that I have endured so that she can know my next words are a line that binds us together, life and limb and hearts and selves. "Like you, I have been hurt. Like you, I have scars."

The words settle in, and so do the feelings, and I can tell that they touch something within her. Moreover, she relaxes her center-self, opens to me, and we touch selves, both of us shuddering at the precious contact. Sharing pain. Sharing joy. Sharing *us*.

Before she can think about it, her hand goes to my head. I'm smaller than her, of course, like all we l'dray, so it's not a hard reach. For a moment she hesitates, fearful of my teeth. But I'm weaker than a human, again, like all we l'dray, and pose no physical threat in any practical sense, and as I splay my ears and lean forward a little, making it easier for her, she begins to stroke her fingers through my soft, well-groomed fur. She's inexpert at it, obviously having had few opportunities, poor dear. But I don't mind, and I don't comment, only close my eyes, and let our center-selves wash over each other.

"It begins with my father," she says, and I simply let her talk. "He was angry that I was born a girl. And so..."

Oh, you poor, poor lost one.

But we've found you now: you're safe.

One of so, so many.

Can we save you all?

...

I must try.

CHAPTER 2: NEW FRIENDS

Location: Interstellar Link, The Professor's
Classroom
Perspective: The Man

"And...I think that about does it for your syllabus and first reading assignments," the Professor finally declared, and I felt a soft wave of relief wash over and through me: there were too many people around, too much of a crowd, and so far it had only been bearable because I was the only human among them and we were all sitting down, letting me focus my attention forward rather than on the too-many eyes surrounding me.

"No, wait!" he exclaimed, his strangely charismatic yet utterly alien face expressing his urgency with the dilation of vast irises, and instantly I and every other sapient in the classroom settled back into our assorted seats: I might not even know the Professor's species or be able to pronounce his personal name even through the translation filter we all shared, but I had to admit, he had a powerful command presence. "There's one more thing, a piece of desperately important advice that you should all know. This is only the first day of class, and so many of you are thinking that you have all the time in the world. This is false: you don't.

"One great danger brought about by living in our post-scarcity society is the belief that we are immune to consequences. That we can get away with procrastination because there will always be those around us to pick up the slack should we fail. Or perhaps there is an automaton that can do the work instead. Perhaps that sort of lifestyle is acceptable for those who sell their votes or their reproductive privilege, but you are in school now, and I assume you are here to *better* yourselves, to *make* something of yourselves, and to become productive, useful members of the society of the Pan-Galactic Republic.

"So, to give you fair warning, because I have seen it time and again: at least one of you students, as in every prior semester I have taught, will have something horrible happen to you. The Worst Possible Thing. I don't know which of you it will be, or even if that poor soul is in this specific class or one of the others I'm teaching. I don't know what that Worst Possible Thing will be, either, but it's likely to come from one of the following, all of which I've seen happen, and usually more than one at a time.

"Perhaps your home will suffer a power surge right at the very moment you're transmitting your final assignment for this class, and you lose all your data, as well as suffering an on-site memory wipe. Perhaps a natural disaster unique to your planet will strike; earthquakes and windstorms are fairly common to most habitable planets, and precautions against them aren't always in place. Perhaps, for those of you who have opted to keep or reinstate your reproductive privileges, you will get pregnant, or your spouse will, and your priorities must change for the sake of your unborn child. Perhaps a loved one will suffer a dreadful illness, or even die, and focusing on your courseload simply becomes impossible. Or perhaps *you* will get sick, and while our modern science can cure most diseases, such cures still take time, time that will have to come from somewhere, and this class is a likely possibility.

"Most of you can probably guess at what your personal Worst Possible Thing might be, or at least narrow it down to a few likely possibilities. Think of them now. Among the founding principles of the Pan-Galactic Republic is the need for constant review of possible hazards and preparing multiple redundant backups to answer each of these possible dangers. Many of the horrible things that might happen to that unlucky soul among you, being acts of God, might not be avoidable, but all the same, if you are prepared when the Worst Possible Thing does hit – and it will – you do not need to fear.

"At least...not so much."

As he finished, I could see the slight crinkling around the Professor's eyes that indicated his version of a kindly smile (and his face *was* kindly for all its alien-ness). It also highlighted his age: with the anti-agathic treatments available from the medical science of the Pan-Galactic Republic, he had to be centuries of Earth-years old for it to show so readily. Maybe thousands.

"After you are done with your classes for the day, I strongly suggest that you go home and back up all your files on at least one separate external system. Two or three would be better. Check on your family members and friends and pets to ensure that they are safe and sound. Make an appointment with your physician for a complete checkup, psychological screening, and pan-immunity treatment, and consider having your reproductive privilege turned off for a time. Keep track of local weather patterns and seismological surveys. Most important of all, don't procrastinate; do your assignments, especially the big ones, as far in advance as is reasonably possible.

"And if you have done all of that, and the Worst Possible Thing still strikes you down," he inclined his head invitingly, "please, come to me and explain what has happened. Our society was built to provide a safety net against the vicissitudes of this mortal existence. Our government is dedicated to serving you – that is the reason for its founding – and has many services that are available. And I, as your instructor, will do everything in my power to assist you in your time of need. I will not lie for you, and I will not cheat for you, but beyond those limitations, I am your servant, a living resource to facilitate your learning, and want only what is best for each of you."

He extended his long-fingered hand in a casually dismissive wave.

"I am done, you may go. See you all next class."

Once again, I felt myself releasing that ball of tension that had formed somewhere in my abdomen. I felt it move down into the pit of my stomach, then rise just a little, settling somewhere around my solar plexus.

Yeah, I need to get out of here quick. Before the anxiety attack hits.

Tapping my desk to send my notes and the video archive of the class to my personal computer, I rose to my feet and turned, waiting for the crush of creatures surrounding me to file down the steps of the auditorium and out of the room. Not quite fully relaxed, but feeling myself getting there with the prospect of returning to my personal quietus I saw an opening in the queue, stepped toward it...

"Wait!"

...and walked right into the path of a giant, talking mantis.

Elongated, irresistibly powerful forelimbs wrapped around me, easily pulling me right past the stairs leading down and into the next row of seats, then lifting me up onto my tippytoes. As the dots that were the bug's eyespots in its faceted, jewellike eyes focused on me, giving the mantis an expression that was almost cartoonishly cute, the grip of those heavy front limbs relaxed slightly, allowing circulation, but didn't release me. At the same time, two pairs of smaller limbs, each ending in complex-looking manipulators that were almost like fingers, began patting me down, exploring my body from the waist up to my shoulders. From the neck upward, the bright pink bug's antennae stroked and caressed my cheeks, my nose, and my hair.

"You're a real human, aren't you?" exclaimed the big pink bug in a voice that sounded almost exactly like a little girl's, high-pitched and annoyingly adorable. "Like, you guys can eat plants and stuff, right?"

"Um...yes?"

"That is so awesome!" she (and though I know other species have different views on gender, I instinctively labeled the bug as female) squee'd happily. "Hey, Bright Spots! Come and look at what I found!"

Following the motion of two more of the multitude of the bug's appendages, they gesticulated toward the upper reaches of the room. I looked up to what I, in my limited human thinking, had considered a "ceiling," but which I could now see was actually where numerous flying and climbing creatures had been seated, suspended, perched, or otherwise arranged while they attended class. From among the throng that were making their way out of a skylight-like aperture, just like the ground-based species were departing by the door at the front of the class,

34

two vast, doe-brown wings spread, and their owner floated gracefully down, setting clawlike gripping feet on the back of a nearby chair as she perched by my new friend's head.

Bright Spots had a body and a head something more-or-less like a very fuzzy brown-and-white moth without the antennae, with wings like a bat, or maybe a pterodactyl, large and intelligent-looking owl-like eyes, and a mouth that was something like a very fleshy, flexible beak. The diminutive creature was only tall enough to reach my chin, and that was even while she was perched on the back of the chair right next to me.

"This one ponders," Bright Spots intoned in a feminine, high-pitched voice, cocking her head slightly to one side. "You are human?"

"Yeah," I answered.

"This one exclaims, most fascinating! This one now queries, you eat fauna as well as flora?"

"Yeah," I answered again, fighting with all my might not to rub my temples.

"Doesn't that make going to the bathroom kind of," the pink bug gave a confused quirk of her head, "you know, weird? And messy?"

"This one chides, Pinkflower," Bright Spots said, reaching out with one of her small, dainty claws, which I now saw were also her only manipulators: she only had four limbs, counting her wings. "This one reminds: many species are sensitive about matters relating to 'private places,' like bedrooms and bathrooms. This one also reminds: these same species have concepts such as personal space."

The pink bug, Pinkflower, twitched, a motion that I interpreted as resulting from a sudden, mind-blowing realization, her jewel eyes pulsing slightly before she instantly unlatched her grasping top limbs from around my torso.

"I'm so sorry!" she exclaimed, folding her many, many hands in front of her in a manner that seemed to be trying to express a state of ultimate contrition. "Bright Spots has been trying hard to teach me about how to be considerate of others and respect boundaries. But you humans are so weird! I mean that in a totally cool way, though," she added hastily. "I saw you, and just *had* to say hello!"

"This one wonders, maybe we can *hang out* sometime?" chimed in Bright Spots, whose name I suddenly realized, big brain that I am, was probably derived from the white spots I'd seen on her wings when they'd opened. "This one also queries: what is your name, human?"

"Joe," I said, feeling *so* much better now that I didn't have a big buggy face right up next to mine anymore. "You can just call me Joe. And yeah, sure. But, um…later, huh?" I shrugged, giving them an apologetic expression. "But you're kinda spot-on about my diet. I've gotta use the bathroom, like, right now."

"Oh!" chirped Pinkflower, all her limbs giving a little upward jerk as she made yet another realization. "Of course: you go and do that right now, Joe. We'll send you our contact information. I'm sure we can find some time in a virtual space to meet up soon."

"Sure," I grunted with a short wave before I turned toward the door at the front of the room, my path of escape now clear. "Soon."

Taking the steps as quickly as I could without being too impolite about it, not that either of those alien girls would've noticed, I was already reaching for my head as I stepped through the door and into the swirling light beyond.

CHAPTER 3: MORNING ROUTINE

Location: Earth, Sunflower City, The Sanctuary
Perspective: The Man

Kah!

That...ugh...that's *not* a pleasant feeling, jarring into the real world all of a sudden. I've heard that most people find the process of transitioning to and from the virtual world of the Interstellar Network Link quite pleasant, like waking up to soothing music after a good night's sleep. But I was in a rush to escape before my social anxieties finally hit me fully and decided that some motion sickness was better than a panic attack. Even attending class virtually, it did little to help. As it is, my hands are still white-knuckled as I grip the crown-of-thorns that serves as my control module while I'm Linked-up, while the Link's many little filaments, previously attached to the major nerve clusters of my body, are still in the process of drawing back into its full-body gyroscopic frame.

For a moment I wonder why I no longer have to use the bathroom –
that's pretty normal for me when I'm right on the edge of escaping a panic
attack – when I catch sight of a yellow-filled filament vanishing into the
Link's frame. There's a "bladder bag" in that cord which connects to the
various pipes that underlie the whole city, and I always assumed it was
just for the diehards who didn't want to disconnect for something as
trivial as a bathroom break. Rude thing! It could've at least asked me first!

Blinking several times, I force myself to postpone the headache and
queasy stomach for later. Instead, I begin filling my internal logs with my
psi-stylus, including all my experiences and knowledge of what I've
learned, no matter how embarrassing. This digital memoir usually auto-
logs, but occasionally I take time to input entries manually. For now, I
leave the psi-stylus to continue writing as I go about my day. Right now,
it's time for an assessment, to make sure everything's where it belongs.

The room itself, my "living room," is a big rectangular cube with
tables, shelves, and plenty of other places for guests and inhabitants to
lounge in whatever manner makes them most comfortable and gives
them a place where they can stay out from underfoot. There's also lots of
free space, which keeps me from constantly jogging my shins or stubbing
my toes and gives my live-in roomies plenty of room to roam when the
mood takes them. Over against the far wall is the Link setup, removed
from everything else so that I can always review the room the moment I
come out.

Up above, most visible of all, are the cats, looking down from their
assorted perches around the room, judging me (business as usual there).
Another shift of my eyes, and there's the sloth, dangling from his artificial
branch, munching on the real leaves growing out of it (also normal). Two

39

bearded dragons, a smaller female sprawled shamelessly on top of a larger male, bask under a sun lamp on one of the many middle shelves, confident in the soft shimmer of the forcefield surrounding them being able to keep them protected from any random acts of feline psychopathy. And they were indeed protected, since the collars worn by all my pets, or "pets" in the case of the cats, are tied directly into Sunflower City's power grid to produce forcefield shields at any sign of danger, as well as to allow tracking of the animals if they decide to go roaming outside. And finally, down below the level of my waist, are five pairs of the most soulful eyes imaginable looking me over, one of them a very lovely light sky blue color, the rest varying shades of amber-brown.

Wait a sec: *five* pairs?

"When I got online, I only had four dogs," I patiently explain to the now five fuzz kids seated before me, their earnest and slightly guilty expressions making it plain that they'd been really, *really* hoping I wouldn't notice this new development. "What exactly happened?"

Yan, a hulking, muscular, adorable beast, part Bernese Mountain dog, part Great Pyrenees, tilts his head slightly, indicating the swollen teats and heavily gravid belly of a mixed-Retriever bitch who had joined my boys. As I arch a speculative eyebrow, she promptly crouches low, carefully owing to her advanced status, and rolls over onto her side, exposing throat and belly and the whites of her eyes in a sign of total submission. Ivan, the blue-eyed Spitz-o-mutt, then interposes himself between me and her protectively, though he still gives me that hopeful look, his tail doing a slow wag, making it as clear as he could that he wasn't challenging me, just trying to say "Please?" the only way he knew how.

From the peanut gallery where the cats perch, I can see that the cats, being cats, are perfectly happy seeing someone else get into trouble. All of them except Elizabeth, of course: she's a fluffy seal point Birman, and she thinks of herself as everyone's stuffy Victorian-era maiden aunt: a fussbudget, but for a good cause. From her perspective, the world would be a far better place if only it were a bit more organized.

"Huh," I half-vocalize, half-grunt, then get to my feet, blinking for a moment at the *ache* that suffuses my body: I'd set the Link to exercise my muscles at the same time I was in the classroom, and I was surprised at how exactly I felt as though I'd just finished a full set of weights (it was biceps day, but that meant my forearms, shoulders, and upper back also shared the ache), followed by a brisk set of aerobics and planking.

"All right: Jane," I address the copper-furred girl. "You follow along and pay attention to what the boys do, because you'll be doing this yourself once you're trained properly. If you need to rest up, or feel your time coming, you head straight for the sacking over there."

I point to the mass makeshift dog bed I'd thrown together, and which I regularly had to replace anyway, so the mess from birthing wouldn't change things much.

"One of the boys will escort you. Now come," I told the assembled motley crew, and started toward the double doors at the rear of my living area.

Of course, they couldn't really understand my words; they don't have the right parts in their brain to process language. Sure, the boys (and now girl) recognize a phrase or two, but true language is something that only humans and other sapients share. Despite the lack of language though, dogs do understand meaning, intent, the bits of communication that transcend language. My body language, the tone of my voice, the countless subtle shades of my scent and the pheromones that I wasn't even capable of noticing, all of that was conveyed to my five dogs as I spoke. So, when I pushed open the first of the swinging double layer of doors leading out, all five of them followed, even Jane, tails wagging. They all relaxed as soon as I'd given her a name, understanding on the most instinctive level that something important had just transpired: Jane was one of us now.

Stopping in the antechamber between the swinging double doors, I reached over to the racks on the left wall and pulled down the forcefield bands. One for my neck, one for my waist, and four for my wrists and ankles. Properly protected, I pushed through the second set of double doors, not really expecting anybody to join me on my rounds except the dogs. Two of the cats, though, trotted along right after us: Creamsicle, an orange kitty with a white tummy, hardly more than a kitten and full of eager enthusiasm for playing with the dogs; and Inky, a black tom whose name I'd taken from Pac-Man. He affected far more dignity than he actually possessed, and had an almost overwhelming need to supervise matters, since obviously without his presence there was no telling what might go wrong. He and Elizabeth get along great. She's been his surrogate mother ever since I brought him home with me, so it's no wonder he's adopted a lot of her attitude.

Before us loomed a space that was vast and bright with an artificial sun dappling through high trees to either side of the double doors, the air steaming with moist, semi-tropical warmth, typical for this part of the Sanctuary. Other parts of the vast underground estate, cordoned off by more of the "soft" forcefields, held every climate that could support life on Earth. Those same semi-globular forcefields acted as lenses through which the light of the artificial sun above us had to pass, ensuring that each section of the Sanctuary was tailored to the specific needs of the life within. From the hill on which I stood with my dogs and cats; the whole Sanctuary looked like an especially lumpy tatterdemalion crazy quilt.

Satisfied by my initial survey that nothing was obviously amiss, I started down the hill, smiling to myself in the warm, gentle breeze that rustled the tall grass to either side of the path.

WHAM!

And *that* is why I wear the bands: if not for their reflexive forcefield generators cushioning the impact of the two powerful, birdlike talons that slammed into my chest, and the subsequent impact of my fall, I would almost certainly be nursing a caved sternum, some cracked ribs, a concussion, and an assortment of cuts and contusions. And that was the owner of those claws being friendly!

As it was, I was still dazed, and not really able to move anywhere close to fast enough as the sharp-toothed maw of the critter that had pounced me clamped down around the softly shimmering "skin" of the field that was suddenly surrounding my head, while two other sets of powerful jaws began gnawing on my feet.

Of course, the forcefields didn't stop the assault on my feet, since the owners of those jaws didn't want to crunch my bones. What they wanted were my sneakers!

Giving the Utahraptor seated on my stomach a shove, I got back up, scowling.

"Hooligans!" I yelled after the spotted hyena and thylacine bearing my shoes away with them into the bush, obviously happy as clams at having pulled one over on the dumb human. "Rapscallions! Knaves! *Poltroons!*" Then I rounded on the drab-feathered theropod who'd been point man (or woman in her case) for the whole operation. "And you!" I bellowed, poking her in the snoot. "What do you have to say for yourself?"

Quite casually, and with utter indifference to my annoyance or the enthusiastic barks of the dogs as they went bounding off after their playmates, eager to engage in some tug-of-war with what would soon be my ex-shoes, the Utahraptor hen closed her rather formidable jaws around my hand, making a trilling-purring sound in her syrinx as she did so. To her, that was affection. Lucky for me that the forcefield immediately kicked in again, or else she'd have probably nipped off a few joints with her cute little nibble!

Wrapping my fingers around the inside of the rowdy lady's jaws, feeling the sharp tips of her fangs prod my skin through the pseudoplasmic membrane of the forcefield, I gave her teeth a friendly tug, which she returned, before releasing my grip and heaving a resigned sigh.

"Didn't wanna hang out in the VR, huh?" I asked rhetorically, before continuing my walk around the Sanctuary, now accompanied by the Utahraptor rather than my dog pack, who were having far too much fun out in the bush with the hyenas and thylacines. Not unexpected: their species-cultures were close enough that they'd developed a playful sort of truce, though they still generally kept to their separate territories; the wolves were too far away, in the cold zone, or they might've joined in as well. Sometimes a maned or Falklands wolf would wander over and hang around awkwardly, though: they're a lot like me that way, wanting to join in, but not really knowing how. "Yeah, I don't blame you: too much time in the virtual feed will rot your brain."

Truthfully, my presence around the Sanctuary is almost optional (I do stress the "almost," though). Walking along the firm-but-yielding path that led between the enclosures, making my morning inspection just like I always did, I noted the various robots that tended each creature, some on wheels, others on treads, a few on legs of a highly variable number, two on gravitic sleds, and a double handful with hydro-jets to propel them quickly and efficiently through the water of the floating aquarium-globes. Each enclosure had a readout display on a stand in front of it, looking a great deal like the information placards in the zoos of an earlier, less enlightened time.

The major difference between those ancient enclosures and these modern ones was simple: the boundary between an enclosure and the rest of the Sanctuary was life-permeable. So, if they didn't want to stay put, the animals could leave any time they wanted: woe betide the unprotected visitor! The readouts gave me a real-time status review of each creature within a given enclosure, and whether they were hooked up to the virtual feeds or not. I could have looked it all up from my workstation back in my living area, of course, but I feel that a personal inspection is an important part of my job.

None of this would have been possible, of course, without the virtual feeds. Each enclosure had what I call "trees of life," pillars that extended an array of connective tendrils like the multitude of tiny graspers on the underside of a starfish, but longer, more flexible, and infinitely more durable. Once one of those touched one of the simpler animals, like the fish or birds or reptiles, they were instantly transported into a habitat that existed only in their minds, but might as well have been completely real: as real as the classroom I'd just exited, or the ache in my muscles where

I'd gone through a workout while attending a virtual class, or the thick, reddened calluses on my knuckles where I'd been hitting a virtual punching bag.

For the more complex animals, like the cetaceans or the primates or the cephalopods, they had to have a rig like my crown-of-thorns, though fortunately most of them quickly "got" their purpose and adapted accordingly. All the animals, whether complex or simple, spend most of their time in their virtual environments. There they live out their complex, intricate lives, hunted and hunting, being fed real food in the real world by the robots when they virtually acquired whatever their needs demanded they eat. Being faced with virtual challenges that stimulated their minds and strengthened their bodies. Simple or complex of mind, the overwhelming majority of the critters around the Sanctuary never saw the need to leave their relatively small enclosures, since they could occupy worlds vastly wider while they were linked in.

A lot like most of humanity now, as I thought about it. That was how I'd read that the Republic handled most of its populace, the ones who sold their votes in exchange for the necessities of life: they were provided the highest quality virtual lives via the Links in each of their habitations. They'd build complex, intricate virtual societies, shared virtual forums and gathering places, tribal centers, and auditoriums. They had whole virtual governments, sometimes, complete with leaders selected from the virtual communities.

But then, weren't most of our social constructs all in our minds anyway? Just because you only knew a friend in a virtual environment, didn't mean your souls couldn't talk.

Or so I guessed. I've got serious anxiety issues, and they get really nasty whenever I'm around people for too long, and that includes virtual people. I've got a variety of workarounds for when I have to interact, and it's not so bad when I'm around fewer than a handful of people at a time, but all the same... I just have to curl up at the end of the day and hug a dog or cuddle a cat or snuggle a sloth. That and a book or three and I'm usually able to get back to work the next day, good as new.

My job, when I do finally make myself go to work, is Chief Zoological Management Officer, Earth Ecosphere. It sounds pretty spiffy right up until the realization that I'm the only person working down here in this not-quite-secret and *very* safe place. So being the "chief" around here doesn't count for much...well, unless you count the dogs. Not the cats, though; anybody who knows about cats will understand. The sloth and the lizards accept that I'm a source of food and affection, but concepts like "boss" just aren't part of their respective species psychologies.

Oh well, at least the robots respect me.

There are three distinct parts to the job, one that's my favorite, since I can do it alone and the robots handle the drudgery bits; one that's a bit harder since I have to think about it, as well as interact with people; and the last that's...honestly, I don't want to think about it at all. As for how I got the job, it's a bit more complicated.

Around two or three Earth centuries ago, some clever soul figured out how to break the Einsteinian speed limit, and suddenly we had an infinite universe all around us, filled with habitable worlds (many of which, incidentally, also had plentiful petroleum reserves, usually the ones with the most life on them). The fact that some of them were already inhabited didn't really bother most of us.

On Earth, faced with unprecedented prosperity, our major world religions reached out to each other, and soon found common ground, forming the World Peace Collective with its well-trained, non-denominational Preachers to tell us how God was on our side, and how we were bringing the blessings of our civilization to the benighted nonhumans out among the stars. Our major corporations soon had to scramble for supremacy, and when the dust settled, only the strongest remained, spreading their influence as they backed various new colonies with lots of representatives down here on Earth to tell us how great the economy was, especially with all that cheap off-world labor, some human, most not. Most importantly of all, we had the United Earth Empire, which fielded a benevolent representative government for everyone who got to stay on the home planet, and kept a firm grip (some might call it a tyranny...but not too loudly) on our extraplanetary holdings.

In short, it was a golden age. At least if you were a human living on Earth. If you were a malcontent, a rebel, or a criminal without friends in high places, there were plenty of places to send you out in the colonies, ensuring that life on Earth remained peaceful and perfect, and that there were plenty of well-paying jobs for everybody.

Some of us could see there was dry rot at the foundations of the United Earth Empire, though. I was one of them. Like in George Orwell's "Animal Farm," I was Benjamin the donkey: a shy academic professional teaching at a mostly forgotten little community college, just working away, day after day, keeping my head down and not causing trouble. The phrase "Those who can't do, teach," described me exactly in those days. I knew that things weren't right, knew that there were so many wrongs we were committing, knew that our leaders were lying to us, that we were lying to ourselves, but I just...I didn't know what I could do, or even where to start, the problems just seemed so overwhelming.

Because I didn't act, because I didn't do *something*, I have to share in the guilt for what the Empire did. For what humanity did. That's only justice.

Around the time that the United Earth Empire conquered its second pre-inhabited planet and had just about finished pacifying the natives is when the Pan-Galactic Republic sent its first representatives, its diplomats and technical experts, to discuss the matter with humanity's leaders. As it turned out, they came from a culture that took the quite reasonable stance that life was the rarest and most precious commodity in the universe, and it should be treasured as such. Sapient life forms – people – were even more rare and more precious, and they regarded anything like the imperial system we'd imposed on other cultures, to say nothing of the mass extinctions that had followed in our wake of colonization, inexcusable.

Given their viewpoint, I think they were surprisingly reasonable: instead of trying to wipe us out, they decided to try giving us stuff, loads of free technology, as well as the training needed to use it, so that we wouldn't need to go around conquering people. Instead, we could have paradise on Earth without having to exploit anybody.

Needless to say, that whole fiasco didn't end well. First our leaders decided that they didn't want any outside interference. Then they decided they wanted to regulate everything being given to us, heavily, keeping it all limited to the elite. Then they wanted to have our official Earth corporations to be the only ones licensed to manufacture and sell what was being offered, usually for exorbitant prices. Of course, the harder our leaders squeezed, the more Republic technology hit the black market, the stuff simply overwhelming the ability of our government to stop its spread, and thus undermining its authority on the most fundamental level. Just by providing their services and technology for free, and making them available to anybody who asked, the Republic's representatives caused a vicious, culture-annihilating economic war, one waged between the Empire's leadership and its common citizenry.

Attempting to turn people's attention away from this economic war, the Empire turned it into a hot war instead, starting off by gunning down the Republic ambassador, a big pacifistic tree-bush-thing named Towering Canopy.

That didn't end well either: the next thing any of us knew, when the Republic's Master of Defense, Garfi Lett, turned his attention onto us, the Republic's armed forces wiped out the remnants of our space fleet who didn't surrender or run away. It all ended in a single battle above one of our more distant colony worlds. For us, it was a catastrophe. For Garfi Lett, apparently it was just another day at the office.

In a panic, the overwhelming majority of humanity's trillions flooded back to Earth, and as we all began to crowd back to the ancestral home, without the distractions afforded by conquest and colonization, it was only a matter of time before we collectively realized how much we hated each other.

Thus began the End.

First the Empire collapsed into nations.

Then nations collapsed into states.

States soon became city-states.

Before long, most of humanity was just a collection of tribes.

And then we got *serious* about killing each other.

All that hate we'd so long deferred, putting it off day after day, letting it simmer, bubbling just beneath the surface of all our interactions, it all came gushing out in a flood of blood, a planet-wide murder-suicide where we unleashed every weapon we could devise, from ICBMs and killer robots to clubs and pointy sticks.

The carnage of the End left our poor little planet covered in vast swaths of wasteland...or wasted land, places where nothing natural could live, not even microscopic organisms. There were bio-engineered plagues and irradiated landscapes and storms that range from flaying sand or ice, to smothering dust or acid snow, to literal fire and brimstone. And if the environment out there isn't enough, there's always the monsters, the only macroscopic life that seems to thrive in the wasted lands. They're not natural, though, and none of them are friendly by any definition of the word.

Well, maybe by one definition. They're not the kind of friends you'd invite on vacation, or to your birthday party, or to come home and meet your folks. Instead, when you've hit that point where your lips are chapped and your face is blistered and all you can do is lie down and stare up at the pitiless skies, they're the last friends you'll ever need, the ones who'll make it all just go away.

My knowledge of the wasted lands is *very* personal. What I was back in the End is what the Republic people call a gene pirate: somebody who smuggles out genetic material, or even whole living organisms, from a planet that isn't legally a part of the Pan-Galactic Republic and so should be off-limits for any sort of eco-exploitation. Except I didn't do it for money. I did it because there was nowhere else for me to go: we were killing our little blue planet. We were doing it because we hated each other so much, we couldn't stop doing everything possible to slaughter each other any way we could. The plants and the animals and everything else that had the bad luck to share the planet with us, they were just collateral damage in a war of species' self-annihilation. So, somebody had to do something, and because I couldn't live with my shame and guilt at not having acted before, I guess that somebody ended up being me.

Back in those days, maybe ten, twenty, thirty Earth years ago, my contact with the Pan-Galactic Republic was this guy named Scintillant Camor. Mister Camor is probably the nicest, sweetest, gentlest guy you'll ever meet anywhere, and you'd never know that he's actually one of the *really* important people in the PGR's government, a Chief Minister and Master. The Master of the Ministry of Life, actually. He's this wizard with genetic engineering, and...oh. Oh, the things he's done. With the help of the technicians of the Republic, at the request of what was left of the Empire's leadership, Scintillant Camor went to work enacting the miracle of Ezekiel's Vision of the Valley of Dry Bones.

He brought them back.

He brought them *all* back.

River dolphins. Bats in colonies, in droves, in *scads*, thick enough to blot out the skies if they ever left their Links and took wing. Cheetahs. Rhinos. Dodos and passenger pigeons and penguins and birds, birds, *birds* beyond counting, beyond imagination. Whales, all of them. Seals and sea lions and things from the ocean I'd only read about in Lovecraftian fiction. Polar bears. Dinosaurs by the boatload (take that, Noah!). Megafauna that were around eons before the quaternary extinction event. Dwarf mammoth!

The technology of the Pan-Galactic Republic includes computers with programs powerful enough to re-create even scraps of genetic evidence into a full sequence. They've also got biochemical processes that can rebuild whole chromosomes from bits and pieces of stuff that's been dead for ages and ages, no life left in it at all. Once they've got the full sequence, then, they've got these artificial wombs – Mister Camor's showed me some of the ones they're using right now to repopulate Earth, set up in these huge facilities on the Moon – of all different sizes, which they can use to grow just about anything from a mosquito to a blue whale. Science so advanced that it might as well be magic or a miracle, so I classify the whole process in the same section of my brain that handles supernatural events. When they've got a working population of a particular type of critter, they send them down to me in the Sanctuary and I work with the robots to set up a habitat for the new arrivals, then help them get settled in.

As for the way things are now, Scintillant Camor has now taken on the task of Earth's re-terraforming, and of Earth in general after the End...well, ended, and what was left of our population officially applied for membership in the Republic. I mean, it just made sense by that point: pretty much all the other planets where humans resided joined the PGR. Not too dissimilar from the rumored individuals that joined when we first encountered them in our outward expansion into space. I believe there's maybe a little bit less than a half-billion of us left. Total, everywhere in the universe. Here on Earth is where about three-fifths of that total still survives, and the bare majority of them live in one place: Sunflower City.

Which is fine by me: it means there's plenty of area for Mister Camor to give to the animals and the plants and everything else after they've cleaned up the rest of the planet. Not back to us humans, though: we had our shot, we blew it, and we should be grateful we're allowed to live at all, let alone in a place as nice as Sunflower City can be.

In the meantime, when I'm not out doing the hard part of my job, I just mind the animals in the Sanctuary, supervising the robots and the Links to make sure nothing goes wrong, stepping in if it does. Mister Camor got me the job pretty much as soon as Earth was legally a probationary member of the Pan-Galactic Republic, and we could just declare the gene piracy stuff retroactively legalized.

The work in the Sanctuary is nice. There are a few animals that prefer not to be hooked up to the Links, like my Terrible Trio, the Utahraptor, hyena, and thylacine; I haven't tamed them, and they're *not* mine, not like the animals who stay inside my living area semi-permanently (all abandoned by their former owners). There are a few smaller critters around as well, like rabbits with attitude, foxes on the prowl for mischief, and an especially polite skunk, but I keep them all safe with forcefield collars, just like the pets.

Sometimes I have to play the role of veterinarian, especially when the VR feed gets a little too brutal, but with all the classes I'm signed up for via the Link, including all the subliminal training that goes on while I'm asleep, I'm swiftly getting up to speed on that sort of business. Republic technology being what it is, and Scintillant Camor wanting only the best for the critters, there's not a lot of health problems short of death that can't be fixed, and even that's negotiable as long as I get there in time and enough of the body's present.

The second hardest part of my job is working with the experts Mister Camor keeps sending my way so they can hash out Link scenarios to help all the critters learn how to be proper members of their respective species. Animals have analogues to culture, after all, even without having language or those other things that identify a species as sapient, and the smarter ones especially need to learn a lot of how they're supposed to live and act from their parents or other members of their kind. Since "their kind" in far too many instances was wiped from the face of the planet, starting over from scratch can get kind of tricky without some proper models. And that's a big part of what makes the VR feed so important.

More importantly, the Link keeps them wild: since most of the Sanctuary's animals are in the Link most of the time, they don't usually notice me, so they don't get used to humans or the idea that we're somehow a source of food. They *earn* their food, at least in their own minds: for herbivores, they have to stay alert while they munch their fodder of choice, because there are predators out there that want to eat them. For the carnivores, they have to actually hunt and chase and take down their prey, then tear it apart and devour it before somebody else steals it from them. Of course, it's all in their heads – the food they eat is actually formulated food pellets – but the VR gives them the experience of all the real qualities of the food the animals are eating in the feed, and the programs make sure they're seldom in lethal danger, however much it might hurt.

The threat of real injury is a kindness in the long run since it prepares them for the real world, where mistakes or bad luck can get you killed. They don't know that, of course, and that's what makes sure they come out wild, and ready to live *in* the wild.

But, as they say, my doors are always open just in case one of my charges needs some special attention, as the Terrible Trio clearly demonstrates. When it's a bunny or a bandicoot, that's just a minor adjustment, mostly to convince the cats that the new arrival isn't food. When it's a moose or a bear or a giraffe or an especially pushy triceratops... yeah, that's a bit more serious.

Statistically speaking, most days I can avoid the third aspect of the job. Maybe today will be another of those days, the "good days." That would make me happy.

Before I know it, I'm back at the doors, my rounds all complete, and all my major limbs and organs still in their proper places: a very nice bonus! A whistle blow is all that's needed before the dogs come running. Creamsicle is already there, since apparently she got tired out and came back to curl up on the flat rock where Inky is still sitting like a highly judgmental gargoyle, and soon after they're both preceding me into my living room. The Utahraptor keeps trying to munch on more than her specially formulated food pellets, probably upset that they don't squeak and bleed when they're bitten, but overjoyed that *I* do, especially when she gets in a nip on the spots where the personal forcefields don't quite reach. Still, she doesn't follow me past the double doors, seeing that as my territory, and to her, territory isn't something you trespass upon lightly.

That's actually a good idea: figure out an automated food pellet that can scream and squirt and stuff, maybe with an edible plastic machine inside as the skeleton. I'll move the idea along to the right parties during breakfast.

Despite all the horseplay (dino-play?), I don't take any offense by it. She's just playful, even if she's rough about it sometimes, so I don't really mind the artificial skin I have to spray on once I'm back inside, or the new sneakers I program my personal fabricator to craft. However, there *are* critters in the Sanctuary that genuinely wish me ill, to put it politely, and they do occasionally decide to slip out of their VR feeds, so I can't ever completely let down my guard. Fortunately, I'm on quite good terms with almost all the big carnivores. Mostly it's just some of the small carnivores, a few of the ungulates, and this one *mean* megatherium.

Stepping back into my living room, the dogs trailing along behind, I can't resist a long, slow sigh: deep breath in, slow breath out. Sure, I love my job, and I love all my charges, whether they love me back or not, but... well, home is home. The cats haven't attempted any murder (that they'll admit), the dogs have had their morning walk, and everything appears to be all clear.

Time for breakfast!

CHAPTER 4: THE QUEST FOR BREAKFAST

Location: Earth, exiting the Sanctuary,
entering Rock Bottom
Perspective: The Man

Breakfast for me, as per usual, came last of all. First were the critters around the house: they take priority. I know there are sources on dogs that say you should make them watch you eat, or something like that, because that proves you're the boss of the pack. Well, maybe that works for them, but I've found that my boys behave just fine as they are, and Jane seemed to adapt to the status quo readily as well. After all, what good is a boss that doesn't make sure your needs are met before his?

So I tug on my work suit, a saggy, baggy job that accentuates all my body's worst features, double-check to make sure I've got all the essentials in my pack, sling it up on my back, then hit the safety seal, which merges the tough micro-fabric with the back of the suit so there's no way to tear the two apart without ripping them both to shreds. If I need it, there's a helmet in there, and once that's in place, the suit's pretty much self-contained.

The "clown suit," as I like to call it, is a makeshift merging of a human design with some PGR tech added in, something I jury-rigged together over the course of many years. The specs I've read about the various parts I'd cobbled into the suit say that it'll be able to withstand the hard radiation following ground zero of a dirty nuke and let the wearer endure a full salvo of fifty-cal across the main chest plate (hidden, like all the armored bits, in the inner lining), and I know that the shoulder plates can take the bite of a deinosuchus, though the body beneath tends to bruise up a lot afterward.

All that protection, even with the muscle mnemonic neural net that integrates the hidden plates with the ballistic fabric of the suit, doesn't mean it's *comfortable*, though, especially that dumb buckethead helmet. Besides, I hate stuff on my head as a general rule. Or jewelry. Or tight clothes. Honestly, if I didn't hate people staring at me so much, and if I didn't have such a desperate and ongoing need for pockets, I'd probably wander around naked.

Once I'm all suited up, then – and only then – it's time to head out into the City.

As I said previously, most of the work tending to the needs of the various creatures around the Sanctuary is dealt with by automatons of various sorts. That means that I'm not essential around the place for most of the day. Which is a good thing, because my *real* work takes a whole lot of my time and energy, and when I come home at the end of it all I usually just pour out food for my personal critters and crash into the webbing in my Link, letting it lull me into a subliminal learning state. So, what's my real work?

That's a very fair question.

Mostly, I hunt monsters.

Leaving my bedroom and pushing my way through the more clingy members of my fuzz buddies, I make my way out through the living room and into the "airlock." That's my name for the front hall, complete with shelves for shoes and pegs for coats, and a big, classic-looking and *very* solid oak front door.

I spend a few extra minutes calling all the dogs and cats and whoever else cares to join in on the fun over to the front door, hook each of them up to their daily play and exercise routines via the little Link cables next to the shoe shelves, unlock the door, and step out onto the streets of Sunflower City at Rock Bottom. Down here, it's usually not that crowded, since the people who actually live at Rock Bottom level are the ones who want to enjoy the bounties of Sunflower City, but don't want to register as citizens of the Republic. For... reasons. That doesn't mean there aren't eyes watching for weakness, because the place is thick with scavengers, but you won't see them unless you know the signs. Above Rock Bottom, though, the whole City is bustling with people in little knots and small crowds; thankfully nothing like the congested agony of the human-built cities of old Earth, though, especially not with our reduced population, so I can usually keep my anxieties from kicking in as long as I don't find myself overstressed somehow.

With that thought, naturally, about two seconds after I lock the door behind me, making sure the magnetic seals fully engage, a man in a very expensive business suit hits the clickway right in the middle of the street in front of me. I know it's expensive because it's the only part of him that survives the landing. Well, that and his designer shoes. Thank goodness for modern micro-fibers! If it wasn't for the incredible stress-resistance of the Republic-made materials of the guy's suit and shoes, he'd be *all over* down here, and I'd be sorely regretting not putting on my helmet.

"Central," I address the empty air with as calm a voice as I can manage under the circumstances. "Were you aware of the man falling from," I looked up, "I believe somewhere near the mid-upper stories of the Mandela Building?"

There was a slight shimmer, and then a glowing blue square formed in the air in front of me: a solid-light touchscreen, complete with a keyboard.

"Certainly, Chief Zoological Management Officer," came a very calm, pleasant-sounding female voice emanating from the solid-light construct.

"Just call me Biff," I tell it, massaging the bridge of my nose. "And glad to hear. Now, can you tell me why you didn't stop this guy from taking the plunge? I'm pretty sure Nelson Mandela wouldn't appreciate people engaging in voluntary euthanasia from off a building named after him."

"Mr. Mandela's wishes are not germane to the present situation," the computer reported calmly. "However, to answer your questions, direct and implied, the deceased individual in question is Percival Villafort Montgomery, known as Peewee to his co-workers in the Central Auditing Department. He specifically requested that I deactivate the containment fields on the upper walkways, and then the gravitic dampening fields all the way down, both as precursors to an act of self-termination, as per his fundamental rights as a citizen of the Pan-Galactic Republic."

"Guy was depressed, huh?" I grunt, crossing my arms and feeling sorry for the poor fellah despite all my wishes to the contrary. "Aren't you supposed to offer counseling services or something?"

"Certainly, Biff," the computer agreed with as much enthusiasm as its non-sapient processors could manage. "I refused to comply with his wishes until he had discussed the matter with me thoroughly, and I had confirmed that he did indeed have a valid reason for wishing to enter the state of non-mortality. In that conversation, much of which I am afraid falls under confidentiality laws and has been automatically deleted from my memory, he informed me that he wished to self-terminate because, and I quote, 'I don't want to see the horrors that my complicity has allowed to come to pass.'"

Now *that* was freaky: at the end of her explanation, the computer shifted over into the dead guy's actual audio recording! Still, the recording did tell me a whole lot of stuff that I couldn't pick up any other way, nuances in tone and modulation of the voice that a text copy or a simple repetition just wouldn't allow. For one thing, I knew that the guy wasn't depressed: he was filled with self-loathing! That, and he was really, genuinely afraid of seeing the end results of whatever it was that he'd taken part in causing, just like he'd said. I mean, sure, the guy was a bit melodramatic, but what can you expect from anybody who'd want to go out in such a public kind of way?

"After our counseling session, I informed him that he could call out for assistance at any time, and I would reactivate the various safeguards," Central continued. "Following a neural scan to ensure his competence, I required him to acknowledge that he had heard and understood me and that he truly wanted me to turn off the safeguards before I would comply with his request. Once he had done so, I directed him to a vertical descent point that would minimize the risk to others and complied with his wishes. That he failed to change his mind on the matter, despite ample opportunity to do so, is self-evident."

"No kidding," I muttered, before I noticed movement from my peripheral vision. "Hey! Get away from that body! That's evidence!"

"No," calmly replied the exceedingly unpleasant-looking individual who seemed to be the leader of the little cadre that had materialized out of the shadows of Rock Bottom. "That," he indicated the body with a jerked thumb while his two companions got to work on the laces of the guy's shoes, "is *swag*."

Oh boy: it's gonna be one of *those* days.

Under normal circumstances, I'd have tried some more negotiation, maybe started some give-and-take diplomacy, offered him information on some of the nice stuff I've found during my various explorations of Rock Bottom and the layers beneath. Seriously, there's enough booty stowed away in forgotten vaults and crevasses and hideaways in this city's secret places to satisfy Blackbeard! (Though probably not Leopold II of Belgium.) On my first day poking around in the under-ways, I crashed through a false floor and landed right on top of a stack of gold bars, each neatly stamped with an eagle-over-swastika, just to give you an idea of the sorts of treasures lying around in humanity's last city on Earth, forgotten and unclaimed.

That guy might have some important stuff on his person, though, and the way he'd said his last words was making me kind of freak out, and if I'm being completely honest, having a guy go splat right on the clickway within spitting distance had gotten my adrenaline going. Besides, those two goons behind their boss were obviously professionals when it came to stripping bodies, and I knew I wasn't going to get the time I needed for diplomacy before they'd vanish off somewhere in the very nearly infinite streets and subdivisions and alleyways of Rock Bottom. As a double-besides, the lead yobo was getting closer to me, and I could see him reaching for something concealed in the small of his back: a high-end warning sign.

So instead of opening with words, I opened with a foot to the bossman's knee, making sure to bring it down at a nice sideways angle for the full cross-shear effect.

Next moment the other two are coming at me, and while I make sure the guy I sent to the ground stays there with a quick jab from my hand stunner, they're rushing me with buzzers: hand-portable chainsaws, a real hit with the lowlifes who end up here in Rock Bottom.

Fortunately, those plates in my clown suit aren't just for show (I mean, if you could see them at all), and I deflect the first goon's thrust with the armored part of my forearm as I drop down and cover up in a nice, low stance, minimizing my profile even more. Also, luckily for me, the buzzers are old-style Earth leftovers, like the hand cannon the lead jerk was pulling before I interrupted him. In contrast, the armor plates on my forearms, where the second yobo's buzzer connected, are solid Republic-tech. Like all chainsaws, if you jam up the flow of the chain, such as by slamming it too hard and too fast into an immovable object, some unpleasant things start to happen, among them the chain snapping. While I was protected by the plates on my clown suit, letting one end of the spiked chain bounce harmlessly off my armored forearm (and one of those whizzing spikes nearly parting my hair!), the goon isn't so lucky, taking shrapnel from his shattering weapon all along his arm.

Another jab of the stunner, and all I've got is goon number three, who I can see is having some significant second thoughts about this whole ganging-up-on-the-little-guy business, especially since the "ganging up" part is no longer one of his available options.

"Hey," I call out to him while he's circling me, though I don't drop my stance, and I certainly don't take my eyes off him. "You get anything off the stiff?"

"Naw man," he growls at me, giving me a quizzical cocked eyebrow behind the dark glasses he's sporting. "Didn't even finish gettin' those shoes clear of the excrement."

Since he's only wearing a tight white undershirt and shorts, not even a pair of shoes to his name, I believe him: there's just nowhere that he could hide anything substantial without me noticing.

Still...

"Central," I address the computer, its solid light console still hovering in the air where I'd left it, even as I reach back into one of the side pouches on my pack, where I keep the emergency medical slap-packs. "Anything missing from the body?"

"No personal effects have been removed," the calm female voice reassures me.

"Get lost for a while," I tell the last guy, whipping out some synthetic skin and slapping it over the shredded bits of his buddy's arm, making sure to hold it in place until the flesh seals up, stopping the bleeding. I keep my stunner in the other hand, though, just in case. "I just wanted to check the guy's ID, anyway. You can strip the body when I'm done: I won't even take his cash, if there is any."

Nice thing about a post-scarcity society: I don't need the money, so I don't need to worry about temptation to do other than what I'd just promised. If these yobos would just get their acts together and ask for official recognition in the City, they'd get the resources they needed, too. They'd probably never get rich — you have to *work* to earn money — but the Republic is really good at taking care of its citizens.

Well...I guess they'd have to sell their votes to somebody, same as most citizens do. But I can't think of many folks who ever used those responsibly back before humanity joined the Republic. At least under the Republic you're guaranteed shelter, sustenance, education, and recreation in exchange for your vote. Quality stuff, too, the fruits of superior technology efficiently applied.

Kind of a shame, really: we humans could've had all this stuff too back in the day, if we'd just quit trying to grind each other down all the time.

The guy takes the pause in the action to think over my offer, and then beats feet. I don't bother trying to track his route once he's out of the critical distance zone and get back to the business at hand.

"Central, can you get a trauma team down here, please?" I ask the computer while I'm poking my way through the...well, *goo*; that's really all that's left of the poor guy. The molecularly enhanced microfibers of his suit and his shoes are the only things keeping him from leaking down the nearest storm drain. "Forensic team, too: I've got a pretty strong suspicion that this is the tip of a very unpleasant iceberg."

"Of course, Biff," the computer replies. "I presume the trauma team is for the two unconscious individuals?"

"Yeah," I growl, unhappy at ending up being a nice guy again: if the team gets here soon enough, which is likely, those two goons will be fixed up as good or better than new before they even wake up, the pain of the injuries nothing but a memory. "Can you please make sure there's Ministry of Peace personnel in the team, too? Might as well get these two signed into the system so they won't have to keep stripping bodies for a living. Get 'em off the streets and hooked up to a Link instead."

"Already done, Biff," the computer reassured me as cheerfully as any non-person ever could. "I presume you'd like me to scan the data card in your hand to present to the forensics team when they arrive?"

"Yes please," I agree, feeling overwhelmingly more relaxed now that I was handing this whole mess over to the professionals, holding the data card I'd found in the guy's breast pocket at arm's length; while Central didn't need it away from my body to scan it, I'd done so out of unconscious habit, just that irrational urge we humans have to try and keep the invisible rays as far away from us as possible, no matter how harmless. "And anything else you can pick up, too. Um," I blink, realization hitting, "I didn't screw up this crime scene, did I?"

"Of course not, Biff," said Central. "I began compiling a full record from the moment Percival Villafort Montgomery demonstrated his desire to self-terminate. Everything that has transpired here is fully and duly recorded, right down to the last detail, provided it did not violate privacy laws. The card you retrieved was shielded from scanning within Montgomery's pocket, however. If it contains any information germane to the investigation of the circumstances surrounding this individual's demise, you have proved a significant support to these investigations. May officials contact you regarding further developments?"

Yeah, sure, pull the other one. What the computer was really asking was if the peacekeepers, led by that crazy dragon lady Benjuro Clee, could come and give my brain a once-over at some point, with a side order of asking if I'd be willing to provide additional assistance with the stuff going down here in Rock Bottom, since I'm a known expert on the region.

"Yeah, sure," I sighed, stuffing the data card in my wrist pocket along with my stunner, letting it auto-seal to ward off the pickpockets. "I'll be available for, um, maybe an hour or so longer before I get to my rounds. I'll be up there," I pointed, a smile crossing my face as I saw my intended destination, six floors up from Rock Bottom in the many tiers of the ever-shuffling City.

Carlscrown Family Bakery. Even the name is a whisper of Heaven.

"I'll let them know, Biff," the computer assured me.

"Thanks a million," I sighed. "Can I have my privacy back now, please?"

"Of course, Biff," replied the computer. "I'm only here when you want me." There was a brief pause. "Or sometimes if you need me."

Scowling, then voluntarily deciding to ignore all the implications that final statement called into my head in favor of a fresh-baked pastry, I headed over to the stairs leading to Sixth Level and started climbing up.

And up.

And...

CHAPTER 5: BREAKFAST CONVERSATION; MOB AT A DISTANCE

Location: Earth, Sunflower City, Sixth Level, outside Carlscrown Bakery
Perspective: The Man

Bliss is the taste of Kouign-amann. I've read that it's the hardest of all pastries to make, and I can confirm it's *darn* time-consuming, having made it once myself, just to prove that I could.

Oh, but the way Carlscrown Family Bakery makes Kouign-amann...oh. Oh. Oh.

For something like this, to fully, *properly* enjoy my breakfast of purest buttery sin, I can't stand up. I can't even stay indoors. Instead, I'm outside at one of the little tables scattered around the bakery's exterior, French bistro style, taking in the wonder of the City while my mouth takes in the wonder that is humanity's most perfect pastry. Alone, and I give thanks to God for the solitude and the pastry, knowing that it's only because of how few humans there are left, and how many of those are hooked up to a virtual feed via the Links in their homes, either for work or for play, that I can eat out-of-doors like this without having my social anxieties spike. I expect in forty or so Earth years that this'll all change and our population will bounce back, so I'm going to enjoy the peace while I can.

Right now, I'm coming down from an adrenaline high, and there's all sorts of messy hormones running through my system as I leave nature's combat state. Dad had some blood of berserkers in the old family tree, or so he told me, and based on my personal experiences he was probably telling the truth (though Dad himself hated violence, may his gentle soul rest in peace; certainly more than he ever found on Earth). When I get into a fighting state, the whole world just centers down on this single point, the rest going to red haze, and my mind and body kick into overdrive, making everything around me seem to slow down while I become pretty much immune to minor distractions like fear or pain. I'm lethally goal-oriented in this state, my concentration and reaction time on a monofilament edge, but in exchange, my whole being just goes to pieces afterward, body and mind. Not necessarily spirit, since that's harder to recharge, so I try to save spending it for when I don't have any other options.

So, if I seem flippant, it's because I'm worn out right now, and the butter-buzz of the Kouign-amann and the gentle sun and the soft breeze of Sunflower City at Sixth Level is what I need to recover as quickly as possible, psychologically as well as physically. If I don't get this happy-time detox in, as soon as my brain kicks fully back into rational gear, I'm going to have a serious freakout as I realize fully what I just did, and what could very easily have happened if anything had gone wrong. I'm just grateful

Mister Carlscrown's not the nosey sort: I just ask for the pastry I save for special occasions, instead of my usual next-to-tasteless fiber-protein scones, and he gives it to me while it's still warm, not once saying anything about the trickle of blood still drying on my forehead where that buzzer blade shrapnel nicked me.

So my mind's floating for a bit as I look up toward the glacially slow arc of one of the City's great "petals," driven by the vast planarian engines that underlie the foundations of the whole artificial island on which almost all of humanity's population now lives. The salted caramel tang of the Kouign-amann is drizzling its way along my tongue, front to back, and I think about what the place of cash is in a post-scarcity society just to further distract myself. Like the cash I forked over to Carlscrown, bright silver-and-gold-and-copper coins interlaced with complex circuitry in exchange for this bit of sweet heaven in my mouth right now.

That coin's a "sid," or Sidereal Credit Denomination, the smallest and least valuable coin in use by the Republic. The other major coins are the Solar, or "sun," which is the most valuable, and the Lunar, or "moon," the middle sister of the family, and they're all based on a given quantity of matter-energy conversion. Or, in other words, you can have a certain amount of energy from whatever source is most handy converted into a certain amount of matter of your choice in exchange for one Credit Denomination, the amount varying by the coin. Heck of a lot easier to back than a Gold Standard!

But why have coins, "cash," at all when it's just so much neater to keep all your money tied up in a virtual-theoretical format, or "in the books," or as credit?

The simplest answer to that question is right in my hand: cash is how you keep the little guy, like Carlscrown Family Bakery, in business, rewarding the hard work and innovation of the common citizen. At the same time, having cash in the economic system means that the government of the Republic is less able to monitor and regulate how people choose to use that money: a deliberate choice by those in charge to surrender power so as to provide the Republic's citizens with freedom, in the same vein as their choice not to collect taxes. In other words, preserving the best bits of what capitalism can do, without necessarily letting its grosser excesses take control. Small time artists get ahead the same way, local talent who don't have the guts to throw themselves into the Arena, risking their lives in exchange for agents willing to sell their material to the Republic at large.

The Arena's fantastic that way: gives creators, singers, dancers, writers, the makers of art in all its infinite varieties a chance to make money on the Link's most popular reality television survival show, fighting robots and monsters and each other on screen in exchange for the chance to get their stuff out to a universe-wide audience if they make it...or even if they don't, posthumous works usually selling just as well as stuff from living creators.

Not that the system's perfect by any means; those three yobos down at Rock Bottom make that pretty clear, and I understand that organized crime and aristocratic elitism are still ongoing concerns in human society. Worst of all, of course, are religions with paid clergy, always popping up and causing trouble, using the cash economy to sneak under the level of official attention, at least until the simoniacs eventually – inevitably, I guess – try to spend all that wealth in a more substantial way, and get noticed and shut down. While I don't know much about the state of affairs beyond Earth, I've heard a few hints dropped that it's like that all over. Apparently, humanity's worse about these "cash-based crimes" than most, but not unique. Degree, rather than presence. As it turns out, civilization is still one long hard work in progress.

Ah well: bad habits do die hard, and there's always a price for freedom. The price being that people can make the wrong decisions with that freedom if that's really what they want. Which I guess is the real test to see if you have it.

... Somebody's watching me, and I blink for a moment, the pastry in my hand hovering halfway between plate and mouth before I turn my head.

"Hey, Mack," the girl standing there greets me with a smirk, probably having been waiting to see how long it'd take me to notice her there, and I suddenly remember: they call me "Mack" around Carlscrown's because that's how I introduced myself before I learned that the Carlscrown family's only daughter was named Mackenzie, "Mac" to her friends.

"Hey yourself, Mac," I reply.

She smells like the fresh bread she's been helping her father bake in the back of the shop as she climbs onto the stool next to me and shares my upward gaze toward the blue skies so far, far above us. There are some flashes up there, some sort of violence going on at the point where void turns into atmosphere, ships shooting at each other over a dispute far beyond my sphere of influence, but I don't think Mac notices it. No, she's focused on something a bit lower, and I adjust my eyes a little so I'm seeing what she is: a crowd of people up on Level Eleven advancing purposefully after a single figure a far-too-short distance ahead of them.

73

There are a few stormy looking clouds above the city, blots in the otherwise clear skies, and I guess that's the reason why.

"What's that crowd for?"

"Lynch mob," I tell her before I resolutely take a big bite of my Kouign-amann and start to chew with all my might, making sure to savor every dollop of baked perfection before I finally swallow.

Deep breaths. That's all: just take deep breaths. Draw in. Hold. Let it out. Slow.

"Why're we so awful to each other all the time?" Mac asks me, her eyes wide and white against the backdrop of her dark skin framed with copper-red hair. We're both too far away to make any difference, and we know it. Mac's just a teen, I guess, but she's smart, almost up to the standards of being an adult, and she's usually able to accept reality when she encounters it without letting her preconceptions get in the way. Cynical city kid sometimes, one of the lucky ones to have been raised in a stable family environment in one of the Protectorates enforced by Republic mercenaries, but I guess we all do what we gotta to survive. Now, if only she could pass those aptitude exams the Ministry of Understanding keeps pushing.

As I'm thinking these thoughts, eyes on her face, I see her pupils dilate, her nostrils flare, and I turn back to the mob. The guy they were chasing's cowering behind this tall, winged figure, one I recognize: a darishi. Mammalian bipedal space dragon, one Sergeant Benjuro Clee by name. Some have wings, like the good Sergeant. Some breathe fire, and this one probably falls into that category too, judging from the smoke puffing out of her nostrils as she stares down the crowd of suddenly stalled humans in front of her. I can't tell what she's saying as she

74

gesticulates with her sharp-clawed fingers, but whatever it is, it's got the people quieting down, whatever screams of hate and murder they'd been spouting now dulled to a quiet background murmur of diminishing discontent.

"Why do those aliens have to interfere with everything we do?" Mac asks next, and I restrain myself from sighing only with an extreme effort: case in point as to what's keeping her from passing those exams she keeps studying for. The Republic's got subliminal trainers that can help you memorize pretty much anything you'd ever need to function in whatever job you might pick, so they're not so interested in book learning. She thinks the tests are there to measure how smart she is, but they aren't: she's plenty smart, and back before the End she'd have had her pick of jobs in any culture that embraced one of the immoral strains of capitalism and didn't care about age. I don't have the heart to tell her that the tests are made to test her cultural adaptability. In other words, she's too human to get one of the nice jobs the Republic has on offer. Too unwilling to adapt to the needs of a vastly bigger universe than just our little Earth. Probably too young, too: the Republic's got a strong bias against hiring people who haven't been proved, and for humans, that means anybody under the age of twenty-five. Knowing her, all those problems will probably fade in time, but for now, she's stuck right where she is until she learns to let go of the bad parts of her humanity.

There's no way I'm going to keep focusing on that crowd of people just a few levels up, on one of the big, broad planes that make up the layers of Sunflower City. Instead, I draw my perceptions back into my center-self, just like I was taught by Scintillant Camor when he was helping me awaken some of my previously latent psychic ability. Doing this is a

75

defensive measure, a way to block out attacks from others, conscious or unconscious, but it works just as well to keep me safe from sensory-emotional overload, which would almost certainly end in a full-blown panic attack. That happens, and I'm no good to anyone; I'll just go back home and cuddle with the critters the rest of the day.

"What was that?" is what I eventually asked Mac instead, having completely missed the last bit of dialogue to escape her lips.

"I asked 'why don't they let us make our own mistakes?'" Mac supplied. "I mean, we've got to get it right eventually. If somebody steps in every time to make us stop when we're doing something bad, how're we supposed to learn?"

Smart! Not smart enough, though, so against my better judgment, I decided to provide answers, whether or not the questions were rhetorical.

"If you're gonna ask a question, Mac, ask a useful one," I tell her, turning my face toward the sky instead, and the little white cirrus clouds that have spread out where once there was a burgeoning thunderhead. "'Why' questions are toddler questions, for when you have absolutely no information on a subject and just need a basic education, or if you don't want an answer. If you're looking for real answers, you wanna ask 'what' questions. Questions that start with 'what' demand as much from the person asking the question as from the person who provides the answer. If you're doing a *really* good job asking the question, then you'll probably end up being the same person who answers it."

Mac glowers at me over that one, her nostrils flaring even more. But I've stuffed my face with another mouthful of her dad's Kouign-amann, my second-to-last, so I'm not beholden to say one darn thing more if I don't want to.

"What gave the aliens the right to impose their laws on Earth?" she finally asks, and unfortunately for me, she waited until I swallowed before she asked the question. Just wish I could stop myself from answering, but there's another compulsion to lay on top of the pile. Guess that was why I used to be a teacher.

"Glad you started with an easy one, at least," I grumble. "We did: the United Earth Empire, or what was left of its core elected government, presented the Pan-Galactic Republic with a formal request for membership, which was accepted, giving Earth and its inhabitants probationary status in the Republic. Since the UEE had at least some of their officers voted into their positions before everything fell apart, that means that whatever they decided to do was done with the tacit acceptance of its citizens. That's us."

I see her expression, look down at my last potential bite of breakfast, sigh, and continue talking despite myself.

"Look, just tell me to shut up when you're sick of it, but once I get started, I have a hard time stopping, 'kay?" I waited for her sullen nod, then pressed ahead. "You know how there's all those flying cars up there?" I point, and she grins.

"They look like a lot of fun," she admits. "Shame they're just for rich people."

"We'll talk economics some other time," I handwave, knowing that if I get sidelined here, I'll never make my way back before I get to work. "Right now, though, those flying cars are a pretty good metaphor for how the Republic works.

"What everybody notices first off is the appearance of freedom and privilege. Hey, I've got a flying car! Suck it, pedestrians! Thing is, there's no possible way the Republic is ever going to let people with flying cars use them however they want. Think of the body count that would rack up having rich maniacs racing around however they pleased, and in who knows what states of inebriation.

"Sure, they can fly to any destination they can think of, but not until they've told the car where they wanna go, let the car's computers talk with City Central to arrange a flight plan, and then hooked up with one of the guidance beams radiating out from the control towers set up all over for guiding air and space-to-ground traffic within Sunflower City. I've been in a few of those things, belonging to friends, and the whole process ends up taking a matter of seconds, tops, and the flights themselves whiz by in minutes to any destination within the City, so unless you're paying attention, you're probably gonna completely miss the fact that you're not actually driving yourself around through the air: the car's doing the flying for you, interacting with the rules imposed by City Central.

"And that's the way it has to be, because if people in flying cars were allowed to go buzzing around whenever and wherever they wanted, it'd make the thirty-plus-car pileups on old America's freeways look like the aftermath of a preschooler's playground scuffle. Because everybody's convinced that they're better drivers than they really are, and that all the problems on the road – or in the air – are the fault of somebody else, and that's what we all think right up until the moment we're in a head-on with the deadliest weapon ever made by humanity, at which point we stop thinking about much of anything anymore, forever. So, metaphor: a car that'll take you anywhere you want, so complete freedom of movement, but you have to let the car do the driving for you.

"Same with the Republic: there's loads of rules running around behind the scenes, but if you stick within 'em, you've also got loads of freedom. And where you don't have freedom, as long as you're not looking for trouble, trying to bust through boundaries just because they're there, you probably won't even notice the boundaries in the first place."

We're both looking up at the showdown between mob and peacekeeper, and I'm relieved to see that there's no brickbats being thrown: if they're listening to Benjuro Clee for as long as they have, that means she's got their attention, and there's a peaceful resolution in the likely future.

"These nights," I eventually continue when I feel Mac's eyes on me, her expression expectant, and my last bite finally swallowed and digesting, "I've been taking this college course through the Link, Understanding the Republic. Just finished the first lecture last night, actually, though I've been reading ahead in the textbooks, so I've got a pretty good idea of what to expect. It's all on history, culture, technology, everything that made the PGR, and how it continues to work. That's why all this stuff's fresh in my mind, I guess.

"The Republic's all about being as hands-off and homeopathic as possible, and it shows in just about everything. Seriously: instead of using antibiotics like we always did back in the old days, Republic medical technology uses these injections that change the way your body works so you enter a symbiosis with formerly hostile microorganisms. So, once you've gotten the shots, your body recruits common cold bugs to improve your lung function instead of trying to fight them, and the germs that used to eat your teeth instead get their proteins turned into catalysts for growing more enamel and improving your breath. Don't fight things: incorporate them. Turn what they wanna do naturally into something you can use."

Extending my hand, I lead Mac's gaze down toward the roots of Rock Bottom with a pointed finger.

"See that foundation pillar there?" I say as I gesture toward the indicated object. "You can't even see all of it from here, it's that big, and all the buildings extending off it get in the way. That's one of the three pillars that support Sunflower City, sunk down through miles of water and crust and right into the mantle of the Earth. They're placed in a set of three because triangles are nature's most stable shape, and that way the City flows with tectonic movement instead of fighting it, so there's no earthquakes here like there'd be on a natural continent.

"They call the whole place Sunflower City because all the layers of the City spread out from those pillars like the petals of some impossibly immense flower. And they're always shifting, going up and down and revolving around the pillars, just like some colossal sunflower turning to always follow the sun, except the layers of the City follow the moods and needs of its inhabitants. If one part of the City needs sun and another needs shade, that first part lifts up and rotates to cover up the second part, slow and steady so nobody even notices it happening. The mechanisms that let this happen are called 'planarian engines,' 'cause they're based on a mechanical model of the primitive neural matter of planarians – flatworms: reactive and regenerative in response to external stimuli. So, the city's even self-repairing...well, to a point, but nothing's absolutely perfect."

"Wait," Mac stops me, blinking with realization. "Are you saying that this whole city is *alive*?"

"Might as well be," I admit with a shrug. "Might even *be* that way for all I know. I mean, it takes in food for its citizens from the sub-aquatic hydroponic farms and clone-flesh banks, and pipes waste out to and takes water in from the treatment and recycling plants way down below the Undercity, just like a living creature. Even the weather seems like the way the City thinks and dreams, reacting to the emotions of its inhabitants. I do know, though, that whatever this City might be, it's made that way by us humans: it's composed mostly of the best pieces of all the other cities we've ever built.

"After the End, back a little before you were born if I'm guessing your age right..."

"Twelve," she supplies, breaking into my narrative, and throwing off my earlier appraisal of her as a teen.

"Anyway, back then, before the Protectorates like where you grew up were established, there was almost nowhere left on the planet that was safe for habitation, so when Earth joined the PGR, the Republic's people had to work fast to make the survivors a place where they could live. Somewhere where they'd feel comfortable. So instead of building everything from scratch, they scooped up huge chunks of pre-existing cities with these massive gravitic manipulation engines, the same equipment they use when they're terraforming a hostile world to make it habitable to carbon-based, oxygen-breathing life. That's why you can see the Sydney Opera House over there," I point, "and Notre Dame over there," another point, "and the Statue of Liberty would be visible in that

81

direction," I jerked my thumb behind us, "if that foundational pillar we're sitting on wasn't in the way."

Then I felt myself growing somber where once I'd been flippant, and I looked down at my thick-booted feet.

"They couldn't bring everything, though," I eventually got out, Mac leaning in closer, since my voice had dropped with the seriousness of the subject. "Vatican City had to stay where it was, somewhere out there, because it was too plague-ridden to be moved; that and too many flesh-eating morlocks. Same with Mecca, the sands of Saudi Arabia turned bright blue with radioactive cobalt dust. And even if Jerusalem hadn't been a bombed-out wreck, the Republic people knew better than to mess with it: the whole incident over the attempted rebuilding of the Hebrew Temple on top of the Dome of the Rock was what officially kicked off the End in the first place, after all. Better to leave that place where it is, dead in the dust of Old Earth."

"That's where all the monsters come from, isn't it, Mack?" Mac asked me next, and I gave her an encouraging grin, grateful for the change in subject. "From the leftovers of Old Earth?"

"You're right. Lots of critters from Old Earth got scooped up along with all the other stuff, and most of 'em went to hide down in the places at and below Rock Bottom. Which makes good sense, if you think about it: nobody goes down there except critters and people who don't want to be noticed, so it's a perfect little ecosystem all its own, where the city systems aren't likely to interfere. At least not until they overflow up onto the surface, of course, like roaches in the walls of an Old Earth apartment building." I shrug. "Which is why I'm not gonna be out of a job for the foreseeable future: somebody's gotta sort through all the transplants, save the natural animals, and deal with the unnatural ones so they don't go around hurting people.

"Speaking of," I segue out as I get to my feet, "my breakfast is all done, and it's about time I got to work. See you around, Mac."

"See you, Mack," she replies with a grin and a wave, which I return before I scoop up my pack, lock it back in place, and set off down the street.

By this point I'm feeling pretty good. Maybe today's not going to be so bad after all.

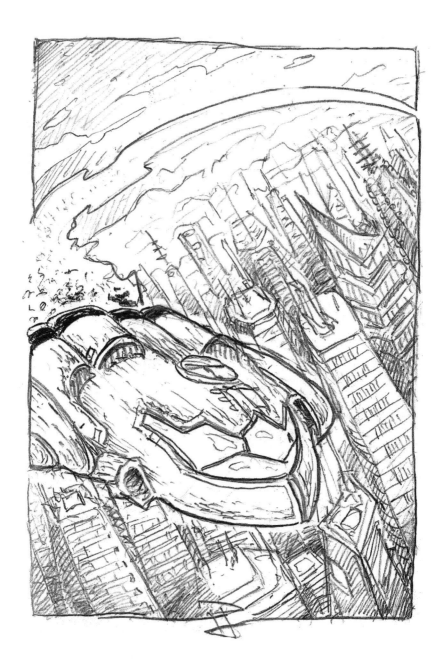

CHAPTER 6: SHOWDOWN IN SPACE; SHOWDOWN IN THE CITY

Location: Earth Solar System, on approach to
Earth above Sunflower City
Perspective: Susan Six

In Susan Six's personal experience, violence was one of the best ways to solve problems, so long as that violence was applied with careful precision and deliberate control. Too often in conflicts, the people who actually caused the problems escaped scot-free. Well, not when she was at work!

Susan Six's ship slowed from faster-than-light speeds just outside the Human Earth solar system (the name so designated on official documentation, when a serial number wasn't used instead, simply because so many species called their planet of origin some variation of "earth" or "ground" or "home"). She smirked to herself with yet another stray thought: amusing how human physics had once been so convinced that traveling faster than light was a physical impossibility. Then somebody built engines powerful enough for the job, and ships strong enough to endure the strain, and Earth's leading physicists all quit in unison.

Susan Six knew of at least seven different ways that speeds faster than light were achieved. Hers was the sneakiest, just sheathing herself in a quantum-independent forcefield and quietly buzzing along through the void of space, independent of time. Strong gravitic fields, such as proximity to suns, tended to interfere with her speed, and overall, the method was one of the slower ones available. But it also had the distinct advantage of making her ship nearly undetectable to all but the most sophisticated of military-grade sensors. In her usual line of work, that was more important than a speedy arrival.

Her ship's sensors began picking up four light civilian-grade frigates around the rings of Saturn. They'd likely just left Enceladus Station, a base on one of Saturn's moons, and an unofficially recognized site for a variety of criminal enterprises linking Earth with the rest of the cosmos.

Though Enceladus Station might not have been officially outlawed, thanks to carefully exploited legal loopholes, many ships that stopped there were known smugglers, pirates, and occasional slavers. The latter of which allowed Susan Six to employ lethal force with minimal questions asked, and an equally minimal docking of her pay for its liberal application: the Pan-Galactic Republic took slavery *very* seriously.

But Susan Six couldn't open fire with all her ship's available weaponry. At least, not right away.

"Dan," she spoke to the empty air of the cockpit, looking up unconsciously as she did so: her ship's Integrated Intelligence was aware of everything the tall, muscular woman said or did within his innards. "How's the hacking going?"

"Rapidly, Miss Six," he reported as promptly as always. "Their systems are cobbled together, hardly even worthy of being called intelligences, artificial or otherwise. Typical cobldp work on one, and leftover United Earth Empire technology on the other three. The lead ship, our target, has some minor Republic upgrades, or I would have acquired all the information we require by now."

Susan Six curled her lip: typical technology indeed. The cobldp were a species of brutal, bloodthirsty icthyoids, bipedal and piranha-headed, only considered semi-civilized at best. Some of their planets were members of the Republic, but more were not, and all of them were reputed to field significant pirate fleets. Thankfully those fleets were notoriously poor in technology, sometimes literally held together with sinew and mucus excretions when they couldn't steal equipment from the more advanced species of the cosmos. These pirates, thankfully, weren't in that lucky category, and only posed a minor danger to her sleek copper-and-gold Long Range Scouting Vessel because of their human accompaniment.

The lead ship, the one that was giving poor Dan a little trouble, was headed by Captain Caddigan Carse, and Susan Six wanted him dead.

Caddigan Carse wasn't his real name, any more than his rank held any military significance. When he first started using the name, he'd been a figure in the colonial government of Winston's Moon, the world where Susan Six had been born. A well-known tyrant from the Empire, brutal and cruel, so much so that even her biological father, the planet's Imperial lieutenant governor, had occasionally mentioned his disgust of the man in his young daughter's presence. According to most historical analysts of the events that transpired on that planet beyond the edges of civilization, the natives of Susan Six's birth-world hadn't been treated well by Carse. This cruelty was the underlying cause for the violent revolution that eventually erupted.

Susan Six's birth parents didn't live to see the aftermath.

She didn't remember too much about the incident, except in dreamlike memories of early childhood: she'd been only six Earth years when it happened, and she'd been hiding in the gardens of her family's palatial estate at the time. Because Susan Six had been hiding so well, she stayed undiscovered by the natives while they torched the manor house and the surrounding fields. Fortunately, they'd decided to leave the gardens since there were some very nice edible native fruits growing there, and the freedom fighters couldn't quite decide what to do with the highly valuable plot of productive land.

They'd still been dithering about it when the Republic's forces had arrived, led by a commander searching for survivors and for opportunities to assist the natives of the planet in rebuilding their devastated culture. By that time, though, Susan Six was the only human on the planet left alive.

All the same, Susan Six didn't plan to kill Carse for her personal loss: the commander of the Republic forces that rescued her and his partner had adopted her, becoming the most wonderful fathers any girl could ever hope to have. Even if they were both big, muscular super-lizards. No, she was going to kill Carse because he kept trying to bring the Empire back! He was a common pirate, a coward and a repeated mass murderer who loved to spread around death and misery, then slip away when the authorities showed up to stop his followers. Despite the manifest evidence of his actions, he still had the *gall* to call himself a "freedom fighter"!

Killing him would at the very least stop him from giving humans a worse name than they'd already earned when they'd had an empire of their own. The way Susan Six saw it, she had a moral duty to do at least that much.

Noticing that she was starting to accelerate faster than was wise, Susan Six eased back, letting her light repulsors slow her down until she was exactly matching the speed of the four crafts before her. They were past Jupiter already; the pirates' sub-light speeds were still incredible, even with their outdated engines. Mars was coming up on the left, the dome cities built on its barren red surface gleaming in the light of the yellow sun that had allowed the birth of humanity.

"After this job, I'm going to go play tourist for a while," Susan muttered to herself, smirking at the signs of humanity's escape from the womb-world of its origin.

"I've downloaded all the relevant data from the computers of Captain Caddigan Carse," Dan chimed, paying her idle words no heed. "And I can confirm that they are, as of yet, unaware of our presence. Before you indulge the external sublimation of your Todestrieb, however, I strongly suggest that you review the cargo manifests of the piratical vessels."

Rolling her eyes but stifling her wish to unleash hot plasma down the tailpipes of her quarry in the face of Dan's wisdom, Susan Six motioned with one hand in the air before her face, instantly calling up the images in question on Dan's hard-light holographic projection. Only a few seconds of scrolling, however, was enough to cause Susan's eyes to harden, her jaw to set.

"No," she declared with deceptive calm. "Nobody will want this stuff, not even as evidence: the manifests alone are enough for that."

"Then I should draw your attention to an unfortunate fact," Dan rejoined, taking over the scrolling function of the data image to cycle it down to a point he felt was especially relevant. "As you can see, this is only the latest of several prior shipments. With the same cargoes, judging from these manifests; these are delightfully well-organized smugglers, I must say."

The only warning the pirates got as Earth filled up the viewports of all the spacecraft was the sudden explosion of one and then the other of the trailing ships. Susan Six was on the attack.

"It looks like I'm going to have to go digging around dirtside for the rest of it," Susan Six growled, bringing the cobldp ship into her sights, then depressing her triggers. "After I send this scum down for a dirt nap."

Unlike the action-packed dogfights that she'd seen in the science-fiction stories of her childhood, Susan Six had always found the majority of space battles to be rather boring, at least from a sense of spectacle.

Usually, you tracked your target on long-range sensors, locked on, and launched your weapons from as far away as possible. If you timed things right, saturated the avenues of escape properly with sufficient firepower, and most importantly, had the element of surprise, very frequently a fight was over before the losing side was completely aware it had begun. She'd heard some experts on the subject describe it as roughly analogous to planet side submarine battles: lots of waiting and watching and trying to get into a good position while keeping your opponents from getting a similar position on you. So, the first three ships died in bursts of violently expelled gas and fire, the remnants soon pulled in a glittering trail into Earth's gravity.

But not Captain Caddigan Carse. No, the wiggling bastard shot ahead of his little flotilla, and suddenly his ship was limned in the fire of atmospheric entry.

"Bet the scum-pot thinks I can't do atmospheric dogfighting," Susan Six declared with eager, savage joy as she hurtled her copper-and-gold craft with gleeful abandon into full pursuit of the fleeing pirate. "Oh, but he ain't seen nothin' yet!"

Location: Earth, Sunflower City, Eleventh Level
Perspective: Billy the mutant kid

The boy didn't look back. He didn't dare! He'd spent enough time running away to know that looking back just lost you precious time. And when an angry mob was on your tail, time was something you were running out of far too rapidly.

During the building of Sunflower City, the Republic had moved quickly, far too quickly for a lot of safety checks. They'd had to: most of Earth was a toxic wasteland, killing or mutating its inhabitants in horrific ways, the rest just barely eking by in the fortified shantytowns called the Protectorates. So, they'd moved fast with their force screen cutters, scooping up huge sections of cities that had the least taint of radiation or toxic impurities, and then reconstructing them onto the underlying foundations laid by the Republic master builders. This process, with its accompanying gathering and transportation of Earth's scattered population en masse, had surely saved millions of lives, but had also allowed a lot of people to slip through the cracks, unregistered and unnoticed.

Until now, at least in this boy's case.

"Suffer not the mutant to live!" wailed the Preacher Man at the vanguard of the mob marching rapidly along the broad clickway of the sunlit thoroughfare. The boy sobbed in terror as he felt their nearness, even if he didn't look back to actually see it. They'd been chasing him on and off for hours now and had finally flushed him out into the open. The mob had been trading out people as they got tired, so the ones closing in on him were fresh, while the boy was run as ragged as a fox ahead of the hounds.

In his exhausted delirium, the boy was distracted by the bright flashes of light from high above, his focus broken enough to look up and see two ships blazing along in the upper stratosphere. They were too high for the sounds of their pitched battle to be heard as anything more than a distant whine and rumble, but the bright sparks of plasma and guided missiles flicking back and forth between the two combatants were clearly visible even at that distance.

Fortunately for the boy, the mob behind him seemed even more distracted than he was, since their muted roar of fury dimmed substantially as they slowed down to look up.

*Un*fortunately for the boy, his momentary distraction meant that, when he turned his head back around to take full advantage of the distraction of his pursuers, it was already too late for him to avoid running right into an all-engulfing darkness. A darkness that was strangely soft and yielding, as he soon discovered when he reached up to try and push himself free.

"You're cute," said a woman's voice in a teasing light alto, "but we should really be introduced properly before we move on to that stage of a relationship."

Soon the boy felt a pair of large, long-fingered hands wrap around his shoulders before the owner of those hands easily lifted him free of the obstruction he'd hit, then set him on his feet in front of the being who'd spoken. At first the boy's eyes went wide, his cheeks instantly blazing as he realized where his head had been lodged, and he started to stammer out an apology: mutant scavengling or not, he still had some common decency.

Then his eyes began to travel up...and up...and up some more. The woman before him was tall, taller than him by head, shoulders, and chest. She also wasn't human.

A surprisingly kind face looked down on the boy, a light smirk playing at the corners of its long, flexible muzzle. There was an instinct in the deepest heart of humanity that knew a dragon when it saw one, and this tall, stately woman in the peacekeeper's uniform was definitely that: a dragon! *Very* humanlike in many respects, but a dragon all the same.

"That's quite all right," the dragon lady said as she kept one hand on the boy's shoulder, the touch gentle, but also utterly unbreakable, preventing him from continuing his headlong flight. "I can clearly see that it wasn't your fault: places to go, people to not see." Her eyes flicked past him to the mob still rapidly approaching, and then back down to him...and especially to the prehensile tail flicking free above the rip in the seat of his pants that had started the whole mess. "Ah, a human purity demonstration? Discovered by that tall fellow in front, I presume?"

He nodded, too bewildered by conflicting emotions to do much else.

"Of course, of course," she said in a calm, bustling sort of voice, even as she so casually set him behind her, the material of her formerly soft and yielding uniform instantly taking on a rigid texture, turning it from mere clothing into deadly serious battle armor. "Just stay right there, please: if you run, I can't promise you any further protection. All right?"

She waited for his breathless nod, then turned her full attention to the approaching crowd, which even then seemed to have lost some momentum, first because of the unexpected lightshow in the sky, and now because of the arrival of the towering dragon woman.

"Before you get any deeper into trouble," the dragon lady said in a voice that was immediately magnified by the sound enhancers built into her uniform, "you should all know that City Central has your identities logged."

She raised a hand, and the gathering came to a complete stop, many people murmuring in confusion and concern as numerous hard light constructs appeared before them, one for each member of the group, each displaying their identification information: names and addresses at the top, more sordid details below.

"That aside, none of you are actually in trouble right now," continued the dragon lady. "There are no laws against public gatherings, so long as they're peaceful. My name is Sergeant Benjuro Clee, and I am this borough's registered peacekeeper. Please take the time to look me up," she added, and with a flick of her long, sinuous tail, the information did indeed appear on the softly glowing squares of light before each person in the crowd. "I am sure that you all have better things to do with your time than...than..."

The tall, stately dragon woman blinked, then her eyes narrowed, her horn-ridged brow furrowing with displeasure.

"Are those brickbats?" she asked, twin trails of smoke rising from her nostrils. "You there! And you! Did you tear off pieces of your cultural heritage? Each of those chunks of masonry is an irreplaceable artifact! A treasure of the ages!"

Already the collection of humans had dwindled, and as the great wings of the dragon lady unfurled, the back of her throat limned in ominous blue flickers, the numbers before her began to diminish with greater rapidity, those who'd had the temerity to bring materials for a proper stoning rapidly dropping their implements as they departed in good haste before the dragon's kindling wrath. With an effort, however, she visibly gained control of her emotions, tucking her wings up in a slow, meditative fashion.

"City Central will have repair trundlers along shortly to put those bits of buildings back in place," she said, her voice once more at its even, pleasant tones, the smoke from her nostrils reduced to a mere hint of vapor. "Now, is there anyone who would care to lodge a formal complaint? While your elected Representative is the person to contact, should you feel that Republic laws need to be adjusted to better suit your cultural requirements, I may be of service on a more limited-but-immediate scale."

"Agent of the Beast!" came the shrill cry of the Preacher Man as he finally overcame his momentary emotional upset at the sudden turn of events. "The Dragon and Whore of Babylon!"

Unlike the sight of damage to the city, these personal slurs, and the far less pleasant ones that soon followed, merely caused the sinuous dragon lady to arch an eye-ridge, her tail flicking in obvious amusement. Hands on hips, her nonchalance just seemed to drive the Preacher Man to steadily greater heights of fury and invective, until his face was starting to turn purple. *That*, at least, managed to raise the dragon woman's other eye-ridge.

"Some of that sounds as though it came from...let me see," she reached out to another hard light construct helpfully projected by the ever-mindful City Central and flicked through a few screens. "Ah, the Revelation of Saint John. Much metaphorical language speaking against the ancient Roman Empire, and empires in general, I might add. Standard Hebrew prophetic language as well, packed full of symbolism, with references to events present, past, and future all at the same time. I admit, I haven't even begun to do proper research on the numerological meanings inherent to the text." Brushing the hard light screens away, letting them dissolve into glittering motes, the draconic peacekeeper shrugged, looking a little abashed. "Dragons in mythological literature are a hobby of mine. Your Earth scriptures are simply rife with them...which, I suppose I must confess, is a large part of my reason for coming here to serve as a peacekeeper until we can get enough local people trained into the job."

The purple-faced Preacher Man's expression contorted in paroxysms of rage, his narrow, wrinkled mouth trying to form proper words rather than the mere incoherencies that presently croaked from his throat, but the dragon woman shook her head.

"Castor Agustus Arrhenius," she stated, fixing him with gleaming opal eyes that had once been filled with kindness and amusement, but which were now sharp with judgment's fire. "Your practices are known to us, including the crime of simony. While a bit of passing the plate is usually ignored at the misdemeanor level, this recent act of civil unrest is enough to bring you to official attention." She paused, several glowing screens of many shapes and sizes flicking before her eyes before she dismissed them with a decisive wave of one long-fingered talon. "Also: aren't you a vocal decrier of licentiousness and sensuality? Especially of the same-sex variety?"

Her long, sinuous neck arched downward, until her eyes were level with the skeletally thin Preacher Man's own, her voice dropping until only the boy and the Preacher Man could hear her as her artificial vocal enhancement cut out automatically.

"What you do in the privacy of your, or someone else's, home is legally off the record. However, I think that you should know that the various acts you've done in public places, such as alleyways and the cordoned-off parts of revival tents, are observed and recorded by City Central as a matter of standard practice. Unless you want them made more publicly known, besides being brought in on charges of paid preaching, then I suggest that you limit your future mob instigation to a minimum. For now, I'm only giving you a warning rather than arresting you, because I hope to avoid future bad feelings in the communities where you preach. If I encounter you a second time in my official capacity, I will take steps to ensure there won't be a third encounter."

Straightening, the dragon woman gave the Preacher Man a polite smile and wave.

"Have a good day, citizen," she said cheerfully, before turning back to face the teenage mutant who'd been standing behind her all this time, mouth agape at the now quite empty thoroughfare, save for the lone gobsmacked Preacher Man, his limp spindly limbs making him look like a puppet whose strings had been cut, a mental image that only grew more pronounced the further away from him they got.

"How...how did you do that?" the boy blurted out at last, his tail ramrod straight behind him as he looked up at the towering dragon woman in awe. "They were gonna kill me, and..."

"Oh, that seems a bit strong," the dragon woman chuckled, resting a hand on the boy's narrow shoulders as she began to lead him away along the clickway. "Maimed a bit, and probably cut off your tail, but I don't think they'd have gone beyond that. They weren't really *into* the act, just caught up in the moment. Of course," she frowned thoughtfully, "that man leading them is an unknown factor." The frown deepened. "I think he might actually have gone for blood."

Then her expression was sunny once again as she looked upward, toward a single copper-gold craft drifting majestically toward the spaceport region of Sunflower City, which was attached by a network of deceptively fragile-looking clickways to the highest parts of its sky-reaching towers. Behind it, a plume of smoke and rapidly dissipating plasma above, and a series of splashes in the water around the City below, were the only remnants of the loser of the dogfight. More fodder for the recyclers.

"They weren't prepared for the superior force that Republic technology and training can bring to bear," she explained. "All that time, I had multiple information feeds flashing in front of my eyes, giving me the prompts I needed for the situation, and also letting me know where my reinforcements were."

She gestured to the edge of the wide clickway, where the boy could see a rather hefty-looking robot peeking over the rail while it clung unobtrusively to the side.

"Containment robots," she confirmed. "Also called spotbots. Equipped with various nonlethal crowd-dispersal devices. There are even more of them hanging on right underneath us, ready to spring into action if things hadn't gone so well, and the dear people had been less distracted by the lightshow in the sky. Good luck that some bounty hunter was blasting a smuggler at the right time and place, according to the latest reports. Now," she glanced down at the boy, making an inviting gesture toward the main cluster of buildings at the center of Sunflower City, "would you care to come with me? I'm afraid you're not registered as a citizen of the Republic, and that means I, well, I fudged a few laws by protecting you. I won't force you, but I think you'd prefer having a safe place to sleep and good food at regular periods, besides education and entertainment."

She released her gentle grip on his shoulder and turned to instead offer him her hand.

"You can call me Sergeant Clee while I'm on duty. What's your name?"

"Billy," replied the boy, hesitating just a moment, then taking the tall dragon woman's extended hand, marveling that the obsidian claws didn't immediately cut his skin.

"Well, Billy, do you want to be a citizen of the Republic?"

"I guess," he replied, scuffing a foot bashfully.

"That's good enough for government work," said the dragon cheerily. "Let's get you to your new apartment."

Location: Earth, Sunflower City, Central Spire
Perspective: Trinidad Del Toro

"You humans are all fatheads," growled the rill, glaring out the window of her office as though the whole city had insulted the quality of her work, watching as the erstwhile leader of the dissipated mob finally wandered off, trembling in fury that was visible even from the middle heights of the building where their office was located. "And that includes you," she added over her shoulder, her eyes almost boring holes through the thick lenses of the atmospheric mask she was wearing.

Trinidad Del Toro arched an eyebrow as he looked over the little alien who was now apparently his boss. Gret looked something like an acromegalic pangolin with opposable thumbs, dressed in an old fashioned-looking gas mask and battered brown trench coat, which covered a set of matte black body armor beneath. Something called a "stat suit," if Trinidad recalled correctly: the ultimate equipment used by the military forces of the Republic. Just like the uniform worn by the peacekeeper who'd broken up the mob.

"If you're not pleased with my work," Trinidad replied, "then you can certainly take it up with Mister Camor."

"Sin's a big fat sap!" she snapped. "That fluffy tailed *idealist,*" and she spat out the word like it was the worst pejorative in her repertoire, "is a motherless bastard, too, for sticking me with this job!" Then she paused, her head lifting slightly as she considered what she'd said. "Still, at least he picked someone who could do the job right. Not like you humans: as a species, you have the hardest time doing the right things for the right reasons. I mean, just look down there: all anybody had to do there was just mind their own business, do their jobs, or at least stay out of the way of the people doing theirs, and the whole situation wouldn't have happened in the first place. But some knucklehead with a New International Bible up his rectum decides he's gotta go on a rampage and prove something, and next thing everybody knows, there's a mob howling down the street, and it takes a freaking fire-breathing space dragon to make 'em stop!"

"Darishi can breathe fire?" Trinidad asked, blinking in mild surprise. Despite the various insults the little alien kept tossing at his species, he didn't feel particularly upset. He'd been told to expect these sorts of outbursts by Scintillant Camor during their interview. He'd also been told that if Gret started spouting off around him, it was a sign of her affection: like a lot of her people, she had difficulty opening up about her true feelings – which ran *very* deep – and so she tended to cover them up with tirades and random profanity and the occasional personal insult as a way to try and drive away the people she was growing to like.

Mister Camor had also told Trinidad that if he'd stick with Gret even after she'd done her best to drive him off, she'd happily die for him if the situation required it. This was something that the l'dray could attest to from personal experience, since she had indeed once taken an assassin's shot intended for himself.

"Those sweater puppies of theirs aren't just for looks," chuckled the waist-high alien. "Not just for feeding the tykes, either: they help to provide emergency calories as fuel for the igniting spark for the combustible gases they produce when under stress. Means the females of the species are a *lot* more dangerous, let me tell you, even if they don't have all the testosterone-built muscle mass and keratinous armor plating of the males."

Apparently finished with that subject, Gret's eyes narrowed behind the thick lenses, and she rubbed the essentially non-existent chin of her long, thin muzzle in obvious thought.

"You oughta know, kid," she finally said, turning away from the window to face Trinidad, hooking her long-clawed fingers before her as she did so, as though she were saying a prayer, "auditing is a spiritual principle. What we're doing in this office suite isn't just about finding all the numbers that don't match. Oh no: we're here to purge the very heart and soul of humanity itself and dredge it clear of centuries of your Earth years' worth of sin. Maybe thousands! By the time we're finished, kid, all the sins of a fallen empire of robbers, slavers, simoniacs, and murdering bastards will be scraped off and burned in the ashcan of history. And you'll be partially responsible for bringing numerical salvation to your people's records. Who knows, it might even help their souls a little as well."

"Hey," protested Trinidad, finally spurred to a response. "The United Earth Empire never practiced slavery! It just..."

Under those deeply scrutinizing eyes, veiled behind thick lenses or not, he soon trailed off awkwardly. Meeting that gaze was next to impossible, not if you were being honest with yourself.

"You're young, which means that, by definition, you're also stupid," Gret explained in a tone that was as close to compassionate as Trinidad had heard from the mean little alien. "Not even into your first century yet. Bearing those handicaps in mind, I'll forgive you this once for taking a crap

102

out of the wrong hole. In future, just remember, I've got seniority in this department, and that means I'm the only one who gets to shoot off my mouth without checking all my facts first.

"Fortunately for you, I need you working with me. All that crap the Republic spouts about post-scarcity and people not needing to work, yeah, it's crap...well, mostly. I mean, our infrastructure and automated systems could all last maybe sixty or seventy of your Earth years before they started to break down if nobody besides the robots were around to maintain 'em, so we've got some leeway. That leeway doesn't mean we don't need people to fill in jobs. It means that we have the time to only take on the people who actually *want* to work in the jobs they get: the motivated go-getters who actively figure out how to be better workers, instead of clock-watching placeholders who're just doing a job for a paycheck and an ulcer.

"Case in point," Gret continued, pointing down to where the darishi and the mutant boy were just barely still in sight. "There's a sharp contrast to your human cops. The general populace wanted them to be super-human, but they really all were blue collar Joes with a badge and a gun and a thin blue line. Now *that*," she jabbed her finger at the dragon lady, just before she walked around a corner, "that's what being a peacekeeper is all about. A peacekeeper is somebody who helps to keep the peace of a community, heading off problems before they get out of hand, instead of picking up the pieces after the mess has already happened, with all the legal backing and firepower support they need to do the job right."

Then she sighed, looking down at her huge, clawed feet before clumping her way over to the desk in the near-middle of the office and reaching up to scoop a thin data card off its top.

"Unfortunately for us, it looks as though this mess has already happened," she declared with a world-weary air. "Some days I wish I was still a taste engineer for the virtual dining environments instead of an auditor. But somebody's gotta do these dirty jobs. Might as well be us."

She shoved the card into Trinidad's hands, then turned toward the door.

"After you humans nearly wiped yourselves out, about twenty percent of your surviving population is now made up of the jerk-bags who got you into that mess in the first place: your politicians and religious leaders. Another twenty percent is made up of criminal types: mob bosses and captains of industry and business professionals. Forty percent are just average, but at least they mostly stay out of the way as long as they're not rioting.

"So while Sin is upstairs, making nice with the twenty percent of your species that's worth a damn, I'm gonna be in interviews for the rest of the day – and every day after that for the foreseeable future – with the forty percent that's made up of psychopaths, megalomaniacs, and compulsive liars, all convinced that they're really important people, and who insist on seeing somebody in authority so they can get in good with the new management. That somebody is me, 'cause I'm the best there is at telling jerk-wads like that where to go and how to get there by the most expeditious route available.

"Since I'm gonna be dealing with the scum of your planet for the next slice of eternity, you're the one who's gonna hafta look into this mess." She indicated the slip of glittering plastic in his hand with a casual wave of her claw. "That card there, fresh from City Central, has a complete copy of all the data that your predecessor in this job tried to take with him when he took a terminal dive off," she let her long-clawed finger waver a moment in the general direction of the window, before jabbing it forward with certainty at a point on a clickway just two floors down from the office, "right there."

"Peewee Montgomery, nice guy, a real pushover, kinda nervous all the time, obviously had a guilty conscience. I was kinda hoping he'd spill his guts in the cathartic way instead of the literal one so I could find out where all the loose money around here was going without the bother of hunting it all down myself. Sin didn't interview him: I inherited the guy, since he was one of the old accountants for some self-important so-and-sos and knew where a lot of bodies were buried in your old Imperial books. Now I've got you, and even if I hate the collective guts of your species, Sin's vouched for you, so you've gotta have *some* redeeming qualities...somewhere. So now your big job is to go through that card and find out what made poor Peewee pull a pavement belly flop. We'd have lost that information completely if some helpful bystander hadn't taken it off poor Peewee's body and let City Central copy the data for us, so whatever's on it must be pretty smelly stuff."

"What makes you think that I won't go over the edge, too?" asked Trinidad as he looked down at the innocent-looking card, turning it over in his immense, calloused hand. "If this former worker of yours couldn't handle whatever is on this card, I mean."

"Like I said, Sin vouched for you," Gret replied over her shoulder as she made her waddling way toward the door. "You're in your job 'cause you wanna work, and your test scores say you've got a knack for accounting. Well, that and that service record of yours." She paused at the door, one heavy-clawed hand on the knob. "Anybody who's a fellow ex-marine can't be all bad, whatever your species disadvantages might be. Means you've got a lot of guts, and you've got the proper training and attitude to keep 'em where they belong."

"Ex-marine…?" Trinidad started to ask his boss about her past, but she was already through the door and on her way to the first of her interviews that day, with somebody named Thomas Cerveau according to the daily logs helpfully floating near his head.

Cerveau? That name was familiar somehow. Not in a good way, either: it was an association from back in his days fighting for the United Earth Empire, trying desperately to keep order in a populace that had grown steadily more destructive, everybody crowding back onto Earth until a critical population mass was reached, and nothing he or his fellow warriors could do could stop the End. The man, Thomas Cerveau, was somebody important, one of the people who'd been hard at work behind the scenes of every political coup.

Then Gret suddenly stuck her head back in the door, and Trinidad's chain of thought was instantly broken when she yanked a thick paperback out of one of the voluminous pockets of her trench coat.

"Hey kid, catch!" she bawled before lobbing it at him, very nearly knocking the wind out of him with the throw as he caught the book with both hands: the little alien had a real arm on her! Looking down, Trinidad blinked as he read the book's title: George Orwell's "1984."

"Just wanted to clarify something," she growled, not meeting his eyes, and Trinidad got the impression that, if she'd been human, she would have been blushing. "You, uh, humans…well, um…I kinda think you're important additions to the Republic," she admitted, her voice lowering until Trinidad had to lean forward to hear her properly. "Just finished that turkey there, and, uh, yeah: nobody else in the Republic's ever made something like it. Tells it like it is. We in the Republic had to learn all that stuff about how a tyranny works from personal experience, getting stomped on by the Tarig Empire back in the day. But that was in the day of my great-great-etcetera-grandmother. That book though, it really lays out all the evil nice and plain, so anybody could get it. Makes it feel...*current*. Timeless, really."

Her head lifted, and even though her features were inhuman, Trinidad could feel the strength and determination radiating from the little rill.

"Which is why you and me're on the job, kid: we're the auditors, and we're here to put the fear of God into the bastards."

For a moment there was a connection between the two people, human and rill, as their eyes met across the distance of the office. Somehow Trinidad realized that whatever her flaws, whatever she might say, he felt loyal to Gret, and would do his best for her at all times.

Her cause was just.

Her heart was pure.

Her mouth was filthy.

"Yes ma'am," is what he finally said.

CHAPTER 7: MAN ON THE JOB

Location: Earth, Sunflower City, City Edge
Perspective: The Man

Dear God, if I've done something to offend You, I'm very, very sorry, and would very, very much like it if You wouldn't take it out on me right now, please. Amen.

...

No dice: she's still there, and she's still talking. And she's still mostly naked.

The lady's name is Theodora Eunice Faraday, and I see her about twice a month, since her apartment is one of several that surround, semi-circle fashion, a pleasant, sprawling little park with abutting forest. The park is very much tame, but the forest isn't, and the robots who wander around the city – called "trundlers" because of their stumpy legs and cute little walk – explicitly stay out of that forest unless I go out of my way to bully them into it on my rescue missions. It's a little piece of Earth's real wilderness that somehow managed to avoid contamination, scooped up by the planetoid-sized builder bots and slapped down alongside the various buildings they arranged into the present neighborhood configuration. When it got scooped up – a patch of land many miles square and teeming with all sorts of random life – the animals that were living on it came as well. Animals, and other things.

Mostly I'm content to leave the animals where they are, since most seem to be doing all right on their own. They're mostly just the small sorts of critters left over after humans had gone through and exterminated all the potentially dangerous or edible or trophy worthy animals. Every so often, though, something comes wandering out of the woods, and then I get a call from one of the inhabitants of the apartment complexes surrounding the place, and Miss Theodora Eunice Faraday meets me at the main entrance to the building in her very-nearly-altogethers to give me an official invitation inside.

Don't get me wrong: I really do appreciate her helping me out. Having Miss Theodora Eunice Faraday let me into a legal private place, no questions asked, whenever I need to locate some poor frightened critter that's enduring the misery of being exposed to humanity and get it somewhere safe post-haste is what I consider a literal Godsend. The Republic's pretty clear about the separation of public and private, and since I'm an official Republic employee for the Ministry of Life, I have to follow the rules. But, as long as someone who lives in a legal private place gives the okay, I'm in the clear, and I save so much time not having to go all the way around.

There are, however, two significant problems inherent to all my dealings with Miss Theodora Eunice Faraday.

"You won't believe what Jamie said she saw. Oh, have you met Jamie? I think you haven't: she's my next-door neighbor. She said that she was working out late last night, really trying out what her Link could do, but when she stopped, she looked out her window and she said she saw something like a white hairy ape down in the central yard. According to her, its fur was so white, in fact, that it looked like it was glowing in the moonlight. Did you ever hear about something like that?"

Yes, Miss Theodora Eunice Faraday, but I'm going to tell you "no" anyway, because you really don't want to know what your neighbor saw.

"It was so nice of you to save that horse the last time you were here. The poor thing looked so thin! I could see its ribs! Watching you work with it; I never knew you could get a horse to come to you like that. Why, it followed you right out of here like a trusting little lamb."

It's called the "turning loose" method, Miss Theodora Eunice Faraday, and if you'd been watching any closer you could see some of its ribs quite literally, because something out in those woods had torn open one side. But I did my best to keep that side turned away from her after applying a "large animal" slap patch, so as not to horrify her.

The horse was probably the last living horse on the planet, and if she hadn't called me in to rescue it, the poor thing would have gone back into the woods and right into the clutches of whatever had nearly killed it. Not that I'm going to bring that up: I'm trying really hard not to spread fear in these troubled times.

"These new apartments are so comfortable, have you noticed? And the floors seem to clean themselves! There's no dust anywhere, not even a speck. Besides that, I can actually tell my place to rearrange itself, growing new furniture, even new rooms, leave for a while to let it work, and when I come back, poof, it's like a brand-new place, and none of my stuff goes missing no matter how much I tell it to move everything around. I just wish they let us have pets."

Well, the whole city is just shy of being alive, and it really wants to make everyone who lives in it as content as possible. As for pets: uh-uh, not while I'm the "they" that's not allowing them. Maybe it's selfish, me being the only one who's got pets in the whole of Sunflower City, but they're all strays abandoned by their owners, and for as long as I can, I'm going to keep that from happening again. But for now, I just nod and make appropriate noises to indicate that I'm listening, no sense crushing hope. Especially since I might change my mind...eventually.

"You wouldn't believe the racket that couple on the first floor are always causing! Fighting and screaming day and night, every time they're both at home! I'm really so glad for the soundproofing that these apartments have. I don't know why they even stay together. Jamie and Bertrand and Babette and Ambika and I all agree that it's just a matter of time before they kill each other if they keep on like this."

In case it wasn't apparent, Miss Theodora Eunice Faraday is an extrovert, and for me, that is a pretty significant problem. Just being quiet and listening to someone talk is hard for me, and I say that knowing perfectly well how hypocritical I am. Being around people as *enthusiastic* as Miss Theodora Eunice Faraday is emotionally exhausting.

The other problem is I think Miss Theodora Eunice Faraday is quite attractive, and I don't do very well around attractive people. Especially attractive people who wear as few clothes as Miss Theodora Eunice Faraday does every time I see her (today it's a bikini top and shorts that are, well...*short*). Me being the socially clueless sort that I am, and still figuring out my empathic senses, I'm not sure if it's just because she doesn't like wearing clothes much, or if she, for reasons I simply cannot even begin to fathom, might perhaps maybe just a little bit be hitting on me.

Not able to tell the difference, and since I wouldn't know where to begin even if she did want me to make the first move, I'm just here to do a job. And if Miss Theodora Eunice Faraday happens to keep brushing against me with her hands, or legs, or other body parts as she talks, or occasionally leans over in a way that shows off just that much more of her from various angles, well, she's just a tactile sort of person, and anything else is none of my business. My eyes stay right on a level with hers when I look in her direction, and when I'm not, my gaze stays focused on the direction of travel.

That gaze, as we walk out of the rear door of the complex and step into the shade-dappled sunlight of the wooded park behind the housing complex, promptly centers on what is probably the last living specimen of a North American opossum. No, not quite the last: she's a mommy, and she's got six little babies clinging to her back. They're all obviously sun-dazzled and very stressed, probably displaced from their home by something unfriendly back there in the woods that I am almost certain I do *not* want to meet, and as they notice me, they give me that blank, innocent-eyed expression I used to see all the time on the faces of the opossums in my folks' back yard when I was a kid.

Grabbing my arm, which ends up squeezing her bosoms against my thankfully clothed body, Miss Theodora Eunice Faraday points and squeals in delight.

"Oh, look at them! Aren't they just adorable? Who knew that there'd be so many animals living so close to us humans, and in the city, too?"

I really should have put on my helmet: it would cover up my blush. Again, though, that's none of my business; my business is figuring out how I'm going to get those poor little critters out of here before they get hurt or, probably worse, go bolting right back into whatever danger they just escaped from out in those woods.

Right on schedule, that's when the whole situation goes pear-shaped.

That couple that Miss Theodora Eunice Faraday was talking about, the ones who fight all the time, they open up the window of their kitchen, and right away the whole park is filled with the raw tension of their mutual hate. While they're still indoors, I can deliberately ignore whatever they're saying, but pretty soon they open up their back door, the man coming out first, followed soon after by the woman.

"I'm the one who makes the money around here!" he yells at her, and I studiously avoid looking in their direction, not wanting to see the fury I know is on his face, or the tears that will be streaming down hers. "You don't have the right to talk to me like that! Not when I'm the one who keeps you living like you do!"

"That's not true!" she wails back, sounding somewhere close to the edge of hysteria. "I make my own money, too!"

Of course, the argument is delivered at the tops of their very agitated voices, and I'm just glad that opossums tend to freeze when they're stressed, because that poor little mama was just petrified. Obviously, she wished she could be anywhere but right there right then. I shared her wish, but I had a job to do.

Let me explain a bit about psionics, or what are sometimes called talents. The subject is important because I'm one of the rare people that can use them, though I'm only an amateur. Pretty good with animals, great at being forgotten (whether I like it or not), but otherwise my talents are erratic. Turns out, I'd been using them subconsciously for most of my life, so when I met with Mister Camor in person, when he tried to help me out, instead he got me in touch with the Universe Soul, sometimes called the Heart of God, and just like that, I was flooded with power I never knew existed.

If that sounds weird, I guess it is, but it's really what happens; with talents like Mister Camor's, or like mine, there's no way our bodies can handle the raw power that it takes to pull off some of the stuff we do.

Seriously, the electrical energy released by a telekinetic's brain just lifting a penny would cause shorts in nearby electronics, to say nothing of the damage it would do to all the delicate gray matter. That's why my powers were so low-key until Mister Camor awakened me, at first by accident, and later on with deliberate training. Now, though, I can do like he does, first calling on my "center-self," the core of my being, and then using that hard core to reach into a source of universal energy, which can then be channeled into whatever powers an individual might have. I don't really understand how it works, or what that universal source actually is, and I've only got the start of an idea of what my powers are, but I've already discovered that I can do some pretty incredible things, and I keep surprising myself.

Now is one of those times where I call on that power, and start to walk forward, leaving Miss Theodora Eunice Faraday by the door while I work my way, nice and slow and steady, toward the poor little mother.

As I walk, I control my breathing, then I reach into my center-self, just like Mister Camor taught me, trying to shove aside all the negative energy the couple are throwing off like gamma particles. Trying not to ask why these two chose to live together when there's an entire city full of people they could have chosen instead. Straining against all endurance to stop myself asking why they're fighting at all when instead they could just choose to be happy.

I'm not going to ask those questions because I know there's no answers that I want to hear.

Finally, I realize that I'm not going to succeed here, that there's just too much negative energy filling the area, filling me and the opossum and Miss Theodora Eunice Faraday all at once. So instead, I try something new: instead of pushing the negative energy aside, I embrace it, pulling it right into my core-self. When I have it, feel it bubbling inside of me, feel it building right below my solar plexus, I *grip* it, deliberately sucking it from the air, from the fighting couple, from Miss Theodora Eunice Faraday, and from the little opossum mama and her babies.

It hurts.

It works, though.

Instantly the little mama's blanked-out eyes clear, and she starts to toddle toward me in that slow, careful walk her kind have when they're trying not to drop anybody.

"Oh, look!" exclaims Miss Theodora Eunice Faraday, suddenly able to talk again, while grabbing my arm and pointing. "She's coming here! All on her own! What a brave little mother she is!"

Keeping most of my concentration on holding onto that cruel energy, I tap the summon tab on my wrist, calling out to the closest trundler; the ones that will answer my summons all have stasis compartments, so I can load small creatures into them for automatic transport back to the shelter.

If I got the chance.

That warning thought comes at pretty much the same time that I feel something hammer against my face, my vision flashes into stars and sparklers for a moment, and I nearly get knocked off my feet.

"He's just doing his job!" screamed the woman, just an instant before I heard the loudly bellowed words, "What're you doing, listening in on us!"

Honestly, it was my fault. With that much negative energy bashing around the place, it had to go somewhere. So now all the bad feelings the screaming couple had for each other were suddenly centered on me instead.

Right now, the woman is too busy bursting into tears to do anything else, which is great for me, since it means she's not joining in on the attack. Him, though, he's still coming at me, punches coming hard and fast like a trip hammer, and I can tell right away that he's got training in how to fight, boxing if I'm reading his style of attack right, and he's got the advantage of reach, since his arms are longer than mine. He's athletic, tall and broadshouldered and handsome, the classic All-Star Athlete beloved of fans far and wide, at least right up until the End killed off sports right along with its fans. No wonder the guy's got so much anger and frustration built up.

With my connection to his emotions, I can feel his intentions screaming through my core-self with the aftereffects of each punch: he'd just been about to hit his significant other. Not for the first time, either, judging from what I'm picking up from her. This time, though, he'd hit the murderous edge, and now...now I was his target, and he wasn't going to stop until I was a bloody smear.

I wish he'd chosen something more productive to do with that negative energy, maybe found some way to sublimate it into something nice instead.

This is what I'm still wishing as I just barely turn with his next brutal straight punch, letting it roll off my chin as I flow into the blow; even as I'm raising my hands, touching them against the thick, corded muscle of his arm, guiding it past me, away from me. That touch tells his body what it should have known all along: it didn't really want to hurt me, no matter how much the brain of its owner might say differently. No, what it really wants is to hurt itself, because it has to: that's the only way to stop the big man from hurting others.

When the guy crashes onto the permacrete bounding the edges of the park, his nose bursts against the unyielding surface like an overripe tomato. This is an act of atonement, his body acting to save me from the sins of its owner. The throw has given me a little breathing space, but I feel the surge of his pride, outraged in unreasoning fury at being thwarted and humbled by the little man in the silly clownsuit. I know he's going to be back up in a moment, that he's not ready to let go of his hate yet, so I take a moment to pop my hand stunner out of its sheath on my wrist and start forward, ready to put him down.

"Stoppit! Stoppit! *Stop!*"

The woman's grabbed a big kitchen knife from a shelf just inside her open window, and just like I could feel the man's desire to beat her bloody, I felt her own intention to use it on him as soon as she got a chance. But I've turned myself into an emotional lightning rod, and there's no stopping the storm now, so all that hurt-desire floods into me. Thankfully, it also warns me of her attack before she's too close for me to do anything about it, and as soon as she's in range, I turn and stop her short with a quick jab of the hand stunner.

The distraction, though, is all the man needs to get back to his feet.

"I'll kill you!" is what I'm pretty sure he's screaming through the busted nose and smashed teeth, again at the top of his lungs, along with a lot of profanity. He's as fast as I knew he'd be, and he's no weakling; he knows how to fight, and with his next punch he sends the hand stunner skittering out of my grip.

Oh no. Oh no, no, no. I can see what's coming, can feel it as I turtle up, dropping into a low stance, getting my guard up, letting his punches flow off and around my raised forearms, letting the rush of adrenaline and endorphins and the armor plates under the suit block out the pain of their impact. I'm turning my shortness into an advantage, making it hard for him to really get a proper bead on me, while at the same time using my lower center of gravity to press down into the earth, making me immovable in spite of all his attacks. But you can't win a fight with defense alone, and it's only a matter of time before one of those punches gets through. Once that happens, I don't think I'll be able to get my defenses back up in time, and the first punch will lead to another, and then another, and soon I'll be dead or badly injured, and I can't let that happen: I have to save the mama opossum and her babies first.

What I can feel is about to happen is I'm about to kill this guy, somebody whose name I don't even know. Training in fighting only improves your ability to control what is already an inherently chaotic state; it doesn't give you superpowers, and a fight is always dangerous; there's always the chance that somebody ends up dead. With those street yobos, they didn't really know how to fight, half-starved and stupid, and

I still had my stunner. This guy, he knows what he's doing, and he's at least as good as I am, probably better. Actually, if he was trained in kickboxing or tae kwon do instead of just his fists I'd probably be finished already. Now that he's paying attention, fighting smart instead of with blind fury, all my tricks and locks and grapples aren't going to do much. Worse, I've awakened all his darkest, most vicious desires and directed them right onto me. So now either I'm dead, or he is.

Making my decision, I start to close, stepping into his punches, using my body to force them around me, rock-in-stream, then shoot a quick kick to his groin. He blocks it, but it throws off his concentration, and that was the whole point. Another moment, and my fist is going to connect with his temple, and he's going to die.

Then, out of nowhere, his whole body stiffens up, and he tumbles right into my arms.

While I'm still processing this, blinking like the idiot I am, I see Miss Theodora Eunice Faraday standing there, holding my hand stunner out in front of her. She looks almost as shocked as I feel.

No time for distractions!

Putting the big guy down on the grass (and I surprise myself at how gentle I am), I scoop one of the animal stasis pods from my pack (two more left) and expand it to operational size. A moment later, I reach the little mama opossum and her five babies, and while I hate the trauma it'll cause her when she wakes up, I scoop her and them all up into my free arm, then plop them into the tube, sealing it with a click and a hiss. Another instant, and they're all safe and asleep, frozen in a moment of perfect crystalline time.

"Please hold this for me, Miss Faraday," I tell her as I press the capsule into her shocked-but-accepting hands and find myself feeling strangely warm and happy when she nods at my instructions, her eyes clear, her expression sober. "And, um, thank you."

Right about then, an unfortunate little detail hits me: I had only packed up five babies. The little mama opossum had six to start.

Well nuts.

"Miss Faraday," I say calmly as my eyes scan the forest, and I see the dark patch where I just know in my heart of hearts the little baby opossum went, hoping that the scary dark would keep it safe from the much scarier humans. "Can you do some things for me, please?"

"You can just call me Doe," she tells me with a smile as she hands me my stunner back. "Like the deer. And that depends on what you want me to do, Nature Man."

I fumble with my backpack until the seal releases with a soft click, and I reach inside for the implements I'd really hoped I wouldn't have to use today.

"Doe, then," and just acknowledging it, and meaning it, means that something's changed between us, and we both realize it as my eyes meet hers. What this feeling is, I really don't know, but I do know that if I don't explore it now, I never will, because this moment's spark will flicker and die for both of us. Just another "might have been" lost to the ash pile of history.

So it goes.

"Doe, could you please give that stasis pod to the trundler when it arrives? And, um, when you've done that, could you also please call the peacekeepers and tell them everything that happened here? If it's all right,

I'd like them to have access to the City Computer records from this area, too. It's really hard to get without a resident's permission, so you lending your help will shave maybe weeks off something they could settle in a few hours, tops."

There's that smile again, but it's a little sad now, and I'm glad I'm pulling my helmet on, letting the baggy fabric grow semi-rigid as I activate the plates that cause it to pop up into a roughly cylindrical "bucket head" shape (a perfect complement to my clown suit, actually), so she can't see my eyes.

"Anything you want, Nature Man. But why can't you tell them yourself?"

Now her expression clouds, and she starts to realize that I'm strapping on a pair of bumpy-looking wrist bracers, my bolt-casters, following them with a short cylinder of brass-bound wood, about six inches long and perfectly fitted for my grip, which I strap to my waist. Finally, I pull out a tactical knife that I shove into a handy socket in my boot, about eight inches of sunken-molecule star-forged ceramic, black and ominous.

"Midway on our life's journey," I say, though I'm only half-talking to her, the rest all for me, steeling myself for what I know is about to come, "I found myself in dark woods, the right road lost." I take two cleansing breaths, and then I look her in the eyes. "I'm going into Hell, Miss Doe." Then I blink and look toward the two people lying unconscious on the grass. "Can you please make sure the peacekeepers take them both in, too? I'm sorry to be such a bother, but, well," I shrug helplessly, "they're gonna need therapy."

She's still figuring out everything I said when I turn from her and walk into the dark of the woods. Another few steps, and I've found what I was expecting: a hole in the ground, where there was once a manhole or some other plug to cover up the terrible places below, to hide them from the eyes of sanity and cleanliness and right. That opossum baby's gone down there, as I tell from the tiny tracks in the soft earth leading right up to the edge, too desperate to escape the evil of humanity present to care about a place of a very different sort of evil.

"Through me you enter into the city of woes," I whisper reverently. "Through me you enter into eternal pain. Through me you enter the population of loss. Justice moved my high maker, in power divine, wisdom supreme, love primal. No things were before me not eternal; eternal I remain."

I pause, then step right up to the edge, soon finding the little handholds I was expecting, set into the side of the access tunnel drilled straight down to Rock Bottom and the dark worlds that lie beneath. This is the place where all the vile sins of humanity poured, ancient and terrible, when our cities were cracked open and brought here and pressed together in more perfect form by a brighter, cleaner, more wonderful sort of people, come from the stars or from Heaven to save us if only we'd let them.

But we would not. And so, the underworld waits, repository of the darkness within.

It will always wait. Patiently.

"Abandon all hope, you who enter here," I say, the words a benediction, before I swing myself over the side and start the long climb down.

CHAPTER 8: RIPPLES FROM BELOW

Location: Earth, Sunflower City, Central Spire
Perspective: Scintillant Camor

There's a ripple of emotional energy somewhere up above, by the Nosebleed Needles that top the spires of the City, and then another down below, in the depths past the place the humans call Rock Bottom, and for a moment I'm distracted from my interview with Peterson Xiang.

Fortunately, the interview is nearing its closure, and I've already helped him purge himself of his worst, darkest, most enervating sources of pain and fear. Free at last, he wants desperately only to throw himself into work for the Ministry of Life as we reclaim this poor blighted Earth, redeeming it from the sin and horror that now renders most of its surface into a deadly wasted land. He came into the office stiff-backed and stone-faced. Now, his shoulders have lowered, and after he got the tears out of his system, he's smiling again.

Given time and meaningful work, the latter of which Gret tells me we have plenty, he can heal on his own. Smoothly. Fully. Completely. Whole once again, in time.

Though dear Xiang is a good person, and I can sense the brilliance of his mind on the periphery of my center-self, he lacks that spark that might have allowed him to take some training in the higher arts of psionics. At least right now: with his soul allowed time to heal, he might grow into that power. When time and resources permit, I intend to bring in some proper experts in the psionic arts, both to help me locate potential talents in the local human populace, and to provide "seed psi" to safely develop those whose powers are only latent. While empathy and telepathy are the most useful of the paths of awakening the self, at least in my personal opinion, a few telekinetics, precognitives, teleporters, or biometabolics would hardly go amiss. Certainly, they would make my job, and Gret's, immeasurably easier.

A pity that man who works down at Rock Bottom with all the animals couldn't come up here to lend a psionic hand, but he really is necessary doing what he does in this mixed-up, chaotic City, saving what life he can, while he can.

Now what was his name...?

But that's not important, at least not right now. What's important is that Xiang, even with his center-self still not awakened, has noticed my wavering attention, and is looking at me with worried eyes. He's sensed my own core-self drifting, identifying troubles as they arise, ripples in the smooth flow of emotional energy in this building.

"Mister Camor?"

Before he can give voice to deeper questions, I'm giving him a gentle, dismissive wave, telling him with the gesture that he's more important than an imminent apocalypse. I was just distracted for a mere nonce, perhaps understandably, but now he has my full attention once again.

"Call me what makes you most comfortable," I tell him with all my honesty. "We are going to be working together quite closely in the future, as long as all goes at the projected rates for our reclamation of your world." I turn, and together we look at the glowing image that springs up instantly before us. "Oh, what a mess we have here," I say, giving voice to my sympathetic pains, brushing a fingertip against the eastern portions of Asia. "The recyclers are hard at work on the ghost cities, but the rivers..." I cannot hold back a wince at the thought of the images I've seen, and what my imagination tells me must be far worse in person. "We have a man down in Rock Bottom who is helping raise a family of baiji, but the sheer immensity of the work before us will occupy many of your biblical threescore-and-tens before they can be safely released into their old homes in the Yangtze. And that's just for a fleeting start."

"I think I can help with that!" the young man exclaims, all eagerness, opening up just a little more to me as I make oblique mention of his Christianity, a barely tolerated religion in his former home even before the great act of self-annihilation began on this poor, tired world. "While I was at university, I was drawing up plans for a water purification system. There was never a chance to do any testing of the designs, or even to use the mainframes for some preliminary reviews of my calculations, but now..."

"Now you have the full resources of the Republic at your disposal," I tell him, standing up and extending both my hands, taking his as I look into his eyes, into the core of his being, and fill him with strength. "Go and do," I tell him. "Miss Barika Das has already been briefed on coordinating the cleanup efforts: she has real talent for top- and mid-level administration and will be your best friend in getting you the resources you need." With the motion of my chin, the image of Earth vanishes, replaced by work orders, which I fill out with a few movements of my eyes. "There, now she has the authorization *she* needs to give you what *you* need."

"Go and do," he agrees, gripping my hands in his own, giving me back a portion of the power I gave to him, and together our strength multiplies rather than being diminished.

Then he steps out, and I sink into the harmless little chair that I had brought in during my mid-morning break, grateful to have something more proper for my position. Despite the sharing of selves, there's always a draining effect once I break the connection, and I have yet to find a way to overcome it, to work past that great barrier. Perhaps with some more time, some more mastery, some more faith...

There's no time for that now, though. Not enough time for much of anything. While, as I've said, I'm only an empath, sometimes I can put enough pieces together to be able to catch a glimpse of what the likely future will hold. This shouldn't be too surprising: empathy is just another sense, and those with only the standard six possessed by most sapients can often put together some very clever visions of the future, to know the oncoming bullet before its flight. With a seventh, as well as many years of experience, I can see what is coming just that much more clearly, even if it is still, as that strange big collection of books dear Xiang likes so much put it, "through a glass darkly." Now I've got the time to properly review what I felt earlier, during the interview, and see the big picture. If I were a precognitive, I might get all the information I needed in a simple flash of insight, but limited as I am, I must pick my way through the tall grass of deduction like anyone else, though aided slightly more than most by my seven senses.

Up above, I felt the personnel of many ships die. They were cruel dark stars, and their winking out hurt like the lancing of a boil, bringing great relief when they passed on. Still, the one who ended them is landing at the spaceport, and I can sense that she's bringing news of more than significant import. If only she can arrive in time, she might put a stop to the great and terrible evil I sense is coming, before it can overflow from the depths like a backed-up sewer.

At the same time, however, down below, more dark star minds are gathering, people with intention to do harm. There were plans in place, squiggling like worms in the tarry dirt of their iniquitous skullduggery, plans that were supposed to have borne evil fruit in the fullness of time, where I couldn't sense it so easily. But the strong one who slew those middle-sized evils above the City woke the greater, darker evils down here, forcing them into rapid, hasty action, determined to harm as many people as possible before they can be slain like their co-malefactors in the destroyed ships, or, surely a worse fate for such as they, dragged out into the purifying light and made to face rehabilitation.

Some of that intended harm – no, most of it – is directed toward me. There is so *much* of it! What could I have done to merit such a vast cloud of cruelty?

Ah, but it is *not* what *I* have done, at least not personally. What I have done which has drawn this oncoming darkness, so great and so terrible it leaves all my senses reeling with its impact against my poor, tired, weak little self, is serve as the single most important representative of the power of the Republic on the planet Earth. I am the head of the Ministry of Life, that branch of our government whose purpose is to preserve and repair environments, terraform planets, and provide bio-products to the whole of the Republic – products that especially include food and medicines for the teeming trillions – and while my purpose as its chief administrator, for that is what the title Master means, is ultimately an innocuous one, it is nevertheless important. Perhaps even vital at this precarious time of transition. One of my ability, age, and experience will be hard to replace. My death will cause widespread chaos on this poor, limping little world, for I haven't yet been able to establish a full support system, and I'm still the acting interim planetary governor. There's enough of a system in place to provide essential services, but Gret and Benjuro Clee are the only other Ministry agents of any real authority. After all, the United Earth Empire was a bitter foe of the Pan-Galactic Republic until it collapsed on itself and then sued for our aid, and most of the leadership of the Ministries still do not trust the intentions of Earth's former rulers and would have been content to leave them to rot.

Irony pale and piercing: I am the lone advocate of Earth and its people among the chiefs of the Ministries. I chose to come here in defiance of their beliefs, determined in an equal mix of vainglory and desperate hope to start this weary, wounded race on the road to recovery. Now I am to be the target of the very people who were most feared by my colleagues. I, and whoever might be near me when they...

Oh! Oh my dearest darling little Birdcry!

"No more interviews today," I say as calmly as I can, stepping out into the office of the secretary that I replaced with my sweet and perfect and priceless daughter, to whom I so wanted to give that dwarf mammoth that the kind man down in Rock Bottom has been keeping for me: her next birthday present. "Please," I continue, meeting my daughter's brown eyes and giving her a gentle touch of my center-self to keep her from being confused or afraid until I can explain matters in their entirety, before turning my full attention to the four humans still sitting and waiting, amusing themselves with various data projections connecting them to their home Links.

"I am so very sorry," I tell them, "but something unfortunate has come up, something I was foolish enough not to foresee before this moment. You are all hired, so please don't worry about that. Come back here tomorrow, bright and early, and whoever is on duty will help you get situated in your proper positions. I think it will be Barika Das...yes," I nod, coming to a firm decision, "she will be your supervisor, and have your duty rosters. Today, however, you must all leave, and leave quickly, and please do not come back, not for any reason."

The hard light projections vanish, and the little wires slide back into their connecting mobile devices, and there is a brief cacophony of voices. With an effort of my fullest self, I fill them all with a sense of mixed urgency and comfort, answering the underlying emotions of their questions without using my voice. They can sense, then, that they *need* to go home, and if they do, they will be safe, and everything will be all right. At the same time, I have given them a gentle antipathy for this place, something that should wear off quickly enough, but which will almost certainly keep them away until tomorrow. These are all good people, smart people, wise people, the bright ones that I need to begin the process of saving Earth and all its inhabitants: I need them safe, and I need them out of here, and I need those things *right now*!

As soon as the room is empty except for me and my daughter, I slump, hands on knees, breathing hard. Helping a person, really reaching into their center-self and helping them to become better, the sort of people who have enough inner strength to save a world, takes a lot out of me. I would have gotten a good part of the strength back, of course, with the give-and-take that is a natural part of the process, which is why I was confident I could help six people in one day — a herculean task by any standard! Now, though, I've pushed out far more than I've taken in, but enough to save four more lives.

Can I save anyone else?

"There is something terrible coming, my dearest one," I tell sweet Birdcry, forcing myself to be strong, to stand up straight, to project calm confidence enough to keep her from being frightened no matter how frightened I am myself. Then I extend my center-self to her, and let her feel a very, very gentle touch of what I felt before, so that she can understand the situation as fully as possible without overloading her developing senses. "It's coming too fast for the peacekeepers, I'm afraid, but we'll alert them anyway. The human woman coming, you will know her, now that you've felt what I felt and sensed what I sensed. Trust her completely: she will keep you safe, no matter what happens, no matter where I go. If anyone can save me as well, she can. Now, we are going to do some needful things, and then we are going to get you somewhere safe."

"Yes father," she says sweetly, eyes full of trust, just as they've always been when she's looked at me, ever since I took her as my daughter, just as the monster-planet of her birth took my wife. Bringing life out of death, light out of darkness.

She will survive this calamity. That I vow to my deepest self.

CHAPTER 9: DEATH AND HELL

Location: Earth, Sunflower City, Under-City
Perspective: The Man

I'd be lying if I said I didn't look up, far up, at the little circle of blue sky high above me and think back on that scene from "The Time Machine" where Wells' Time Traveler is looking up at his last sight of the world above before he lets the morlock tunnels take him. I waver just for a moment in my determination.

...

I really hope there's no morlocks down here: I don't have any good experiences with them.

Every time I go into the underworld, I hesitate. That's because whenever I go into that place where all the bits and pieces that make a place like Sunflower City come together behind the scenes, I always end up leaving bits and pieces of me behind.

Incidentally, I'm being literal.

Natural creatures roam around down in these dark places, so my job regularly takes me down to find them and bring them up to where they're safe and can be prepared for relocation into the waiting world as it's cleansed of the taint of humanity's End. But there's a lot of creatures down here whose natural status is...questionable, at best.

Like that deinosuchus that dragged me into a sump pit and rolled me around for a while. For that big guy, I grabbed the stunner out of the wrist pocket of my chomped limb before I drowned and gave it a good, long jab until its primitive nervous system realized that it was supposed to go to sleep. I'm pretty sure he was made by humans, probably part of the copious experiments with monster making that took place around the End. But now, the deinosuchus is safe, and we've more-or-less made up after our initial misunderstanding. I mean, as much as anybody can make up with an archosaur, but at least now it gets food that isn't me, it doesn't have to live in a sewer, and I'm fairly sure it's not planning to Captain Hook me at some point in the future. Fairly sure.

Or the smugglers who were dealing out "scrubbed" Republic weapons, guns and stuff that had been deprogrammed, their biometric guards removed so they could be used by anybody. Since this is a pretty difficult and very dangerous process, I can understand why those weapon dealers were so protective about their operation, and don't really begrudge them the bullets they sent through my bicep and my hip, so long as they're willing to forgive me the bolts I sent back their way, and the peacekeepers I sicced on them as soon as I was sun-side again.

Or that pack of super-rats that tried to cut out my heart on a bloodstained altar right after I declined the honor of being a deity in their cannibalistic proto-religion. I did my best to explain that my present job keeps me way too busy to be a god, but it didn't go over well.

Or the slurps.

Or the cordy-creeps.

Or...

Some have said that the hardest parachute jump is the second one, because that's when you know what's coming next. That is a saying that I can confirm in this situation, except this is more like my sixtieth, starting back when they were first building Sunflower City and had some pest problems the robots couldn't reach. Under the circumstances, I think I'm allowed a little melodrama. For just the briefest of moments, I considered going back up the ladder and into the light. After all, I had five opossum babies and their mother, and that was probably enough living genetic information to save their species, even if my hunch was right and they really were the last of their kind.

Then I thought about what it would be like for me in that situation, small and weak and alone and scared, no mommy, no brothers or sisters – *alone* – except for the big, scary things out in the dark that want to eat me, or maybe just to hurt me because that's what they do, what they *are*.

...

So much for going back.

The whole undercity is a weird patchwork of little bits and pieces of the undercities of a thousand different metropoli all just crammed together more-or-less at random by the big machines that made Sunflower City, then reshaped to suit their new purposes, housing the countless tubes that make the city above run, taking food and water and data in, sending waste out, and connecting people via the postal service.

As I walk along, letting the digital overlay in my buckethead helmet project a view of the place onto my visor when there's not enough light, I can see the openings of pipes of various sizes up, down, left, and right of me, and I work hard to keep plenty of distance between me and them.

Keeping distance is a rule for survival, because I've had run-ins with slurps and snapjaws, both keen on springing ambushes from openings like these. Some of these pipes don't lead anywhere, leftovers of the chaotic building process, while others are meant to serve as maintenance access points, but there's not really any easy way to tell the difference until you've started to get a feel for things down here, for sensing the way the robots were "thinking" when they were last shuffling everything around.

Under my feet, I quickly skirt around a pit that drops off into nowhere, one of the "dead end" pipes, probably packed at the bottom with hardened clay or a metal plug, and it's almost certainly a long way down; it would be easy to starve to death at the bottom of one of these, even if the hapless explorer survived the fall. As I walk, I watch the floor turn from checkered black-and-white tiles to smooth metal to hard-packed natural earth. Soon, I also see what I was hoping to find: tracks. Little handprints, and the slash-line of an immature prehensile tail.

Click. Shifting my visor into the infrared, I soon detect the heat signature I was hoping for as a quickly fading presence in the clammy dampness. Lingering just long enough for me to extrapolate distance all the same. I'm close, and I thank whoever happens to be listening that lost baby opossums don't seem inclined to move faster than a wobble-foot amble.

Since I want to catch up to the little guy before something else does, I decide to sacrifice a bit of stealth, and draw my "sticky-stick" from my belt-clasp. It's made of living wood, and it's a fantastic little piece of Republic technology: I put a little gentle pressure in the right way on the pseudo-brass that binds the wood, and then I watch it grow outward at an incredible rate. There's a very slight friction differential to it, so it sticks to my hand just a little, ensuring that I won't accidentally drop it.

Once I've got the sticky-stick out to the size of a hanbō, about three feet of smooth, well-polished bludgeon, I stop the growth and tap my new weapon against the side of the square-cut earthen tunnel. There's a soft "ping" in my head as my helmet's sonar sensors start tracking the tiny vibrations my tapping produces, and the heads-up display starts building a map of this place. Well, *most* of a map, anyway: there's always places where the sensors just can't quite reach, so relying too much on the digital overlay is a surefire way to get lost. Or worse.

Still tapping every few steps, up, down, and to each side, getting as complete a map-out as I can, I keep my eyes moving, letting the sound enhancers in my helmet feed information to my ears. This receptive state lets me become almost superhuman, merging with the machines crammed into my clownsuit and buckethead, working with them to pick up and absorb and react to more data than I could ever handle on my own. I've spent years using this stuff, and it's second nature to me now, a lot like how people can become one with a car or a plane. Me, though, I'm one with the suit, and I let it take me along.

Good thing, too: it's how I notice the slurp before it notices me.

Slurps are one of the many monsters humans unleashed around the time of the End. We'd been building monsters for a long time before that, mostly as part of larger experiments to see how far we could push our genetic engineering skills. Part of those projects included the eradication of type 1 diabetes and Down syndrome, among other congenital issues, so I can't say that they were wastes of time. Still, when the labs were all finally opened to release all the interesting ways we'd devised to kill off our species, living weapons in the ever-growing arsenal we were using against each other, those were certainly interesting times.

What's the old curse? "May you live in interesting times?"

Slurps, though, are a mishmash of several natural critters all amped up with something extra. They're very large, dangerous lizards, based more-or-less on Komodo dragons, except they've gotten a big smack of panther chameleon, and probably some anole as well just for good measure, as well as something else that I just couldn't guess, except that it makes them more bloodthirsty than any reptile ought to be. From the monitor lizard side, they've got size and speed and strength, and a symbiotic relationship with flesh-eating bacteria in their mouths that first paralyzes you and then starts to digest you alive. From the chameleon side, they've got long, sticky tongues, also coated with that same bacterium, and barbed on the end, and a set of iridophores that let them change color to blend in wherever they go. Oh, and they've got a chameleon's claw-hands, sized up appropriately, and perfectly capable of ripping a full-grown human to pieces. So they're next to impossible to see, either in the standard human range or the infrared, they can hit you with their tongues from across a room, and all the while they're reeling you in, the barb on the end is injecting you full of killer bacteria so you won't be able to struggle much, but will almost certainly still be quite alive and conscious and *aware* while the lizard sinks in its teeth and sucks out your slowly liquefying innards.

The only reason I notice the slurp that's sitting in a pipe forming a T-junction with the main tunnel is because one of its eyes flicks in my direction, the other focused on the little baby opossum toddling along right in front of it. I'm a bigger threat – and a bigger meal – but the opossum is obviously a nice little snack, and it's *right there*. For a lizard's brain, proximity is darn important. Which means I'm almost out of time.

Just as the slurp's opening its maw, and I'm watching the dark dots of its eyes snapping into focus on the fuzzy baby, I pop my free hand up, the bolt-caster makes its sharp *click-CHAK* sound as its projectile breaks the sound barrier, and just like that, the slurp is dead, about half of sixteen inches of rebar sticking out of the back of its skull.

Before anything else can happen, I'm running forward, jerking the second of my three "small animal" pods out of my pack as I go. The opossum is dazed. Poor thing. It's not sure what to do, and so it just goes limp as I pick it up, as carefully as I can, and place it into the stasis pod. Clicking it shut, I hear the soft hiss of the gentle gasses inside as the padded interior turns red. Then I watch through the clear plastic along one side as the little guy gives a great big yawn and then curls up, nodding off almost instantly. Soon the red turns to blue, and the readout on the side lets me know that my new friend is safe and comfortable in the stasis field.

As I'm packing away the opossum, looking around the tunnel with proper watcher's eyes, that's when I realize that I'm in trouble. Apparently, that slurp wasn't just some stray monstrosity of the depths. No, it was put there on purpose. I see a chain on one hind limb, encouraging it to stick around on sentry duty, which is kind of the original purpose of slurps: low-maintenance guard creatures. The chain wouldn't keep a slurp in place if it really wanted to break free, but the sucked-clean skins of its prior meals make it obvious that the big lizard had been feeding well. Not seeing any reason to slip its chain, it stayed put, a watcher at the crossroads.

Watcher for what?

I scan the walls. They tell an interesting story. First, there's Cyrillic graffiti on the walls. Only so many creatures that live down here can write after a fashion, even if they can't use actual language, but this graffiti isn't just mimicry of human territorial markings. Instead, it's real writing, real language. Language means people, and there's only one sort of creature that comes to mind when I think of people living down here by choice.

Morlocks.

For those who didn't live through the End of humanity, the morlocks were a direct product of the total warfare of that time. Morlocks are humans partially chimerized with some old-style homo erectus stock, and maybe some other proto-humans from way back when, a deliberate step backward on the evolutionary charts. It's enough to give them these big, chompy teeth, sort of like a baboon's. They've also got a set of carnassials, which tends to make their mouths look a little overstuffed, besides keeping them from closing their lips completely shut. Their eyes are massive, too, and they're frankly incredible pieces of biological engineering, able to see into both the infrared and the ultraviolet, almost as complicated as a pigeon's eyes. Perfect for seeing in complete darkness, and unlike the creatures described by Wells, they can see in full daylight as well, though they don't like it, and much prefer the dark places. They're all albinos, too, making them more suitable for a troglodytic lifestyle, and most have short, downy hair all over their bodies.

What is most notable about morlocks, however, is that they are uniquely designed to get the maximum possible nutrition out of cannibalism. A variation of humanity that could eat other humans without suffering from the many ill effects that come from cannibalistic acts. No spongiform encephalopathy. No transmissible parasites. Nothing except pure nutrition, fats and proteins and essential amino acids.

Knowing about morlocks is all anybody needs to understand just how bad the End was: their makers actually thought they were a *good idea*. For all I know, they might have been right.

Now that I'm really looking at it, the wall writing tells a complex story. It's not all Cyrillic, as it turns out, printed in neat block lettering telling trespassers what they can expect if they wander into this area. There are also bits that have been scratched out, deliberately defaced, and sometimes scrawled over with old-fashioned spray paint. Words copied for their looks rather than their meaning. Whorls of colorful patterns that are the beginnings of art. And, in case I hadn't caught onto who was doing this writing, a variety of prints made by little paw-hands. Where the morlocks convey cruel, cold, but ultimately rational intent, these markings are all about emotion and raw impulse in the moment.

Super-rats.

With sinking horror, I realize I've walked right into the middle of a turf war between two of the more organized factions of the underworld. That slurp was stationed here at a major contested point between the morlocks and the super-rats to keep down the cross-traffic, probably forcing a state of involuntary truce. And I just took it out. Now hostilities can resume. Neither side is likely to be happy with me.

And I just broke the sound barrier with my bolt-caster.

First comes the tapping.

Morlocks have ears like owls, these fur-covered holes in the sides of their heads, one set slightly higher than the other to improve their parabolic hearing. This lets them pick up sound incredibly well. When they start tapping on the walls, they're looking for a sonar picture of their turf, one that's about as good as what the tech in my buckethead can make. Maybe better.

Now I'm hearing those soft, murmuring voices, and worse, some are coming from back the way I came. There must be side tunnels or hidden passages I didn't notice on my way in, and just like that, I'm almost surrounded.

One point that nobody in their right mind ever forgets about morlocks: there is never, *ever* just one.

Those voices in the dark could be kind of pleasant, soothing even, if I didn't know they use those same tones when they're busy in their kitchens. Yet another reason why I try to use the Link for subliminal classes instead of natural sleep: true sleep means dreams, and dreams mean nightmares.

All the same, I don't panic, even when I start to hear the pattering of bare feet on the slick, damp, hardened clay, and the soil, and the moss on the pipes. Instead, I check my equipment and make sure everything's in place. The opossum's safe and secure in my pack, which is sealed up tight, and that's important: the little guy is the reason I have to get out of here alive; rule one of survival is emotional preparedness, after all. The bolt-casters are set to go, the one around my free hand's wrist automatically cycled to the next length of rebar, while I've got the sticky-stick in a nice, firm grip in my ready hand.

When I'm sure I've got all my gear good to go, I take off!

Running away is the primary reason why I made such a good gene pirate: it made sure I stayed alive for the next job. It's also how I burned off the worst of the pounds I'd put on around my middle before the End hit. I was a pad-chair academic before humanity came home to commit planet-wide murder-suicide, and my knowledge of fighting was generally limited to what I'd studied in a classroom setting – I never did any competitions – and the occasional stick-up while I was heading home from work, or the other minor altercations that are part of normal life. Well, *my* normal life, anyway. Fortunately, I was obsessive about working out, using it to take the edge off the worst of my anxieties and depression, so at least I had a bit of a head start when the End hit. If not for that, I think I'd have probably died the same way most people did. Well, that and a lot of plain luck, of course; needless to say, if I don't stay constantly active, my survivor's guilt cripples me, if something else on my laundry list of psychological-emotional disturbances doesn't get to me first. If not for genetics and my unwillingness to watch what I eat, I'd probably be as thin as a rail, no good for morlock purposes.

As I'm running, I'm tapping my sticky, keeping it around chest height as I stay close to the side of the wall that seems most likely to have a turnoff. The tapping keeps up my sonar feed, and I see the little red "pings" that tell me that they're closing in. Way too many of them, and all over the place. They're up ahead, too. There's no way to avoid them all, so all I can do is pick where I'm going to fight.

I round the next bend in the tunnel, and I just slam on through the massed pale bodies arrayed against me. There's a flash of ghost-pale bodies and wide, horrible eyes, but they vanish as I swing my sticky, and I can feel the *crunch* of bone once, twice, and then I'm through, shouldering my way past the little gang without looking back. The speed and sudden ferocity of my attack is all that's keeping me from being surrounded and overwhelmed by those awful clutching fingers. I've felt them before and I am *not* going to feel them again: they like to take their meat alive, and they think fear and pain just add flavor.

CLANG!

A grate drops from the ceiling of the tunnel and slams down in front of me, a big, heavy steel thing. It blocks the tunnel before me completely, and a glance is all I need to know it's impossible to break through with the time I've got.

I dart down another passage, and now I'm lost, losing sight of my way out on the ever-updating mini-map in my buckethead's systems.

CLANG!

They're herding me. They've set this place up, a perfect trap, like people used to make in castles. The idea flashes into my head: this is how they've kept out the super-rats, by building a series of grate-controlled funnels, letting them decide where their enemies will have to go. To do that, they'd have had to hack into some of the wireworks down here, letting them flip switches and shuffle grates how they like. Morlocks are good with their awful, clutching hands, fantastic at making things, at tinkering with machinery even when they don't have the education to really understand what they're doing with it. Almost as good as super-rats, truth be told, though super-rats seldom make their own...

A spear suddenly cracks against the back plates of my armor; guess they're not planning to take me alive after all. Whoever I just killed back there must've been important to them if they want to just turn me directly into meat without any "tenderizing" first.

I can't stop, can't turn and fight, can't pay nearly enough attention to the path before me, because I can hear those pattering, slapping feet on the chill, damp moss, and I know that they'll overwhelm me if I give them the chance.

Another second later, and a final gate slams behind me just before the tunnel angles downward, and I hit a moss-slick slide. Just like that, all my forward momentum turns against me, keeping me rushing headlong down a long slope, and I'm just lucky the moss is soft enough that I don't get torn up too badly, and the angle isn't so steep that I get more than briefly stunned when I come to a stop with a bump and a tumble.

Sitting up and taking in my surroundings, I suddenly decide that maybe I'm not so lucky after all. I've been plopped down right into the middle of another T-intersection, one arm of that intersection being the way I came. Looking right, I see a tunnel, possibly a chunk of mine shaft snatched from somewhere in the mountains, heading off beyond sight. To my left...

Slowly, making no sudden movements, I get to my feet. A pair of slightly luminous red eyes off in the dark glare back at me. Strings of electric lights shine on the walls here, adding credence to my idea of it being a mine shaft. There's just enough of that light for me to see the owner of those eyes as it lets me take in the full extent of how doomed I am right now, savoring the scent of my fear as the blood freezes in my veins.

The morlocks just herded me into the lair of a super-pig.

Super-pigs aren't a prehistoric resurrection created by human science like the deinosuchus was, even if they look something like a daeodon with gigantism. No, what super-pigs are, in strictly scientific terms, is *dangerous*. Their genes aren't just made of pig either, though the idiots who created them thought they might make a good source of meat in the lean times of the End, right up until the super-pigs ate them first. Besides wild boar genes, and domestic pig genes, there's also a mix of hippopotamus and chimpanzee somewhere in the chromosomal smorgasbord. Just enough to make something that was already huge, aggressive, and surprisingly smart a little psychopathic as well. It's like something out of Roald Dahl's "Dirty Beasts." There's an anthropophagic pig in there — first poem in my edition of the book, actually — and it's downright pleasant compared to a super-pig.

The hulking shape lumbers out into my vision, snapped back into proper color now that there's enough light for the visor's digital projection to shut itself off. It's big, *really* big, taking up way too much of the tunnel, those beady red eyes fixed on me, and I'm less than happy about my life decisions right now. Coarse, dark brown bristles cover its body, some long and sharp enough to serve as quills, and its slavering, sloppy mouth, big enough to fit my whole head inside, has a pair of upward-curling tusks, each about the size of my forearm. This isn't just some big suidomorph, though; you can tell because it's not resting on all fours like a proper pig ought. It's got hands, heavy, knot-knuckled things, awkward and brutal and clumsy and cruel. Hands big enough and strong enough to tear me right in half if they got hold of me.

A string of drool dribbles from the flaccid lower lip as it turns its head this way and that, its snout snuffling the air, sighting me, scenting me, sizing me up slowly and methodically. It's confident because it's eaten plenty of my kind, enough to know that we're small and weak and delicious. I know it's a human-eater because there's some cloth scraps scattered around on the ground behind it. The remnants of clothes, but nothing else, not even shoes: just like the more standard sort of pig, they gnaw up bone and skin and *everything* with equal relish. I'm just glad I don't have an olfactory feed in my buckethead because I really, really do not want to smell this monstrosity or its environs, not with what I know about the stuff they like to live in, roll in, and occasionally snack on.

With a glance behind me, I can see a pit right at the edge of the guttering electric lights, a few red-brown smears around its edge, and I'm figuring that's why there isn't too huge a buildup of waste around the lair. The morlocks probably hose the place down every so often, or maybe the pig itself shoves the worst over the side; I mean, that chimpanzee part has got to have some say in the housecleaning around here. Still, it's an exit point, and as much as I know I'm not going to like it, I'll take what I'm given.

It's smart, though. It knew what I was planning, and it out-thought me. Before I have a chance to move, to escape by the only egress, it comes at me – fast, so monstrously fast – and I don't think about it, just spin, swinging my sticky two-handed and smashing off most of its length on the super-pig's too-thick skull. There was so little room for maneuvering, I have to wipe a hand across my visor to clear the drool that splattered there as the pig sped on by.

Slapping the sticky-stick back onto my belt, letting it rest up for later, I bring up both of my bolt-casters as the pig rounds on me, its movements even more hindered by the cramped space than I am, giving me the only edge I have. So, I use that edge for all its worth and just open up with both bolt-casters, letting the powerful electromagnets in each of the wrist-mounted weapons straighten out the curled bolts of rebar wrapped tight around the bracers, then launch them at super-sonic speeds through the barrel on the top of each. They're cheap weapons, dirty bits of makeshift technology I patched together during the End, but rebar is still plentiful, and with a few Republic-level additions, they're ideal for monster slaying even now.

The crack of the discharge reverberates through the tunnel, made even louder by the crackle of electric fire along the bolts' lengths. The sound is almost as loud as the roaring squeal of the super-pig as it charges at me again, heedless of personal danger. The big porker makes a prime target, and both of my shots hit, sinking right into its massive shoulders and plowing into the muscle-corded meat beyond.

WHUMP!

Too focused on shooting, I didn't pay attention; the big guy barrels into me. It was a sideways angle, not direct, and I didn't get a tusk for my troubles, but the hit makes me see stars and sparklers. On the bright side, I spin all the way around, so I'm facing the super-pig as it wheels for another pass.

Lifting my arms, I start snapping off rebar bolts as fast as I can.

WHAM!

Too punch-drunk to remember to keep moving, it rams right into me. But I got a heart-shot in. It should be dying now, bleeding out on the inside, but it's got me speared on one of its tusks, the sharp ivory stuck up between the plates of my belly and my chest. So, I'm dying too.

Not dead yet, though.

147

We're barreling down the tunnel now, with me up on the super-pig's snout, getting jostled around between the tusks, one partway stuck into my abdomen. I use the pain to sharpen my thoughts, to kick off the daze of being hit, the haze of hurt. If the pig reaches the far wall of the tunnel, it's going to smash me against it, and then it's going to gore me to pieces, its last act before it dies.

So, I make myself act, yanking my knife out of my boot sheathe and hacking wildly at the side of the super-pig's face, at the connecting tissue keeping the tusk attached to its skull. It's so sharp, it cleaves right through flesh and bone, and the pig is squealing and roaring loud enough to make my head ring as I grab onto the tusk and work my feet up and *shove* with all my might.

The pit. I was right in front of the pit! The pig's clattering past me, its weird trotter-like hind feet making such a strange sound alongside the hard-knuckled fists of its twisted hands as I hit the refuse-slick ground. I skid along the floor on my back, helpless, unable to stop myself even when I slam the knife into the stone, flipping myself over in the process: it's too sharp, and just gushes through the offal and sticky moss coating the floor! Another second, and it might've caught, but now...too late...too late...

There's a cruel, sharp moment of clarity as I find myself in freefall, plummeting down a pit whose depth I cannot even guess.

Reacting like I'd been taught, I splay out my limbs in readiness for landing after a fall, tucking in my chin and preparing my body to work with the impact rather than just go splat. Reaching out with the knife, I feel it shudder in my hand as I use the friction of contact with the wall of the pit to turn myself over so I'm going down feet first, legs slightly bent, ensuring I won't land on my back and risk endangering my pack and its precious cargo; it's made to be rugged, but I don't want to take chances.

The knife's throwing off sparks at it cleaves through the pressed rock of the long pit, and with my other hand I whip out my sticky-stick as well, letting it grow until it smacks into the other side, the friction sizzling the wood away almost as fast as it can grow, and I'm just hoping the combined drag will slow me enough so that when I hit the bottom I can –

CHAPTER 10: AN INTERVIEW; EVERYTHING GOES TO HELL

Location: Earth, Sunflower City, Central
Spire, Outside Stairs
Perspective: Thomas Delmonte Cerveau

Standing at the top of the stairs leading from the hovercar drop-off to the entrance of the shining building that was Central Spire, provisional headquarters of the government of Earth, was Gret, scowling down at the motorcade that came rolling up, led by an obsidian-tinted car.

One by one, the luxury hovercars disgorged their contents, consisting almost entirely of humans in suits and dark glasses and the obvious bulges of firearms under their jackets, along with those that were carrying "bodyguard briefcases," guns with their triggers concealed within the handles of ersatz luggage. Just the sort of escort to be expected for one of the most important men in a now-fallen empire.

The one notable exception to these dapper-dressed gunmen got out of the second-to-last car, his door opened by one of the interchangeable goons. Once the car's occupant was out, standing at his full and most impressive height, his face tanned and ruggedly handsome, his shoulders broad, his waist slim, he looked up the stairs at the alien. Gret, in turn, stared down at Thomas Delmonte Cerveau.

Even with the artificial height granted to the creature by the broad, white marble stairs, Mister Cerveau's eyebrows raised incredulously: the alien was *bizarre*. Looking something like a sawed-off, hunchbacked survivor of the trenches of World War One in a gas mask and long coat, the little beast was under half the height of Mister Cerveau.

"You're the pinnacle of what your Republic has to offer?" Mister Cerveau quipped as he reached the top of the stairs, looking down his nose at the little creature whose slim, masked muzzle only just barely reached the level of his thighs. "If you're the most formidable sort of creature the Republic can field, it's no wonder you never invaded Earth with ground troops."

"Same back atcha, beanpole," snapped the runt, roughly prodding him in the knee with one thick, oversized-looking claw, punching a single neat hole in the hand-tailored fabric before it turned and started a slow, trundling walk toward the vast glass doors fronting the building. "Now c'mon, you've already wasted enough of my day making me wait on you. Don't you humans understand punctuality?"

"Other people wait for me," answered Mister Cerveau, his broad mouth setting into a tight line, a vein standing out prominently on his temple as he glared down at the maggot-textured skin of the alien's naked head where it was visible around the face-enclosing, thick-lensed mask. "You should have been briefed on who I am long before I arrived."

"Yeah, yeah," huffed the runt, the automatic doors parting as it stumped through them, paying the numerous armed, suited men no mind as they fanned out in the lobby all around the pair, some of them going so far as to draw their weapons from their ill-concealed holsters as though expecting an attack at any moment, from any side. "Everything about you is public access now that Earth's joined the Republic, same as for every public figure. You're Thomas Delmonte Cerveau. Rich guy, back when United Earth Empire money meant anything. Newly broke. One of the key players in – what was it? – five or six of the big secret conspiracies that made your old military-industrial-religious-criminal-government complex work. Mastermind behind the consortium that made sure you humans kept using up your supplies of natural petrochemicals, the single rarest and most versatile resource anywhere, for *fuel* of all things, right up until Earth's supplies literally went up in smoke, so you had to go conquer other planets to get more. Married to a wife with chronic neuroses from being constantly bullied, and father of two sons, because you made sure the neonatal labs only inserted Y-chromosome sperm into your wife when you were making her go through those fertility treatments. Almost killed her both times, too: poor thing just wasn't meant for having babies. Probably too inbred, if I understand the way the old Imperial aristocracy used to work, and how much most of your reproductive endocrinologists suck at their jobs."

The casualness with which the runty alien made these comments, never once rising above a slow, inevitable, plodding gait while walking toward one of the building's many elevators left Mister Cerveau temporarily speechless, his mouth agape, his face growing bright red as the full implications of those words sank in. With a visible effort, the muscles of his neck standing out dangerously, he made a casual gesture to the suited gunmen. One of them gave a single nod right before Mister Cerveau stepped into the elevator with the alien, and the doors clicked shut behind them.

"You seem to know a lot about me," growled Mister Cerveau as he heard the elevator rise. "Which means you probably know that I own this building."

"Used to," huffed the runt, before there was a soft chime, and the doors of the elevator swung open, hardly any time having passed despite the miles of distance going up. "And you only owned maybe," the alien cocked its head to the side, still stumping along as they stepped out onto the floor, "about a third of this heap back when it was in its original location. The rest's all tossed together from five or six other skyscrapers and hotels and stuff, forge-fused by the constructors when they were putting Sunflower City together. Rush job, nowhere near our best work, but not too bad under the circumstances. As for knowing things, meh, that's easy these days: most information's freely available on the Link, and every time someone important tries to conceal something embarrassing, the journalist hacks in the courier service just smear it around that much more thoroughly. Seriously, you oughta see the stuff they post about me."

They were making their way along a raised walkway overlooking a large cluster of cubicles, perhaps two or three hundred of them, forming a complex maze of makeshift workspaces. About half of those workspaces were occupied, human employees busily tapping away on their computers.

"Terrible ergonomics," growled the alien with a dismissive wave at the small sea of workers. "Typical human-made crap thrown together by the lowest bidder. It's a wonder any of these poor saps can do any work at all, especially in these damned cubicles and with those damned supervisors left over and running things the way they did when you humans were still calling all the shots. If your stupid planet wasn't still on probation, I'd get this crap tossed to the recyclers and replaced with proper engineering from back home...or maybe some good blid stuff. They were putting the fine touches on bureaucracy when your species was in its first Stone Age, so they're aces at office equipment." The hunched little alien turned its head to glower at Mister Cerveau with small, beady black eyes that were just barely visible through the thick lenses of its mask. "But here you are, so instead, I have to put up with the crap you left behind, Mister Cerveau, and I spit in your mother's ashes every time I put my claw through one of these flimsy keyboards or have to bawl out a supervisor for pointlessly stressing my employees."

"I'm sure the feeling is mutual," sneered Mister Cerveau, following the stunted creature as they entered an office at the far side of the room, many large windows making it seem almost as though the walls were made of glass. "You just don't understand how to motivate people into doing their best work," he added, closing the door behind them, then surveying the tiny, Spartan office with an air of ultimate disdain: he'd wandered into the realms of Middle Management! "That's what the supervisors were trained to do, and you should trust their methods. You can get the best out of employees by making them work harder and paying them less. After all, there's always somebody else willing to do the job."

"Theory X managerial strategy, yeah," grunted the hunched-over alien as it stumped its way to one of the human-sized office chairs, which creaked ominously as the little beast climbed up into it and plopped down on the unpadded seat. "Read all about that one. And that heartsy-crapsy Theory Y stuff, too. See, Mister Cerveau, that's the sort of crap you need to know when you're making people do stuff they don't wanna do in the first place, and hafta motivate 'em somehow to do it anyway. Especially when there's a practical limit on how many people you can hire for any given position. Things're different now: work in the Republic is supposed to be meaningful and... naw, 'fun's' a stupid word; not accurate, either. 'Fulfilling.' Yeah, that's better. If it happens to be neither, then we hire somebody to make a machine that can do the job so the people who'd been doing that work can go home and recover for a while. Haven't quite caught up to that around here," the alien added with an annoyed glance out at the maze of cubicles. "Right now, I'm stuck making these poor lumps work themselves out of their jobs, doing manual data entry for all the old records left over from what's left of your planet so we can get it permanently inscribed into hardcopy; standard anti-thought control stuff, you know."

"That sounds completely divorced from reality," replied Mister Cerveau with a light snort of derision. "Remove pressure and competition and people lose their fighting trim. What's outside this office right now, that's more in line with the way the real-world works."

"And what about the ones who don't like to compete, Mister Cerveau?" asked the runt, peering up at him through the thick lenses of the mask, its expression...curious now, rather than irritated. "The smart, dedicated, hard-working people who just don't do well when they're being constantly weighed in the balance, threatened, intimidated, and brow-beaten into submission? The ones who don't need to be bullied to get them to work and get more education on how to do their jobs better, just audited and peer-reviewed every so often to make 'em keep perspective on what they're doing, and where they need to improve?"

"That's just the nature of competition," Mister Cerveau declared with a dismissive wave of his hand. "Where there are winners, there must be losers. Sacrifices that must be made in the name of a more perfect species. Your Republic's way of doing things just results in a weak, flaccid worker, not good for anything outside of his narrow comfort zone. That or a pathetic leech, a drain on the public dole, typical of socialism." He spread his legs, his hands almost unconsciously brushing downward, as though to indicate himself as the very pinnacle crafted by his ideal vision. "The Empire required sacrifices, but the results, I am sure, speak for themselves."

For a long, long while, the stunted, hunched alien looked up at Mister Cerveau, its eyes unreadable. Then it snorted, waving a claw toward a collection of chairs that had been shoved up against one wall.

"Pull up a seat, Mister Cerveau," the alien directed. "You ever heard of the trolley problem? Also called a catch-twenty-two. I ask 'cause it sounds like you're presenting me with one."

"What?" Mister Cerveau answered, blinking, then shook his head. "I'll stand; I don't expect to be here much longer."

"Suit yourself."

Location: Earth, Sunflower City, Central
Spire, Trinidad's Office
Perspective: Trinidad Del Toro

Frowning in concentration, Trinidad found himself starting to really like Republic technology. For one, with the microscopic circuitry encoded directly onto his corneas, he didn't have to make use of anything as crude as keyboard and mouse. After he'd gotten used to it, he could manipulate data pretty much by just thinking about it, the micro-movements of his facial muscles enough to convey his slightest impulse into action. Which meant he didn't have to confine himself to the prison of a desk, something he'd been dreading ever since he'd taken on a respectable office job like his mother had always wanted for him.

Instead, he could do all the work required of him while moving around his office, whether walking, jogging in place, or, as now, performing a slow Bando kata, taking his time and keeping to the simpler forms so as not to disrupt his view of the hard light screens as they moved to stay level with his eyes. Due to Earth's probationary status, the technology was extremely rare for humans, but Scintillant Camor was the head of a Ministry, one of the most powerful officials in the entire Republic...and Gret was one of the most short-tempered: as soon as Mister Camor had vouched for him, Gret had pushed through an order to get Trinidad the tech and training he needed to do the work she wanted him to perform as quickly and efficiently as possible, which meant goodbye to carpal tunnel and swivel chair spread, and hello to working on his feet while he pored over the records left behind by his deceased predecessor.

Peewee Montgomery had been incredibly methodical, incredibly thorough, and incredibly steeped in a conspiracy so far-reaching, just learning about it shook Trinidad's faith in his own species. Earlier, when Gret had said that forty-percent of the humans who made it through the

End were bad people, and that most humans had a hard time doing the right thing for the right reasons, he'd written the words off as just a part of her general tirade against the universe at large, trying to get a rise out of him to see how he'd act when angry; he'd had drill sergeants who'd tried the same trick on him, and they'd been about as successful. Now, though, he was starting to think that she might have been generous in her estimate. Piecing together what he'd learned from Peewee's records, Trinidad Del Toro was horrified at the tale those numbers told.

"Gret was right," he muttered to himself as he looked up and down the financial records of a fallen Empire.

The United Earth Empire had been practicing slavery, of that there was no doubt. There were shipment manifests of aliens transferred between planets, and even a cursory cross-referencing into the conditions on such transports was enough to make Trinidad's blood run cold.

The horror didn't stop there, though: humanity, as in times before, was just as eager to enslave itself. The Empire had adopted wholesale all the most aggressive, expansionistic, profit-focused strategies of humanity's most savage times, and in such a system, where the people in charge lived lives of luxury and hedonistic excess, secure in the knowledge that they had the might which gave them the right, there was the overwhelming majority who were squeezed ever tighter. Those who couldn't be squeezed for anything else, naturally enough, ended up as sapient livestock: the proof was all there in the numbers, neat columns of facts and figures that had never appeared in any news report. Numbers that had once been people, lives destroyed in the name of progress.

Secrets buried and nearly lost and forgotten forever, if not for the random act of a stranger on the streets of Rock Bottom.

After he'd swallowed this initial bitter pill, Trinidad could more easily start to process the rest of the story the records told, which was a tale of conspiracy and corruption that ran all the way to the top of humanity's leadership. Certain names came up again and again, names of colonial leaders and criminals, like Caddigan Carse, who'd been given the governorship of a new colony to give him political legitimacy, explaining his methods of controlling the native population. There were the names of religious leaders, like Castor Agustus Arrhenius, one of the chief advocates of the Empire, preaching its holiness before God every week and humanity's divine right to rule. And there were the names of many prominent politicians and, of course, the leaders of business, the semi-private, Imperial-commissioned enterprises whose efforts brought wealth pouring like a tide into the Empire.

Thomas Delmonte Cerveau's name was one of the most prominent in that last group. He was the one who'd championed the use of fossil fuels as the financial foundation of the Empire, after all, and the need for more had been the principle driving force behind humanity's outward expansion. Now Trinidad's memory churned, and he recalled how frequently the pre-End news had featured Cerveau's name, usually associated with opening some new frontier, or the fantastic new wealth and affordable products made possible thanks to cheap alien labor.

That same set of conspirators appeared time and again throughout the records, always quietly profiting from every event of cosmic expansion as the Empire made its inevitable way outward, dominating planet after planet. They even appeared alongside the sale of arms and research, as well as development budgets for a host of twisted biological projects that presaged the End, selling weapons and diseases and monsters to anyone who'd pay for them when the rest of humanity returned home to put a final epithet on the various conflicts that had been simmering under the surface for so long before that flashpoint.

Now, with the End past and the rebuilding of Earth just started, those same names appeared again, this time right alongside the Republic budget for that rebuilding. These humans had been the ones to engineer the unconditional surrender of Earth and its application to the Republic. As liaisons with the Republic, before Mister Camor and Gret had arrived to properly set things in order, and while the great builder machines were still constructing Sunflower City to house humanity, they'd been the ones to tinker with the books, using cat's-paws like poor Peewee Montgomery. They'd rerouted resources intended to be used to create the City, causing old and obsolete materials to be used instead, especially in the underground, where few people ever went. Then they'd used criminal contacts to directly translate those resources into black market money, money that went to two purposes. The first, naturally, was to line their own pockets: these people were survivors, after all, and they were always looking for ways to make sure they stayed on top with a golden parachute in case everything collapsed. The second of these purposes...

The hard light constructs shattered as Trinidad plowed through them, he wrenched open the door to his office, and went tearing off toward the stairs down.

He chose the stairs because, of course, the elevators were already in use: Thomas Delmonte Cerveau's goon squad was on the move.

Thinking that she'd have some time before the next mission, Susan Six was only halfway through her tropical-flavored smoothie when Dan relayed an intercepted peacekeeper communication to her stat suit.

"Political dissidents are strongly suspected of being in operation in Central Spire," came the dispassionate report from City Central. "Calling all available peacekeepers: political dissidents are strongly suspected of being in operation in Central Spire. They are presumed armed and dangerous. Head Minister Scintillant Camor and Head Earth Auditor Gret are suspected primary targets."

"No rest for the wicked, huh, Dan?" Susan chuckled as she reluctantly slid the smoothie to the end of the counter, then dropped another coin down next to it. "Keep this cold for me," she told the attendant with a smile that made the poor boy's acne-speckled face break out in still more pimples, before she turned and strode purposefully toward her ship.

A matter of minutes later, Susan Six was streaking along on her sky cycle, letting City Central's navigation beam smoothly guide the little personal craft right up to the roof of Central Spire, the tallest of the many buildings that made up the shining city, its brightness rising like a pillar of light toward Heaven. As she stepped out onto one of the flat landing areas on the roof, mostly intended for use by sightseers and maintenance workers, the tall woman in the gleaming copper-and-cobalt stat suit frowned as she looked up: she'd just felt a drop of rain.

"Dan," she spoke softly, her suit rippling slightly as it hardened into rigid plates, a brief flicker around her face the only sign that her head was now encased in a forcefield. "Is there any precipitation scheduled today?"

"I'm afraid not, Miss Six," replied the near-sapient AI. "The cloud cover you are seeing is the result of recent emotional developments in the populace of Sunflower City. Presently the planarian engines are reacting as they were designed, adjusting the flow of weather patterns around the city to better acclimate to the mood of its inhabitants."

"And since there's a revolution in progress," Susan Six concluded as she drew her carbine in one hand, her sword humming to life in the other as the roof access panel slid open automatically at her approach, "we're about to enter the eye of a hurricane. Good to know."

```
Location: Earth, Sunflower City, Central
Spire, Gret's Office
Perspective: Thomas Delmonte Cerveau
```

"See," the alien explained, "the trolley problem's this old psychological game where you're in a trolley at the top of a hill, and suddenly the brakes go out, but you can still change which rail you'll travel. So, you're hurtling down the hill, and there's two branches on the line: one will make you hit one person, and the other will make you hit a whole crowd. Just like you right now, I guess, from how you see things: either you can choose to run over a few weak people, but make the survivors stronger, or you can relax all the rules, like how you think the Republic does things, and let a huge number of people get run over the next time they land in a pickle. The catch-twenty-two trolley," the alien reached up to tug an imaginary bell-cord. "Ding-ding! Well, what about it, Mister Cerveau: which would you pick?"

Mister Cerveau rolled his eyes.

"A stupid question: you pick the track that runs over the least number of people. The greater good and all that."

"Yeah, figured you for the type. Well, you're wrong!"

The alien drew itself up to its extremely unimposing full height, standing on the chair, and prodded Mister Cerveau in his other knee with one sharp-pointed claw tip, leaving a second tiny hole to match the first.

"The right answer, Mister Cerveau, is either option C, or option D, or maybe even option W."

"Option-" Cerveau blinked. "What are you talking about? There are only two choices in the problem!"

"The choice is a false one," answered the little alien, the smugness sounding loud and clear in its high-pitched, almost girlish voice. "If you'd read the book by Joseph Heller, you'd know: the catch in a catch-twenty-two is that you're being forced to choose between two undesirable outcomes by some scum-bucket with a gun and delusions of grandeur, just like whoever thought up that dumb trolley question in the first place.

"The right answer to a catch-twenty-two is to say to Hell with the choices that jerk-wad gave you and make up something else instead. For the trolley problem, you could shove something under the wheels, either stopping or derailing it. You could jam the rail-shifter halfway, so you go off the rails, then race to the back of the trolley and jump off while it smashes into a brick wall. Depending on what you happen to have in your pockets — and believe me, Mister Cerveau, I've got a *lot* of stuff in my pockets — or what set of skills you've got either in yourself or among your fellow passengers on the runaway trolley, your options extend even further. Pretty nearly infinite, actually! And nobody has to die at all! It's a dumb problem, and you're dumb, too, for thinking up a situation where you can claim that doing something rotten to people is somehow justified in any way. There's no 'greater good,' Mister Cerveau: there's just good."

The sneer in the alien's voice was heavy and obvious, even through the translation device in the clunky atmospheric mask and the soft hiss of its efforts to breathe in Earth's thin air.

"According to the appointment book, you're here to ask me for a job, Mister Cerveau," the hunched alien said next, after giving the towering human before it plenty of time to stew over its words. "Problem is, you're with me 'cause Sin doesn't think you're hirable material, and I don't care for you much, either. You haven't asked for or used my name once during all the time we've been talking, and while I'm no empath, the looks you've been giving me are the same as the ones I've seen on the leaders of lynch mobs. Unless I'm way off the mark, I'm guessing you don't even think of me as a person. So right now, if you're wanting me to find you a job, it's gonna be a hard sell."

"Actually," said Mister Cerveau, casually pulling a very large pistol from his coat pocket and resting the muzzle against the naked top of the little alien's wrinkled, pink-skinned skull, "I'm here to inform you that there is going to be a change of management. Effective immediately."

"Are the bad people coming now, Daddy?" asked my precious, perfect Birdcry. I have to struggle not to squeeze her hand too tightly as I lead her toward the lavish executive break room I'd noticed upon arriving that morning, and had hitherto ignored, as its emotional currents reeked far too heavily of the wickedness of its former users to encourage a healthy appetite. I risk a look down at her, and the memories of our first meeting come flooding back.

There was my wife, pregnant and dying, the coils of a carnivorous vine wrapping around her more quickly than my pathetic survival knife and even more pathetic strength could resist. Our center-selves touched one last time, and I felt the life within her that would never be born, and we all shared in a final familial communion.

Then they were gone, and I was alone on a world that ravened with *hate*. Hate for me, the intruder, the invader, the parasite.

Later, much later, I learned from the planetary scout patrol that found and rescued me that the whole world's ecosystem was a single living entity, sentient, but like an especially large, crude animal. Not a person, but most certainly self-aware. Anything that wasn't a part of its systems was regarded as an enemy, to be killed whenever possible, and made miserable when it was not. Invading organisms like me and my wife, of course, were like blood-bloated ticks from the perspective of the planet, and in less than a day after our forced landing following a near-miss with space pirates, the planet itself decided to make its displeasure at our presence known.

I would have died there, on my knees in the tattered remnants of our little camp, if Birdcry hadn't come to save me. She'd taken me by the hand, spoken to me in her soft, melodic voice, and led me to where more of her people were waiting. While I didn't speak their language, the Republic translators in my ears and eyes and my own empathic abilities soon helped me to learn enough of their speech to begin communication, at first with simple gestures, then with words, and finally with sentences. Over the course of many Standard weeks, I grew to love Birdcry as though she were my biological daughter, even as she took to me as though I were her biological father.

Birdcry, as it turned out, had been orphaned by the same planet that had left me a widower, and my two grown sons bereft of a mother. Her shared loss with mine led her to depart from her people's normal, natural caution – the planet regarded them as an especially tenacious sort of parasite! – to bring me into the fold of her tribe-family. That act of saving me, as it turned out, led to the salvation of her entire people: the planet was well into the process of wiping them all out. When the scout service arrived, following my emergency beacon, they soon summoned more ships, enough to ferry the entire liptani species away from that death world. Some chose to settle on another world, a jungle planet much like their old home, but without its active malice. Others, especially their many orphans, chose to be adopted by various families in the Republic and learn our ways. Birdcry was of this latter group.

She should have gone with someone else, my first impulse in the face of this overwhelming danger declares. I should have known that there

167

would be the wicked and the cruel who would happily endanger her to get at me, and at the Ministry of Life, and at the Republic. There were a number of families who should have taken in my sweet Birdcry, who would have raised her as she deserved.

Even as I finish this inner emotional protest, however, I know that I did the right thing: we love each other, and while I am not a perfect parent, Birdcry knows that I do my best to give her the love and attention that she needs while also fulfilling the requirements of my profession. Her presence in my present place of employment is evidence of our relationship. She played the part of receptionist in this office because she recognized that I had a job to do and was doing my best to integrate her into a natural place in fulfilling that job, while giving her precious time. Time with her daddy, time spent getting an education, and time getting to meet the various interviewees, and even a chance to play with some of the less inhibited ones while I was right there and could keep a careful empathic watch over her and them to ensure she was never in any danger.

Though I did the right thing, all the same, my daughter is in danger because of me. Whatever else takes place, I must make this right.

"Yes, my dear one," I tell my daughter, and now I do squeeze her hand, though not *too* hard, as we enter the disused break room, a thin layer of greasy dust on many of the surfaces. "They're on their way now."

Stopping before the sink, I yank open the cupboard doors beneath it, nodding in satisfaction as I see the sizable space amidst the bare plumbing. Republic plumbing technology means that very little space needs to be spent on water pipes, which means that the old-style human design has plenty of room left over. More than enough to make a perfect hiding place for my priceless daughter.

"You remember how to hide, Birdcry?" I ask her, needlessly: staying hidden is the first skill any liptani had to learn on their home world, or the planet would eat them. She nods, though, her eyes shining with her complete faith and trust in me, her daddy. "Good. Stay hidden until the woman comes. She'll be a human, but you'll know her right away: she'll make you feel safe. She'll make the bad people go away. You can trust her completely; if anyone can save me, she can. If not, your older brothers will take you into their families and make sure that you're not left alone ever again."

"I don't want to live with anyone else!" exclaims Birdcry, her large, dark brown eyes starting to brim with tears. Then she swallows, wipes her eyes, and shakes her head determinedly. "I...I'm sorry, Daddy. I didn't mean..."

"It's all right," I tell her, kissing her forehead; she's from a people who lost their loved ones almost daily, and adapted by growing just that much more closely attached to each other, that much more loving and gentle, all the better to cooperate and ensure that their orphans would always have someone to take care of them. Her reaction is normal, natural, healthy. But she'll survive, even if I do not, emotionally as well as physically. "You have my permission to be happy, Birdcry. You don't have to feel guilty for my sake just because you live, and I do not. I wouldn't want you to suffer that way, even if I can't be there in person." I kneel and touch my brow to hers, my purple fluff squeezed against her short, mottled brown-and-green fur as I let my strength flow into her, ensuring the survival of her heart no matter what might happen. "Will you do as I asked? Will you stay safe?"

"Yes, Daddy."

"Good girl."

Closing the cupboard doors to conceal my daughter from sight, I turned and made my way back toward the office where I'd held interviews. After all, I need to give the invaders what they expect to find, and absolutely no reason to go hunting for my daughter. As I walk, I reach into my suit pocket and pull out a long, narrow syringe, popping off the cap with my thumb. Shaking my head ruefully, I lift the sucker-tipped end toward my face: this is going to hurt.

```
Location: Earth, Sunflower City, Central
Spire, Emergency Stairs
Perspective: Trinidad Del Toro
```

About six years ago was the last time Trinidad Del Toro had been forced to kill anyone. A year ago was the last time he'd held a firearm, and only for some practice. A halfhearted attempt to maintain the old skills that had kept him and the members of his squad alive during the End.

Now he was looking down the stairs to where two dark-suited bodies lay, their necks broken, holding a pistol in one hand, a submachine gun slung over his shoulder. Neither of the two human-made weapons were his, of course: after all, Sunflower City was supposed to be civilized, and he was in a civilized job. The most dangerous items he was supposed to be carrying were official records!

Fortunately for Trinidad, while he'd been a bit lax on his firearms training, he'd stayed quite current in hand-to-hand combat practice via the Link connection provided by his Republic citizenship, making full use of the various virtual environments to keep his reflexes sharp. Since he was well over six feet tall and sufficiently heavily muscled to be occasionally mistaken for industrial equipment, the fight on the stairs against the two goons had been over in seconds. They were dead, and he was armed.

"Central," he called out to the air, feeling a surge of relief when he was answered by the immediate appearance of one of the orange-colored solid light projections that marked the computer's active presence. "Can you locate Gret? Is she still alive and in the building?"

"Just follow my screen, Trinidad," City Central promptly replied in its pleasant female voice, using his first name, just like he preferred. "Chief Auditor Gret is still alive, though she is in peril: her interviewee, the man I have logged as Thomas Delmonte Cerveau, has a pistol of significant caliber pointed at the unarmored part of her head. I have not yet completed calculations on her chances of survival if he pulls the trigger. I apologize for my tardiness in this matter, but my sensors are not in full operation around Cerveau or his various employees: they are all carrying dampers, which are actively hindering me."

"Nobody's perfect," muttered Trinidad as he kept moving, never once staying still as he rushed down the stairs, sometimes even grabbing both rails to slide down just that much faster, keeping the orange rectangle always in view as he went. "Just him with Gret, or does he have any goons with him? And what about innocent bystanders?"

"Two by the elevator," the computer immediately reported. "Most of the normal employees were in the process of leaving when Cerveau and Gret entered her office for an interview, so as far as I am able to tell, all employees have either exited the building, or will be gone before you reach Gret's floor. Though my connections are being scrambled, keeping me from directly interacting with the elevator, I can sense its movements, and know that the rest of the armed assailants in this building are presently on their way toward the floor where Scintillant Camor's office is located. I strongly suspect that the head Minister is their intended goal, though I cannot say certainly what their intentions might be."

"Revolution, Central," explained Trinidad with a frustrated grunt, before he heaved himself over the side of the stairwell, dropping several flights before catching the rail and swinging back onto the steps and continuing his downward rush. "They embezzled Republic resources with the help of Peewee Montgomery so that they could buy black market weapons and equipment, even carve out a hidden base somewhere down under the City. Peewee slapped Cerveau's name all over the records as the mastermind behind the whole plot: he must've had a really guilty conscience. Too bad he didn't come clean, or we might've been able to stop this before it began."

"An old Earth adage involving ounces of prevention and pounds of cures comes to mind," Central quipped casually as Trinidad rounded the last flight, and went barreling toward the doors, bursting out into the floor...and right into the sights of two more of the black-suited goons.

CR-CRACK! CR-CRACK!

"I always forget how loud these things are," grunted Trinidad, shaking his head as he spared the two double-tapped corpses no further attention: he had a boss to save. Another few steps, another door shoved open, and he was tearing across the observation walkway above the maze of cubicles, Gret's office dead ahead. And through the glass that surrounded the interior...

"Oh no," Trinidad panted as he ran as fast as he could – too slow!

172

The looming figure of Thomas Delmonte Cerveau glared straight into the eyes of the little rill taste engineer and pulled the trigger of his very large pistol.

```
Location: Earth, Sunflower City, Central
Spire, Executive Offices
Perspective: Susan Six
```

Blocking bullets with a sword always looked cool. Susan Six supposed that was why she always took every opportunity to do it. Of course, it didn't hurt that the sword was neutron-enhanced, high gravity-forged steel, reinforced with a plasma-based forcefield, and sporting a sonic disruption function for when she wanted to saw through things, or amp things down to use the flat of the sword like a hand stunner. What also didn't hurt was the way her stat suit enhanced her already superhuman reflexes to the next level: both her fathers had heavily encouraged her to get all the best combat enhancements, and her father in the military had been more than happy to help her qualify for them, as well as her military-grade stat suit. Bright copper orange and gleaming metallic blue were *not* stealthy colors, of course – actually, they made her into a bullet magnet – but when she could parry a bullet more easily than an unenhanced person could swat a fly, that didn't really matter.

What mattered was that the moment Susan Six had stepped into the top office level, the entire floor had turned into a war zone! The first thing she'd done as soon as she walked out of the service stairs was snap up her carbine to mow down a pair of suited goons who'd spun, sporting automatic shotguns. This was why the carbine in her off hand was still steaming as it let off excess heat in preparation to continue firing, which was the main reason why Susan was parrying bullets instead of laying down more plasma fire. Cutting the weapon down to carbine size had required removing the main heat sinks and range extenders, but those hardly mattered in the close quarters where Susan Six made most of her living. Her weapons were well-chosen for her present opponents: about half of these black-suited thugs were equipped with spiders!

Not arachnids, of course: "spider" was the slang name for an especially gruesome neurological weapon, a fat central processing unit with five fingerlike projections. Pressed against the head of a carbon-based life form with a standard nervous system and the arms would wrap around the head before the whole contraption bored its way into the skull, leaving a telltale spiderlike mark on the face. This very permanent alteration to one's brain served as a quick, cheap, and highly illegal combat enhancement: it boosted your pain tolerance, which also had the useful side effects of allowing you to exert more strength and endurance, almost as though you were under the effects of a permanent adrenaline and endorphin high. Besides that, it also rendered you pretty close to invulnerable to psi influences: even an empath as powerful as Scintillant Camor wouldn't be able to do much to stop the goons from carrying out their orders; he'd have enough trouble just detecting them in the first place. The illegal part of a spider's effects were twofold, though: first, it made you really receptive to orders, especially from people you regarded as authority figures before the treatment; second, when you died, you'd get up again, and then keep on going as a shambling flesh puppet until somebody either heavily damaged your head or spine, or did some serious tissue damage to what remained of your person.

According to the smuggler's manifest that Dan had hacked away from Caddigan Carse, there were any number of crates filled with spiders already delivered to Earth. Not surprising, since Carse had been in the habit of using them to get dead slaves up and running again back when he'd been a colonial governor, filling the native population with superstitious dread. Which meant that this group of rebels were equipped with everything they needed to field an army of corpses.

Not that this mattered much to Susan Six: her blaster carbine was tied to a targeting reticule her suit projected onto her eyes, and that along with her superhuman hand-eye coordination was more than enough to ensure a perfect count of headshots. And when her gun was in its cooling phase, her sword was perfect for dealing out more than enough tissue damage to ensure these goons didn't get up after they went down the first time. For her, everything ahead of her was almost in slow motion, acts of clinical violence.

Detached as she'd been trained to be, she noted the placement and purposes of the enemies arrayed against her. The two by the stairs to the roof were a delaying action, intentional suicide troops to keep off any official response until they'd finished their dirty deeds, whatever those were. The three that met her in the vestibule leading to the main office of the executive suite opened fire the moment she stepped around a corner, but that's when her superhuman reflexes turned aside their bullets with a wide sweep of her blade, before she cut them down on the upstroke, sending their bodies sprawling.

Nobody in the main office, though. Just like that, Susan Six felt her suspicions confirmed. But why did they leave a rearguard at all? Unless they were searching for something...or someone.

Realizing there was something she was missing, Susan let Dan fill the heads-up display before her eyes with red outlines, the heat signatures of those goons still remaining on the floor. Sure enough, they were definitely looking for something. Smirking as she decided to interrupt their search, Susan Six tested a dividing wall, and soon found it far less than adequate to resisting the raw power she could bring to bear in her armor. With an explosion of old-fashioned Earth plaster and drywall, the shining warrior burst right into the middle of her foes, blade swinging in a blazing arc of electric fire.

A few minutes and many fatalities later, the upper floor was dead quiet, and the few minor scores the weapons of her foes had made to the plates of her orange-and-blue armor were already repairing themselves. The same could not be said for the various disassembled bodies on the floor.

"Dan?" Susan Six spoke to the air as she stalked the corridors of the executive suite, weapons still ready for immediate deployment as she nudged open door after door, slow and careful, letting her sensors do as much preliminary reading as possible. "Where's Scintillant Camor? He's not among the bodies, as far as I can tell, but..."

Movement! As Susan opened the door to a slightly dusty kitchen, her carbine immediately trained on the wide-open cabinet under the sink. Several other cabinets were also opened, the goons obviously having made a quick and dirty search of the room before her arrival. But she'd seen movement – she knew she had! – so where...?

Eyes lifting, Susan Six watched as one of the cheap ceiling tiles shifted, and then went tumbling to the floor of the kitchen. Above, she saw a wide-eyed, fuzzy face peering down at her, belonging to a being that looked like a cross between a brushtail possum and a wallaby, except three times as adorable.

"Are you the woman my daddy said would rescue me?" asked the little liptani girl peering from her hiding place in the ceiling: liptanis were natural born jumpers and climbers, agile as any Earth monkey.

"Yeah," Susan Six told the little girl, sheathing her weapons and raising her hands to let the soft-furred youngster climb down. "I guess I am."

Location: Earth, Sunflower City, Central
Spire, Gret's Office
Perspective: Thomas Delmonte Cerveau

Smoke was still filling the room while Gret stood there, calmly looking up at Mister Cerveau as though he hadn't just fired a bullet at her head. Said bullet was still visible as a flattened disk where it had smacked against her skull...and completely failed to penetrate.

"Dumb mistake," said Gret as she calmly reached up and broke Cerveau's wrist with a squeeze of her hand, the gun clattering to the floor. "You big beanpoles always assume I'm wearing all this gear because I need protection. Naw, it's the other way around: I'm wearing this dumb suit to protect *you* from *me*." She glanced over to the door as Trinidad Del Toro came bursting in and gave him a casual wave of her other claw. "Hey kid: glad you could make it."

Still in shock, Cerveau couldn't even try to resist as the little alien hopped down from her chair and whipped his legs with her tail, flipping him onto his back before she walked over to put an astonishingly heavy

177

foot on top of his chest. Just that pressure alone was more force, more sheer *weight* than he could ever hope to resist; she had him pinned!

"That's right, just relax and get comfy," growled the little alien. "And if you don't, I'll put my foot down. Considering where it's resting, I don't think you want that. We rill come from a high-gravity world, Mister Cerveau. What that means is, our bodies are *dense*. I've got all the mass of a critter half again your size, all packed down into a one-third package. And here you come into my office with that teeny, little popgun, assuming that anything less'n a man-portable mass driver is gonna pop a cap in my cartilaginous ass."

Casually, while Trinidad just gaped in utter shock that his boss was not only still alive, but even more ornery – and sassy! – than ever, she ground her foot from side to side, and Cerveau finally cried out, the pain of his shattered wrist mingling with the agony of the pressure right over his heart. When she relented, lifting her weight off him, instantly his whole body went limp, and he looked up at the ceiling before his face set in defiance.

"You...you won't win," he tried to sneer, though the effect fell somewhat flat. "We've already infiltrated the building, and there are those among us with weapons that could bring down the ceiling on top of you." A derisive curl of his lip soon turned to a grimace of agony, but the arrogance of his voice remained. "There's nobody left here who can stop us from taking our prize. And whoever has him controls the destiny of this planet."

"Sin," sighed Gret, shaking her head, giving Trinidad a look and a nod that sent him running to the elevators, even though she knew it was already well past too late. "Poor, dumb, idealistic sap. Shows what good intentions get you." Behind the cracked lenses of her gasmask, her eyes began to glisten with tears of frustration. "Maybe you've got a point: Scintillant Camor is kinda the only one who's got the vision to save your planet; nobody else in the Ministries wants to touch this world with a ten-digit pole. So yeah, destiny of the Earth and all that. But not to control it. Naw, you bastards have just blown this whole popsicle stand to Hell: once Sin's out of the picture, Earth's gonna be on its own, quarantined off from the rest of creation while you stew in your own filth for the next Standard century."

Taking her foot off the prone man, Gret lifted her mask to wipe away the tears streaming from her eyes. Strong she might be, tough she certainly was, but she was just one little rill, and her fastest speed, even in this low gravity, was about equal to a human's brisk walk: her legs just weren't made for anything faster! There was no way she could stop these idiots from taking Sin hostage...and if she couldn't do that, there was no way she could save the world from their attempt at planet-wide murder-suicide.

"You poor dumb bastards," she whispered hoarsely in her own buzzing language, without the benefit of her mask's translator. Cerveau understood, though, and felt a dark chill as the truth of her words sank home.

CHAPTER 11: THE MAN'S IN OUR PLANS

Location: Earth, Sunflower City, Central Spire, Outside
Perspective: Trinidad Del Toro

Looking up at the sky, Trinidad's expression was grim: it was a maelstrom up there, clouds churning in an ominous slow spiral, flashing with blue and purple and red electric flickers, the light sprinkle of rain supplemented with the occasional clatter of tiny shards of ice against the softly glowing clickways.

Seated nearby on the back bumper of one of Sunflower City's flying ambulances was Gret, her head quite bare save for a clear plastic breathing mask, occasionally growling unhappily at the vulture-headed doctor – a vlok by the name of Doctor Salvee, and present chief of Earth's medical services – who kept caressing the little rill's head with fingers that, to human sensibilities, looked freakishly oversized, with two too many joints. Apparently the vlok species had evolved as scavengers who'd quickly learned to work in close cooperation both with each other and with the major predators of their world. This gave them a keen life sense, so when a vlok was touching you, they were giving you a complete checkup. When the vlok in question was also a trained medical professional like Salvee, the information she could derive just from casual contact was astounding. As an example, she'd told Trinidad what he'd had for breakfast right after they shook hands on their first meeting.

That same sense of cooperation was also what made the vlok, well, endearing, Trinidad had to admit. The bruise-purple naked vulture-like head and fleshy beak were off-putting, as were the sharp eyes that seemed to be sizing you up for a menu. Doctor Salvee, though, was professional, polite, and seemed to genuinely care about the wellbeing of those around her. When she asked, "How are you feeling?" you got a sense that she really wanted to know...and not just because it was almost time for dinner.

"Lousy," of course was Gret's reply. "Don't need a quack to tell me I've got a concussion. And yes, you are so a quack, Salvee, even if you're descended from a different sort of bird!"

"I'm not actually an avian at all..." the doctor protested mildly, but Gret was already continuing her mid-level tirade, and Trinidad was unable to stop grinning down at her, finding her even more adorable now that he could see her small, spiny-plated body clearly, including her small button-black eyes in a pinkish-tan face with a long, narrow muzzle.

"Glad the spotbots dragged off that jerk in the black Mariah," she explained, fixing Trinidad with her slightly out-of-focus eyes. "Couldn't bear to admit around him that I talk a good game, but that bullet really rang my bell. Lucky for me he was using hollow points instead of depleted uranium, or we might not be having this conversation. I'd still be alive, sure, and I know I'd have still kicked his keister, but…yeah, there'd be a lot more mess to clean up. As it is, I'm not gonna be going anywhere with you and the two super-chicks."

She motioned with a heavy claw toward where the human bounty hunter Susan Six and the darishi peacekeeper Sergeant Benjuro Clee were standing, chatting amiably as they reviewed the footage City Central had acquired from the office building towering over them. Trinidad hadn't really paid much attention to the pair in all the excitement before then, the gray of the gathering storm dulling his senses almost as much as his concern for his boss. He did notice, however, that the dragon-lady was the one holding the hard light screens: Susan Six had Scintillant Camor's daughter perched on one broad, armored shoulder, while she shared a brightly colored drink she'd acquired somewhere with her little passenger.

"Hey!" Gret hollered over. "You two get your fannies over here! And the fuzzball, too, I guess. My guy Trinidad here's gonna go with you on whatever hunting expedition you're planning, and he's gonna need a briefing!" Then she blinked, glancing at the broad-shouldered man with a slightly quizzical expression.

"Yes, I'm going," he affirmed to the unasked question. "I've got to do whatever I can to save Mister Camor: he brought me out of a very dark place."

"He does that for everybody," Gret huffed back, but Trinidad could see the momentary softening of her expression underneath the clear plastic breathing mask when she said it: for such an inhuman – and surly – creature, she was remarkably easy to read. Then she reached down into one of her many deep pockets and dragged out a smooth metal cylinder with a plunger on one end, one of the injection ampoules used by the Republic for its various drugs. "Here, I was planning on giving you this for your birthday, but now's as good a time as any. Stuff's called mite, and if you're gonna go after Sin, you're gonna need it: just jam it into whatever body part's most handy. It's not really legal on this planet, per se, at least until Earth's off the probation list, but ya know: needs must. That, and the quacksalver here owes me some favors."

Taking the silver-colored tube, Trinidad looked it over for a moment, then at Gret...and then at Doctor Salvee, the weak link in this information chain.

"It's a mitochondrial enhancement boost," the doctor promptly explained. "Tailored for humans, of course, as shown on the identification symbols," she added, pointing at the many little runes stamped onto its surface. "The mitochondria are the primary aerobic energy generators for many carbon-based, eukaryote-celled species, a group that includes everyone here. A single shot of 'mite,' as it's frequently called, vastly improves the efficiency of the body's mitochondria. This has the practical effects of reducing fatigue, increasing rates of healing, increasing reflexes, and generally boosting all the body's systems, making tissues tougher and more resilient. It's also the first essential enhancement necessary to allow other genetic and implanted enhancements without endangering the recipient."

"Which is another way of saying it's the only sort of body boost you can safely get in the Republic that doesn't require either powered armor, a hospital, a lab, or a machine shop," added Gret. "I'm pretty sure it's not against your religion, though if you're really worried about it, I'll let you give the most available clergy a buzz through City Central before you go shooting up. Still, you're not going anywhere without it, 'cause that place means death for anybody that isn't a superpower like Susan Six or the big draggy...or me on my good days."

"Which is not today," declared the vulture-faced doctor, watching with keen eyes as Trinidad held the ampoule in his hand, hefting it, letting his eyes shift between the tube, Gret, and Salvee. Then, giving a short exhalation and a nod, he jabbed it against the big muscle of his thigh and depressed the plunger. There was a soft hiss, and that was that: Republic docs had long ago figured out how to make shots painless.

Their *effects* could be another matter entirely, of course...but at least for right now, Trinidad didn't feel anything different, which must have showed in his expression.

"I dunno about you," said Gret, "But *I* feel a whole lot better. Now what's up? Lemme see those screens."

This last was said just as the two women stepped into grabbing range, whereupon Gret did indeed snatch the nearest hard light construct out of the air. While she was fiddling with the screen, Trinidad finally took the time to get his first good look, up close and personal, of Susan Six and Sergeant Benjuro Clee.

If it wasn't for Gret, Trinidad wouldn't have known much about either of the two women. The little rill, disregarding her injuries while they'd waited for the arrival of the peacekeepers and the doc-wagon, had shoved a screen into his hand, and so he'd been forced to speed read his way through lives of heroic service that read like a series by Jack Kirby and Stan Lee. In the flesh, though, well, they both *looked* like super-heroes from the comics he'd loved so much as a kid, and Trinidad suddenly found himself believing every word he'd read.

Susan Six was tall, blonde, and her muscled physique was obvious even under her bright blue-and-copper stat suit. She was almost as tall as Trinidad, and her shoulders were pretty close to as broad, but all the same she was obviously every inch a woman, her physicality just enhancing her appearance. The transparent forcefield of her stat suit served in place of a helmet, as was quite common for anyone in a profession where they might have to both face combat and social situations, letting her head and especially her almost embarrassingly elfin and lightly freckled face remain bare, though she kept her sun-lightened tresses tied in a casual ponytail, done back with a scrap of blue ribbon that matched the color of her eyes.

Standing next to the bounty hunter, Trinidad finally fully realized that Sergeant Benjuro Clee was *tall*, which put her shoulders about even with the top of his head. Her height looked *right* on her, though, natural, and enticingly sinuous. The effect was enhanced by her long, muscular, and highly flexible tail, and her almost equally long and flexible neck, taken altogether making her obviously and inherently feminine in all the best ways, even with her stat suit presently in rigid mode, turning it into a suit of bright blue-and-yellow armor plates. The underside of that neck was a brilliant metallic gold, as were the long-spiraled horns that swept backward from just above her equally golden eyes, while the back of her head and neck were a scintillating metallic forest green. Nine feet tall, and every inch of her a stunning specimen of womanhood, species differences irrespective.

As he sized up the women, Trinidad knew they were doing the same to him, but this didn't bother him: it was only fair, after all. His body was tall, solid, heavily muscled from years of hard work in the gym and in the field, his ink-dark hair shaved down to a scanty stubble well-suited to combat situations. The one point of discomfort Trinidad felt was that he was wearing a buttoned-up white shirt and slacks rather than the military uniforms to which he'd grown so accustomed in times past. At least Gret hadn't insisted that he wear a tie to work.

"They go all the way down, by the way," the green-and-gold dragon-lady said with a teasing quirk to her mouth, which made her cheeks dimple adorably.

"What?" asked Trinidad, breaking quite abruptly out of his inner thoughts.

"My scale colors," explained Sergeant Benjuro. "I'm green all the way down the back, and golden all the way down the front, at least until," she stroked her long-fingered, obsidian-tipped hands across her inner thighs, "right about here, where the gold shades into green on the inside parts of my legs. I just guessed that you were curious, based on the way you were looking me over, Mister Trinidad Del Toro."

"I'm terribly sorry," Trinidad gasped out, taken aback: had it really been that long since he'd had a significant other – or any dating experiences, for that matter! – that he was so painfully obvious about his interest? "I certainly didn't mean..."

While Susan Six laughed, her face beautiful in the joy of the moment, the darishi lifted a finger to Trinidad's lips, silencing him quite effectively as she bent her supple neck low, putting her long, elegant muzzle right next to his ear.

"Actually, I rather hoped you did, Mister Del Toro," she stage-whispered, before flicking her ribbonlike tongue around the lobe of his ear in a teasing little lick. "You're not bad looking yourself, and your service record is...*impressive*. After we get to know each other a little bit better – and I expect we will, since I'm likely to be here on Earth for quite a long time – I was even thinking about asking if you'd like to get married."

Normally confident, competent, and calm in the face of enemy action, Trinidad's brain promptly shut down.

"Buh?" was about all he could manage as the brightly smiling dragon-woman straightened, then turned so as to include him in the little four-person huddle that had formed around the hover-ambulance and pulled another hard light construct out of the air, courtesy of City Central.

"Slutty space dragons," grumbled Gret.

"I've never slept with anyone to whom I wasn't married," Sergeant Benjuro mock-huffed at the little rill as she passed out screens to everyone, except Gret of course, her grin widening a little more.

"Yeah, and how many people *have* you married, anyway?" Gret shot back. "Everybody knows you darishi are polyamorous. I mean, how's adultery even possible when you just keep getting married to more and more people?"

"As easily as with any other species, I'm afraid," the dragon-woman replied with a light shrug, an expression of regret on her face. "A sad reality of our licentious modern life, I suppose. We darishi are nomadic by nature," she explained, turning an eye toward Trinidad. "And always have been. I think our wanderlust was why we were the first species recorded as having made it into space. But the long distances of our relationships made things complicated until some genius realized: why not just have people marry into clans, rather than to individuals? We've also always been, well, a bit xenophilic..."

"Understatement, much?" snorted Gret.

"...so, when we met other sapient species, it was hardly a great leap to just include them in our ever-expanding family units. You would be simply *amazed* at the wonders it's done for diplomacy within the Republic: most persons of importance are related somewhere along the line by marriage into a darishi clan, which always makes for a very pleasant starting point for any decent relationship, let me tell you. Why, even our dear Gret here is married into my clan. A little bit distantly, but it's still a direct line."

"Wait," said Gret, blinking. "Wait. Are you saying Deeray's related to you Benjuros?"

"His Majesty, King Karkrimmon Deeray, is related by blood or marriage to *all* the darishi clans," laughed the dragon-woman. "That's why he's the king!"

"I'll murder the bum!" snarled Gret, only for Doctor Salvee to rest her oversized hands on the little rill's shoulders, gently but very firmly holding her in a seated position. "I'll wring that fork-tongued philandering son-of-a-snake's...!"

"Please, Gret," pleaded the doctor, and Trinidad could have sworn that the tips of her fingers glowed softly where they touched Gret's shoulders. "I've turned off your pain receptors for now, but you're in no condition to get worked up. If you insist on antics like this, I'll turn them back on."

"Yeah, all right," grunted the little rill, her shoulders slumping. "Fine. We've got more important things than regicide to do right now, anyway. Kinda the opposite, actually: we've gotta go save Sin before those bastards kill him." Then her face turned down, and her slim mouth tightened even further in obvious annoyance. "By which I mean *you three*

189

gotta go save him: much as I wanna, with my head like this, I'm a liability in a fight. The quack here tells me I might have an aneurism or something if I got hit again, and I can't have you three distracted while you're down in those tunnels."

"Just two, I'm afraid," the dragon-woman corrected with an apologetic expression. "The weather should make the reason pretty obvious: people are getting steadily more worked up all over the city now, and we peacekeepers are already woefully understaffed. It's the simoniacs, whipped into a frenzy at the Republic's ban on paid clergy. I'm going to have to work a triple shift just to keep the next three riots in the works from taking place." She shook her head ruefully. "It's a good thing we darishi don't need much sleep."

"Tunnels?" asked Trinidad, his brain finally kicking back into gear.

Sergeant Benjuro held out one of the hard light constructs that were her ever-present companions, showing a wire model cutaway of the building towering above them. She tapped the upper floor, where Scintillant Camor's office had been located, and Trinidad and Susan Six leaned in close as a recording of past events began to play.

"Daddy," whispered Birdcry.

Stepping out of the executive break room, the purple-furred I'dray looked around, while the sounds of shouting and heavy running footsteps could be heard coming rapidly closer. Visibly steeling himself, Scintillant pulled something out of an inner pocket of his coat, a small metal cylinder, and then brought it up to his eye. His muzzle curled back in a sharp-toothed wince, and his grunt of pain was clearly audible even as the angry voices came closer. Tossing the little cylinder into a nearby wastebasket, the slender foxlike man brushed down the front of his suit, then stood calmly as the many tall, dark-suited men came barging into the corridor.

"What did my daddy do to himself?" asked the fuzzy little girl.

"We'll tell you soon, sweetie," Susan Six whispered, glancing at Clee, who nodded affirmation to the promise.

While most of the men spread out around the floor, two going into the break room, the camera followed the knot that stayed around Scintillant, two of them holding tight to his arms, one of them roughly jabbing him in the back while leaning in close, barking short, sharp commands. The l'dray didn't resist, but simply let the large, muscular men force him to the elevator.

Mere minutes later, as the men were starting to organize themselves for what was now obviously the search for Scintillant Camor's daughter, as well as to run a delaying action against any official response, a flash of light and sound tore through the corridor, followed by the living hurricane that was Susan Six, sword plunging straight for the chest of the nearest of the dark-suited goons.

That, naturally, was the moment when the darishi tapped the screen with a sheepish wince at Birdcry, cutting off the feed. She needn't have bothered, though: at the first sign of violence, Susan Six had promptly covered the little girl's eyes with one hand.

As the clip ended and the wire model of the building popped up once more, Sergeant Benjuro's claw traced one of the elevator shafts that ran down the middle.

"I had the staff back at the station run a check with the financial data you deciphered for cross-referencing," she explained with a nod at Trinidad, giving the shaft a light tap with a claw tip, which started a little glowing elevator model running from the top all the way down the shaft...before it just kept on going, vanishing from sight. "Turns out, when our conspirators were stealing funds by using substandard construction materials, they also arranged for hidden bolt holes in many major buildings. The elevators in those buildings drop down into the system of pipes and tunnels that runs underneath the city, beyond where Central can reach. As far as we can tell, that's where they've got their home base, because there's nowhere else that we couldn't have already found by now. Worse, they've blown the nearest of those elevators, so you're stuck going in the hard way: through the tunnels around Rock Bottom."

"There's a big blank zone down there," growled Gret. "Sort of like how you can't see your own guts, that's why Central can't see into it so well. It's a nasty place, nothing like a proper underground should be. Just mashed together from all the bits and pieces of a thousand of your Earth cities. Crammed with all the monsters from those cities, too, since the builder robots were programmed to take pains not to hurt anything living while they were doing their jobs. All the stuff you humans made to kill each other during that nasty business you call the End: it's bred and thrived down there in the dark. Miss Six here also tells me these jerk-wad idiots are using spiders, like those ones you saw on the feed, so that means you're going right into the middle of a combat zone filled with monsters, enemy troops, and frickin' zombies! So, you're gonna need some expert help at the whole monster-slaying gig, besides somebody reliable to bring your two back up to three."

Reaching out while Clee held the hard light screen for her, Gret pulled up a personnel file.

"Meet the Man from Rock Bottom," she announced.

Trinidad and Susan Six stared, blinking in gape-mouthed astonishment. Clee's face wasn't nearly so surprised-looking — she obviously knew the person — but it was also obvious she had some doubts of her own.

"*This* is Sunflower City's monster hunting expert?" Susan Six was the first to exclaim, voicing the disbelief of her two companions.

On the screen was a slightly plump-looking, balding little man dressed in a camelhair sport coat, tan slacks, and very thick-looking glasses. He was standing next to several other instructors, which made his lack of height all the more apparent. In the background were several buildings at a college campus, probably somewhere the exact opposite of prestigious from the look of it. A note on the side of the image set its date as four years before the End. He wasn't ugly or even unpleasant in appearance. Something about the way he carried himself, about his expression, his manner, made Trinidad think of a pet rabbit he'd had as a child. But whatever else might be said about this man, he was memorable. At least, Trinidad *thought* he was memorable...right up until he tried to read the man's name.

"Yeah," Gret grunted, wincing as Salvee continued to work her glowing hands against the back of her head and neck. "I didn't believe it, either, when I first met him. I understand he got a vision enhancement on the sly, one of Sin's little gifts along with the sparse Republic tech he's got for his personal use, so no glasses anymore, but the rest of him looks about the same. Just flip over to his records, though, on the next page, and don't look at his picture while you read 'em. Sergeant, you know the guy best, since he works with the peacekeepers a lot from what I understand. Fill these two in on the Man."

"He's got a pretty sad story," the darishi stated, giving a slight shrug, her expression wistful. "But you can read that later. What you should know about him is that he's friendly, soft-hearted, slightly autistic, almost crippled by social anxieties, and has terminally low self-esteem. Before the End he was just a minor academic with a doctorate in something I don't understand at all, another degree in education, and still another in animal science, though he seems to have gotten that one mostly for fun on the side. The education degree is how he got his job as a teacher at a community college, which is what he was doing when the End hit. He did a lot of work with various animal conservation groups, too, volunteering his time and resources quite freely. That work was enough for him to show up on the Ministry of Life's radar, as one of the advocates for letting the Republic relocate Earth animals in danger of extinction to locales far away from humans, which is how we got that old picture. It's also how he first met several Ministry of Life personnel, including Scintillant Camor during a diplomatic visit before the war between the Republic and the Empire broke out; there's some speculation that that's when he first started to manifest active psi. Then the End happened, and he vanished for a while from all available records.

"Three years after the End started, he suddenly reappeared on the radar by contacting members of the Ministry of Life that he'd met personally. Somehow in all that mess he'd gotten access to a military-grade communications device and used it to reach out with an offer: he wanted to help the Republic save the various life forms of Earth. We have no idea what sort of things he'd done to survive to that point, but before too long he was globetrotting, working as a gene pirate...or maybe a 'gene privateer,' since he was working exclusively for the Republic, and doing it because he felt it was right, rather than for pay. He was fantastically successful in this role and while, again, he has neglected to share details, considering what life was like on Earth at that time, he must have survived a situation akin to the most brutal of war zones...for *years*.

"After the Republic took charge of Earth, our Man met with Scintillant Camor and was officially recruited as Earth's Chief Zoological Management Officer. Mister Camor, one of the most skilled and powerful empaths in the Republic, was only able to treat his various emotional disturbances to a certain degree, which I'm sure Mister Del Toro here, as a recipient of Mister Camor's attentions, will agree is quite surprising. This was because, during the interview, apparently Mister Camor dug a little too deeply with his power, and accidentally fully awakened our Man's previously only half-realized psionic potential.

"He almost always has consciousness recordings running, something he decided to do as a way to ensure his ethical behavior as well as to fully document his activities, so we have a very nearly complete history of his activities from the moment he first got a Link connection. That's a summary of his career's highlights right there," she added, pointing at the screen floating in front of the two humans. "As you can see, it's...well...it's rather surprising, really."

There was a pause as the two humans scrolled slowly down the screen.

"Huh," said Susan Six, blinking.

"Wow," said Trinidad. "Who *is* this guy?"

"More importantly, how is he even still alive?" chimed in Susan Six, shaking her head. "After *this*!"

"I have absolutely no idea," Clee admitted with a shrug, before she sighed. "And knowing who he is is...well, that's an ongoing problem. According to Scintillant Camor's report on the Man, part of his talent is that, unless you're right there talking to him, or have some other good reason to keep him in your mind, everybody tends to forget all about him. He's made a game of it: since nobody remembers his real name, he just makes one up when he's introducing himself. Funny thing is, people tend to remember the fake names better than his real one, and once he's shared one with you, then as long as that's your focus, you won't forget him. And before you ask, no, I can't remember his real name either. But, um," her golden cheeks darkened to the verdigris of corroded copper, "I do remember that he told me I could call him Al. But only if he could call me Betty." She shook her head. "Some human popular cultural reference: I really didn't understand it."

"It's from a song by an old-Earth musician named Paul Simon," Susan Six said with a laugh. "'You Can Call Me Al.' My dads discovered his stuff while they were trying to figure out how to raise a human girl and loved it. Of course, my military dad never admitted it, but I caught him singing along a few times, when he was sure nobody would notice."

"I'll have to look it up," said Clee, smiling brightly. "It sounds like it might be fun. But back to our subject, our Man's talent also enhances peoples' reactions to him, so you should be aware of that, since it's almost certain to color your behavior around him. If you're a nice person, you're going to get along with him fantastically well. You'll probably also feel protective toward him, like you would toward...well, Miss Birdcry here," she chuckled with a smile, reaching out to very gently beep the liptani girl's nose, making her blink her large, expressive eyes. "On the other hand, people with a lot of aggression and other nasty emotions tend to see him as an easy target, the perfect victim, somebody they can bully or even kill without fear of repercussions."

"Which would explain some of these incidents," said Trinidad, still scrolling through the summary report. "He attracts monsters."

"But still not how he made it through them," added Susan Six. "Is there anything else we ought to know before we go and recruit him?"

"Hmm," mused the darishi, rubbing her delicately pointed chin with one hand, the other scrolling down yet another of the many hard light constructs that were a ubiquitous part of her presence. "Well, two things about him, I suppose, and then that one thing about Scintillant Camor that we promised Miss Birdcry," she added with a gentle smile at the indicated party, "who has been so very patient with us. The first, he's got a smattering of assorted psi talents: a sliver of telepathy; enough psycho-metabolism to help him heal faster and act as a surprise boost to his physical abilities; a little precognition to warn him of some dangers before they arrive, sometimes. Besides his main talent of being forgettable, he's at least equivalent to a free-level empath, which rises to near-expert level when he's dealing with most animals. He hasn't had the formal training or accreditation to be a true expert yet, and he often makes mistakes, especially when he's dealing with sapients, but Mister Camor's notes here indicate that he's got quite a bit of potential for growth, if he can just get past his fear of people.

"The second thing is, um," she blinked. "It appears he's already wandering around in the undercity. He's got a Link connection active, so I'll give you the signal frequency; just follow that, and you should eventually make your way to him…eventually. Admittedly, it's still a crazy quilt maze down there, considering how quickly this city was thrown together to save humanity from the wasted lands of Earth, but you're both a lot better trained than our Man, and you'll both be better armed and armored than him once I let Mister Del Toro raid the peacekeeper wagon's locker – as a loan to an emergency deputy, of course – so I expect you'll be able to handle most threats you might encounter.

"Finally," and now Clee's expression turned deadly serious as she looked at Gret, "I think Gret is most qualified to explain what it was that Mister Camor injected into his eye in that video, since she's the one most currently briefed on its use."

"Cryogenic gel," Gret said with a slight sigh. "It's the stuff they stick into you right before they put you under for a cold sleep. You know, for when they need to put you on ice until a doctor can arrive, or when you're stuck in an emergency life pod, and don't know how long you'll be there. Situations like that. Normally you feed the stuff in through a vein, nice 'n slow, but for a fast jolt to your system, when you're in a pinch, you can inject it straight into the eye. Hurts like Hell, though. Lots of important people in the Republic carry the stuff around so they can shoot it up in case they're worried they might have somebody try to kill 'em. Great stuff. It gels up all your organs so they stay in one piece, even when you're being hit with something that would normally kill you. You'll still look dead, but it's a whole lot easier to resuscitate you afterward. Not a guarantee, of course, but it gives your odds a massive boost." She glanced over her shoulder at Salvee, before wincing at the too-sudden movement and slowly returned to facing forward. "That about right, doc?"

"A good summary," agreed Doctor Salvee. "Of course, there's a serious disadvantage to using cryo-gel without a sleep capsule: without the mitigating environment of a capsule, you..." She paused, looking up at Birdcry, who looked down trustingly from her perch on Susan Six's shoulder. "Um...well," she cleared her throat, making her head bob in a way that was so very birdlike, "you have to receive treatment within a rather narrow range of time, or there could be serious consequences."

From the way the doctor said, "serious consequences," Trinidad and Susan Six shared a quick glance, and silently they both realized just how bad that euphemism meant things were going to become.

"How long do we have?" asked Susan Six.

"Twelve Earth hours," the vulture-headed doctor responded promptly. "Counting from now, that is. However, based on what I saw of the ones who took Scintillant captive, I don't think the cryo-gel's effects will be the limiting factor here: their patience will be much more easily strained. As Gret pointed out, the gel only *improves* the recipient's chances of survival through otherwise fatal events; it's not a guarantee."

"Then we'd better get moving," Susan Six declared, bending down to let Birdcry climb next to Doctor Salvee, her long, prehensile tail wrapping around the vlok's skinny forearm. At the contact, the doctor looked down, blinking several times in surprise. Most people tended to be wary of vlok, at least until they got to know them personally; it was just a result of their "scavenger's vibe." The liptani, though, had immediately decided to trust Doctor Salvee, and soon climbed up her arm to perch on her narrow shoulder, where she could better observe what Doctor Salvee was doing to Gret with wide-eyed interest.

"I'll be back soon, okay hon?" said Susan Six, bending close to Birdcry, touching her face. "We'll save your daddy, I promise."

"I know, Miss Six," said the girl. "Daddy said that if anyone could, you would. Twice."

Susan Six grinned.

"Kid," she said, "you just made my day."

THE PROFESSOR'S INTERLUDE: QUANTUM LESSONS

Location: Interplanetary Link, The Professor's Classroom
Perspective: The Man

Perhaps many of you have been wondering how you could possibly have a class in real time, with real students and a real teacher, when there are so many practical limits on how fast communications technology can deliver a signal along the satellite network that connects our entire culture across such impossibly vast distances. While faster-than-light travel isn't terribly difficult in our present age, the same cannot be said of data transmissions. If you have not been wondering about our apparent real-time classes, or why you have had flashes of these lessons as you have been going about your daily routines, or perhaps why you found yourself talking about parts of lessons in idle conversations, I want to bring these matters to your attention now.

The answer is twofold. First, you received the entirety of the content of the lectures in this class in a single massive burst of data beamed

201

directly to the subliminal parts of your brain the first time you logged into our virtual classroom. As time has gone on, your conscious mind has gradually been reconstructing those lectures, working them into your permanent memory. This is also why your memories of these lectures might occasionally be out of order: that's just how your brain works. For simple memorization, such as for the vocabulary of various languages, or the principles of mathematics, or medical anatomy, this would probably be enough, and combined with some practical lessons and lab work would make you proficient in the subject in question in a fraction of the time required for normal studies, and with a vastly greater store of information recorded in your permanent memory than students of prior eras would ever have experienced. This ease of memorization via subliminal burst technology is the reason why the Republic has enough doctors, engineers, lawyers, linguists, and similarly skilled professionals of the highest quality to meet its needs, when such training was long and laborious and highly uncertain before the advent of the technology.

Besides the subliminal burst, however, the Link connection to this virtual classroom also employs temporal programming technology, which incidentally is what has made the original purpose of the Interstellar Courier Service slightly less relevant today than in prior times. In reality, you all log into this classroom on your own schedules, based on your local planetary times. Almost none of you are actually here at the identical time as your classmates, or your instructor for that matter. Instead, the virtual classroom is hooked up to a system of programs so complex, no single person of my acquaintance is able to completely understand how they work. These programs work together with a series of quantum engines integrated into a vast communications satellite network that spans whole galaxies. These engines are based on those used by the fastest starships presently produced, and when networked together, they are used to recreate the classroom environment in real-time. Your actions and interactions, your questions, your comments, and your class- and lab work are all compiled and integrated into your overall experience of the classroom construct as though you were actually there with everyone else taking the class.

In other words, for all practical purposes, even though many of you are separated by the infinite and infinitely expanding void of space, while you are in this classroom, you are together. Here. Now. Your classmates are as real as you are, and your interactions are just as real. Please treat each other with appropriate respect and, most especially, kindness. After all, we all have our individual trials and difficulties. Because of the miracles of technology, however, if you help someone here, even if it's only to provide them with an appendage for easing weariness and a kerchief to soak up their sorrow excretions, you really are helping them.

Whenever, wherever you touch the lives of others for good, you have changed reality for the better.

CHAPTER 12: A LITTLE HELP FROM MY FRIENDS

Location: Interstellar Link, The Professor's
Classroom, post-class
Perspective: The Man

The lectures were fascinating, and they absorbed my entire attention. When you're on the boundary between life and death, your mind does odd things. Sometimes you see visions of the afterlife. Me, I seem to have been kicked into the virtual lecture hall where I'd started the day, right on the tail end of another lesson. Probably a weird side effect of my psi-stylus' remote connection to the Link system. Being the academic that I am by initial training, I suppose this isn't the worst way to go out of this life.

Reviewing myself, feeling out my body as gently as I can, careful not to disrupt the dream-state in which I'd found myself, which might have kicked me from my remote Link and tossed me unceremoniously back into the real world, just a cursory self-examination made my present state obvious: I was screwed.

Cracked and-or broken ribs, one of which was digging into my lung. Assorted contusions and hematoma. Internal bleeding...yes, but I'm not sure how bad it is just yet. Still being alive is a good sign, but unless I get a proper diagnosis, rather than just relying on my personal experiences with the many ways my body can be dis-integrated, there's no telling how long I'll stay in this state.

Yeah, not happy right now. Not happy at all. And the lecture was done, too, so I didn't even have that to distract me anymore. Right now, the only thing I had left to do to keep my mind off my troubles was look around at the rest of the class as its various attendees made their way out of the virtual doors and vanished from sight, one by one. While I'm not the kind to just resign myself to death, right then it looked as though I might just be stuck in this half-dreaming state until I sank too low for even that, and everything just...floated away. For good this time.

"Human! Human Joe!"

Nuts. I didn't die fast enough.

"It's good to see you, Human Joe!" exclaimed Pinkflower, looking down at me from an upside-down angle as she hovered over where I was seated in the virtual auditorium, the rest of the place pretty much empty except for her and Bright Spots. Then she paused, her antennae and those big grabby forelimbs of hers visibly wilting as she saw my present state and realized that I was not all right at all.

"Oh, Joe," she said, her many smaller handlike appendages poking and prodding me with a degree of skill and gentleness that I wouldn't have expected from a giant alien praying mantis, her little girl's voice carrying a note of genuine anguish. "You're hurt really bad."

"Occupational hazard," I explained, trying to smile, though I'm pretty sure it ended up being more of a grimace. "Don't worry about me: I've been through worse."

This was true, strictly speaking. What I didn't mention was that the few times I've been in a state like this, right on the edge of being dead, I'd had somebody, usually City Central, within crawling distance who could get me some immediate triage followed by emergency medical services. Right now, not so much: I was all alone down in that dark hole, and though I'd somehow managed to connect to my home's remote Link, I didn't think it would be a strong enough signal to reach the City's emergency services, since that was on a separate channel. Well, not in time, anyway, not as deep as I was right then. At least City Central would know where I was, and eventually somebody would come to see where I'd gone. I'd hate to leave one of those gaps in the records of Sunflower City. Missing person cases are the pits. The stasis pod on my back should still be working, too: no wasted life.

"This is no time to be a hero, Joe," Pinkflower chided me, her many hands trying to reach inside of me in a way that I found rather disconcerting, especially since they completely failed to make any sort of contact. "You need help right now, and... can you let me into your Link connection? I think I can access whatever you're wearing remotely and maybe make some emergency fixes."

"This one explains, Pinkflower is training to be a physician," Bright Spots told me as she gently floated down onto the chair beside me, fixing me with a gaze that I knew involved a lot more than just mere observation. I could feel her own Link trying to access mine, with or without my permission. "This one also opines, she's quite good, actually. Her teachers all say she has a knack for it."

"My species doesn't consider the practice of medicine sufficiently feminine," admitted Pinkflower with...was she blushing? "We're supposed to be warriors, after all. But it just seemed so *right*, I had to answer my calling."

"This one questions, what sort of outfit are you wearing, Joe?" asked Bright Spots, the confusion and annoyance in her voice both obvious as I felt her penetrate my clownsuit's defenses; which shouldn't have been possible, but now I knew who the hacker was of these two. "This one opines: this is...strange. It's not strict Republic technology. Some sort of hybrid system?" She blinked at me, and I could sense the incredulity in her alien features. "This one questions aghast, did you stitch plates of Republic armor onto some sort of alien meshwork?"

"My clownsuit," I affirm, nodding before I remembered how much it would hurt when I did that, realizing at that moment how she'd gotten past my Link's security: she'd accessed the emergency services function, and since my suit's Republic parts could sense that I was indeed in a state of emergency, and she was indeed trying to help, it had let her slip inside. "A human-made suit of reactive fibers. The best stuff the military of Earth had for making hazmat suits...I mean, suits made for dealing with hazardous environments and materials in a combat zone. It's air-conditioned and everything. I kinda had to bolt on the plates myself, though," I admitted sheepishly. "Scrap parts I salvaged. That's why they're not perfect protection, keep shifting around at the worst times. I'm from Earth, and that's still on probationary status in the Republic, so they couldn't spare a complete stat suit. Not that I blame 'em, I mean, can you imagine what might happen if some dirty rotten so-and-so managed to kill me and swipe a military grade stat suit? They say they're made for just one person, but I'm sure somebody would figure out some way to rack up a body count with it, or at least its weapon systems."

"Such an uncivilized-sounding world, your Earth," Pinkflower said, marveling, even as I could feel her hands starting to touch my flesh in the real world while Bright Spots got to work hacking into the Republic side of my tech, allowing the physician-in-training access to my real body through the virtual bits of the suit, all her actions being mimicked by the reactive technology in the armor plates until, even with the time and space separating us, she might as well have been right there, performing surgery on my real-world body. "Is it really that dangerous?"

"Exhibit A," I growl through gritted teeth, mostly because it was the best way to keep from whimpering at the pain of what she was causing: she was good, that much I could tell immediately, but good or not, there was no anesthetic. Getting the equivalent of surgery done by hand, since some of her fingers had tiny edges to them that worked serviceably as scalpels or sewing needles, was, shall we say, *uncomfortable*.

"This one exclaims, I've hacked your Republic parts!" Bright Spots did indeed exclaim, sounding rather excited, even hopeful, as she finished her part of the work she'd been doing in tandem with Pinkflower, the hacking complete, letting Pinkflower work without distraction. "This one hastens to add, it's not a perfect connection; I had to do my best with what I had available. This one assures, however, it should start to interface more directly with your body, now, almost like a proper stat suit."

"Is it enough?" I asked Pinkflower, since she was the medical expert here. "I mean, how much of me can you get back together?"

"I... I think it'll be enough," the big beautiful bug said pensively, her hands and those teeny little fingers of hers a blur. "I've gotten your ribs back into place, and Bright Spots has reinforced them with the biometric integrative circuits in the plates. Same with the internal injuries: I think I've gotten the hemorrhaging under control, so your body can start to heal instead of falling apart. As long as you're in the suit, it should hold you together all right. You shouldn't do any heavy lifting until you get to a real doctor, though," she warned. "You're in no shape to do...whatever it is that you do."

"Hunt monsters, mostly," I deadpanned, continuing to grit my teeth as I forced myself up to a proper sitting position in my chair as Pinkflower finished, her assorted appendages withdrawing. "Sometimes the sort that's also people." Then I stopped and looked at my two rescuers, my mouth open, my words sticking in my throat. What could I say? They just saved my life. They didn't have to do that, but they did anyway. "Thanks."

"No problem, Human Joe," Pinkflower said, her antennae wiggling happily, while Bright Spots' beaklike mouth spread into an obviously happy expression, even if it wasn't anything human. "Maybe we can get together sometime when you're not...you know?"

"Yeah," I agreed, chuckling. "I'd like that."

Surprisingly, I was telling the truth.

"Um," I hedged, rubbing the back of my head, which had stopped hurting, incidentally. "You should know, my name's not really Joe. I just...well...I throw out names whenever I meet new people, 'cause it's easier for me to keep my distance from 'em that way. I'm scared of people, and... well, I guess I'm scared of a lot of things."

"This one expresses incredulity," Bright Spots interrupted. "You hunt monsters. How can anything scare you?"

"Yeah, I know," I admit, clearing my throat. "It's just...social situations are scarier for me than stuff with claws and teeth, is all. I don't know why." Then I pause, frowning. "No, I do know why: it's because I'm afraid of being hurt, just like all the other times. Bad stuff happens whenever I get close to people. Or animals for that matter. Or anybody or anything." My eyes turned toward the floor. "Usually, they end up dying. Or trying to hurt me. Or worse."

"We won't die, Human Joe," Pinkflower told me gently, putting one of those big graspers of hers on my shoulder, her touch surprisingly soft, delicate. "And we won't try to hurt you. But if your name isn't Joe," she continued with dawning realization, "what shall we call you instead?"

"Joe's fine, I guess," I tell her with a smirk, meeting those big buggy eyes of hers. "But if you've just got to know, my real name is actually- "

Naturally, that's the moment when my systems come back online, and I wake up.

CHAPTER 13: THE ACCIDENTAL DEITY

Location: Earth, Sunflower City, Under-City
Perspective: The Man

Maybe it's just me. I mean, I've never heard of anybody else having problems like this coming out of a Link connection. Whenever I do it, though, it's just...sort of this full-body ick factor, like I'd just finished purging my whole inner cavity.

Probably because I basically died there, before my two new friends brought me back. Thank goodness the clownsuit has filters to catch all that stuff. Makes sense, though: I'm knitting my body back together, and a part of the healing process is expelling damaged material, especially when whatever damaged you has any number of contaminants. I don't even want to think about what diseases are on the tusks of a super-pig, considering what it roots around in...or *who*, as the case may be.

Before I open my eyes, I commence the standard full-body check. Long bones are still intact, which is a fantastic start: if they weren't up to specs, I'd be crawling my way out of here. Shifting my body around reveals that there's something still not perfect in my guts, but I don't think it's hemorrhaging anymore. I'd say that Pinkflower did a fantastic job with the tools she had available. Bright Spots and her saved my life: that gushing sensation has turned into the post-scab itch, when the body's putting itself back together rather than actively falling apart. I press on the abdominal plates of the clownsuit – gently – and can feel the bruising that will soon follow, but as I push myself up, nice and slow, I can tell that my body's enough together for me to keep on going. For a while longer, anyway. Hopefully long enough to get me out of here.

Before I get too optimistic, which might impact my survivability down here (a healthy Murphy-based attitude is a necessity for survival, in my experience), I open my eyes and look at my surroundings.

Looks like I've landed in the middle of a midden. The whole place around me is big piles of trash and...let's say *residue*. Fortunately for me, the reason that I don't have any broken bones (outside of the rib cracks that are still bothering me) is because I landed right in the middle of one of these piles. A glance around confirms that it's just old rags and bags, not...well, the other stuff making up some of these piles. I mean, it really shouldn't matter if you're being objective about it – a soft landing is a soft landing – but I'm not really all that good at being objective, and landing in a pile of pig poop is just gross. I deal with that quite enough when I clean out the pens to give the robots a break and get a healthy dose of reality in the form of smelly hard work.

As it is, I'm never going to get this suit clean again, ever.

Of course, there's a problem with my present location, because *of course* there is: it's on fire. Most of it seems to have been extinguished when I landed on it, so it must not have been blazing too brightly before, but all the same, there's fire all around me, and it's closing in again now that I've been holding still for a while. Actually, a lot of these trash piles are on fire, and as I get to my feet (oh *wow* but that hurts!) I can figure out why pretty quickly.

As I said before, morlocks don't like light. It doesn't incapacitate them, but they usually go out of their way to avoid it whenever possible. Same with foul smells, like burning trash, which messes with their other enhanced senses. In other words, I've landed right in the middle of another buffer zone between the two major factions down here: up top was the super-pig, and down here are the trash fires. Which means that there's super-rats around here somewhere. For all I know, they could be watching me right this instant. Whether I can see them or not, and I have no way to tell for how long.

Warm.

Huh?

Warm. Want warm.

That's not a voice, exactly. More like my brain putting together the meaning of a strong external emotional impression. Makes sense, as I think about it: the stonework around here is cold, and I imagine most of the tunnels are clammy. So, if there's an animal around here that likes warmth, and doesn't like cold, then of course it would be attracted to the trash fires. And once it got in range of my empathy...

Looking around, I see the culprit: it's a snake. Big one, too. I can't really make out a lot of details right off, not in this light – the fire is making my buckethead's visual sensors flicker in and out in annoying ways while they recalibrate after the beating they took – but I can see right away that the big fellah is about to make an awful mistake: he's heading right toward the rekindling blaze that I just vacated.

No, I send to the big fellah. *Fire bad. Ouch!*

I poke around inside my memories, and once I've found something appropriate, I send the snake the emotional response I had as a kid watching the Christopher Reeve classic, "Superman 2," where a snake got burned by some villain's heat vision: fun movie, but that scene really upset me! Again, it's not words, just emotional impressions, but it gets the message across. Right away the snake stops moving, then turns its head toward me, forked tongue flicking out.

Smiling inside my helmet, I hold out my hand, offering my own warmth as an alternative. There are people who don't like snakes, but I think they're adorable in their own way. Like any animal, you just have to accept it for what it is, and then look for the right way to love it. Reaching inside, I find my joy at being in the big fellah's presence, my excitement, my depth of emotion and sensation, and I share it all. It's an invitation, not a demand, not forcing anything on the big guy, just, well, *offering* to let it take part in my love of its presence.

Of course, the offer of body heat helps.

As soon as the big guy (and I'm fairly sure about the "guy" part, judging from the thickness and taper of his tail, as well as his general emotion-projection) starts toward me, I know that things will be all right. More than all right, actually, because I seem to have been more persuasive than I'd expected: the big guy's got friends. Or, well, whatever it is that snakes have.

The big fellah is kind of drab and desert-y in coloration, but as he wraps around my wrist (his grip's *strong*!), I admire the diamond shape of his head, as well as the pretty white and black and gray diamonds all along his back. The color contrasts sharply with the bright forest green of the next snake to approach, which is long and whiplike and has highly visible scales in the drab gray stonework around us. The next to approach is red, yellow, and black, and its head is small and conical. And there's still more coming, all of them wrapping around my arms, my legs, wherever they can get a grip as I crouch down and let them come into contact, sharing the heat emanating from the clownsuit's various systems. They've been cold down here for too long, but now they're here, and I'll keep them safe. They can feel that through our connection, and I feel them all accepting it voluntarily, no force required from me, not even the gentle nudging I sometimes have to use with mammals. Instead, they give of their emotions freely, just like I give of my warmth.

Of course, this also means that I'm covered in a sizable passel of snakes, most of which are highly venomous. While I'd deliberately shut off the part of my brain that was trying to warn me that I was letting a rather sizable male diamondback rattlesnake wrap around my arm, and a green mamba wrap around my ankle, and a coral snake wind its way up to my thigh, while a common brown snake is pressing itself friendly-like against my belly, I'm perfectly well aware of the creatures in question, of the threat they could pose if they were so inclined. But we're all friends here, and my new friends all know that I don't mean them any harm, and that they can't eat me – I'm too darn big – so there's no point in initiating any hostilities. Lucky there's no cobras or water moccasins in the mix: they always take a bit more coaxing to get them to be reasonable, which might unsettle the others; calming down that mamba was quite hard enough.

I wonder how they all ended up here. Not only are they all from different places, but normally I'd expect snakes of different types to try and eat each other, or...well, something besides staying in the same general vicinity. But these guys all seem to have found a state of homeostasis. Probably too busy trying to avoid the super-rats, or too sluggish from the chill down here, to bother with trying to hunt each other. They're hungry, too, that much I can sense, though at least the cold of the tunnels has slowed their metabolisms, keeping their energy from depleting into the critical ranges.

If I had to guess, I imagine that they were dumped and forgotten somewhere as part of one of the innumerable monster-making projects that cropped up around the End. One of the skyscraper-sized robots that built Sunflower City probably scooped them up as part of some forgotten laboratory whose materials it intended to use, and whatever container they were occupying cracked open when they were set down, giving them a chance to head underground, away from the surface and anybody that might hurt them up there.

Snakes are, regardless of species, a much-maligned sort of critter, and they know it on the deepest, most instinctive level. Just about everything is out to get them, which is kind of awful for a creature that, in the most extreme cases, is almost blind and nearly deaf, and has to rely on smell and heat-sense to perceive the world. I imagine having to live like that, without sight, without sound, and everybody in the world wanting to pick on me, and I feel a sense of sadness. And despite it all, there's still rattlesnakes, who've evolved that rattle for the specific purpose of warning the creatures that want to hurt it that it could hurt them back. These creatures can feel enough of my love for them to know

216

that they don't need to bite me, because I don't want to hurt them. They don't quite understand altruism, of course, but at least we've got the start of a working relationship here.

Slowly, carefully, I unsling my pack, lay it on the ground, and pop the seals. There's still plenty of room in the stasis pod with the baby opossum, so I press a few buttons and do a partial unfreeze, just enough to get it open without waking up the little guy. To the snakes, the baby doesn't even register as alive. The chill from the interior makes the snakes hesitate, especially when compared with the warmth of my body, but as the warmth heats their brains, they're starting to feel those hunger pangs more keenly. So, I focus on the vat-grown feeder rats back home, on the warmth and safety of the enclosures, and on being *anywhere else* than this awful place.

The lure of food gets to them, eventually, and slowly they uncoil from my body and slither their scaly way into the pod. Nice thing about snakes is a lot of them can fit into a really small space. Not like they're concerned about social boundaries, after all. Which is good because there's nine of them, but they're all stuffing their way into the pod, coiling around each other nice and snug. When everybody's as comfortable as they're going to get, I snap the pod closed and activate the stasis field. There's a brief flash in my heart as they all react to the single moment of cold, and then everything goes peaceful as they drift into a soft, squamous dreamland.

Now that I've got time to realize it, all that empathic effort took more out of me than I expected. I'm breathing a bit hard now, and can feel my heart pounding in my chest, neither of which I'd noticed while I was concentrating on getting the snakes into safety. This psi stuff really takes it out of a guy in a physical way as well as in emotional fatigue, and the toll creeps up on you.

About that moment, when I'm taking stock of the costs to my body and psyche that I've already paid out, I look up, and notice that I'm staring down the barrel of an AK-47. I'm not much of a gun buff, but the banana clip and overall shape of that particular gun is pretty distinctive. Lifting my eyes a bit more, I look into a furry face, its lips curled back in a snarl that was surely intended to be intimidating. And yes, the teeth *are* pretty scary, but nevertheless, it's just a rat. A big one, sure, almost human-sized and standing on two legs, but a rat all the same.

I like rats.

***

So now, I'm sort of a prisoner of the super-rats. This doesn't bother me too much because I can hear them playing Mozart off down the tunnel as we walk down toward their lair. Mozart's a good sign because that's what they play when they're in a good mood or want to get in one (I can recognize one of Papageno's solos from "The Magic Flute," though it's a bit scratchy; they must be using an old record player). They tend to play Beethoven, or sometimes rap, when they're in a bad mood, or working themselves up to going on the warpath. I once tried to get them interested in Barry Manilow, but that didn't go so well: that group tried to eat me. Which hurts my feelings a little: I *like* Barry Manilow!

This is a new group, though, one I've never met before, and as we step into the larger cavern where they've got their nest, I can see that they're not on a war footing at all. It's mostly females and little ratlings, and they all keep their distance from me. I'm a scary human, after all, and they're in no mood to mess around with a human, whatever his relative size. Even the two young males keeping their guns trained on me aren't really looking for a fight. After all, if they wanted to kill me, they'd have tried it while I wasn't paying attention to them back in the trash piles. I'm pretty sure the clownsuit would have deflected the bullets from their outdated weapons, but, well, why take chances when you don't have to? The whole place has the look-feel of a hobo camp, just little piles of bedding made into comfortable-looking nest-domes, most of them propped up with sticks, while more trash fires keep the area reasonably well-lit.

Based on what I'm seeing, I'd guess that these super-rats have managed to keep the morlocks out of their home turf in this region by pure bluff and raw moxie so far, but either they've lost a lot of their numbers, or they didn't have that many to begin with, and right now they're just living each day in the dread of knowing that the only things keeping them from total annihilation are a bunch of trash fires and a bare handful of old machine guns.

To be honest, I kind of like super-rats, and I feel sorry for them as well, and I try not to hurt them whenever possible, even on those occasions when they've tried to kill me. They're a genetic tatterdemalion sort of creature, originally composed of several different populations, some made on purpose, others by accident, that have now formed a composite culture out here in the wild, free of the labs that spawned them. Rats have been one of the most common and long-running lab animals used by humans. We've done things to them over the centuries that make me feel ashamed to be a member of my species (not that *that's* hard to do!). Finally, when we got serious about genetic manipulation to create weaponized species to fight our wars for us, especially to terrorize our civilian populations, keeping them tractable and submissive, turning rats into one of our first bioweapons just made good sense, since we had so many of them, and already knew so much about what made them tick.

The weaponized super-rats, the ones that were made the way they are on purpose and released on purpose (as opposed to the ones that escaped from captivity on their own, "Rats of NIMH" style) were made to act as living monkey wrenches. So, unlike just about every other monster we've made, they're not necessarily hostile towards humanity. Instead, they're actively interested in our *stuff*.

Poor things: they were made to want so very badly to have everything that people have, but without actually being people. Desire without capacity. This makes them restless, constantly trying to fiddle with or steal human things, because we're the only people that they know. Perfect for a biological weapon intended to incapacitate an enemy force or population center by messing around with or outright stealing things, especially the big, shiny, important-looking things that keep civilization running smoothly, but for a critter that's supposed to fulfill a natural function in the world? Not so much.

Still, they do get some satisfaction out of using tools and making things out of other things. Whether those tools or things work or are used in the manner they were originally intended is completely beside the point. The way they wear clothing makes for a pretty good example of what I mean: one of the pair of males that brought me in, the tough-looking one, is wearing a button-up shirt and a tie, but no pants, while the other, a chubby little fellah, is wearing a pair of very expensive-looking cross-trainers, and...well, that's about it. But they're wearing *clothes*, darn it! Surely that's enough! Or at least that's the impression they seem to be trying to make, and I've always found it equal parts pitiful and adorable.

So far as I've been able to tell, super-rats really aren't that bad, at least from my perspective, so long as they stick to *objects*. I've sacrificed more than a few of my own clothes and shiny stuff in prior encounters, back in the wasted lands of Earth, to keep them happy, and after that we've gotten along great. Stealing shiny stuff and fiddling around with it isn't even a problem now, because Sunflower City's trundlers tend to patch up the lesser messes they create, while the maintenance staff handle the bigger problems. They also keep down a lot of lesser monsters that might otherwise diminish the quality of life for the people living from Rock Bottom on up, and at least keep the nastier ones sufficiently contained that I'm usually the only one who encounters them. Which is entirely my fault, of course; if only there weren't so many things down here that need saving...

No, super-rats are only a problem when they steal *ideas*. Like a group that tried to copy religion. Naturally they went in for the flashy kind, the sort with big buildings and bloody sacrifices and all that. At first, I thought they were just being friendly, if a bit over-enthusiastic when they invited me into their community, but when they tried to sacrifice a half-dozen rat-maidens to me as their new god-figure, I had to put my foot down. Needless to say, my relations with that group rapidly deteriorated after that point: those ratgirls were *mad* about having their big scene interrupted!

But these guys, all they want to do is stay alive. No risk-taking from them, not even to the extent of trying to bring down a human like me, who wasn't that much taller than their biggest male. They just wanted to keep an eye on me, and make sure I wasn't down there to cause them any trouble.

As we hit the rough center of the ramshackle encampment, one of the tougher-looking females, hard-muscled and scarred up around her chest and belly and missing the tip of her tail, hurries over, and she's carrying something *very* interesting: it's a headdress. A headdress that I find familiar, tickling the old memory banks the more I look at it. She's waving it around as she comes running up, squeaking and gesturing emphatically.

Super-rats might not have any language, but they're no mean shakes at communication when they put their minds to it. Right now, I'm finally twigging to what she's trying to communicate about the same time that I remember exactly where I last saw that broken headdress: it was being worn by that important-looking morlock whose skull I bashed in during my headlong, controlled-panic rush through their tunnels; at the time I didn't even register more details than I needed to kill my way through, but with hindsight recreation of the moment, my memory fills in all the blanks in astonishing detail, obviously having been working overtime in the background while my conscious self was more interested in the business of staying alive. From the pantomimes I'm getting from this she-brawler, I apparently brained one of the morlock leaders that was causing this little group the most trouble; probably the same guy who'd figured out how to weaponize the slurp and the super-pig, if I had to take a wild stab in the dark.

Not too wild a stab, as I soon deduce, based on the tusk-like motions one of the motherly-looking ratwomen is making now with her hands:

222

apparently, she knows something about the showdown that got me dumped down here in the first place, maybe from a peek up the hole during my fight with the pig. And there's another joining in, one of the ratlings, old enough to start having that sharp gleam of near-personness that most of the older super-rats have, wiggling his tail like a snake, and then curling it around himself and hugging it, as though it were his best friend.

Judging from the way everybody's looking me over now, furtive-like from the sides of their blue-rimmed eyes, I think I might've accidentally started another cult.

(Oh, but I am going to *love* trying to explain this one to God when I finally meet the guy: "Honest, I didn't mean to impersonate a deity, it just kind of *happened*.")

At least the super-rats have stopped pointing guns in my direction.

A few moments more, I'm watching the super-rats making their various gestures and squeaky noises, most of the community joining in at this point, certainly no longer afraid of me in the slightest. I have to exert pretty close to all of my willpower to not make any unfortunate "squee" sounds over how adorable they are — that is *not* a good way to start diplomatic relations with a warrior-hunter-gatherer proto-culture! Typical of any religion in the conceptual stage, the worshiper-base are naturally ignoring any potential input from their object of worship. If the clergy in the original Ecumenical Councils couldn't be bothered to open with prayers for guidance from God, why should a bunch of high-end rodents think of asking *my* opinion? At least they've got the excuse of not having language!

While the older members of the pack jabber and gesture, one of the little rat-girls wanders over to me and looks up, her thumb stuck in her mouth. I give her a shrug and my best "it's not my fault" look, hoping she can see it through my visor. She returns the shrug, so I offer her my hand. She takes it, and we both turn our attention to where everybody else is still set on squeaking about what to do with this weird human that's stumbled into their midst, both of us about equally bemused by the spectacle.

After much demonstrative body language, chest-poking, tail-tugging, and vigorous gesticulation (and two more ratlings deciding that I was less weird than their adults, my other hand and my leg now serving as hold-points for tiny pink proto-hands), the tough boy-rat that originally brought me to their camp rounds on me and points, right at my chest, in a fashion I found highly indicative. Of what I had no idea, but he did it with *feeling*.

Once he's got my attention, he turns and points over to a roughly human-sized opening on the far side of the campsite. As I look away from the shine of the trash fires, I realize with a steadily rising uncomfortable feeling that the super-rats' shelter is a place I find highly morbid by nature: it's apparently a transplant from one of the European catacombs, bones of all shapes and sizes mortared up in the walls in a most visible style. The builder 'bots did a fantastic job of recreating the place!

The young male wants me to follow him, though, and it seems to be important not just to him, but to everybody there. Even the little ratlings let go of me when they realize what the male is suggesting, and now they're all looking at me with...wait? Is that *hero worship*? I know what the expression is supposed to look like from all the old films I love watching, but it's supposed to be directed at...I don't know, big mighty heroes and heroines, godlike of physique, glorious of action, infinite in wisdom; you know, somebody like that. Not a squat, dumpy animal control worker who just kind of ended up where he is via a series of unfortunate events.

Ah well, in for a penny, in for a pound, so with no ratlings holding onto me anymore, I take the hint, and follow the young ratboss to wherever he wants me to go, so I can take a look at whatever problem he's got and, in true heroic fashion, fix it. Somehow.

About this time, as I'm right behind the skinny, tough-looking guy with the tie (and I admit to being impressed: it's actually tied, not some tacky clip-on), heading down a long, winding flight of cobwebby stairs, probably into an area mostly forgotten by everybody except the super-rats and the spiders and other bugs (normal and otherwise) hanging out down here, I realize just how thoroughly I've been winging it up to this point. If I'm going to have any chance at all of getting my cold-sleeping charges back up to the surface in safety, I'm going to have to start making proper plans. Especially if I'm going to be dealing with a problem like whatever this rat-guy thinks is important enough that it requires a god-hero to fix it, even a cut-rate one like me. Fortunately, anything that super-rats might need help handling isn't likely to be all that bad. I mean, they're smart and all, but they're just animals, and the problems of animals are ultimately small in scale as a very general rule, meaning that it's just going to deal with some problem that impacts their immediate survival.

Stepping off the Frankensteinian staircase, I can see lights up ahead, past a final archway, white and dazzlingly bright after the darkness of the passage and the red glow of the trash fires. Electric lights, which means I was completely wrong: this is a people problem, and people problems are *complicated*.

The super-rats made the right call in bringing in another person to handle this one. Tough luck that person happened to be me, but what can you do?

Looking back at the ratguy, who's sidled back as I walked forward, I can see he's not into this. Obviously, whatever's past this point scares him spitless, and he'd really, *really* rather not go any deeper into the frying pan if he can avoid it. At the same time, I feel a surge of genuine gratitude and admiration for him: he's willing to come with me, if I want it, even when it's obvious that he thinks going anywhere near whatever it is up ahead is probably going to kill him.

"You've done enough," I tell him, hoping he'll get the hint from my body language and the tone of my voice (trying to keep the active empathic influence to a minimum in the process: I don't want another mess like what happened with the opossum mommy up surface-side). "You're brave and you're strong and you're smart and you're a great guy. All the ratgirls are gonna worship you! And, uh, ratguys, too, if you're into that kind of thing. But you're not much good to any of them if you die down here, are you?" I give him a wave, and then point back up the way we came. "I'll take it from here. Go take good care of your family. Make sure they grow up healthy and strong and smart. And get them moved to someplace without morlocks as soon as you can."

Whatever of what I just said got through to him must've been enough, because he high-tails it like a streak of greased lightning. And that's that. No sense in delaying the inevitable.

I turn around, and I walk into the light, coming out on a little overhang right above a nice, long ladder overlooking a massive artificial cavern, lit from above with the glow of an artificial sun. This must be one of the backup forcefield-contained "pocket" fusion reactors that they keep in case there's any interruption of the power flow from the solar microwave collectors. From this point, I've got close to a perfect view of a whole community – a community of humans! – that must be hidden away from everybody up above. City Central can't reach down here very well, if at all, not with all the monsters and other obstacles always messing with her communications, besides the weird and more-or-less random architecture of this place. And as I look around, I start to realize that the way this undercity was built must have been done on purpose, to suit the mind of someone truly twisted. Twisted enough to make...this.

The City of Dis, at Inferno's deep.

After seeing the way the super-rats acted, I was already pretty sure this quest was going to be something bad. Well, I was wrong, and I'm not ashamed to admit it: it's so very, very much worse.

CHAPTER 14: THE TEMPTATION OF SCINTILLANT CAMOR

Location: Earth, Sunflower City, Dis
Perspective: Scintillant Camor

Of course, when I surrendered without resistance to the men with spiders in their heads, I knew that matters would be bad in the hearts of such people, wicked enough to kill their souls with the vilest sort of corrupted machinery, while letting their bodies continue to serve as hollowed-out shells. And I knew that whomever their leader was, if they would allow such abominations, or even encourage them, they had to be vile beyond words.

Also of course, I was wrong: they were worse. So much worse than I'd imagined.

The evil of this place was like a scent in my nostrils, so awful that it was making me want very badly to bury my head under a pillow and pull the sheets up over my whole self and never, ever come out again.

That wasn't possible, though, since I was shackled, wrists and ankles and neck, to an extremely uncomfortable metal chair, which seemed to be the center point of a rather complex set of implements intended to inflict pain in many interesting and creative ways. Fortunately for me, at least in the short term, the primary operator of these machines was not actually all that interested in causing pain, at least not as an end in itself. No, whoever he was (and I got the very clear impression that this person was male), he was a professional, and took great pride in doing his job well. His job just happened to be as a professional torturer, but I can appreciate an expert wanting to perform well in his craft. After every one of his operations, he carefully cleansed all of his tools, keeping them as spotless and ready for service as possible, which had the fortunate side benefit of also scrubbing them of the lingering emotional residues. If this were not so, I...don't think I could have lasted long: the temptation would have simply been too strong.

The temptation of the incubus within me.

Of course, once this person gets here, I expect that I will have to endure some horrific experiences, but that's just my body: when the torture gets bad enough, I'll make myself go away, and then whatever happens next won't really matter. It might not matter at all, since a true professional at the craft of torture will know how to keep my body alive in spite of positively horrendous tissue damage, so even when I send myself somewhere safe, if (*when*, I have to keep hoping!) I'm ever restored to a position where I can risk coming back, then I can probably do so without having to worry too much about dying. Oh, it will hurt, make no mistake, and I'm not very well-suited for dealing directly with physical pain, but at least experts like Doctor Salvee can eventually put me back together, and I can return to my precious daughter and my work at saving this poor, wounded little planet.

But...do I *want* to save Earth anymore? What I'm sensing here, as I cast myself outward, seeking a clearer picture of my surroundings, is starting to lead me to doubt.

No. What I am starting to want – what I really, really, *really* want – is to make what I sense stop.

It is an abomination.

Child slavery is just the start of the monstrosity. I can feel their young hearts beating, chained by fear and pain and the aftermath of unspeakable abuses. They are too damaged in spirit to even hope for deliverance; some may be too damaged to be healed at all. And I know how they came to their present state: we moved so fast, built Sunflower City so quickly, allowed so much fiddling about the details from the fallen leaders of Earth, allowing them the benefit of doubt when we should have been vastly more cautious, even at the risk of being tyrannical, of violating our core beliefs in the free will of the individual. In all that haste to create a place where humanity could be moved to live in safety before their wasted lands consumed them utterly, we failed to perform an adequate headcount.

Here, above me, I sense children, lost and forgotten, the orphans of a doomed civilization. How many others of these shadow people have made their way to Sunflower City, above or below or in the borderland place called Rock Bottom? How many others live in the margins, unseen, unrealized, and unsaved?

The thought, the realization, it staggers me. It leaves me sick to heart and soul and stomach.

There is a vast amount of activity going on in this strange, hidden, forbidden city below the paradise I and my colleagues and friends tried so hard to create. While I'm no engineer, there is a feel to places, an emotional gestalt composed of the combined selves of everyone, past and present, living there, and through that feeling I can sense this place expanding, spreading like a cancer beneath the healthy-seeming surface. Not only are they sucking the life from one of the backup generators, but they must also be tapping into the tubes and pipes that keep Sunflower City fed, robbing the people above for their own continued, parasitic survival.

The cancerous metaphor feels steadily more apt the longer I consider the situation.

While letting my empathic center-self wander this terrible place, this City of Hell, I come across its malignant heart with a horrible start, so sharp and sudden it makes my eyes snap open, my own heart quite literally skipping a beat: I hadn't encountered *that* sort of evil in a very, very long time.

Above me, almost directly above me, the work all over the City of Hell has ground to a stop. There is a pulpit erected before an audience swiftly gathering, some fearful, others eager, none of them willing to risk the consequences of daring to miss hearing their great leader speaking.

The Preacher Man.

At times like this, I am glad that I lack telepathy or any significant extra-sensory perceptions. If I'd had such abilities, I would have seen and heard the Preacher Man, been exposed to his sermon directly, and possibly been tainted by the vitriol of his words. As it is, I feel the poisonous gush of the emotions he sends out into his audience – not just into willing and misguided adults, but into the child slaves dragged from their labors and forced to endure this abomination! – and through the nuances of those emotions, I know the subject of the sermon.

An old joke comes to my mind, a human joke, about one of their leaders of prior times. This leader, a quiet sort, not prone to wasting words, went to church on the established holy day and listened to the sermon. After it was finished, he returned home, and his wife asked him what the preacher spoke about.

"Sin," was the reply. Naturally, his wife was hardly satisfied with such terseness, and asked what the preacher had, specifically, to say *about* sin.

"He was against it," was the quite natural response.

Not the Preacher Man.

Since my nickname *is* Sin, bestowed upon me by my dear friend Gret while we were learning some of the human languages together, I tend to have an interest in the subject, hence my cross-species religious studies. Humans typically recognize seven major motivations for sin (often mistaken for the sins they beget): sloth, gluttony, lust, envy, wrath, greed, and pride. As I felt the sermon, I sensed those abominations pouring out of the Preacher Man in waves, inundating and engulfing his audience, crashing into them, crushing them down, filling them up, drowning them in filth.

He began by appealing to wrath. Hate, fear, and just a teasing touch of envy toward the Pan-Galactic Republic, telling his audience of our crimes against them, the Chosen, the Elect, the Saved. According to him, they were forced into the city of Hell, cast down from the light of the world above, from the very light of God and the sun, because the Republic had banished them, had forced their fall, had stolen from them their rightful, deserved places in the Light. Those above, the vile aliens and their collaborators, were traitors akin to the Evil One, the First Sinner and Rebel, turning and spitting in the very eye of God with our blasphemies.

We were monsters, cruel and wicked and filled with the sins of our pride, our wealth, our prosperity. To illustrate what sort of monsters we were, he began to describe, in detail so explicit, acts so graphic, so extreme, even to hear them vicariously through the ears of his audience made my own ears burn and my stomach churn.

Of course, he did have a point: the laws of the Republic have never banned anything that takes place between consenting adult sapients within their homes or other private places. In our defense, however, one of the first requirements for ensuring that decadence does not claim a society is regulating sexuality. For we of the Republic, that regulation is self-imposed, or derived from our religions, as the individual feels is best, not forced upon us by governmental law. Some licentiousness certainly takes place, but not nearly to the extent and degree that might be expected from a society of the Republic's size and population.

From the way the Preacher Man described us, though, we…I can't repeat what I felt him saying, can't even bear the thought of describing it. My mind immediately returns to my precious wife, to my equally precious daughter – as much a part of me as my other children, even if we don't share a species – and I quail to think of what he told his audience we did to our loved ones. It is obscenity past endurance.

And the adults in the audience lapped it up and crowed hungrily for more.

Soon, too soon, the Preacher Man began to evoke the baser impulses in his audience: greed and gluttony and sloth. The desire to take what isn't yours from those who you imagine don't deserve it (even if the justification for being deserving eventually sums up as "you weren't strong enough to stop us from taking it"). I, in form deeply caricatured, was a subject of this part of the sermon, apparently intended as a hostage, a key game piece that the Preacher Man and his cronies intended to use to take what they felt should have been theirs in the first place. And of course, there would be plenty to go around, or so he claimed, flattering the adults in his audience and dazzling them with images of a paradise and prosperity they'd wrench from the grasp of the vile invaders and usurpers. They would ascend unto Heaven upon the backs of the pretender-gods who'd descended from the skies to steal what was rightfully theirs.

They believed him. Every adult in the audience believed him without question, without thought. Throughout his preaching, he'd called out to them, and they'd responded, letting themselves grow ever more caught up in the frenzy of the moment's emotions, consumed by his spirit speaking to theirs. Their emotions rose high and burned hot, and I could feel the power of a spirit raging about in that great chamber above, tearing this way and that through the audience, making some begin to babble, and others to convulse.

They'd called a spirit there, but it was no Holy Ghost. No, to tell what sort of spirit had been summoned, and eagerly accepted into the hearts of the congregation, all you had to do was look to the children.

They were terrified. Terrified beyond the ability to feel anything else, even their senses starting to fail them as they were frozen in place in the pews where they'd been chained, physically *chained*, to keep them from escaping this gospel of hate.

Were they exposed to enough of it, many of them would succumb to its lure, in time. The rest, the ones who had the courage and the purity and the good sense to resist...

There was blood on the hands of the Preacher Man. The blood of the innocent.

There was a far worse sin upon him, however: he had never shed that blood himself. No. He had others do his killing for him. Not enough that he sinned: he made others into sinners, into murderers, driving them from one act of darkness to another until their eyes were too caked in filth to see the horrors that they had become, and their hearts too past feeling to care.

Something welled up in me, dark and terrible. How dare this Preacher Man decry the sins of others when his own spill over in gore and filth? How *dare* he accuse us of any sin at all, when he oppresses orphans, when he enslaves them and drives them to death and grinds down their hearts until they start to believe monstrosity like his and those who follow him is *normal*!

How dare he!

In the past, before the tarig found my people, we were monsters. Emotivores: emotion eaters. We fed on pleasure, and pain, on life, and death. Those primitive l'dray lived alongside several other sapient races with whom we shared our home world...and fed on them. We would lure them in with promises of ultimate sensation, seduce them with gently whispered words of darkest, forbidden sin and sweet, sweet wonders.

And we never lied. Oh no: we delivered. We gave our precious, darling victims *exactly* what we promised. In the process, we devoured their souls, flaying their lives with pleasure and pain and joy and sorrow and rage and calm and every madness that could be conceived until they were left lifeless, empty husks.

Those were the original "gentle ones," the most expert at luring in prey and giving them every reason to stay, quite willingly, right to the moment of shuddering, sweet demise. The ones who took other I'dray under their wings, who trained them, raised them properly, and sent them out into the world to spread our special gift.

Then the tarig found our little world and conquered it. Not that it was hard for them: the various sapient species living on it were just starting to tinker with steam power and clockwork when we were simply steamrolled and crushed under the cogs of the Tarig Empire's war machine.

True to their nature as conquerors and masters of life as well as limb, the tarig gene-forgers remade my species. They tempered our predatory natures by mingling our genes with those of the other species on our planet, the ones we'd once regarded as our semi-consensual prey.

These reborn I'dray, like myself, were cursed so that we wouldn't just feel, we could feel *sorry*. Sympathy, as well as empathy. Faced with such new and strange sensations, we soon became docile, eager-to-please pets and playthings. Being a Gentle One meant one who could soothe the inner hurts of another, who could reach inside of them and heal the wounds the eye cannot see.

But the tarig...they were too wounded for us to heal. When the Resistance rose up at last to overthrow these terrible overlords, we had to join them – *we had to* – because the evils they'd committed were too deep, had scarred them in their deepest souls. For all the evils they'd done to others, they'd done far worse to themselves, until we all saw –

oh so clearly – that only death could save them from such horrors as they'd inflicted.

Mercy killing.

Even so, despite all the efforts of our conquerors to change us, from those times up until this day, there are still throwbacks among we l'dray. Predators. Emotivores. We call them incubi.

Now I feel myself, in the fury of righteous indignation, reaching deep into the ancestral energies of my species and seizing tight hold of the forbidden but never forgotten sense-knowledge of the power that those ancient incubi could use. I let it fill my center-self, soaking it red, bright and bitter. Trading pity for power.

Too many people think that empathy is the weakest of all the powers that might manifest. The one with the least combat application. How, they ask, can knowing what someone is feeling help me win a fight?

Fools.

Have you ever been so sunken into sorrow that your irises, your *sclera*, leaked out all their color with your tears?

Have you ever felt anguish of body and spirit so intense that you were left paralyzed, your limbs bereft of strength?

Have you ever experienced pleasure so great that your spine was *arched*, *stretched*, *contorted* until it *snapped*?

Have you ever been so wracked with guilt that your pores sweat blood?

This Preacher Man, these humans, these vile and wicked and disgusting sinners, they will soon know what it means to have the full horror of a Gentle One unleashed upon them! I will teach them the Thousand Pleasures and the One Great Pain! What evils they have

237

wreaked upon the innocent I will visit upon them a hundredfold and more, until they are caught beneath the weight of their own sins like fruit in a winepress, pressed down and *squeezed* of their vital-most juices!

For the Greater Good of us all!

But...could I do these things, and look my daughter in the face ever again?

If ever I see them in whatever life lies beyond, could I dare to take my lost wife and dear child, unborn but no less real, in my arms, my hands and heart clean?

No.

"No," I tell the empty room, softly, softly, and I feel the killing red recede, then withdraw.

The sudden departure of the powers I'd started to call up leaves me weak. Spent. Empty. For a time, how long I cannot tell in this place without clocks or the light of the sun or the moon or the stars, I sit there, bereft of the ability to feel anything at all.

Then it passes, and life resumes.

Ears twitching, I hear a heavy foot tread, the tromp of a man of great size and strength. Someone with the body of a butcher. The door clanks as keys turn in the lock, and then it swings open. I raise my head and look into the eyes of the man who is to be my torturer, his body thick with black, wiry hair, his massive forearms bared to either side of his white apron.

He's frozen there, mouth agape beneath the surgeon's mask that only barely covers his thick beard, no longer the calm, clinical professional. Instantly I sensed his difficulty: he was only told that he was to work on an alien. Nobody told him that the alien in question would look like an inoffensive little canid with fluffy fur and pretty purple eyes.

Despite everything he's done, and in spite of everything the Preacher Man has done to him, there is still the capacity in this man to soften at the sight of a small, furry creature in distress.

"Hello there," I say, smiling gently. "My name is Scintillant Camor. What's yours?"

He hesitates.

"John Martin," he finally says.

We can work with this: both of us as one. Together, we can help him heal.

CHAPTER 15: RED, BLACK, AND WHITE

Location: Earth, Sunflower City, Dis
Perspective: The Man

Looking down at this city below the city, the city I now call Dis, I can see the people, all of them humans, moving between buildings in varying degrees of ramshackle. This is one of those cities, like so many back in the Hell we humans made of our planet, where the refugees came and built, not expecting the settlement to be permanent, but as days stretched into weeks into months into years and nowhere else presented itself, the temporary structures gradually got built upon, and the community itself built outward from the primitive beginnings.

Obviously, just based on how short a time Sunflower City has been here, this place hasn't been around nearly as long as some of the refugee cities I've seen and sometimes visited, but it's still got all the makings of one. Built up for a similar reason, too, if I'm any judge: these are people who refuse to join with the new society up above. Back in the wasted lands, that was often understandable: after the big collapse of the End, petty tyrants were always rising and falling, over and over again, and every time some new regime came in, they'd start killing off anybody who disagreed with them, or maybe they'd just kill a bunch of random people to prove a point about how awful they were, and how everybody should fear them and not try to overthrow them (fat lot of good that ever did, considering the turnaround time for a typical tyrant during the End). So, a lot of people gravitated into places nobody wanted, threw up enough shelter to reach basic survivability levels, and hunkered down to wait things out.

Here, though, that's not a good thing. See, up above, in the society that these people are actively rejecting, is bright sunshine and clean air and everything they could possibly need to achieve the fullest sort of happiness and life-satisfaction. I've seen the people of the Republic, and the average citizen is clean, healthy, happy, satisfied with life as it is, but also constantly looking for ways to improve so that they can give back some of what they've been given.

These people, down here in the dark and the damp, have rejected life-satisfaction for something they thought was more important.

I can feel what that something is with every breath I take, until I don't want to breathe anymore, just to make it stop.

One of the key differences between animals and people, and probably the biggest reason why I prefer the company of animals, isn't too hard to understand: people lie. To others, to themselves, and they'll even try to lie to God or the gods (to varying degrees of success). Most psychologists, across all species, agree that a major part of a person's social development hinges upon developing the ability to lie until it becomes ingrained, second nature, a part of standard interactions with other people, and so much so that we don't even realize we're doing it most of the time. Lies are so much a part of the societies that people have developed, in fact, that we'll give money to professional liars, even when we know that what they're presenting to us is, by strict definition, a lie. In fact, some of the lies those professionals tell are so good, they wrap all the way around until they tell truths that the plain truth just couldn't convey nearly so completely or so well. Hence the origins of humor and poetry and all great literature.

The depths and breadth and all-pervasiveness of lies in the human psychology, though, is why nobody realized this city was down here: it was wrapped up in a great lie, a darkness of such magnitude that no sane person, not a precognitive, not a telepath, certainly not an empath, would ever consciously locate the place, out of simple self-preservation. Not until after they were ready to try and extend the lie beyond their boundaries.

There is an evil here that kills the soul. If I stay here too long, it'll kill mine, too.

Down there, I can see the training grounds for soldiers. About half of the trainees going through their drills look to be somewhere around the prepubescent stage of life, eight to twelve. Child soldiers in training, a practice that I saw way too often back in the End. Back when, just to stay alive, I had to…no, I don't want to think about that. I won't think about that. I can't think about that.

Maybe this time I can save a few.

Children are the major workforce around here, too; that's what I'm seeing from my vantage point up on the lip of the bowl of solid bedrock where this city has been built. Children in chains. No wonder so many of them prefer being child soldiers. Beats the alternative, that's for sure. They're being beaten about the same, yeah, but at least the ones beating the child cadets are slightly older children: they don't have the same strength as the adults doing the beating of the child-slaves, making them haul and lay the stones to turn this place into something more permanent.

All around, I see adults wandering from place to place, furtive, mock-purposeful. Pretending that whatever they're doing has something to do with "official business," and so they shouldn't be stopped. The only people who don't have that look to them are the ones in the scary uniforms, black-and-red with high white collars and round, broad-brimmed hats and mirror-shaded dark glasses. They'd look sort of like generic clergy if it weren't for the body armor they're obviously sporting beneath the clothes, the clubs they're toting in their hands, and the various guns about their persons.

Just as I've almost got the layout of the place figured out, and have stepped up to one of the long metal ladders leading down into the depression of this Hell city (I can see elevators at various strategic points, so the ladders must be there for emergencies, or left over from the place's original construction; either way, nobody's monitoring them, while the elevators are sure to be guarded), I get a shock as a great big bell starts to clang, and immediately everybody stops whatever they're doing and starts toward the big building – the only real building in the entire place – at the center of this community of the determined damned. Even the kids, whether getting beat by clubs in the chain gangs, or beat by fists and feet out on the training grounds, are rounded up and herded toward the building.

244

Since the place must be important, I took a closer look.

One look, and I know what *that* place is, all right, and I turn away pretty darn quick, keeping the bad memories from coming back too hard and fast for me to handle, and instead focus on getting myself down the layers of ladders. Sure, part of it's done up like a church building, especially the front bits, where the kids are being herded at the end of the line of the citizens of Dis, but I'm not buying the lie. Not this time.

That place is a House of Terror. Doesn't matter what it's called, that's what it is; I get my title for those sorts of places from the Hungarian museum of that name, and it fits. Whether it's run by a religious organization, like the Inquisition or the Guidance Patrol, or by a political institution, like the Gestapo or the Oprichnina, it's all the same in the end. It's the sort of place any decent tyrannical regime builds to keep safe the people it wants safe, and the people it doesn't want... otherwise. The former class typically includes the tyrants themselves and their chief sycophants, set up in a nice, cushy sort of bunker in case they feel especially paranoid that day. The latter category includes all the prisoners who are still in the process of breaking.

Having been in that second category on a few too many occasions, I'm getting steadily less and less reticent about what I know I've got to do down here.

During most of the times I've ended up in those awful places, I got beatings, maybe a bit of mutilation. Some broken or at least cracked bones were always par for the course. Once, a power drill was taken to my funny bone. Twice, hot irons. Three times, flogging, one of those times with an old-fashioned scourge strung with jagged chunks of goat bone (or maybe sheep: they look so similar). Once, I had something done to my teeth that still makes me wince at phantom pains every time I start to chew, long after the Republic people put my mouth back together again, better than new. Every time, thankfully, my captors quickly figured out I didn't have anything to tell them – I was just an eccentric animal lover who'd wandered into the wrong place at the wrong time – but they always felt the need to go through the motions anyway before, eventually, they tossed me somewhere and forgot about me, giving me time to affect an escape, typical black torture thinking. Thankfully I've never been in the clutches of a professional red torturer for more than an hour at a time (the dental work was during one of those light sessions), or I don't think I'd have ever gotten free of the Houses of Terror: red torturers take their jobs seriously. But one time...oh, that one time.

They made me go through white torture.

Let me explain, for those who read these psi stylus recordings later. Let me tell you about red torture, black torture, and white.

Red torture is the sort of stuff the Chinese were famous for back in the day (Imperial or Communist, it doesn't really matter), and which sometimes shows up among more conscientious regimes, the ones that feel a need for professionalism. Ideally, a good red torturer is a trained medical practitioner, someone who knows exactly how far a body can be stretched before it breaks, and then keeps from going *quite* that far. Barely. If a torture session involves knives, drills, saws, or even more fine equipment, like drops of water or drugs or equipment specifically designed to twist natural motions of the body to their horrific extremes, then it's red, so-called because the victim and the torturer usually develop a pretty intimate relationship during the whole process.

Eventually, many red torture experts figured out that they didn't even need to cause actual damage: waterboarding or dry boarding, for example, or constant exposure to music that you hate. The point of red torture is to cause maximum suffering with maximum precision and the minimum amount of damage to the subject's body, as well as the intensely close relationship between torturer and victim (who you eventually wish you didn't have to disappoint by not telling them what they want to know: they're being forced to do such terrible things only because of your stubbornness). The best red torture sessions will make experts debate ad nauseam whether or not they're actually torture, or cause comedians to make jokes about it. Roman-style crucifixion was the direct result of red torture methods with the safety taken off: an unnatural position coupled with a few strategic penetrations of the body at key nerve clusters, plus public exposure and ridicule, plus time. It's all about the victim, making them the most important person in the room. Or the road. Or the hill, as the case may be.

Black torture is brutal, and there's no question about it being torture. Of course, since black torture doesn't take much education or equipment (though I don't mean to imply that there's no skill involved), just a complete disregard for life, it's probably the most common sort of torture used, past, present, and future. It starts with a beating, just to drive home how cheap your life is; broken bones are the norm. Then, typically, you get tied up and thrown somewhere and forgotten for a while. Sometimes the place you're thrown happens to be underwater. When you're remembered, it's just so that you can be brutalized, bones shattered, joints dislocated, all to demoralize you, depersonalize you, break your psyche down the same way that your body is being broken. The ubiquitous oubliette is *the* standard in black torture, where the victim is dumped down a dark hole, usually breaking bones on landing at the bottom, before it's sealed up. Sometimes they're remembered later and pulled out for questioning. Sometimes not. That tenuous boundary between torture and death is the defining point of black torture, never really knowing when the brutality will go too far, or if you'll just die from neglect, forgotten in the dark. Your only hope in black torture is to break quickly and completely, and hope that whatever you tell your captors is enough to make them stop, if only for a little while.

The end goal of all torture, though, is just that: to break you down. To destroy your sense of self. Once you've been broken, then you lose all reason to keep resisting your captors. You'll do anything they want, because nothing has purpose for you any longer; eventually, there's nothing of *you* left to resist. Even if your body continues to live, you've died inside.

With this in mind, and after having gone through sessions of all three types (though I'm so glad my red sessions were cut short on the grounds of my being too insignificant), I think white torture is the worst of them all.

White torture is where you're put into a plain room, usually with bright lights – slightly too bright – and white walls. There are no windows. All surfaces are muted, dulled and smooth, creating a minimum of stimulation of the sense of touch. For me, there was a smooth white plate on one side of the room that I knew was a one-way mirror, though I understand that sort of thing is optional to the process. There is no way to tell how long you've been in the white room. Your belongings are taken from you, of course, but that's to be expected of most imprisonment. In white torture, though, that also includes your clothes.

From my later studies, apparently there is some variation in the sort of dress you're allowed. Sometimes they give you a loose gown, hospital-style. Sometimes you're forced into a straitjacket. Other times, just some simple, plain clothes. For me, I was left naked, and the temperature turned way, *way* down.

And then I was left there. Alone. In complete and absolute silence except for my own body.

That might not sound like such an awful thing, especially not to somebody like me, with my...well, my "issues" with people. Except it's not true what you might have heard about introverts: we need to be around people, too. We need company. We need contact. Just like anybody else. Moreover, I'm a human, and humans are omnivores: all of evolution has adapted us to seek out variety, even unpleasant ones, as part of properly stimulating our brains.

White torture denies you that essential contact, and almost all essential stimulation. It's just one step down from total sensory deprivation. Maybe that just makes it worse, because there's this huge blank gap filled up with cold, stark white, and there's supposed to be *something* in it...but there isn't. All there is, is the white.

Every so often, I would fall asleep. When I woke, sometimes there would be food, and sometimes there would be water. Also, bland. Also, white. There was a white bucket in a corner, covered by a white sheet, for my waste. When I slept again, sometimes the white tray on which the food had been brought would be gone, the bucket cleaned, and other times it wouldn't. A few times, I detected traces of caffeine in the water, bitter and sharp (and *such* a rush of sensation after all the white!), and I knew they were using chemicals to adjust my metabolism, to throw off my biological clock. That and it made me have to use the bucket in the corner more frequently, and that just added humiliation to everything else. Additional depersonalization, besides robbing me of essential nutrients and moisture, making the periods of hunger and thirst that much more acute.

Actually, all things considered, I think I did all right: I didn't start hallucinating until... maybe the fourth or fifth day.

They were products of my own personal Hell, the Hell within everyone's innermost soul. For me, it was a vivid recreation of my memories. All the worst ones. The times when I was selfish. When I was cruel. When I was thoughtless. When I hurt others. Those times, around ages five and sooner, when I stepped on little bugs because I was bigger than them and I could get away with it and because they looked interesting all mooshed up. The times, ages four through eight, when I was a bully. Those few occasions, teens and onward, where I went to dances and other social mixers, or tried to, and found myself utterly engulfed in a state of paralyzing panic unlike anything I've ever experienced before or since. Every instance of resentment for having to give up my time to help others. My pride at feeling that I was better than others because I thought I was smarter than them, coupled with the whiplash on finding out, again and again and again, how stupid, how useless, how incompetent, how weak and impotent, how clumsy and foolish and maladroit I really am. That and the betrayals by friends, leaving me alone and bewildered and sunk into humiliation. And every death.

250

And worst of all, those times when I did nothing. When I could have acted, should have acted, might have acted...and didn't. The source of the all-consuming guilt that drove me to become the Republic's gene pirate on Earth, desperate for some way to assuage my guilt for believing in my deepest heart, rationally or not, that the whole End and the mass extinction of life on Earth was all my fault. Because I didn't act when there was still time.

Over. And over. And over again.

The memories themselves were bad enough, but the really bad part, the part that still sometimes creeps up on me when I don't watch out for it, is the way those memories *warped* while I was hallucinating them. Memories are mutable things, constantly shuffling around in our heads, and for me, they changed. And the more times I relived them, the more they changed.

Later, after I got out, I had to retrace all the physical artifacts, photos and diaries and my own written journals, besides news articles and the ephemera of Earth's Internet to recreate a more accurate picture of what actually happened in my past. Even so, there are parts of my life that feel like sucking on the socket of a missing tooth, places where there's something *off*, and even knowing that what I think I remember isn't always accurate can't rationalize away the times when I just want to curl up in a ball and cry until I die. And where the objects or people or animals that served as mnemonic devices for my memories were absent, lost or destroyed or dead, that piece of my memory is blurred forever. I don't even remember my torturers, because they never bothered to ask me any questions; as far as I can tell, I was shoved into the House of Terror as a matter of routine, the usual treatment for a wanderer, as I always was during my gene pirate days, and when the next regime came around, nobody thought to check on me.

Fortunately, by the time I was put into white torture, I was already well acquainted with emotional anguish: I'd had a nervous breakdown in my thirties after...after a very bad day. After that event, my emotions went so haywire, I was physically robbed of the ability to move except by main force of will: I might as well have been paralyzed for all the strength I could muster, all my movements like those of an invalid three times my age. Nobody helped me through that: I had to guts my way back to full mobility on my own, and it took me almost three whole months, to say nothing of the years of emotional turmoil left behind. So, this time around, when staring madness in the face, I'd learned all sorts of ways to fight off the nerves, the fidgets, the heebie-jeebies, and the howling fantods.

Mostly that meant calisthenics and katas.

No, really: you'd be absolutely amazed at the wonders you can do for your psychology when you've worked yourself to exhaustion, the body is just leaking clean, cleansing sweat, your veins are rushing with endorphins, and you're simply too tired (and too stinky!) to be humiliated, or depersonalized, or much of anything else. Besides that, I've never had any problems talking to myself, or even answering, and I've spent literally years filling up my head with subjects of potential self-conversation. Body and mind constantly active, I held on.

Mostly.

That's probably the reason why, when there wasn't any food delivered for a while, I started to get suspicious. Hunger will do that to you, and when hunger gets to be one of the few sensations you're able to honestly experience, it wasn't too hard for me to decide to act on it. In my case, I used the white metal tray they'd left me, and got to work breaking the one-way mirror set into the wall in my room. Sure, it took a while, but considering I had nothing *but* time (time and hunger and thirst, that is), that was hardly a concern.

Nobody stopped me, and so eventually I did indeed break out. As for how that felt, seeing colors besides white, tasting the food left behind in somebody's lunchbox (even coffee, and I *hate* coffee!), getting to put on a leftover uniform after breaking open a guard's locker...there are no words. There can never be any words.

Once I was past the initial euphoria, I went down the halls of the place, unlocking doors and opening them wide and calling to the prisoners inside, urging them to join me.

As far as I know, I was the only one who ever left.

Turns out, as I found out later, there'd been four or maybe five regime changes while I was going through the white torture, all in the span of about a month. The guards couldn't have cared less: they had jobs to do and didn't really care about for whom they were doing them. I can almost respect that kind of professionalism. Almost.

The only reason I got out after the last regime change is because it was accompanied by a monster attack, something big and slobbery with lots of teeth sent over from one of that micro-nation's neighbors, and after it went through there just weren't enough people left in the entire country to maintain the place. Turns out, making monsters was just coming into vogue, and it was one of the most effective ways ever developed for slaughtering people wholesale, even better than nukes or sarin. (And just think of the terror factor!)

253

Getting close to the doors of the House of Terror, I can hear the voice of the preacher inside. Beyond that, I deliberately close my ears: I've been through enough hellfire-and-brimstone when trying to fit in around various communities during my globetrotting days amidst the horrors of the End (religion was one of the most commonly cited justifications for the atrocities perpetrated, but also a major reason for stable communities to form in the first place), and I'm just glad that the walls of that building are thick enough for me to be able to ignore the individual words being said. The tone was quite enough for me to get the general idea even if the raw emotional impact wasn't. The fact that these people inside were accepting anyone who'd preach like *that* as their spiritual leader is the final nail in their collective coffin. Except for the children, of course.

As I'm pulling up my buckethead's internal displays and fiddling with the combat HUD, telling it who I wanted "painted in" with what colors, so I could tell without much conscious thought who was an enemy (bright red, for all adults with weapons), who was a "maybe" (dull orange, mostly for the kids with guns and anybody adult and un-weaponed), and who was a "friendly" (soft baby blue for the kids in chains), that's when I feel it. It's a wave, a shuddering that rocks through the entire city of Dis, and for a moment, despite everything I told Mackenzie Carlscrown about the construction of Sunflower City (was that really eight hours ago?), I think that I'm at the epicenter of an earthquake.

Then I realized that it's Scintillant Camor.

Back when he talked to me, tried to help me, and ended up awakening the stuff that's made my life so very interesting these days (though I suppose the latent versions of those abilities have been with me for most of my life), I got to know the purple-furred fox-thing pretty well.

254

That's not really saying a lot, considering what he does for people, but I think I noticed stuff that others missed. One of which was the core of razor wire he's got under all that fluff.

Since I'm an empath-in-training, I can feel what he's doing clearly, and it drives me to my knees, and then to all-fours as the weight of power starts to build. The thought of using empathy as a weapon had never occurred to me before this point, and it shocks me, horrifies me...and yet it also makes perfect sense. I don't know what Mister Camor is doing down here, but if he can feel even a fraction of what I do about this place, about these people (and I'm not kidding myself: he can feel so very much more), he's well within his rights to massacre them all.

Even the children.

Even me.

No way I've got a basis for being self-righteous here: I was just about to start killing as many people down here as I could justify, and the only reason I wasn't going to use any psionics is because I'm nowhere near strong or controlled enough to pull it off. Mister Camor, though, he's got the power to wipe this place from the face of reality, snuffing out every living soul within the city at his whim. I knew that when I first met him and shook his hand and looked into those pretty purple eyes of his and saw someone who could understand the sort of loss I'd experienced.

When you've travelled long enough through Hell, you start to recognize the signs of your fellow travelers. Of course, you also start to recognize the permanent residents, which is why I and Mister Camor had come to the same conclusion about what ought to happen down here. He was just going to be more efficient about it than me.

Inside the big church building, the preacher's voice raised high and higher, a mockery to Heaven itself, and I look up even as I feel my nose starting to bleed, and know I'm going to die first because I'm not being protected, temporarily anyway, by the waves of emotional darkness that man in there is throwing out, and I'm okay with that because it means I won't have to kill everyone myself: it's all taken out of my hands. That knowledge brings me peace.

And then, suddenly, unremarked by anyone except myself, the pressure stops building, and then recedes.

Mister Camor had decided to spare this city.

Well, I haven't!

Getting back to my feet, I give a soft sniff, and my buckethead's internal systems promptly clean away the blood that had been leaking from nose and ears and eyes. Probably for the best that Mister Camor's backed down on using the "nuclear option": means the kids have a chance to make it out, at least. Unfortunately, that also means I'm the only one available to fix this problem.

Now is my last chance to check my tools. I clench my fists, and I feel the hum as my bolt-casters power up, turning slowly as I run a test of their systems, each turn-and-test accompanied by a soft click. I reach down to my sticky-stick, just for another test, and instantly it leaps up into my hand, the auto-holster working fantastically well as always. Then I pull off my pack and find a handy place nearby to stow it, in a little alley between two buildings, well out of the line of fire. But before I tuck it away, I make sure to retrieve my last empty stasis tube: I've got plans for that chunky thing, and I'm about to void its warranty.

The sermon's winding down now, and I'm starting to feel some doubts. But then I hear the clank of chains, heavy and cruel, as the children are marched toward the big front doors of the place, the first forced to leave, and I just close my eyes for a moment as those doors creak open, nice and slow, and I know in my heart that this is my best and only chance. Somebody has to do something, right now, or those kids are going to be taken off to a fate worse than death. That much I know for certain, whether that fate is to end up as child soldiers or slaves or...no, better not to let my mind go into what I know always happens to children in the clutches of truly evil adults.

It was worse than I'd imagined. So much worse now that I can feel the oily shadows of the community with the empathy Mister Camor awakened in me and know what it means. And worse still than I really *could* imagine, because to do so would mean sending my mind to a very bad place, and maybe never coming back. I'm already close to a breakdown after the emotional rollercoaster I've been riding today, to say nothing of physical strains, and I don't have a whole lot left to give. But what I've got, I *will* give. All of it.

Anything to make the guilt and the fear just go away.

Still, me being me, I know that whatever I do, I am going to mess it up royally, mostly because I'm a screwup by nature: any successes I have are flukes or acts of direct divine intervention, and I know it. But there's nobody else available, and my conscience is working overtime, as per usual. When the only memories you've got left are the awful ones, where you were an awful person who did awful things and thought awful thoughts or were too selfish and cowardly to do anything at all, there's a lot of incentive to try, oh-so-desperately, to make up for your sins. And I have so many sins.

After all of this is done, I'm going to go back to my safe, secure home with the baby opossum and my load of snakes, far, far away from people, and I'm going to cuddle with the dogs and cats and rats and bats and horses and sloths and elephants and snakes and nurse sharks and Utahraptors, and then I'm going to curl up in a ball under the covers in my bed and just be completely alone for a while. Just until I don't hurt so much inside, or the peacekeepers decide that I need to go with them on murder charges for what I'm going to do down here, or assault charges for what I did up top. Whichever comes first.

Right now, though, I've got a job to do.

CHAPTER 16: KEEPING THE PEACE

Location: Earth, Sunflower City, Street-
level outside Central Spire
Perspective: Sergeant Benjuro Clee

"Hey, Billy," chirped Sergeant Benjuro Clee into one of the hard light screens surrounding her, this one containing the face of the boy she'd rescued earlier that day. "How's it hanging?"

"Semi-prehensile, same as always," the incredulous kid replied immediately. "How can you be so cheerful all the time, Sergeant Clee? You've been out on the streets all day, the news says there's hail and worse weather starting to hit hard, and there's a riot in progress!"

"These things tend to cancel each other out, Billy," laughed the space dragon, motioning to the sky. "A proper mobbing relies on nice weather to keep up its momentum, so I expect most of the crowd converging on our position will give up in the near future, once they find out we're serious about holding the line. After all, most of them are just here because of complaints they have with the way the interim government is running things, and they can get those noticed much more quickly by filling out a form in the comfort of their homes. As for me, I love my job! I get to meet all sorts of new and interesting people, and then do my best to help them. That's how I met you, after all."

"Well, uh," the kid stammered, his cheeks visibly coloring, "yeah, thanks for that. Thanks for letting me crash at your place, too. But just until I can get a place of my own!"

"Not a problem," Sergeant Benjuro replied with a shrug that did a variety of interesting things to the flexible mesh of her stat suit in its non-rigid mode. "I only need a fraction of the sleep you humans do, and I still feel like a tourist around Sunflower City, so walking my beat is the same as being on vacation. The novelty will wear off in an Earth month or two, of course, but with City Central making filling out reports so easy, I'm not likely to lose my enthusiasm and joie de vivre for years to come."

"You're actually serious," Billy deadpanned, blinking. "You actually like Earth."

"I like meeting people and getting to help them," she clarified. "And I like Sunflower City. Speaking of which, have you finished that homework assignment I gave you? About where you came from?"

"You mean helping that computer lady fill out a map and the full story about that place underground where they're keeping kids?" Billy growled, fury at the injustice he'd suffered showing clearly on his young face, an honest emotion that felt so clean after all the time he'd been forced to hide everything for fear of his life, his tail (an unfortunate side-effect of puberty) included. "Yeah, I'm all done with that. Do you want to come and pick that up or something? I'll do anything it takes to help you stop the Preacher Man from...." He trailed off, his ability to express what he'd seen, what he'd experienced, what he'd almost been a part of if his mutation hadn't been discovered, and his humiliation at the circumstances under which his tail *had* been discovered more than his young body was capable of enduring just then.

"City Central's already shared it with me, hon," Benjuro assured the boy with a comforting smile. "Handy effect of instant communications and rapid-fire permission form completion. You just rest up for now, maybe try out some of the functions of the Link system and stay hunkered up safe indoors: it's not really fit for anybody out here right now. Once this bit is all finished, we'll get to the next steps in getting you somewhere more permanent than a peacekeeper's apartment-ow!"

"Sergeant Clee!" Billy exclaimed.

"No worries, Billy," Sergeant Benjuro reassured him, rubbing the spot above one eye where a chunk of rock had bounced off moments before, then giving the teenage boy who'd thrown it a glare so searing, he promptly dropped the hunk of brick he'd been gripping in his other hand and fled back toward the ranks of the protestors as fast as he could across the clickways. "But I'm going to need to focus on my job right now. I'll see you at the end of my shift. Bye!" She let that screen vanish and, looking mildly peeved, turned toward the little cluster of humans around her, each of them sporting the uniform of a deputized peacekeeper. "Now, what *is* it with you humans and brickbats?"

"Longstanding tradition, ma'am," replied the most sizable of the deputies, a barrel-bodied man with a masterful set of well-groomed whiskers. "It's not a proper riot unless someone starts tearing up the local pavement for ammunition. Why, I'd feel downright insulted if there wasn't a hail of masonry to accompany a public hue and cry."

"We're just lucky the clickways are luminous pressed molecular diamond glass," muttered the dragon almost under her breath before turning her full attention to the mustached man. "Deputy Gaunt," Sergeant Benjuro acknowledged the man, before blinking as she looked him up and down in earnest. "You and your positively magnificent moustache will take charge as my lance deputy and get our little group organized into defensive lines. Is that acceptable?"

"Yes, ma'am," was the prompt reply, while the newly appointed lance deputy (and his moustache) bristled with pride before he rounded on the short double score of gathered deputies. "Come on, you lot, you heard the sergeant! Let's get a perimeter set up!"

There weren't many of them, of course. Only thirty-seven individuals made up the entirety of the peacekeeping force on Earth, and the only one fully trained at the job in that district of the City was also incidentally the only one of them who wasn't human. The other three fully trained peacekeepers had their assorted appendages full keeping the situation buttoned down in the rest of the city, bereft even of Sergeant Clee's level of deputized aid.

The thirty-three humans gathered there weren't completely without experience or preparation, thankfully, each of them having been selected, though not fully interviewed and assisted, by Scintillant Camor (with the strong advice of Sergeant Benjuro Clee, of course, acting in her capacity as official liaison with the Ministry of Peace), but even as survivors of the End, facing down four separate slowly converging masses of angry-looking people, some waving signs, others brandishing weapons both makeshift and professional, was more than a little bit daunting. More daunting still was the harsh reality that the only defense they had against the overwhelming numbers of that crowd were the badges they'd been handed by Sergeant Benjuro after they'd responded to City Central's alert that they were needed for duty, and a motley collection of riot shields of various makes and models, castoffs from the police forces of a hundred different dead nations.

Crouching slightly to make the most use of the makeshift cover (little good it did to his sheer immensity!), Lance Deputy Gaunt set his matte black shield against the friction of the clickway at his feet, fixing his steely gaze through its eye slits. Next to him, a rail-thin, freckled redhead made her best Clint Eastwood impression through the clear plastic riot shield she was holding, finding it almost as inadequate as Gaunt's own.

"Fun times ahead," she chuckled humorlessly.

"If your idea of fun involves Molotov cocktails," agreed Gaunt, before he glanced at the woman. "Your name is Bramy Wolfe, isn't it? How does one get a name like that?"

"Think I'd tell you?" she scoffed. "And especially a Limey? Not a chance!"

"Kiwi, actually; and you're a Yank," affirmed the Lance Deputy. "At this point, though, I don't think our backgrounds matter anymore."

Glass shattered against Deputy Wolfe's upraised shield, her squint-eyed, sunburned glare flinching only slightly at the assault before she and Gaunt started breathing again: it was just an empty bottle, not one filled with any of the many flammable or explosive materials that it could have held.

"Guess not," she finally agreed. "Formerly of the Wily County Fire Brigade, Dogcrotch Georgia."

"London Metropolitan Police," Gaunt growled out of the corner of his mustached mouth, grunting softly as an especially large chunk of hail shattered against his blue helmet. "Formerly of the New Zealand Police before...well."

He shrugged, giving Wolfe a look, which she returned with a knowing nod: of course, she understood. They'd all endured years of the End, struggling desperately to hold civilization together while all around them the citizens they'd sworn to protect strove most diligently to tear that civilization to shreds. New Zealand and Australia had avoided the initial exchanges of chemical weapons and the first crude weaponized teratogens, but Australia's arid outback had ended up being the proving grounds for the most successful monster-making operations backed by various world governments.

Everybody knew about these secret operations now, of course, after the monsters had proved impossible to contain, some so hardy they made their way across the waters to New Zealand and points further north. Just like everybody now knew that the United States and Russia and China had done the same out in their rural regions, as a way of testing the effectiveness of their Frankensteinian creations on isolated populations under what were supposed to be controlled conditions. The monsters had been meant to terrorize civilian populations, making them fearful and compliant, more eager to accept the domination of the governments that would, theoretically, protect them from such threats. Naturally, as was typically the case with such projects, the monsters had soon proved far

265

better made than their creators had ever expected, breaking free by the trainload to wreak havoc on nations already on the edge of collapse.

Shared horrors united the two human deputies. Unconsciously, they drew together a little more tightly, until their shields pressed against each other, forming a firm defensive bulwark. As their shields locked, so did everyone else's all along the line.

Behind that line, Sergeant Benjuro had another glowing projection before her pointed snout. From the circle of hard light came the sounds of blaster fire and bullets, interspersed with grunts both feminine and masculine, and the occasional near-human scream or shrill squeal of the completely inhuman as they fell before the weapons of Susan Six and Trinidad Del Toro.

"Hello there, Susan Six," she greeted in her usual chirpy tones. "I hope I haven't caught you at a bad time."

"No time like the present," the blonde woman chuckled, right before her body lunged forward, and something offscreen splattered glowing blue ichor across her cheek with a hiss like a steam kettle, the forcefield surrounding her head immediately causing the goo to drip away. "You wouldn't interrupt unless it was important. But we're just finishing off the last of these cordy creeps, anyway." She looked over at what was presumably Trinidad, nodding in satisfaction at the cries of battle and multiple loud crunches that could be heard. "He's fun to work with."

"Oh, you found Al's notes!" Benjuro exclaimed, clapping her talons while her tail waved happily. "I'd hoped you'd find that file in the data load I gave you."

"Big rule of bounty hunting," Susan Six said with a grin. "Always check the mission data logs. Right after the rule to always maintain your own weapons." Then she shook her head, her expression making it clear how impressed she was. "That little guy has got some ridiculously detailed write-ups on everything we've encountered down here. Of course, the map notes attached are already outdated – I don't know why he bothered in the first place with the city's planarian engines shuffling things around down here all the time – but he gave some pretty handy descriptions of the telltales for when you're entering something's territory. Helped us know to bring out the flashbangs to drive off the morlock hordes, and to watch for fuzzy stuff on the ceiling."

"That was the, what was it, cordy creeps?" asked Benjuro, honestly interested.

"Yeah," Susan Six affirmed. "Product of a mutated variety of Cordyceps militaris. It's this fungus that infects bugs, then hijacks their bodies as a framework for growing more of itself. Except this sort takes the buggy form and runs with it, literally. Basically, it means that we've been fighting human-sized daddy longlegs and centipedes for the last fifteen minutes." Her grin grew wider. "Fun times!"

"Glad that you're enjoying yourself," Benjuro chuckled. "But I think I might be able to help you with the lack of accurate maps. Someone made it out of the place where I'm sure our friend Al is heading, knowing his predilection for finding the worst available source of trouble, and they've given a fairly detailed description of their route to City Central, which has recreated it in visual form. While it won't stay current for more than a few days, that should be enough for your purposes. I'm sending the data stream to you right now."

"Got it," said Susan Six a moment later, before blinking. "Wow. That's...yeah, that's helpful, all right. Surprisingly big place. And close, too, if we don't run into too many distractions."

"I know what you mean," Benjuro commiserated. "You overlook a problem for just a little while and end up having to do extensive fumigation later."

"That's what I'm paid for," laughed the bounty hunter, before she shook her head disbelievingly. "And yeah, you were right: merging his signal with this map, it turns out our guy's already right in the middle of that place. If it's the hotbed of revolution that we think it is, he's gotta be in some serious trouble by now. I just hope we can- "

"Little help here, Susan!" came Trinidad's voice, sounding a bit stressed, before some truly hideous sloshing, gargling sounds drowned out his voice entirely.

"Gotta run!" Susan Six exclaimed. "Ooh, that's a new one! And here it is in the Man's guide! Looks like it's a..."

Then the screen before Sergeant Benjuro's eyes shattered into a cascade of motes that showered to the ground at her feet. Giving a light snort as she brushed one of the swiftly fading motes from the bridge of her snout, then shrugging, she turned her attention back to the situation at hand.

The situation, as it turned out, was grim.

Shields locked together, the peacekeeper deputies had clenched jaws and tensed bodies, while the sounds of the occasional pistol shot spanged off their defensive line. Nobody had tried to take a shot at the towering dragon-lady yet, most likely because the mist and the hail reduced visibility too much, but she could see that it was only a matter of time. Her gleaming eyes swept across the different ranks of the humans advancing on their position before the steps of Spire Nine, or Central Spire, the big building that had proved to be central to so many events that day.

"That," she said with sudden but absolute finality, gently shouldering her way past the line of defending deputies.

"Is," she continued, her stat suit instantly hardening into rigid plates, a brief shimmer around her head marking the activation of her otherwise invisible helmet-screen, while her wings flared wide.

"Enough!"

With that final word, radiance streamed from her outstretched wings, a wave of raw force that sent the foremost and most aggressive of the human mob tumbling, while the rest came to a sudden and complete stop, eyes wide and watching. The deputies around the towering dragon were bathed in golden light, and under the protective field being projected from their sergeant's wings, the hail slid harmlessly to either side and the mist parted, leaving them warm and dry while all around was cold and wet and miserable.

"I don't like to raise my voice," Sergeant Benjuro said, her tones now calm, but also irresistibly firm, the voice of a mother whose wrath has been roused by especially recalcitrant offspring. "But you have endangered the lives of my deputies. Many of you seem to believe that this is a combat zone, you versus the forces of...John Law, I believe is the term. Or 'the Man.' The forces of oppression. You are wrong. For my deputies, this is supposed to be a training exercise, to give them a proper taste of what it means to be a peacekeeper. For some of you, this is a misguided attempt to get attention drawn to your grievances, whatever those might be. For others, you are here to start a riot, an attempt to keep the forces of justice bogged down while your allies keep a good person hostage, and then to make your demands after you seize control of our temporary center of government. All involved groups decided that now was a perfect time for such insurrection, since we haven't finished the process of setting up a local representative government, which sadly includes a lack of fully trained peacekeeper forces.

"Before we continue, I want you to know this: peacekeepers are *not* police!" With this statement, the dragon's nostrils flared, spouting great gouts of steam from the furnace churning inside her belly, a heat haze distorting the air before the little knot of deputies. "We are public servants, and our job is to do just what our title suggests: we keep the public peace. If a fire starts, we fight it. If any natural disaster threatens, we rush to the rescue. If your beloved pet is stuck in a tree, we climb up to get it. If someone goes missing, we find them. If people try to hurt each other, we stop them. That is the beginning and end of our job! *We keep the peace!*"

Then Benjuro's golden eyes turned sad.

"Too many of you come from places where the agents of your government, local or general, were there to ensure you stayed frightened and oppressed. I understand that you need some time to learn that the situation has now changed. Of course, there will be an adjustment period: we're right in the middle of interesting times while we try and get Sunflower City up and running properly. We would be farther along, in fact, if a faction among you hadn't kidnapped the only person here with full authority to act in the name of the Republic. Some among you are responsible for taking Scintillant Camor!

"Whoever you are, you are the reason that public works are slowed, that a full representative government hasn't been implemented yet, and that this planet is still on probation, with the rest of the Republic watching from afar. Scintillant Camor believed in you, in your species, in your planet. Knowing him, even in captivity, with the ones who stole him doing who-knows-what to him while he's in their power, I think he believes in you still, and believes that you can become so much more. That's why we built this city for you. That's why I'm here to serve you to the best of my ability, and all my deputies as well."

The dragon's long-fingered talons spread to indicate the stalwart little band huddled around her, only the tallest of them reaching the height of her chest as she stood fully erect. Then her talons lowered, and she swept her gaze across the massed crowd. A low murmur rose from the edges of the mob as they saw the immense, well-armored cicada-like robots come crawling over the rails of the broad clickway on which they stood and realized that they were surrounded. They'd been surrounded all along!

"Now stay where you are, and we'll soon see which of you even need to be here," Sergeant Benjuro Clee concluded, drawing up a cluster of hard light constructs like playing cards, then dealing them out with rapid-fire precision. The glowing circles rushed to their intended recipients in a flash, popping up and displaying messages. Some of the screens showed videos. Others piped up with audio only. Still others were just text. And as the people in the crowd received the information being shared, they began to break up, to disperse.

"What was in those things?" asked Bramy Wolfe, mouth gaping in astonishment – and she was hardly the only one!

"Odds and ends," her commanding officer replied with a cheery grin that made her scaly cheeks dimple, quite spoiling the intimidating presence she'd been presenting before. "For some, they're pieces of useful information, things they didn't know that invalidate their reasons for being here in the first place or calls from loved ones needing them at home. But for most, they're official complaint forms, allowing them to file grievances with City Central for review. Some of those grievances are legitimate and potentially very complicated, by the way," she added. "Take the complaint by the Catholic community about the Republic's fertility management requirements: that's going to take word from on high to resolve, an issue made even more sticky by the harsh fact that after the End they don't have either Pope or Patriarch anymore, or even enough Cardinals to elect new ones. Or the concern by numerous ethnic groups that the neighborhoods where they live are being subjected to discrimination by their fellow humans. Goodness! The typical Republic citizen couldn't tell the difference between all but the most obvious of your racial differences! We're going to need experts from your own species to help us sort that whole mess out, and finding experts who don't have their own biases..."

Deputy Wolfe whistled, shaking her head in understanding.

"Yeah," Benjuro sighed. "But there *are* forms for that sort of thing, and City Central really does want to help. So do I, naturally, or I wouldn't wear the uniform and carry the badge. And so, I expect, do all of you. At least the ones that will be staying on after today, of course. That's why the crowds are clearing up: the weather is miserable, they can't push us around, and the immediate need to draw attention to their various plights has been removed. So, they're withdrawing for the time being, to give us a chance."

"To prove that we have the right to be the ones running the show," said Lance Deputy Gaunt.

"Exactly," agreed the gold-and-green darishi, her gemlike eyes sparkling. "Which leaves," she extended a talon toward the much reduced yet still significant crowd of humans milling before them, "them."

Turning their attention from their commanding officer to the remaining people standing on the softly glowing clickway plaza, even the most inexperienced of the deputies could see that these weren't mere protestors: every one of them was holding a weapon openly now that the "civilians" were out of the area; no public relations scandal to worry about now. Some of their faces were grim. Others had confident smirks. A few were even giggling in anticipation of the violence to come. These men and women were an armed force of revolutionaries, soldiers not just willing but eager to kill for their cause.

"These," Benjuro said with a long sigh, "are prime examples of why we of the Republic don't allow simoniacs, or paid clergy. The practice encourages turning religion, a good, natural, wholesome part of any functional, healthy society, into a tool for the mongers of power and hate. Isn't that right, Pastors Jones and Kaschak; Preacher Simmons; Fathers Guinness and Gutierrez; Doctor Olowe?"

"You can't speak to us that way, you scaly hell spawn!" screamed one of the addressed people, one of only a few that wasn't carrying a weapon openly, standing close to the rear of the group. "You don't have any right to dictate on matters relating to the souls of our flocks!"

"Neither do you, Elias Kay Simmons," Benjuro replied mildly, letting City Central carry her words, even at that conversational tone, to every ear that mattered. "How many of the poor and ignorant have you rendered penniless with your eagerness to slurp up every last coin they had to offer, believing you when you told them that it would somehow negate any debt they might have had in the coffers of Heaven, besides pouring out blessings in their trials on Earth? And don't you *dare* to smirk, Emmanuel Jones! With how many women – and girls, I am ashamed to admit – have you had illicit sex? Or you, Sophia Maria Olowe: how much pomp and circumstance did you demand from your followers, having them carry you like a barbarian potentate on a gilded palanquin to and from your pulpit, while driving about in a vehicle whose cost would have fed and housed and educated the poorest families within your congregation?"

She folded her arms.

"Money, politics, and religion have no place in the same sphere of influence, and yet you all seem determined to have them engaged in flagrant ménage à trois! Now go home and sign up for classes in a respectable trade so that you can become actually useful to society."

"Attack!" came the cry, this from a figure almost at the very vanguard of the small army, sweat glistening from her brow as she raised her weapon, an automatic shotgun, high. "For God and glory!"

"This is your idea of a training exercise?" asked Gaunt incredulously as he and the entire cluster of deputy peacekeepers raised their shields once more, watching as guns and bombs and even more primitive weapons – swords and machetes and sickles and pitchforks – were raised against them. "Dear Sergeant Benjuro, far be it from me to express any doubt in your methods, but surely you could have found a somewhat more...stable situation for teaching us our new profession?"

"Or maybe given us some cool armor like yours?" groused Deputy Wolfe.

"Oh, this is the best sort of situation!" exclaimed the dragon-woman with a laugh like clinking copper coins. "I was just watching to see how each of you react in what you believe to be a potentially lethal crisis. You've all done wonderfully well by the way, and if you take the badge officially, I'll be happy to call you my fellow peacekeepers once you've completed your training regimens on the Link. But for now, yes, I do agree that this has gone on far enough. Spotbots, do your duty!"

While Sergeant Benjuro had been talking (and likely the primary reason why she'd been talking at all with people who obviously weren't ready to listen), four of the minivan-sized, bug-like robots had positioned themselves at each rough corner of the mob, angled slightly so as not to be facing directly at each other. While the general shape of their chassis, and especially the bulbous "eyes" on their heads (covering a powerful sensor suite), were highly reminiscent of a cicada made of brightly shining brass clockwork, the backs of the spotbots lacked wings. Instead, there were the seams of ailerons, which suddenly popped up at Benjuro's command. Instantly, each of the four spotbots extended a device that looked somewhat like an oversized electronic bullhorn dusted in a bright metallic blue coating.

Then the spotbots opened fire.

"The rill are the first sapient species recorded as creating robots designed for lethal combat," Sergeant Benjuro said in her usual cheerful tone of voice, even as all around the plaza the armed members of the mob began to fall down, some throwing up all over themselves or others, others crying out as they clapped hands over their ears, and some simply passing quietly from consciousness. "Like your nuclear arms race, it was the big conflict where they nearly wiped themselves out in planetwide destruction. They were only saved because some of their most advanced electronic brains spontaneously awoke to peoplehood and started asking their creators some rather troubling questions, like 'Why are you making us hurt people?'

"During the councils to establish the basic laws of the Republic, the rill shared their perspective on the subject, and it was decided that if killing had to be done, it should be done by people at the trigger, not a machine." She flicked a claw casually toward the suddenly prostrate masses now sprawled around the plaza. "But there's no restrictions on using nonlethal weapons, like these sonic disruptors. The setting the spotbots are using is specially tuned to throw off the inner ears of humans, though they can be adjusted to affect a wide range of creatures."

The dragon-woman smiled as she looked toward the horizon, where the red blaze of the setting sun was visible at last. Lowering her wings, the soft glow that had been protecting the deputies faded gradually, letting their helmets clink with the last few hailstones dropping out of the rapidly clearing skies.

"Come on," she called out to her fellow peacekeepers, grinning brightly over her shoulder. "I'll show you how to fill out the forms for incidents and arrests. Welcome to the peacekeepers!"

Gaunt and Wolfe traded another look.

"We're right in the thick of it, huh?" said the freckle-faced redhead.

"Too right," agreed the man with the magnificent moustache.

CHAPTER 17: SCINTILLANT CAMOR SAVES

Location: Earth, Sunflower City, Dis
Perspective: Scintillant Camor

Almost always, when I work someone through their pain, the first reaction to come out is recrimination.

"My parents are to blame!"

"Society is to blame!"

"Bad luck is to blame!"

"Life is to blame!"

"God is to blame!"

This recrimination is the first layer, the topmost dross. These reasons, these recriminations, this shifting of blame, all of them are only there to cover the cruelest truth.

You are to blame.

That truth is our reason for covering it up, for spreading blame around as much as possible. If we – and I do include myself in the same category as everyone else – were to face this truth immediately, without prior preparation, it would shatter us. To bear the full weight of responsibility for what we make of ourselves...no, it's too much. It's too much for anyone.

But that's why I'm here: to give the strength, the encouragement, the reassurance needed to help the sufferer through the first layer, and into the second.

It's not the last layer, though. No, not by far.

"It's all the Republic," John tells me, sullen, glaring down at the floor as he sits on his metal folding chair, resting his elbows on its reversed back. "That's the root of what went wrong for me. I mean, look at their name! How *dare* they call themselves a republic? *We* were a republic!" His heavy fists clench. "Right up until they ruined everything."

He was a dentist. He had a happy family, a wife and a son and maybe a daughter on the way. They lived on Earth, and they were happy. Business was good. Money was excellent. He left home every day, sometimes to work, sometimes to play his favorite sport, "golf" (whatever that was); his wife stayed home and tended house every day; his son went to school and spent time with his friends, his clubs, his sports, every day. A positive routine. Boring, but it was safe, and they were happy.

Then came the first glimpses of trouble on the news. While he didn't think of them at the time – they were so insignificant, all about stuff literally light years from Earth, that they only tickled the back of his subconscious – there were reports from the outer systems, from the edge of their great empire.

"And why shouldn't we have been an empire?" he queried, glaring at me. "We were united for the first time ever! The whole damn planet! Everybody got to vote, and everybody got to be a full citizen. Business was booming! The economy was fantastic! Unemployment was the lowest it had ever been in...well, *ever*! Science advanced by leaps, by bounds, and our brave explorers and military forces were always pressing on to a bold new frontier! God was on our side, and we could throw all the chops we needed to prove it!"

He didn't say anything about the people on the edges of that empire, the people who weren't human, and therefore weren't people. He also didn't say anything about the underclasses among humanity, the forgotten ones, the ones left out and quietly shuffled aside. They didn't slip his memory: they just weren't in his conscious thoughts. Nobody thought about the prosperity that their suffering, far away, where no news crew ever bothered to go, had brought about. Only the worst bleeding-heart types even mentioned them, but of course it was only a way to bring in votes or stir up pointless controversy, so who cared what they had to say?

"The first time I realized that something was about to change was at the arrival of the first delegation of official representatives from that so-called Republic," John explained. "Led by some big bushy tree-thing that called itself Towering Canopy. I was doing a root canal that day, the news playing in the lobby, and I just sort of overheard it. Not like it really mattered much: we'd been seeing the pee-gees all the time on the news ever since my parents were kids. Never anything big or important. They were just kind of there, a presence that mostly kept to itself and stayed out of our way. We all guessed they feared us," he added with a hopeful half-smirk in my direction.

"When you got home, you learned that the delegation meant something more important than you'd initially thought," I prompted him. "Your wife was watching?"

"Yeah," he growled, low and dark, the memory making his entire body clench with the force of the emotions it evoked. "She was telling me how that ugly tree-bush-thing was there with gifts. Mostly it was just advice, information, so at first, I wasn't listening to what she was saying. She was just droning on about how these pee-gee clowns were giving away free advice on how to improve efficiency and minimize waste, how to implement robots, how to build and arrange cities, how to make efficient food production, how to enhance our quality of medical care. All hippie crap, but that last one got my attention, and onto the internet I got while I still could. Turned out it was just a false alarm: I mean, who gives away anything for free? Naturally the government people didn't buy it for a moment."

"Then," I added, letting the word hang in the air for a long, long moment.

"Then," he continued with a forced sigh. "They were just probing us out, trying to find a handle where they could grab and crank us. They wanted us to quit expanding to new worlds."

We wanted you to stop invading other people's planets.

"They wanted us to give up the greatest economic prosperity we'd ever had in the history of forever!"

We wanted you to free the people you'd enslaved.

"They wanted us to cut our military down to nothin'!"

We wanted you to stop killing people and taking their resources.

"And then they wanted us to start using their weird, new age, spacey crap," he concluded with a contemptuous curl of his lip. "Well, the government people didn't buy into stopping growth, exploration, military power, or the economy..."

"But they did buy into free stuff."

"Yeah," and the word was a long, slow sigh, the sound of old memories from a past you wished you could forget.

"Medical stuff first," John told me, shaking his head, not meeting my eyes. "Part of the first wave of imported developments? This treatment that worked with the germs in your mouth, turning them into symbiotes instead of invaders, so they started helping to build up your teeth and gums instead of breaking them down.

"And just like that, I was out of a job."

The words hung in the air.

"That's," he began, and then he choked up. Waiting a moment, I watched his whole big butcher's body trembling as he fought for control, and eventually gained it. "That's when everything went to Hell."

When the first time that he hit his wife was, he couldn't remember. Didn't want to remember. How often, he wanted to remember even less. After he'd lost his job, he'd been so angry, so frustrated, so in need of some sort of comfort, and all she had for him was her constant nagging, making everything out to be his fault. And his boy...

"Kid was never home after that point," he told me, and our eyes met. "I loved the kid to death, and I was so scared, and the whole world – the whole universe! – was falling apart, and we needed to stick together so bad, and..."

"And none of you could quite reach each other," I said, my voice soft. "There was a great gulf that had opened up between you, separating you, imprisoning you each in your own small, ever-shrinking worlds."

"That's probably why she left," John said, continuing the thought I'd started for him. "Just...too much distance grown, and all of it apart. I think she took the kid with her; I don't know. Never saw either of them again. Don't even know if they're alive or not."

Now I caught his eyes, held them as I felt out the imprint that those lives had left on him. Then I sought outward for them, for the faint glimmerings of personalities that matched in some recognizable way.

"They're still alive," I told him when I knew for certain. "I don't know where, and I don't know their present state, but they're both somewhere on this planet."

"I...I don't wanna see 'em again, though," he forced out, breaking his eyes away from mine. "Not after...naw." He stood silently for a moment, then launched back into his tirade as if he were trying to run away from his thoughts. "All the big corporations and the government and everybody tried so hard to slap a price tag on all the new technology, but the pee-gees were just *giving it all away*. Anybody who wanted it could have it, all of it, if they could just find a Republic supplier. Stuff that made *everything* that Earth and its people had accomplished, had worked and bled and died for over so many countless thousands of years...pointless.

"So, everybody started to fight over the changes that were coming," John explained. "The pee-gees, they said it was because they wanted us to not need to expand and conquer anymore. They said they wanted to buy off the planets we'd taken."

We were paying a blood price for the slaves being forced to produce cheap products for the people of Earth, to take Earth's heavy industry, to shoulder as much of the burden of Earth's most hazardous professions as was possible. And when it wasn't possible to have them perform those tasks on their home planets, then the people of Earth would kidnap them and move them to where they could be best exploited. Teach humanity how to make robots to fill the same role, how to take heavy industry into zero-gravity, to find the best asteroids for mining? A small price indeed, compared to what was gained.

"Guess you pee-gees should've expected what came next," he added with a sneer. "When some nutjob gunned down that Towering Canopy guy."

When a well-equipped Imperial sniper tried to murder a pacifist, one of the kindest, most gentle beings I have ever had the privilege to know and call my colleague and my friend. As much as the representatives of the United Earth Empire tried to cover it up, to play it off as the work of a lone shooter, and then as a rogue terrorist organization, and then as common criminals made upset at the losses to their profits we'd inflicted, their efforts were amateurish at best: the entire attempted assassination had been planned and implemented and authorized at the very highest levels. A short, casual conversation between a key individual in their government and one of our Expert-level telepaths, with another two to confirm the results of the first, was all it took to reveal the truth, to say nothing of the overwhelming burden of physical evidence the messy idiots had left lying around, expecting us to be too naïve and foolish, or perhaps too afraid of a war, to think to see what was right before us.

I thank God that bullets didn't work as well against the Big Tree as they would've against beings of weak flesh like mine! Even so, he was still left in critical condition, the radiation from the depleted uranium rounds used against him requiring special attention to prevent him from being poisoned, and when we had him back in our midst, we realized…

"Everybody realized, after that happened, there was no way there wouldn't be war," John chuckled ruefully. "And why not? We were at our strongest ever. All you pee-gees had ever shown for the last couple centuries was this peace-and-love crap, and we'd mopped the floor with every bug-eyed monster we'd met. Of course, we'd win!"

But you didn't.

"But we didn't," he said, his eyes haunted. "Everybody who knew, they all did their best to cover it up, to keep us civilians from finding out. They couldn't, though. I mean, how do you cover up having the whole entire damn space navy blown to pieces!" He shook his head as though he were trying to shed the past like water. "Hundreds of ours to every one of their ships, and they didn't even get their paint scratched.

"And back down here, the whole world started to fall apart, just like my family. While our soldiers died on alien worlds, far from Earth, Earth stopped being paradise. People started flooding into all our cities, into every town, as they fled the colonies, and just like that, the whole planet started to get crowded. Too crowded. And when we hit a critical mass of people…everything started to split apart."

No non-combatant of the Republic was ever in any danger, and we took pains to communicate this truth. Instead, we tried to give the outer colonies technology that would let them live in homeostasis with their local ecologies, just like we'd tried to do on Earth. We thought (*I* thought),

284

in our idealism, that just removing the need for ecological exploitation or conquest would help humanity accept peace with us, and free the people that they'd enslaved. When our good intentions proved instead to be a highway to Hell, however, and we annihilated every military force that they sent against us, humanity split into two incompatible camps: the minority who decided to accept our offers of union, and the overwhelming majority who chose to flee back to their home world, likely with the intention of regrouping in preparation for rising again later.

Another good intention, with a similar end result.

There was no way I was going to ask John anything about the End.

He told me all about it anyway.

"Our leaders, all of them, political, military, religious, business, from global to local, they all started shooting out noise, and all of it contradictory. On the one hand, they called for peace and cooperation in our 'hour of greatest darkness.' On the other they called everybody else a traitor, subtly at first, but soon without any pretending about politeness. Everybody else had caused us to fall, not them. Everybody denouncing everybody else on the nightly news, revealing all the dirty secrets they'd been hiding for years and years. Saber-rattling as our empire broke up into nations, and then into nation-states, and then into tribes. Diseases that started killing us in the streets, and soon we find out that our own people, all the authority figures we'd trusted at the highest levels, were the ones who had them created and then set loose, trying to unite us with a new crisis. No surprise, then, when they started doing the same with bigger things, monsters made to keep us all too afraid to resist them."

Monsters that in too many cases were made using the knowledge and technology that we'd shared with the people of Earth. That I'd been foolish enough to authorize.

"Murder-suicides and massacres all the time on what was left of the nightly news. Scandal, war, and the only people staying safe were the richest percentage, the ones who could afford the protection to keep what they'd taken. We couldn't even trust the law around our homes. *I* couldn't trust the law, not when I got pulled over because a cop felt surly. I got frisked, my car probed, and then they brought in a K-9 unit. And after it was done, nobody cared, because they thought I was lucky to get off so easy! They'd figured out all sorts of ways to spy on us in our homes, and people were getting dragged off in the night and never heard from again. And that was just the start.

"The first atrocity in my hometown was when the local corner gas station got burned down. The owners were foreigners, after all, so of course they should've known it was coming."

Though the words were unsaid, I felt the confession all the same: I, John Martin, was part of the mob that did it.

All of them, scared. So desperate, they would do *anything* to be free of that fear. Even transfer that fear onto someone else. Even kill.

Anything for relief. Anything to make themselves believe they weren't powerless to stop what was coming next.

As John Martin had said, though: that was just the start.

There is no way for me to describe what he told me next. Not as I was, accepting the whole of his center-self into my own, *feeling* everything that he'd endured, sharing the pain of every memory so clearly that they might as well have been mine, except that I lacked the thoughts to match up with those sensations. Poor John had endured horrors that nobody should ever be forced to face, and somehow, he'd survived, but not without lasting wounds on his deepest, innermost self, a heavy weight of old emotions that he'd tried so hard to bury and forget even existed, but which now came bubbling – *gushing!* – to the surface, breaking through all the old barriers.

All I could do was share the burden.

There is a deeper layer, one more true, purer, that lies past the layer of accepting personal responsibility for the pain of your life. That next layer is the cruelest one, because it can leave you adrift in a universe that no longer makes any sort of rational sense. We build these layers of protective deception about us for exactly that reason: we don't want to lose ourselves.

As I said before, the first layer is to blame others. John realized the lies he'd been telling himself in a sudden start as I told him everything I knew – how I'd been part of the Council Body that had decided to declare war on the United Earth Empire, and why, sharing every intimate detail of that event, and how many of us – myself included – wept at the lives we knew were going to be lost. Human lives, not ours: we knew what would happen, and it cut us to our deepest souls. We'd been watching humanity from afar for so long, standing idle in the hopes that we were wrong in our initial assessment. That's the greatest problem with the Republic: we're so afraid of making mistakes, of leaping to hasty conclusions, that we tend to take a very, very long time before we act.

My dear friend Garfi Lett, the Master of the Ministry of Defense, is a prime example of our thinking: he's slow to anger; he hates fighting and prefers whenever possible to let diplomats do the work that others might leave to soldiers. Once he has gathered irrefutable evidence that fighting is what is required, however, he is *very* good at it. Presented with the evidence of the atrocities of the United Earth Empire, with ecological devastation on a galactic scale, families torn apart by the worst aspects of slavery, new religions forced onto subject peoples intended to make them more compliant, and countless acts of petty cruelty and tyranny, to say nothing of continued expansion with every sign of spreading even more of the same as far into the cosmos as possible – a universe-wide Manifest Destiny of blood and horror! – even poor Garfi had to come to the inevitable conclusion.

With our selves intertwined, John knew that I couldn't lie, no more than he could. Just as I experienced his horrors, he experienced mine. With that sharing we passed the first layer together.

The second layer is to blame yourself. That is only right and just. But justice is pitiless! And justice alone isn't...it isn't really *just*, if you can understand me. And that's because of the third layer of realization.

The third layer is simply this: sometimes bad things aren't anybody's fault. Sometimes they just happen.

Without a firm grounding, this last realization can tear the soul apart. When I met and tried to help the man whose name I can't remember (and whose center-self I feel somewhere nearby, I realize with a start), he had deep scars on his soul left over from where he'd almost been torn to pieces with the savagery of this last, cruel truth.

He'd survived, though, and he'd done it by clinging to the same truth that I now shared with John, reaching out to him and taking his soul in the gentle embrace of my center-self: we are thrust into the fire and plunged into the water to reveal our weaknesses. If we can only survive the refining of fire and water, storm and flood, our weaknesses will be seared away, and all that will remain is *strength*. Immortal. Endless. Forever.

But then we both shuddered together as John relived something far worse. As I held his center-self with my own, he twisted like a serpent, and I felt the sting of a horror that he would never escape fully: he'd done things that were unforgivable. When he'd been lost and adrift in a world that no longer made sense, he'd been found by a man who was also a monster. This man, the Preacher Man, took him in, built him up, and shaped him into the tool that the Preacher Man needed to establish his new order, the great movement that would finally take back the Earth and cleanse it of all sinners, mutants, and aliens, leaving it free for the faithful alone.

There are flashes of faces, of voices, of the people he'd personally hurt in the name of the Greater Good on the orders of the Preacher Man, Arrhenius. They almost escape me as he recoils from the truth, tries to bury it back deep inside, undoing all our progress, but I catch them, hold them, bring their echoes to the fore of this poor man's emotional memories. In heartbeats he relives the first time he used his dentist's drill to deliberately cause pain. The first person he killed with his bare hands (an act of mercy!).

And I am there with him, reaching out, letting him rest his head on my shoulder as he cries and babbles, and I take the weight on myself, take all the burden. No, he hadn't lost all feeling: he'd buried it, tucked it away deep, *deep* inside of himself, where he'd put the person he really was away, up on a shelf to be forgotten; given enough time and neglect, that person might have died forever. Now, I'd reawakened those feelings, and what he feels is the anguish of a damned soul in Hell, someone who has done unspeakable things in the name of a cause...

"No," he sobs. "I did it for me! I did it because I was scared, and I hated being scared, being weak! Being pushed around!"

That doesn't make it right.

"No."

You hurt inside. You hurt with all the pain you inflicted on others. All these years, you've been tearing yourself up inside.

"Yes."

You want to be forgiven, but you're too ashamed to even begin to look for the words to ask.

"Yes."

Ask me.

"Please," John gasps out, his tears matting the fur of my cheek, my shoulder. "Please, forgive me."

That's impossible, John: I can't forgive sins.

He pulls back, horror on his face as he meets my eyes. I hold his gaze, and my center-self reaches out to his, and he knows that I am feeling with him, bearing together what I cannot take away.

Oh, but it's such a weight.

"There is no way to undo what has been done," I tell him, words this time, not just feelings. "But...let me show you something that might help. It's dangerous, but it's the only way I know."

Inside ourselves, he takes my hand, and I guide him upward. Up, and higher still. To the source of all power. To the heart of God.

No, I don't go with him. That would be indecent. Also, too personal for me to understand anyway.

What he experiences in that place beyond places, I don't know, but when he falls back down, I catch him, and I carry him – gently, so gently – back into his body, and I can feel that something has changed inside of him.

Darkness has been made light.

Now his eyes open, and he's wondering, wandering. The great burden of his guilt has been taken, but he's had it for so long, he doesn't know what to do now that he's been healed. There's the question in his eyes as he looks at me.

"Now that you are healed," I tell him, "stop doing what makes you hurt. Fill in your life with something better instead."

"Something better?" he asks, and he's reaching out again, trying to make me into a replacement for the Preacher Man who led him down the dark road. He's a follower by nature, lacking self-direction for so long that he's forgotten how. We'll fix that, of course, given time, now that he's allowed the opportunity to enter him. For now, let's start with something simple: a suggestion of direction, of ultimate goals, to do something he knows is right, but leaving the method to his discretion.

"There are children here, John," I tell him. "They're prisoners. Slaves, whatever your Preacher Man might call them. Given enough time, he's going to do to them what he did to you."

Another flood of impressions hit me, but I'm ready for it; expecting it, all the emotions poor John has been hiding within himself, trying to ignore until now, when I've brought his true self back from the dead. Shock and horror and outrage, of course, all the natural emotions expected from seeing the innocent and the powerless being abused. More guilt as well, from not having acted immediately, but I help him control that, keeping it from crippling him. Guilt is like any other pain: it's there to tell us when something is wrong, so that we can make it right. As right as we can make any of our many, many sins. The most important part of making them right, though, is the trying, however futile it might seem.

Then another impression hits him, a bright light that shines through everything else as he stands up, blinking, wiping tears off his thick, hairy arm.

He knows what he needs to do.

"I'll need help," he says, and then starts to reach for my restraints.

"Yes, Brother John," says a stern, reedy voice from behind John, its owner obscured from my view by his substantial bulk. "You do indeed."

We both feel the shock of cold fear at that voice: the Preacher Man has returned.

CHAPTER 18: THE MAN MAKES A STAND

Location: Earth, Sunflower City, Dis
Perspective: The Man

As I felt the waves of emotional energy radiating off Dis, this little Hell-city, this place for the damned and the dammed, people who refused to give up the darkness, the bigotry, the hate that nearly exterminated our species, the seed of killing determination took deep root in my guts. Some of those reviewing my thought-journals later might ask why I did what I am about to do. The answer is a fairly simple one.

Here, in this awful place with a searing red artificial sun blazing overhead like the furnaces of Hell itself, my gut tells me that what I'm about to do is the right thing. Thinking over my actions later, I can analyze that split-second decision in much more detail, calling up and reviewing all the little observations I picked up and reviewed subliminally while I made up my mind, fixing my will like steel on the bloodshed I was about to enact. I knew that the people who were living here were an incarnation of the mob, an embodiment of the deliberate Evil (and I use the capitalization on purpose) that we humans regularly embrace, given physical form in the shape of a city. This city. The city of Dis. They were determined to tear down the bright and shining city above us, Sunflower City, not because they thought that it was evil, or Evil, or even just bad, but because it was better than them, the embodiment of a way of life that had nothing to do with the monstrosity they'd allowed into their hearts until they'd become monsters themselves. A place where they had no place.

So, I was going to stop them because they were monsters who were doing their best to make everyone as miserable as they are. Later, if they succeeded, they'd dress it up as some sort of crusader's holy war, but it's really just the crabs-in-a-bucket effect backed up with guns.

Well, all of that, and because they were abusing children. Seriously, some of those kids in the chain gang couldn't have been more than six! While I'm nowhere as good at empathy as a Gentle One like Scintillant Camor, I know in my deepest self that the shackles and the beatings are the least of what's been done, and will be done, to these little ones. There's a hungry sort of darkness radiating off the Preacher Man as I feel him start coming down and around from his pulpit, and its tentacles are wending their way toward the younger side of the kid-coffle; the side that can't fight back so good. But I am not going to let it happen anymore, or else I'd just die from self-loathing at not stepping in and doing *something* when I knew it was the right thing, even though I knew I was gonna do it wrong.

When the huge and heavy doors to the big church in the middle of the town swung wide, I didn't hesitate, didn't even bother to announce myself before I let the targeting systems of my buckethead's visor draw a tight bead on the dark-suited thug at the head of the kid-coffle, and shot a bolt right through the center-point of his forehead.

I was a little surprised when a squirming, red-smeared thing with twitching metal legs spilled out the back of his skull, but I'd already entered my berserker's mindset by that point, so I didn't spend more time than was absolutely necessary to make a mental note of it for consciousness-review later on. Instead, I focused on the next slave driver in line, and felt the *churr-CHACK* of the boltcaster as I sent another six-inch length of rebar speeding right through the left-center of his body mass.

Rushing up the way-too-many steps, I was grateful once more for all the physical training I do. Chubby I might be, but it's the kind of chub that gives me endurance when I need it. That's my fighting style in a nutshell: turning weakness into strengths. For instance, I'm desperately clumsy, so I compensate for it by almost constantly practicing my katas, using my imagination to fill in what the motions would mean in a real-life situation, to visualize each strike, each block, each throw until I can *feel* them humming through my body, so when the time comes to act, I just act, not giving my body any time to revert to my native failure-prone self.

Same with my hand-eye coordination: I humble myself, accepting that I can't do it on my own, and by humbling myself, I don't fight the systems of my suit, either the targeting programs of the buckethead, or the clownsuit's muscle-reflex guidance systems. Instead, I let myself become one with them, subsuming myself just the same way I ride horses (or bears, or dinosaurs, or sharks), and become just a minor part of something much bigger, better, and more competent. My only purpose is to give the system will and direction.

This is how, once I hit the doors of the church, ducking to one side to use them as cover, I snap up my right hand, leveling the stasis capsule that I'd wound up with one of my rebar bolts, turning it into a makeshift artillery shell, and land it with a swift parabola right into the middle of the cluster of child-soldiers still in the chapel. By that time, they were just barely starting to whip their guns up and around by forced instinct, while their child-officers – and the adult ones as well – try to screech orders to get them into full readiness. Completely unprepared.

Like I said, I'd voided the warranty on the capsule: I tore out the wiring that keeps the containment fields, well, containing. Without those forcefields in place to restrict the flow of the ice-cold null-time within the capsule (which incidentally have the side benefit of making a functioning capsule almost indestructible), the result was an explosion. Not the kind of explosion that sends too-small body parts flying everywhere, though: this was a burst of temporal waves/particles, and instantly almost every kid in that gun-toting cluster froze in place, knocked outside the normal flow of time. Of course, the effect wouldn't last more than an hour in a best-case scenario – those containment fields are also what keeps the temporal energy flowing in an infinite loop – but hopefully I'd have finished what I needed to do by that point. One way or another.

There were two of the soldier-kids who didn't get caught in the burst. One was somewhere in his tweens, the other almost old enough to be one of the adolescent officers, peach fuzz just barely starting to show up on his face.

The tween acted first, his wooden-stocked rifle snapping up with all the speed and skill you'd expect from someone trained in brutality and murder without conscious thought.

Churr-CHACK! clacked my bolt-caster, and I couldn't help but blink when I saw the length of rebar sticking out of the muzzle of the kid's gun, while the kid himself was knocked off-balance by the impact.

"Huh," I say in some surprise, before whipping out my knife and chopping through the lock-point of the chain holding the kids bound together. I grab hold of its freed end and give it a good, hard *yank*, setting most of it rattling to the floor, minus the part I was still holding, my knife sheathed once more, my right-hand wavering between the two jackbooted minors. "Don't pull that trigger, kid," I call out to the tween, who thankfully pauses for a moment, apparently expecting to be dead, then when he starts to scowl at me, I look to his older fellow with a shrug and a jerk of my head toward the barrel of the gun. "You tell him why: I don't think he'll believe me."

This, thankfully, makes the older kid pause and turn his head, his eyes widening when he sees the chunk of metal blocking the tween's rifle. He drops his own gun to snatch that lethally boobytrapped firearm away from the heedless kid just before he can cause a potentially fatal backfire on his weapon. And that tells me everything I need to know about him: the older kid gave up his gun to save somebody!

There's the tromp of booted feet now, and the secret police types, the majority of whom had been manning the choir section just below where the Preacher Man had been standing to deliver his tirade, start moving to intercept. There's a bunch of them to either side, too, though thankfully the pews and all the people starting to panic at the explosions and killing are very effectively blocking them off, at least for now. If the Preacher Man starts taking charge, I'm pretty sure that these fanatics will get their act together most ricky-tik, so my window of free action is closing very rapidly.

"Run," I tell the older girl at the head of the line of kids, obviously put there for her level-headedness, which I can see right away when I look into her eyes. "Keep everyone together as best as you can, and run for the alleys," I continue, keeping my voice calm and level as I lean in close enough to make sure she can hear me, putting a bit of the force of my Teacher Voice into the words, though not too much. I didn't want to scare her, and certainly didn't want to hurt her or any of the kids behind her. "If you can, make for the ladder up," I turn slightly and point, making sure that her eyes follow my finger. "Don't scare the rats, and they'll take care of you until I can get there. All right?"

I wait until I see her nod, feel the determination rising in her, mingled with the instincts of protectiveness that seem to come to her so naturally. "Be safe," I tell her, sharing a piece of my center-self with the words to make them a true blessing, and instantly she's reaching down, taking a small hand in each of hers, before she's off down the stairs, leading a chain made of hands and arms and many little people instead of thick, cold aluminum.

Turning my full attention forward now, I see the teen and the tween looking at me. The tween's just got hate in his eyes, enough hate to kill me with his thoughts alone if he'd had the talent for it. The teen...he's got some softness there. I meet his eyes and reach out to that softness; I've only got seconds left now, and I need all the help I can get.

"Go with them," I tell the older boy, and I feel myself touching the parts of his center-self that want to be a protector of the small and the weak. "Take your gun and keep them safe. That's what a gun is for, isn't it? Don't shoot the rats, though: they're friends." He hesitates for a moment, and though he doesn't turn his head to look at the kid whose broken gun he grabbed and threw away, I can feel the connection: a comrade-in-arms, even if there's no friendship. "They need you now," I tell him, and this time I add the force of my Command Voice, not holding back as much as I did with the girl. "Now!"

He's off in that instant, scooping up his rifle and racing past me. I make sure to keep a piece of my consciousness focused on him just a little longer, not so confident in my judgment as to trust that I hadn't made some mistake about the boy's character. He doesn't stop, though, too focused on reaching the fleeing kids right before they disappear into the rows of houses, and moments later I feel his presence join theirs, before they all flit away, outside of my reach.

Good timing, that: the tween's gotten his courage together by that point, probably in large part because the darksuits are closing in, and it's easy to be brave when you've got the advantage of numbers on your side. A fist swings at me just as I turn my full attention back, and I'm lucky he's just a kid, his reflexes and coordination still in development, or he might've connected, as distracted as I was with all the variables involved in getting innocents out of the line of fire.

But he *is* just a kid, however messed up in the head he might be, and it's easy enough to step into the punch and gently ask all the force he threw at me to go somewhere else. It happily obliges, and another moment later the kid's flipped himself over a pew in the back of the church, landing flat on his back across three ushers who'd been thinking about making themselves into problems, unarmed civilians or not. They all go down in a tumbled heap, ideas of throwing themselves into the fray quite forgotten as they instead start focusing on the business of sorting out whose limbs belong to whom.

By that time the first ranks of the darksuits had made their way down the aisles to either side of the church, and they've all got weapons out. Luck's still holding for me, because they've pulled kill sticks instead of pistols or other guns. Obviously, they want to take me alive, probably for a session in the House of Terror so they can find out who sent me and how much I know about their vile little community of soul-murderers before they get down to the happy business of making me hurt for the fun of it. Also obviously, they don't quite realize that, empty hands notwithstanding, I've got firearms primed and ready on my wrists, while they just went for the close quarters combat option.

Naturally, I take the opportunity to educate them on the error of their ways before they figure it out on their own. I back toward the open doors, spreading my arms to either side, the bolt-casters on each wrist trained almost straight out until my body's gone all cruciform. My peripheral vision's always been really good, even without all the visual enhancements from the buckethead, and I use it to scan out which side's gotten closer, then turn my head to let the HUD paint my next target, feeling the *churr-CHACK!* of the bolt-caster rattle up my arm as I sink a shot into the main body mass of the nearest darksuit, then turn my head to the other side so the buckethead's targeting reticule can find me something else to shoot.

Just when I'm starting to settle into a nice rhythm of turn-and-shoot, with the occasional turn-shoot-shoot-turn to keep them off-balance, and the darksuits to my sides are finally starting to realize that they brought kill-sticks to a bolt-caster fight and are reaching for holsters and back-straps while I'm doing everything I can to thin their numbers before everything turns into a serious hairball, that's when I hear the scream. It's shrill and piercing, the scream of someone who's just experienced a moment of ultimate, horrified realization. In this case, the realization is that the person's life didn't matter much to the thugs who run this hell city, ranking several steps lower on their list of priorities after shooting me dead.

God must have been watching out for me right then, because that scream hit my berserker-fueled reflexes, and I drop and roll behind the nearest pew as the darksuits who'd been coming down the middle of the church open fire. Wood chips and sawdust fly everywhere, filling the air with a fine splintery mist, while depleted uranium burns through everything: the only cover advantage afforded by the pews was keeping me out of immediate line-of-sight! This was driven quite firmly home for me when I felt a stray round ping off my buckethead, making my HUD go on the fritz for a moment.

The loud declarations of one of my gun-nut friends from before the End echoes in my mind, that armor was only bullet *resistant*, and the term "bulletproof" was a deadly myth. This rings in my head almost as loudly as the ringing in my ears before the buckethead's sound suppressors kick in, and I scuttle out the still-open door, still flat on my belly. I'd gone in all High Noon to give the kids as much time as I could, trusting that my clownsuit's armor plates would minimize the damage these yobos could inflict on me. Kill-sticks, like the ones these yobos have, are lengths of nanoconductive material that transmit direct jolts of electrically guided psi-feedback straight to the nervous system. It's not Republic tech, but it's based on it, which means it's *very* dangerous. Getting hit by one, besides the blunt trauma from a sturdy club, causes pain like an unanesthetized root canal all over your body, and it persists until you pass out, or until you die, depending on the magnitude of the jolt. While my armor would give me a few seconds between contact and reaction, that's only enough time for me to have a margin for error. If I'm lucky.

As for depleted uranium, it was the most common ammunition material during the End, when people stopped caring about the environment in favor of murder. During the End, I'd taken more than a few hits from DU bullets and shrapnel, and a few more afterward from the criminal element that crops up down in the underground, and it's never been able to penetrate the neutron-sunk, Republic-made plates of my clownsuit. At least not yet. On the other hand, I've taken pains to get hit by as little depleted uranium as possible, which I consider a very good life philosophy, so I haven't gotten anywhere close to a full stress analysis.

Now, I'm a few steps down the broad stone stairs, and that's when I come up to my knees, just in time to see the darksuits boiling out of the front of the church like a metastasizing cancerous centipede. About this time, I realize that a lot of these guys have holes in their armor-plated suit coats, and I'm fairly sure I'm the one who put those holes there.

They...got up again?

A glance down, and I see the guy I shot in the head having the decency to stay where I put him.

Time to change tactics.

While laying down a few rounds of cover fire, still aiming for their main body masses to slow them down, I fiddle with the buckethead's targeting systems a little more, telling it to go for headshots instead of center-of-mass. Taking a breath, I let it out slowly as I shift my aim upward just a tad, and then open with everything I've got.

Churr-CHACK! Churr-CHACK! Backstep, belly drop. *Churr-CHACK!* Up to one knee. *Churr-CHACK!* Backstep, drop, roll, up to a crouch. *Churr-CHACK!* Drop prone.

Varying up my motions every so often keeps me from falling into a pattern, making myself too predictable. Making me too easy a target. All the same, I'm taking my time now, not wasting shots, and that's a good thing: a glance to the lower right of my HUD shows that I'm running very low on rebar. While I'm still not letting myself think about the shots, which would make me miss, I'm letting the suit take the split-second time it needs for a perfect headshot. There's a red waterfall flowing down the steps now, and I have to gauge each movement so that I'm firmly planted before I do anything fancy so as to keep myself from slipping in the gore puddling around my knees and smearing my belly and chest every time I drop prone.

The slowdown in shooting has a predictable result, though: the darksuits are finally starting to make headway. At first, I kept the drop on them because they kept pausing to aim, and whatever it is that's making them get back up from any shot that isn't to the head also seems to make them pretty stupid, and they take way too long drawing a bead on me.

I can hear the voice of the Preacher Man screaming from the safety of the church interior, ordering them into ranks, and as soon as they get those orders, they comply, allowing me my last and only glimpse of the

Preacher Man, one of him fleeing behind the podium, then down a hidden staircase. Leaving his minions to their fate, whatever it might be; typical megalomaniac, trying to live to spread Evil another day, as though that was something important.

That brief bit of direction is enough, though. Now some of them hold back, pistols and rifles up, while the majority start coming down the stairs, kill-sticks drawn and crackling with cruel black lightning. They don't even seem to care about shooting each other, because I take two loud, pinging shots that whizz off the plates on my shoulder and thigh that originally came punching through the chest and stomach, respectively, of the two darksuits at the front of the charge.

Blowing out the brains of those two in the front, then taking down four more in the back, slotting them right in a line to save aiming time, I take another step down, the last one, and find my foot placed onto solid stone, still clear from blood slick. I've got room to really move now! I'm out of bolts, so I pull out my sticky and say a silent prayer before I step forward, the hardwood tip punching through the spot right between the eyes of the first darksuit with a muffled *crack* sound, followed by a sound so disgusting as I yank it out, I blot it from conscious thought, before I swing first to one side then jab to the other with the opposite end of the sticky, both times causing cruel disintegrations of flesh and bone and flesh.

There's sweat flowing down my forehead, enough that the buckethead's systems can't catch it all, and neither can the clownsuit as I start to feel it dripping down into my boots. Every step makes a little squick-squick sound, before I blot it out with a brutal crunch against bone, sometimes just one, sometimes a second when the first was just to shatter a limb, preventing an attack, followed up by a skull shatter or neck break or spine crack. Shots that would paralyze a normal human seem to work all right, but it's just to limit mobility: they keep trying to squirm around anyway, even when there's no spinal cord connection to allow more than the most minimal muscle-driven motions. So, I follow up with heavy stomps of my feet when I can spare the time, the squick-squick of my boots' interiors gooping together with other liquid and crunching sounds that I can't bear to think much about.

Someone shoots down into the melee, and I twist behind a darksuit, jerking his arm behind him into a figure-four lock. Of course, the dummy doesn't hold still, so I break his arm, then grab the gun in his shoulder holster, jam it against the side of his head, and pull the trigger. A moment later, and my buckethead's interfaced with the gun in my hand, calculating firing solutions, and I'm snapping off more shots, first to get myself a little space, and then to clear the top of the stairs of the few remaining shooters, and finally I empty the magazine into the next darksuit to come charging at me before I finally get my act together and nail him between the eyes. Tossing the pistol aside, I step into the fray once more, screaming like a demon to vent all my fury, all my hate.

I hate this! I hate this! *I hate this*!

I don't want to do this! I don't want to kill anybody! I don't even want to *hurt* anybody! And I hate all of you for making me into a monster! For making me into this cruel, twisted, unfeeling *thing* that just snarls when a kill-stick gets through, once, twice, then a third and fourth time, all from different darksuits. Of course, it's different darksuits, because after they get in their hits, the thing that I've become destroys them, smashing the sticky right into them, tearing through bone, ripping off limbs, sending heads flying as though I were using a sword.

Then...then it's all quiet, and I'm just standing there, the broken ends of my sticky growing back like a crystal formation in time-elapse. There's blood and gore and assorted goop that doesn't belong on the outside of a person smeared all up and down my clownsuit, and the only reason my vision isn't blocked is because my buckethead's visor has a slight charge to it that repels contact with moisture and dust particles. So, the corners of my vision are all fouled up with the residue that spreads off and away from the visor, dripping down onto my shoulders and chest.

On the ground, nothing moves except for a few of those metal spider-things. That's easily fixed with a few well-placed stomps and jabs. There's a lot of mashed-up meat that used to be people scattered all around on the ground, but I just...I just can't think about that right now.

I just can't.

None of the bodies are children. Swinging my head around, flipping through the spectrum so I can see through the nearby buildings and walls, I confirm this: no casualties. No little heat signatures swiftly fading in the aftermath. They were all clear.

Thank God.

Then I hear the tromp, tromp, tromp of heavy-booted feet, and I lift my eyes, knowing before I look what I'm going to see: more darksuits. Lots more. Too many more. They're up at the top of the stairs, and they've all got guns. I'm just...I'm just exhausted. The last thing I ate was my breakfast pastry, the last thing I drank a sip of the clownsuit's internal water supply before I climbed down into this hell-city. I'm wobbling on my feet, and my vision's blurred, and my hands are...

My hands are firm as I lift the sticky and grip it tightly, squeezing until I can feel my knuckles turn white inside my gauntlets. Then I snap the sticky down, smacking the butt of one of the rifles dropped by a darksuit in the melee. As it flips into the air, I snap my sticky back into its holster, and catch the rifle before it hits the ground.

How in the world did I do that?

No, don't think about it: you think about it, you can't do it anymore.

So I scream again, my throat feeling like it's going to burst like a bag of blood, and charge the stairs, gun raised. There's flashes from up above, and a hail of DU bullets splatters against the stone of the steps like radioactive rain. Then I feel the first hit, and it nearly spins me all the way around.

Am I aiming? I see darksuits falling, mowed down. But I'm also feeling more hits, seeing the bright sparks as they ricochet from my clownsuit's plates, the flickers of static across my vision as they hit my buckethead.

That's when the first bullet penetrates.

It's right in that fleshy bit between navel and spine. But I got lucky: I'd turned slightly at that moment, so the bullet passed right through, missing anything important. Feels like I just got punched by somebody *very* big, fists like hams. But I've been punched before...heck, I've been shot before! (I mean, it was awful, and getting shot again was really, really not on my to-do list for today, but still). So, I turn and keep on going.

And get shot again.

Some clever sod got off to the side and shot me right through my thigh, right between the plates on the front and rear of my leg. When I try to move, I drop.

Forward mobility no longer an option, I stay on my knees, point the gun up the steps, and shoot. And shoot some more. And just keep shooting until the magazine finally runs dry with a very unhappy sounding *click*.

Tossing the gun, I grit my teeth, and I drop down onto all-fours. If I can't walk, well...I can crawl.

"You are not getting past me," I growl. "I will not stop, I will not rest, I will not *die* until they're safe. Until they're *all* safe. I will not..."

I don't know where the next bullet went...

Hawking up a blood-loogie against the inside of my buckethead, finally leaving a lasting red smear, I heave myself forward with a roar! How I'm standing, I don't even know. How I made it to the top of the stairs, I can't even begin to guess. But I'm grabbing the nearest of the darksuits in my hands, and I feel his neck crack like all those guns as I twist his head almost all the way around, channeling all the pain I'm feeling straight into him.

Everything's getting black around the edges of my vision now. The pain's so intense that I'm having a hard time focusing on anything else. Coherent thought's...it's not good. Not when I've got this pain on the inside of my abdomen like my guts are being squashed on a blacksmith's anvil, the hammer coming down over and over and over again.

(Liver shot, my brain helpfully supplies, ever the font of useless information: hits to the liver *hurt*.)

At that moment, right when I'm spending more energy fighting my body's limitations than killing the darksuits, having a hard time reaching them anyway as they keep falling back every time I catch and crush one of them to keep up the hail of fire, another loud sound tears through the air, a very authoritative *SHRACK*, and I expect that's the end: that's the sound of a plasma blaster, and that's Republic tech, and if they've got Republic tech, I'm dead and just don't realize it yet.

Except I don't die. I'm just standing there, barely on this side of being conscious, and I'm surrounded by more darksuits than I can count, and then *they* are there, right in the middle of the bad guys. Shining knights in future armor, one male and built like a brick outhouse, the other a blonde reincarnation of Boudica filled with the fury of her Celtic gods, ponytailed golden hair streaming behind her like a battle standard. Where they pass, their guns flash, her sword swings, and the darksuits die, falling like wheat before the scythe of the Reaper Man.

"Wow," I gasp, awestruck at the sight of these two Republic-enhanced god warriors. Then, despite not wanting to miss a single moment of such perfect art in motion, even if it's the killing arts, I can't stop myself from looking down at the spreading red stain in my gut region, thick and gooey and already seeping out around the plates, staining the armored fabric of the clownsuit.

"Huh," I manage, before my senses finally shut off.

CHAPTER 19: DIS; THE FINAL SHOWDOWN

Location: Earth, Sunflower City, Under-City
Perspective: Susan Six and Trinidad Del Toro

"Gracious, Trinidad," Susan Six quietly exclaimed as she let her eyes scroll down the document floating before her eyes, using her peripheral vision to parry the downward swing of the heavy metal pipe wielded by the near-humanoid creature attacking her, before deftly lopping off first its arm and then its head with her softly humming blade. "For a little guy, that man Al was certainly thorough in documenting all the monstrosities he's encountered. See?" With a nod of her head, she sent a copy of the document she'd been studying over to Trinidad's suit.

"These creatures he calls 'trolls.' The result of hybridizing a silicon-based lifeform the United Earth Empire encountered with primate DNA. Now it's starved of carbon, and if it doesn't gobble up carbon-based life

311

as fast as it can, it ends up turning to stone, a process hastened by exposure to ultraviolet radiation. How in the Great Eggfather's name did creatures like these even get down here? One or two I could understand, but six so far..."

"By the Prophet, woman!" Trinidad gasped desperately, jerking his head to shove the document projection out of his immediate field of vision, getting his heavy rifle up only just in time to block the double-fisted crushing strike of the roughly humanoid, blocky-featured shape in front of him. "This is no time to be reading the funny pages!"

"I'm sorry, Trinidad," Susan Six said contritely before leaning over, placing her blaster carbine on Trinidad's armored shoulder, and blowing the head off the creature in a shower of grit. "I forgot that you're so new to all of this. And still only wearing a hardsuit for the very first time."

"More than any other human from Earth has access to," Trinidad laughed in the post-combat rush, his eyes sweeping the area for more foes, finding none. "I can't believe I'm not even breathing hard, and we've been fighting our way through these tunnels nonstop for...what? An hour now? Two?"

"Almost three Earth hours," Susan Six informed her partner, reaching out to point at the chronometer softly glowing at the upper right corner of Trinidad's peripheral vision.

Trinidad was amazed by so many things right now: how he was moving so fast, his thoughts turning almost instantly into actions, every movement like greased lightning. How he didn't feel tired even after hours of brutal, messy combat, hand-to-claw with some of the most hideous creatures he'd seen since the time he'd defended the Capitol Building during the fall of Washington, D. C. And how, in spite of all the various goos and goops and ichors that had been spraying all over during their blood-soaked tour of the underground, not a drop seemed to have stuck to either him or Susan Six.

"Static resonation," she answered his unasked question, noticing the movement of his eyes and guessing what he was thinking, even as she motioned for him to lead the way forward. "It's the same technology that keeps most modern apartments from building up dust or unpleasant smells: most foreign matter just flows right off a good Republic-made suit until it hits a critical point and has to recharge. Your hardsuit's going to hit that limit sooner than my hard-plate plastron stat suit, but even with all these creatures down here, I don't think either of us will be getting actually messy anytime soon."

"Glad Miss Clee let me take the suit," Trinidad said with sincere feeling, looking down at the rigid plates of the armor. Apparently, it was a last-generation model of field-mobile battle-platform, not pretty to look at, but solidly built, especially around his vitals. "But to answer your question, based on what Gret's told me, besides the underground apparently being a prime breeding ground for the monsters that make it here with chunks of human cities, there's multi-mile flexible pipelines that stretch out along the ocean floor, searching around like a plant's roots for nutrient-rich soil and water to feed into the various systems that keep Sunflower City alive. The monsters just slip inside of those around the coastlines and follow them to where their favorite food is – people.

"Speaking of suits, though, is a stat suit really that different from this hardsuit?" he couldn't help but ask, glancing over his shoulder at Susan Six's lean, svelte form, all copper-and-blue, and visible even in the near-total darkness thanks to his suit's vision enhancement. A stark contrast to his own dull gunmetal green carapace. "Besides the fashion statement, that is."

"Yeah!" Susan Six laughed as they continued down the slightly dripping tunnel. "I mean, I've also got synthetic-organic filaments laced into my bones and muscles, letting me build them up beyond normal human maximums, as well as tripwire boosts to my autonomic nervous system. But my stat suit lets me exceed even those limits. In my suit, I've got all the power that you've got in that hardsuit, but instead of having to rely on the whimsy of macro-engineering, I've got forcefield reinforcement down on the molecular level that gives me even more protection without any loss of mobility or agility, and neural extensions that bond me to my weapons, making them literally a part of me.

"Of course, a hardsuit's not really going to get in your way, and over time it'll learn your body inside and out and adapt accordingly, but it's never going to be quite as smooth as a good stat suit." She flashed Trinidad a grin. "Though by the time you're allowed to get one of your own, you might be too attached to that old thing to let it go, and it to you. Just like any piece of Republic tech, it's already tied directly into your biometrics: nobody else is going to be able to use it without your express permission. Or maybe Sergeant Benjuro's or Gret's, if they enact some of the emergency overrides..."

Susan Six trailed off suddenly, and they both fell silent, adjusting their speed so that they were walking side-by-side in the tunnel, shoulders almost touching. Up ahead was firelight and the sound of voices, and in a place like the underground, voices meant you were about to go up against something that could think. Those were the *really* dangerous threats!

314

Angling themselves slightly away from each other, an overlapping field of fire at the middle of their peripheral ranges, Susan Six and Trinidad edged their way cautiously into the light, taking in the scene before them with more than a little surprise: it was rats and children!

The scene was almost Dickensian, urchins gathered around a trashcan fire, less because of any cold (though it *was* chilly down there) than as a way of staving off the horrors that lurked in the dark. Just beyond the light of the fire, though, things took on a far more macabre cast. The entire room was a leftover from some necropolis, the walls lined with cemented-in skulls and assorted bony body parts. The dry bones looked down protectively on the huddled, rag-clothed refugees and their fuzzy hosts, and a sense of sanctuary filled the area, an impression that instantly made Trinidad's heart begin to slow, his grip on his gun relaxing. This was a protected place, a place where no blood should be shed.

Then one of the oversized rats started up with a loud *squeak!* of alarm, pointing at the two intruders (and Trinidad saw that it had actual thumbs on those little pink hands). A moment later, a lean, muscled male in shirt-and-tie jumped between the pair and the gathered group, before he swung the ominous shape of a gun up to bear.

"Squeak!" challenged the chest-high rat, showing his teeth.

"Huh," mused Susan Six, apparently not bothered by the sudden brandishing of firearms. "An AK-47. I didn't know they existed outside of museums." Then, holstering her blaster, she raised an appeasing hand. "Just relax, lil' guy. We're not here to —"

BANG!

Judging from the rat's startled expression, his shot was as much a surprise to him as it was to everyone else.

His newly heightened senses boosting once more with another rush of adrenaline, Trinidad watched the bullet fly straight toward the plastron plate covering Susan Six's chest. There was the spark as it ricocheted, deflected and distorted by the armor's curve, then another spark as it glanced off a nearby wall, the bullet now spinning in midair as it tumbled with inevitable momentum toward...

Oh no.

A little girl rat, clutching a stuffed toy, and herself hugged tight by a six-year-old human girl, gave a short, sharp half-gasp as the bullet hurtled straight toward the forehead of the toy...and the tender fur and flesh and bone behind it.

Then Susan Six was there, the bullet quivering between finger and thumb, its tip leaving the most miniscule of burn marks between the stuffed toy's glass eyes.

"Squeak!" the gun-toting rat squealed in anguish, dropping his rifle as he ran to the side of the children and threw his arms around them both. "Squeak...squeak..." he cooed softly, his whiskers tickling their cheeks as he rocked back and forth.

Seeing the crisis passed, the other rats took a long look at the adult humans who'd come into their midst, then pointed as one toward a passage leading out the other side of the room.

"I'd say we've found the trail of our man Al," chuckled Susan Six, chucking the bullet over her shoulder before pulling her carbine free once more. "Looks like he left a blessing on these kids before he sent them up here." She glanced at her companion, shrugging at his questioning look. "It's an empath thing: a protective aura that encourages peaceful interaction. I don't know the specifics, not being a psi user myself, but I know it when I see it. Or feel it, in this case."

"What's down there?" Trinidad asked, turning to the two oldest children, one a girl who couldn't have been more than fourteen, the other a boy maybe sixteen. "That's where you came from, isn't it? We were told there were people keeping kids as slaves, and we're here to save them." He smirked. "Looks like we were a bit slow on that count."

"This guy came out of nowhere," the girl answered, nodding in affirmation to Trinidad's questions, asked and unasked, a glance down at the shackles still attached to her and the other children's ankles answering still more. "He's still down there, I think, covering our escape. We only just made it up here by one of the elevators," she nodded at the boy, apparently the one who'd made that possible, "and the rats were waiting to take us in, like they were expecting us..."

"Then there might still be time," Susan Six cut her off, her expression grim. "Come on," she motioned to Trinidad. "Time to save the universe again."

A people person, Susan Six was not!

Giving the two older kids an apologetic shrug, Trinidad followed as close on the heels of the bounty hunter as he possibly could. When they reached the top of a long ladder leading down, she didn't even bother touching it, she just dropped over the edge, trusting in the gravitic dampeners on her stat suit to take the impact. Trinidad, naturally, was a bit more cautious, sliding down the ladder as though it were a firehouse pole, but even that minimal amount of delay was enough to ensure that he was three steps behind Susan Six as they tore through the tight-packed buildings of the artificially sunlit city below the City, more than human speed and reflexes letting them cover distances in seconds that would have taken them minutes without their enhancements.

Before they both came to a sharp halt, blinking.

"Huh," said Susan Six, surveying the assorted carnage.

"Wow," said Trinidad, looking up at the figure of the Man at the top of the stairs, his baggy-looking beige-orange suit smeared up and down with drying gore.

That was all the time they spent before they were racing up those stairs, passing one to each side of the Man as he dropped to his knees, and Trinidad noticed the rectangular visor on the front of the cylindrical helmet suddenly stop glowing, the light winking out as the Man apparently lost consciousness. And no wonder: there were numerous holes punched through his suit and into the meat beneath, each oozing life.

He didn't spend more than an instant taking this fact in, however, as he and Susan Six tore through the scant remaining defenders, black-clad spiderheads all of them, then past the doors of the towering building that dominated the center of the hidden city. The screams of panicking people filled the air, a milling crowd pouring out of the double doors and flowing around the two warriors and the kneeling Man behind them in a headlong rush from the killing ground that had once been a church.

Not just a church, though, Trinidad soon realized.

"This is one of those standardized government buildings," he informed Susan Six even as he turned to rest a hand on the Man's shoulder, blinking in momentary surprise as a flood of diagnostic data appeared before his eyes, the Republic-made parts of the Man's armor communicating with his own about the status of its wearer. "With a church-looking overlay, but otherwise it's the same. They were popping up all over the place during the End's balkanization, pretty much required building for a petty dictator wanting to carve out some territory. Should be easy to navigate, too, provided you can bust through some heavy blast doors."

"They're just steel, aren't they?" she asked, arching eyebrows in surprise as the Man's visor suddenly lit up again, his head lifting as he regained consciousness. "Sheesh: you're a regular badass berserker bunny, aren't you?"

"Call me Ishmael," grunted the Man, the strain relaxing from his voice almost immediately as Trinidad pressed a "slap patch" against one of his chest plates, letting his armor analyze, collect, and then distribute the dose of painkillers and regenerative through his system. "They've got Mister Camor down below: I could feel him while I was getting here. I saw the Preacher Man escaping into the back of the church, so there's probably stairs going down."

"On it," said Susan Six, and just like that, she was racing through the church, tossing pews aside or just breaking right through when they got in her way, ignoring the cluster of stock-still boys gathered near the front, their skins turned into monochrome blues by a lingering stasis field.

"Uh," Trinidad stammered, caught between concern for Ishmael and his need to catch up.

"I'll be your rearguard," the Man offered, and Trinidad could have sworn that the visor cocked slightly into a wry expression. "Besides, I have a stasis tube full of snakes I need to collect."

"Oh," replied Trinidad, blinking: this job kept him meeting the most *interesting* people. "Well, uh, good luck with that."

Only half-hearing Ishmael's reply, Trinidad sprinted after Susan Six. After all, somebody needed to show her the way.

Location: Earth, Sunflower City, Dis
Perspective: Scintillant Camor

John Martin wasn't fast enough, of course: I'm still locked tight to this torture chair. Physically helpless, but hardly much of a threat even if I was free. He's flanked now by the two black-clad guards, ready to act if he tries anything against the Preacher Man, and I know that they won't be receptive to my powers: they've been corrupted by spiders, and I can feel the void where their selves used to be. Only brute force will work on them now.

So brute force is what I'll have to use.

"Father Arrhenius," John begins, raising his hands beseechingly. "You don't understand." He flicked his eyes to me, and then back to the Preacher Man, his shoulders slumping. "I just couldn't. We were talking, and..."

"And you let yourself believe the lies this perverse creature told you," the sharp-featured human declared, each word like the knell of doom. Then his features soften, and he raises a hand in benediction, his smile that of the benevolent God in Heaven. "If only for a moment. We have all strayed at some time, Brother John. You know that better than most, as intimately acquainted with sinners as you are in your profession. You also know, in your heart of hearts, that sinners in need of judgment will say and do anything to escape their just recompense."

For a moment I feel John's wavering. He's alone now, adrift in a hostile universe. I freed him from the Preacher Man's influence, and from the pain and guilt of his past. Now the Preacher Man has torn him free from my influence, and John will have to make this decision entirely on his own.

Our eyes lock for just a moment, and I know how the Preacher Man grew so powerful, so influential: he's like me, an empath. A powerful one. Such power isn't something I would have expected from a human confined to Earth. As I consider the matter, though, it does make some sense: the Preacher Man is a dark star, someone who happily sucks out the juices of the heart of God itself for quick, easy power. The power to control and dominate.

As I take his measure, of course, the Preacher Man takes mine. Takes it and dismisses it with a contemptuous curl of his lip. I'm nobody, of course, nothing, not compared to someone with ambitions like his.

Like all Masters of the Ministries, I'm ultimately just a craftsman, a reasonably skilled worker at a trade who happens to also be an acceptable manager of people and administrator of my organization. This job is mine because I had sufficient merit in my field and was sufficiently trusted by others in the same Ministry and could work well enough with the Masters of the other Ministries to be granted a position of ultimate trust and responsibility. My greatest desire right now is to see my daughter's face when she first gets to ride on her very own dwarf mammoth.

The Preacher Man's greatest desire is to hold the Earth in the palm of his hand and gather the stars like pebbles on a beach.

Knowing how much of a nothing I am compared to him, the Preacher Man seems to swell in size, towering over all of us in the room, a dark and terrible figure of doom, his smile of haughty satisfaction enough to betoken the victory he knows he's already won.

Then John Martin speaks.

"I'm the sinner, Father Arrhenius," John says, low at first, his head bowed. Soon, though, he raises his head, his great hairy hands clenched into mighty fists. "I see that now. I've made so many mistakes – too many – and I've done things that I told myself were what I *had* to do. But they weren't, and they aren't, and I'm done with it. I won't be a butcher anymore." He looks at the Preacher Man, his expression entreating. "Please, Father Arrhenius, we've got to let the kids go. We've got to stop all of this." As he spoke, his expression turned to wonder as the truth of his words shone a radiant light into his innermost soul. "There isn't any need for it."

"Judas!" snarled the Preacher Man, and the burly, black-haired man was swept aside by the deceptively spindly-looking cenobite's arm. He rounds on me next, his eyes almost literally blazing with the fury of a thwarted tyrant. "Kill him!" he snaps at the two minions. "Kill-!"

If he'd been serious about killing me, he shouldn't have met my eyes. Instead of acting at his command, the two guards are sent sprawling, just like poor John was, at the shockwave of psychic energy that bursts out from us as our center-selves lock in combat. None of them can move as the conflict between us rages, the veins on the Preacher Man's temples and neck standing out in hideous scarlet-and-blue traceries. He's strong! Strong enough to brainwash an entire congregation – an entire community! Perhaps even an entire army, given enough time.

So, I don't match might against might. That's one of the most basic laws of conflict, so basic that even I know it: withdraw where your opponent is strong, strike where your opponent is weak. Just like dear Garfi taught me. I cast up a shield, a baffle of flash and glitter to distract this dark star, knowing in an instant that though he's been trained, he's never actually faced true combat of wills before. While he focuses on slamming his self against that brief obstacle – and oh! but those blows hurt! – I let my true self slip behind, a needle straight into the heart of darkness.

That, of course, is the ultimate weakness of his sort of power: it's a towering fortress built atop a foundation of sand. Quick power, but weak roots. Roots that I now seize upon.

With a rending *scream*, the Preacher Man falls to his knees! Gritting my teeth against the pain I share with him, I reach into his deepest self and rip out the parts of him that allow him to manipulate others, then slam shut the door that is his conduit to universal power.

"I'm sorry," I tell him, breathing hard, feeling the trickle of blood from my ears at the strain of my act – from the desperate self-control it took to keep from killing him in the process! "I can't let you hurt others anymore."

With the drop in my powers, and the complete dissipation of the Preacher Man's, the two guards are up again. They're almost mindless and don't feel pain or fear, only the need to obey their last order: to kill me.

Just as I'm about to accept my fate, knowing that at least my last act was to do what I felt was the right thing under the circumstances, suddenly John is there, bellowing a war cry from deep in that massive chest as he plows into the pair, sending them sprawling. They're still dangerous, even for someone as physically adept as him, and while one of them struggles with him on the floor, the other scoops up his dropped weapon and levels it once more at my heart.

BANG!

For a moment, I wonder if this is what it feels like to die. Less painful than I'd expected. The bullet must have killed me instantly. Then I see that John is standing there in front of me, wavering on his feet, his eyes blinking rapidly as he shakes his head, a gory hole sprouted like a blood blossom in his back — the exit wound. I glance down to see an entry wound in my chest, and know that I'm dying now, but not dead, the cryo-gel in my system slowing the loss of my vital fluids just enough.

John sacrificed himself to save me.

Scooping up a surgical saw from his tool rack, John spends the last of his life cutting down first one of the guards, then the other, not seeming to notice as the one who'd shot him empties his sidearm into my friend's burly body. Once he's very thoroughly killed them both, however, his arms and thick, armored apron smeared with their viscera, he stops, wavering, then sinks to his knees. John falls back, and his head lands on my lap, while I lean forward to press my muzzle against his forehead. It's not much, but I reach out to him, reach *into* him, and take firm hold of his life's energy. While I can't heal him, as long as I live and keep that essential contact, I can keep him from dying.

That's when the Preacher Man stands up again, grabbing a hideous-looking bladed implement from the row of John Martin's torture-tools as he rises, and I feel his hate like brimstone as he advances on us. On me: I'm the one he wants, after all.

No, John, I plead with him as I feel his intent before he's consciously aware of it, begging with my heart rather than my voice. *Don't do it, you can live, you can...*

"I can do the right thing," John says, and his voice is so calm as he stands up again, breaking our contact. "For maybe the first time ever."

He's there to catch the first lunge. If he weren't dying, maybe he'd have been able to overpower the Preacher Man. He's weak now, though – too much lost blood – and he's slow, and I cry out as the horrible long knife plunges straight into my friend, and I instinctively grab hold of his final pain, cutting it off, making his passing gentle. A step into sleep.

The Preacher Man spits in derision on the body of John Martin as my friend collapses to the ground, then turns his full attention back onto me.

"What a waste," he declares with contempt. "I thought you might be useful as a piece in this grand game after you'd been properly persuaded." He raises the bloody weapon and starts toward me once more, revenge for what I took from him written in his eyes. "But now I think you're more trouble than you're worth."

There's the lunge, and I close my eyes, calling up the memory of my hand on my wife's cheek.

Closing my eyes, as it turned out, was the best thing I could have done. There's an actinic flash, and in my weakened state the sudden shock might have done terrible damage to my eyes.

Opening my eyes again, blinking away the spots, I gape in wonder at the sight of the legendary human bounty hunter, Susan Six, trained by one of the mightiest ganhammen warriors, educated by one of their best scholars. Behind her is Trinidad Del Toro, looking almost as wonderstruck as myself at the realization that they arrived just in the nick of time. On the floor in front of her, his right hand and the killing knife seared away in an instant, the Preacher Man can only gape up at her, as overwhelmed in the moment as the rest of us. She really is something quite amazing.

There's someone even more amazing, though, someone who's not there in person, though without him, Susan Six wouldn't be where she is, standing over my would-be killer.

All the events surrounding this moment snap into my mind in a picture of perfect, crystalline clarity. They all revolve around that man whose name I cannot remember, whose face I cannot recall: a bit player, a backstage worker, nobody of any importance. But his efforts, slow and steady, cleared the way. Because of him, there were no innocents to be taken as hostages, no contingent of guards and fanatics led by a fully empowered Preacher Man to ambush my saviors, bringing out the *real* arsenal of black-market weapons they'd prepared for the job. Because he was here, the two heroes were able to follow his lead, find him, find this place, and then find me.

In the very nick of time.

"Don't kill him," I tell Susan Six just as she points her blaster at the Preacher Man's head, while he kneels before her, clutching his cauterized stump. "I'm not strong enough to survive the shock of another death. Let the justice of the Republic have him."

"I thought I *was* the Republic's justice," the gleaming knight-justiciar chuckles, then sends the Preacher Man tumbling to the floor with a burst of stunning force from her weapon's nonlethal setting. "But suit yourself."

A beat, and Trinidad is next to me, sparing only a glance at poor John Martin, enough to know that the man was well past help, before he's fast at work with a medical kit drawn from one of his hardsuit's many useful little pouches, stabilizing me. I can tell from his hesitation that he's relying heavily on instructions from his onboard computer, flashing directions before his eyes, but he's fast enough for the job at hand.

"Like I said," Susan Six laughed, her own readout showing my improving condition. "We just saved the universe again."

"Yeah," chuckles Trinidad as he sees me past the point of danger with a final injection to break down the cryo-gel in my system before it becomes a danger. "I guess we just did."

PROFESSOR'S INTERLUDE: PERFECTION

```
Location: Interstellar Link, The Professor's
Classroom
Perspective: The Man
```

The Pan-Galactic Republic is not perfect. I am not the first to have noticed this, and I will not be the last. I hope that you have noticed the flaws in our system of government, and that you are thinking of ways in which they can be remedied.

The founders of our government, drawing light out of darkness, freedom out of slavery, specifically built means for adjusting and improving the Republic into its foundations. They very deliberately put strong limits on the ultimate powers of its functionaries, allowing its citizens as much privacy and agency and opportunity for growth and development as possible, while still providing for their needs and maintaining an essential social order to allow all of this in as safe and healthy an environment as is possible. In practical terms, this means that the Republic has very few overarching laws, most of them having to do with regulating the flow of currency and information or ensuring fundamental rights. There are, of course, plenty of laws on the local level, but even these must pass through a rigorous process of review by the Ministry of Peace before they can be implemented.

Naturally, in any system where the freedom and privacy of its citizenry are considered essential rights, there are going to be those who make mistakes as part of exercising those rights. More to the point, there will be those who sin, which I define as actions that individuals know to be wrong, which they do anyway. By that definition, I believe that we have all sinned in some fashion. I believe we will continue to do so for the duration of our lives, and possibly long after. But I also believe that, as long as we are willing to put in the effort, we can get better, and the process of committing errors, trying out the wrong ways to do things before eventually coming to a right conclusion, a right way of life, is our right as sapient beings, and a necessary process that we all must endure toward the ultimate goal of obtaining self-perfection.

Many of the original founders of the Republic explicitly stated that they believed in this philosophy as well. To quote "Slow Thought" of the wassut people's Council of Master Thinkers, acting as the spokes-being for the original founding assembly of the Republic: "We recognize that what we have wrought is not perfect. It is, however, the best we could do at this time. We only hope that the system we have put in place will create an atmosphere of understanding and striving for enlightenment so that, when a more perfect system of government comes along, the citizens of our Republic will be prepared to recognize it and adopt it without reservation."

CHAPTER 20: SCINTILLANT
SURVIVES; THE DATE

Location: Earth High Orbit, Sunflower City
Synchronous Satellite
Perspective: Scintillant Camor

There's a touch on my cheek, soft, exploratory. Through that touch, I feel an equally soft, sweet innocence. The creature touching me has no malice in its heart; she's young, inexperienced with the ways of malice, used only to the most tender care.

Opening my eyes, I look into the wise-beyond-years, brown-eyed gaze of my dearest daughter's dwarf mammoth.

"Daddy!" Birdcry exclaims, grabbing my hand in her excitement, and I can feel how she's only barely restraining herself from throwing her arms around me; obviously she's been warned that such actions might be dangerous, considering my still-fragile state.

Leaning forward, I kiss her forehead, then I turn and do the same to her quadrupedal companion. This seems to puzzle the little giant, who rubs the spot with her ever-questing trunk, obviously uncertain how to feel about the gesture. It makes Birdcry giggle, though, and that's enough.

"We thought you were going to die," says Barika Das, her face visible on a screen near my "bed" (it's actually a gravitic couch, so I'm floating slightly above the surface, my whole body supported on all sides by protective forcefields to prevent me from suffering accidental injury). The relief on Ms. Das's pleasant features is obvious in spite of our species differences. "We... we all were just so..."

She trails off when I smile at her reassuringly, then let my eyes flick to the hulking figure standing in shadows, his eyes conveying far more emotion than his scar-seamed face ever could. Ah, Garfi Lett, you always were a worrier. "I've spoken with Salvee," he tells me, cutting right to the point as he approaches the bed. "You're hurt bad, but you'll heal. Full recovery, she says, but it's going to take time." His mouth actually manages something approaching a concerned frown. "The psychological damage is going to take longer, though: you're in no condition to get back to acting as Earth's interim governor." A flick of his eyes and a slight shifting of his stance, and just like that, Miss Das is included fully in the conversation. "I came in person to officially transfer the post to Barika Das, as senior head minister in this region of space. After conference with our colleagues in the Ministries, we all agreed that she was the most viable of the available candidates."

His bluntness makes sense, as does his avoidance of wasting time with emotional displays. After all, even if he's due to trade off his position as Head Minister of Defense in the near future, as part of the usual cycling of key personnel to prevent burnout, there are countless tasks that still require his attention. For him to have taken even this short time shows me just how much he was worried for my safety.

"It's only temporary, of course," Miss Das is saying, perhaps babbling a little in her joy at my continued survival and her bewilderment at being so suddenly thrust into a position of extreme authority. "Just until you can return and finish what you started."

She's going to say more, I know, but I raise a hand, then rest it on Birdcry's shoulders, pulling her up onto the floating bed so that she can rest next to my heart, her cheek pressed against the soft fabric of the comfortable hospital tunic. Confused at this odd arrangement, the mammoth calf pokes her trunk at the space beneath me, then tugs gently on my fluffy tail. I can feel the waves of quiet delight coming from the little giant, but I make sure to temper the emotion slightly with a sending of my center-self so that she doesn't get too rough in her enthusiasm. Always a danger with little children, of course.

"Yes," I agree. "I will return. But I trust you, Miss Das, and I trust everyone that I cleansed of their inner demons. That was why I had you meet with me, after all: to free you of the pains and weaknesses that might have ruined your ability to perform at your best. There aren't quite enough to meet the full needs of Sunflower City, to say nothing of reconstructing Earth, so you'll have to work a holding action. The work will be difficult, and it will be hazardous at times. All the same," I rest my cheek lovingly against Birdcry's, letting my eyes close as I reach out to Miss Das over the gulf of space separating us, lending her what strengthening power I can, even knowing how much it will exhaust me, "I believe you can do it, if you all work together. Will you accept this commission, Barika Das?"

"Yes."

The word is small, frightened, and she looks it as well. But then she sets her shoulders and sits up straight, and I can feel the determination within her rising strong and solid.

"Yes, I do," she affirms again, and this time she means it.

Out of the corner of one half-opened eye, I see Garfi's nod: he'll convey word to the Masters of the Ministries. As for me, my daughter and I will soon relocate from this satellite facility, most likely to Mars, that being one of the safest locales in this solar system. You can't get to Mars without passing many layers of security, and a truly awe-inspiring web of privacy screens, placed for the benefit of the sacred rites of the humans who travel there, but applying just as much to persons like myself, seeking a place of peace and healing.

"We're not beaten, Garfi," I tell my old friend, letting Miss Das hear our intimate exchange so that she'll know the value I place on her. "Just... delayed. For a short while."

"We'll see," Garfi replies, before he starts to turn and leave, and Barika quietly ends her visual feed to let me rest. He stops partway through the motion, though, and looks back at me, right at the moment when the mammoth calf is trying her very best to climb up onto the gravitic couch with both me and my daughter, who is already well on her way to falling fast asleep in her relief at having me back and safe.

"Just a thought, Sin," he says in that deep, calm, quiet way he has. "The humans had an Empire, right?" I nod, waiting for him to continue. "Have you ever heard of an Empire without an Emperor?"

Oh dear.

"This is just the beginning, Sin," Garfi says with the voice of predictive certainty that has seen him through so many military campaigns. "There's still a villain out there. Someone who can empower someone like Castor Agustus Arrhenius. That sort of power doesn't pop up in a vacuum. Not without someone to awaken it, and then to train it. And eventually we're going to have to deal with whomever they are. Or whatever."

He continues his slow walk to the door of my cozy little room, but pauses one more time in the vestibule.

"I'm glad you were right, Sin," he says, so softly I have to strain to hear.

And then he's gone.

Yes, he's right: this is just the beginning. For now, though, we're past the great storm. Now is a time of healing.

Cuddling my daughter close, while the big little calf settles on top of my legs (thank goodness for the forcefield sheath protecting them!), I sort my cares away with a gentle meditative technique and let myself settle into a healing sleep. The humans have a saying that I feel is most appropriate for this situation: "Sufficient is the day unto the evil thereof."

Location: Interstellar Link, Sunflower City
Simulation
Perspective: The Man

Standing out in the bright sunshine, all storms past and forgotten, I can't help but look up and smile, feeling the wind on my face, rustling my clothes. I love wind; I love the way it energizes me, flows through me, ties me to everything that it's touched, and carries a part of me away to touch everything beyond the horizon.

The sensation is so real, so real...but I remind myself that it's the Link making a near-perfect simulation of the situation outside my door right this instant. I need to remind myself of that fact, because the thought that where I am and what I'm doing isn't completely real also gives me the courage to stay where I am and keep doing what I'm doing.

What I'm doing is...um...well, I guess it's kinda sorta maybe a little bit a date.

Opening my eyes, feeling my pupils contract, I can see the glow from Susan Six's ship as she leaves the atmosphere, riding the point between the blue of Earth and the black of space. While I left out everybody else in Sunflower City when I was compiling this simulation, keeping the streets empty, I kind of wanted to watch her go. She's this superhero, you know? I never saw a real-life superhero before she and Mister Del Toro showed up and saved the day. And now she's off to save the day somewhere else, just two short weeks after our little adventure. Just knowing that people like her and Mister Del Toro are out there, it's...well, it's a nice feeling.

Just to wrap up my little adventure, I let my mind slide back over the closing bits, and all the things that remind me that it's all right for me to feel happy right now.

Miss Six and Mister Del Toro got me and Mister Camor out of Dis, and all the kids, too (while I, of course, brought out my little opossum friend and every one of those snakes: they're all settled into the Sanctuary quite nicely). They were even nice enough to let the super-rats come along, and I understand that they've been relocated to one of the cities on the moon and are probably back to their normal mischief by now. The kids, though, are all being taken off-planet for proper counseling and reconditioning before being made available for adoption; after the abuses they went through down there, they need some professional work to heal up inside, and there's nobody better for that than the empaths of the Republic.

Still, it's not a totally happy ending, not with Mister Camor out of commission. Since he's the one who was driving the reconstruction effort on Earth, that sets everything back by the same amount. Still, it's not a hopeless situation: Mister Camor already picked out these two people, Miss Das and Mister Peterson, to take over the top spots around here, and they're really sharp, and there's Miss Gret acting as Earth's chief auditor, and Doctor Salvee to keep up the flow of necessary food and medicines, so we've got enough leadership to keep things in Sunflower City from falling apart in the meantime. Just, well...the rest of Earth's gonna have to survive on its own until Mister Camor can get back in the saddle.

At least his daughter's got her dwarf mammoth as well as her daddy back.

As for keeping order, Sergeant Benjuro and her three comrades are hard at work breaking in the new human peacekeeper outfit. From hearsay through my contacts up in the big office (i.e. Miss Gret), she's engaged to get married in a few months, too: Mister Del Toro is a lucky man! She's the liaison between Earth and the Ministry of Peace, and Mister Del Toro is our resident superhero (I think his official title is Security Supervisor, but it's a position with a lot of leeway), so I'm glad that they're both happy.

I'm also glad Sergeant Benjuro decided not to charge me with anything. Turns out, Republic law is a lot less...well...*demanding* than Earth's laws ever were, not like I'm sure how Earth's laws would have handled my case, probably as an assault charge at least. With Miss Theodora Eunice Faraday – I mean Miss Doe – being kind enough to provide City Central with permission to share the video feed of the whole incident at her apartment complex with Sergeant Benjuro's office, she glanced through it once while I was sitting in her office the day after everything happened (I couldn't stand for long at that point: I was missing too many bits), then looked through my unedited consciousness logs, a process that took less than an hour, told me I was in the clear, and sent me home to get back to healing up.

"There are four big reasons for punishing people after they commit a crime," she explained as she casually brushed aside the hard light report forms, dissipating them back into the ethers. "Lots of little reasons too, but these are the big four: first, to stop somebody who's likely to do similar crimes and get them off the streets; second, to discourage others from doing the same. That ties into the third and fourth, which is to show how powerful a justice system is, to demonstrate legitimacy, or that the system *can* act; and then to teach the perpetrator a lesson – get their attention by breaking them out of their cycle of bad habits with an arrest – and get them rehabilitated if possible.

"With you, you were attacked, and it's pretty obvious you were just defending yourself. It's also pretty obvious you went out of your way to keep your attackers alive. Those aren't the signs of somebody who's likely to be a repeat offender. Also, it's pretty obvious you feel awful about it, considering you turned yourself in, saving me the effort of finding you, even considering how badly torn up you are right now.

"I already spent most of yesterday showing off how big a stick the Republic can swing, and right now I think we all really need to start showing everybody in this city how rewarding it can be to be law-abiding citizens. So, if anybody's got any objections to my just tossing out this case, we'll just say it's sentence served by community service down in the under-city, and call it even."

Off-kilter from such a sudden dismissal of one source of my stress (but when am I ever completely without stress?), I had to check with City Central to make sure that I'd heard right. I had, and so here I went, to my home, to make sure all the animals were safe and sound and happy and whole.

That was all two weeks ago. One of *those* days. But the time afterward has been nice and quiet, mostly spent with me staying home and healing up; Doctor Salvee visited to help me get better faster, and I could track my rate of healing by how many times she came by, and for how long. Now that she's not coming by anymore, and I'm getting back into my physical fitness routine, it's time to get some important tasks done. I spent a good chunk of this morning on the Link, setting things up for me to make good on a promise I'd made.

After all, they'd saved my life; the least I could do was give my two new friends a tour of my hometown.

There's a slight distortion in the air, and just like that, there's Pinkflower and Bright Spots, the little brown pterodactyl-moth-thingy perched on the big pink bug's shoulder.

"Human Joe!" exclaimed Pinkflower, as exuberant as ever, scooping me up in a powerful hug. Considering how many limbs she used, it was easily the most *comprehensive* hug I've ever received. "Human Joe, you're safe! You're alive! We were so scared we wouldn't see you again!"

"This one exclaims," Bright Spots breathed, floating over to clutch my shoulder in her manipulator-grippers, then bending to nibble on my hair with her fleshy beak, "oh Joe, we're so glad to see you again. This one explains: we saw the news articles, and we weren't sure that you would make it out alive from the crisis."

News articles? Huh, well, I guess it makes sense, as important as Mister Camor is and all, and how he was a hostage. At this rate, Earth's going to get a reputation as...I guess as what it is: a nice place, if it wasn't for the people living here.

Serves us right.

"Glad to be seen," I chuckle, deciding not to linger on the topic of what may or may not have been in the news, giving Pinkflower a gentle hug back, which seemed to be enough prompting for her to finally release me...well, eventually, after which I very softly touched the side of Bright Spots' beaklike mouth, noting its slightly leathery texture. "That was kind of one of the harder days I've had, I guess. But, well, it's over now, and I'm off-duty. So would you like to see the city where I live?"

Weird how clearly I can read the emotions on two very inhuman faces, but both Pinkflower and Bright Spots seemed completely taken aback by my reaction. They probably didn't understand that, for me, the best way to heal up from trauma is to put it into the background of my mind. It's sort of like wrapping up a wound: you know it's there, but you protect it and keep it from getting opened again as much as possible, and as long as you did the job right, after a while it heals up on its own. Mostly.

Right now, what I needed was something gentle, something fun. Getting to do that with somebody...honestly, the only company I've had on any serious level for *years* now is animals. Animals are nice, but they're not people. That's as much the best thing about them as it is the worst, but sometimes...sometimes I just need somebody to talk to who can talk back.

There is nothing quite like a good conversation for the health of the soul.

Maybe they didn't understand, but those two wonderful women didn't object as I led them up from the Link's version of Rock Bottom. Without the people the place wasn't so bad, but there's not really a whole lot to see down there. I mean, there *is*, but it's...it's all subtle stuff, small things, like the plaques on grave sites and the date-printed cornerstones of buildings and street signs leading to places that aren't there anymore. Stuff that I've always found inspires my imagination, but not what I'd share with anybody until I got to know them better.

Definitely not on a first date.

So instead, I took them up to see the Sydney Opera House.

It was within easy walking distance, so I figured, well, why not? *I'd* only read about the place, and I'd always wanted to go, and neither of my companions seemed to mind in the least, so away we went. After a stopover at Carlscrown Bakery, that is: a proper date is supposed to be food and an activity, after all. Thankfully the virtual food was just as appealing to all the senses as it was in real life (seriously, the Link is just amazing!), and when we were all properly fortified, Pinkflower with a

340

Cornish pasty, Bright Spots with a slice of kale cake, and me with a trdelnik (really tasty, even though I can't figure out how to pronounce it), in we went.

Without all the crowds that must normally fill the place, it was breathtaking. Enormous. Awe-striking. We entered room after room without anyone to accost us, anyone to bar our way. Somewhere in the distance we could hear music, as of an orchestra tuning up, but even when we opened the doors to each performance hall, we never caught sight of a single real person. Nobody except ourselves.

"This one realizes, there are others using this simulation," Bright Spots informed us, flickers of light in front of her large eyes revealing the screens she must have called up on her home Link. "We're hearing them practicing together, learning to perform together, each of them apart, but also in one place."

"The miracles of the Link," I murmured. "We'd never even know about each other if not for…"

Pinkflower, though, wasn't paying attention. Darn ditzy bug! Instead, she was following another of the many phantom instrument sounds toward one of the imposing double doors, the main set if my sense of direction wasn't completely out of whack. We were about to enter the main concert hall!

For a moment my anxiety spiked, but then subsided almost immediately. While I hate heights with an abiding passion, and I dislike open spaces, the room was empty – once again the miracle of touring a place via the Link saving me from my own fears – and I couldn't help but allow myself to simply stand and admire the sheer scope of the beautiful room, my eyes drawn up, up, ever and ever upward. I felt Bright Spots' similar movements on my shoulder, both of us sharing in a moment of soft sensation, letting the emotional impressions of the room fill us and flow through us. She wasn't an empath, but I was, and I let her feel everything I sensed, and she freely let me share in her own feelings, every rise and fall of emotion from the ghosts of music past.

This was a place where history glowed.

Pinkflower wasn't concerned with such ephemera, however. No, she had a most definite goal in mind, and as soon as I and Bright Spots realized it, we hurried after her. While I didn't know what degree of effect we might have on the real world through our Link access, I did *not* want to have to explain to the caretakers around here that I let one of their instruments get damaged by an overenthusiastic alien mantis!

Of course, my fears were groundless. Because of course they were. Pinkflower stopped before the great Grand Organ, its many spires and tiers of pipes ascending row on row, and just gazed upward. No connoisseur of architecture or emotion here: she was captivated by something of concrete, definite *use*.

"Oh Joe," she whispered reverently. "Oh Bright Spots. I have never seen an instrument so...so magnificent. I have never even conceived that such an instrument could be possible!" She turned her head all the way around to look at us, her eyes looking massive with wonder – and I thought that couldn't have been possible, big as they already were! "My people live in high forest canopies. There's no room for such wonders. No room for anything heavier than could be lifted by two strong imagoes. But I learned how to play the key-pipes when I was just an instar – father insisted! – and I understand the principles."

Her head turned back around, and she stepped forward, one of those myriad manipulator limbs brushing – oh-so-gently – across the keys of the Grand Organ.

"But not enough. Not yet. With time, with patience, with practice, however..." Her whole body trembled in a gentle ecstasy. "What music I will make. A sound to reach up to Heaven."

She paused then and seemed to catch herself, her eyes shifting from glittering flamingo pink to a softly luminous bubblegum color. A buggy blush.

"If only someone will work the stops."

That's about the time that I finally decided: maybe things weren't so bad after all. Because, well, it's an infinite universe expanding infinitely into infinity. What that means is there's just *got* to be room for all of us: nerdy bat-moths; silly mantis medics; gorgeous green-and-gold space dragons; empathic fox people; pangolin curmudgeons; superheroes and bounty hunters and every child they saved and every last animal in the Sanctuary.

And maybe even room for me.

ABOUT THE AUTHOR

Stephen Eric Johnson has been publishing creative writing on various online sites for over two decades, mostly out of a deep need to tell stories for the enjoyment of others, be it in person or by text. Presently he's a teacher while working on his Ph.D. Whenever he's not at work, he's plotting out his next story to tell.

The author's social media:
https://www.instagram.com/gideonkalvejarvis/

The author's websites:
http://godsindarkness.wikidot.com/
http://godindarkness.blogspot.com/